Breath to Breath

CARRIE MALONEY

For Tom —
whom I love for at LEAST 2
reasons: You know how to
make me laugh... and you know
a hundred ways to kill a man.
Love,

Praise for Carrie Maloney's ***Breath to Breath***

"A stunning, smart, big-hearted debut from Carrie Maloney! *Breath to Breath* is at once startlingly brave and comforting in its frankness. For animal lovers, people lovers, and lovers of insightful, beautifully-crafted stories about falling into grief, and daring to live again."

- Elisabeth Finch
Writer for *Grey's Anatomy*, *True Blood*, *ELLE*

"*Breath to Breath* reads like a river with all of its currents and eddies. This soulful tale captures the passions and struggles of a veterinarian in western Wisconsin—and the changes she sparks in the people around her. The revolving carousel of characters and their four-footed companions draw you into their world. But you don't need to be an animal lover to keep turning pages—just a lover of life."

- Chris Bleifuss, DVM
(A real-life Wisconsin veterinarian!)

"Wow! *Breath to Breath* truly expresses our emotional connection to animals—what we get from that relationship, and what they shine back onto us. Meanwhile, this book is a roller coaster ride of human interaction. The story reminds me of so many struggles in my own life that I had to overcome to pursue my calling. Carrie Maloney has crafted a book that kept me on the edge of my sofa!"

- Jennifer Kachnic
President of The Grey Muzzle Organization

Cover design by Maureen M. McIlhargey
Illustration by Aleksandr Mansurov

ISBN-10: 0990685403
ISBN-13: 978-0990685401

For Mark, my favorite human.

ACKNOWLEDGMENTS

So many people to thank, such a small page.

To Roy Finden, who read every chapter hot off the computer and never stopped cheering me on. To Dr. Chris Bleifuss and Dr. Marcy Armstrong, who tirelessly answered my unending questions about veterinary medicine. To Linda Zespy, who wrote with me, coached me, inspired me. To my writers group, for their lovingly brutal feedback: Tim Hodapp, Cathy Gasiorowicz, and Barbara Brown. To my dear friend and designer extraordinaire, Maureen McIlhargey, for crafting the cover. To the amazing Kelly Germain, who polished up the manuscript in its final days. To all four of my Maloney siblings: Christine, Constance, Meighan, and Matthew, each of whom gave of their smarts and artistry. To Jay Gilbertson and Ken Seguine, for their wisdom and crazy kindness. To Dr. Thomas Thul, for his medical advice and bone-rattling jocularity. To a host of friends (bless you all), who read versions of my manuscript and gave me priceless insights along the way. To psychologist Dr. Jack Stoltzfus, who helped me get inside the heads of a couple of whacked-out characters. To Julie Mayo Haddad, for her sage literary advice. To Former Polk County District Attorney, Karen Olson, for her expertise on Wisconsin animal abuse laws. To my husband, Mark Given, who found a hundred ways to help me.

And to my editor, author Roland Merullo (*Breakfast with Buddha*), who initially helped shape this work and made me a better writer.

Teaching a child not to step on a caterpillar
is as valuable to the child as it is to the caterpillar.

(attributed to) BRADLEY MILLAR

1

Anna worked her way through the alphabet, sounding it out as if it were one long word. Then she started at the end of the alphabet and pronounced the word backwards. Next, she reached for the stack of client files on the seat beside her. She arranged them from thickest to thinnest, then from most tattered to least, and finally according to the color of each folder as it would appear along the visible light spectrum.

With a soft moan, Anna dropped the files back onto the seat and checked her eyes in the rearview mirror. Still a bit puffy, they'd lost most of their redness, so she reached for the ignition. But if she turned the key the motor was going to shut off, and the next logical step would be to get out of the truck and into the morning. She took a baby wipe from the glove compartment and began working the dashboard. It was, however, hard to ignore the personal summons coming through the radio.

"Okay. It's about seven minutes after eight or so, Milk River, Wisconsin, time. And yes, it's Monday. So you might be wondering why we're not doing our weekly call-in program, *All of Us Animals*, with veterinarian Dr. Anna Dunlop, yeah? Me too, I guess."

The announcer, Eddy Rivard, spoke as he always did—with a voice that sounded like it was lounging back on a grassy hill.

"For those of you keeping score, this is the first time in all these years that Dr. Dunlop has ever been late for a show. Or for anything, far as I know. But you've got me in the meantime, and I'm not goin' anywhere. Hey, I read something yesterday that might tickle you animal lovers who've tuned-in. Did you know that the crows in your neighborhood can actually recognize your face?"

Looking through her windshield up at the squat, sandstone building, home to WLCM-FM, Anna nearly smiled. It would never occur to Eddy to panic about having to fill an extra hour of airtime if she didn't show up at all. He would just—talk.

She pushed her limbs into action, turning off the engine and stepping one boot outside before realizing her door wouldn't open all the way. In an entirely empty lot she had parked tight up against the wooden, hand-carved lawn sign and would need to scrape herself along its very Eddy-like message to get out.

WLCM-FM: WELCOME to today and all the interesting things in it!

She cut across the brown grass, the October wind trying to turn her jacket inside out, and let the waft of coffee and microwave caramel corn pull her down the hallway toward the studio.

When she realized how long she'd been standing there, Anna released her grip on the homemade rosary in her sweater pocket. She stretched the stiffness from her fingers and rested her knuckles against the studio window. But the message to knock got derailed somewhere between her brain and her wrist. She stood there blinking and breathing, her gaze in the general direction of Eddy on his perch behind the control board. With his chair tipped back, shoulders and head bobbing against the foam rubber wall, legs dangling, Eddy had assumed the position he most preferred. It seemed precarious for a six-foot-two, 210-pound man, but he'd had the same chair and habit for as long as she could remember, without incident.

He spoke animatedly into the microphone he'd brought close to his lips. A boom mic on a long arm, it swung easily to accommodate Eddy's full use of his small space.

Anna leaned to turn the dial on the wall speaker, letting his soft voice, with its faint Hawaiian accent on certain words, seep into the hallway with her.

"You should try it, yeah? Toasted almonds on your oatmeal. Serious. I can still taste 'em. Oh, and I put brown sugar on it, too. Right from the freezer. Did you know that if you freeze your brown sugar it won't dry up and get hard? But I saw on some cooking show that if it turns to rock in your cupboard, you can just put a piece of bread in the bag to soften it back up."

With the grace of an eagle lifting a trout from the river, Eddy dropped his front chair legs to the floor, grabbed his yellow plastic mug of ice water, and launched himself back into bouncing against the foam wall. His shiny black hair swayed just below his ears.

"Well, I guess we've about covered my entire breakfast, yeah? Pretty exciting radio, so far." He took a drink of water. Still swallowing he said, "If Anna doesn't get here soon, I might have to tell you about this tiny paper cut I got last night…"

Anna straightened her shoulders, tossed her jacket onto a chair, and re-found the oversized rosary in her sweater pocket before tapping on the window. Eddy looked up, bursting into a full-face smile, and eagerly waved her in.

"Wait, here she is! Come in, come in! It's Dr. Dunlop from down at the vet clinic. We can start the show. Hi, Anna."

Making no effort to mute the sound of Anna plopping herself into the chair at the guest microphone, Eddy flashed her another smile full of white teeth and good nature.

"Hey, Eddy. Sorry I'm late." Anna kept her mouth by the desktop microphone as she shrugged her bag from her shoulder.

"No worries, no worries."

She was keenly aware of being studied. For some time now, in anticipation of how she might feel on this particular day, Eddy had been urging her to cancel this week's show altogether. But Anna had wanted none of that. Now, however, with each of her thoughts coming a beat late and every word an effort, she was beginning to doubt the wisdom of her decision. She tipped her head toward the open microphones in a *Let's do this thing!* gesture.

"You okay?" Eddy's tone was so caring, it would have sounded phony from anyone else.

"Yeah, sure. I'm fine. I've had a rough day, that's all."

"Anna. It's only twenty after eight."

"True, but I had to spend a lot of my rising-to-greet-the-day time outside swearing at my truck."

"Your truck? Again?"

"Yeah, the same problem. It rolls over fine but doesn't want to fire."

In a sing-song voice he said, "I'm tellin' ya, you should get rid of that rig." Bringing his mouth closer to the microphone he said, "If any of you out there needs a Ford pick 'em up truck—for parts only—please let us know."

A moment later, his big toothy smile stopped being one.

Anna, speaking fluent Eddy, could see he wanted to retract his last statement. She offered him a tiny shrug that said *no big deal*, hoping it looked more genuine than it felt.

They both knew she would never get rid of the truck. It had been Tony's. With almost a quarter of a million miles on it, the black pickup was cosmetically pristine but needed its inner workings nursed lovingly along by her meticulous shade tree mechanic: Eddy.

"Well, hey," said Anna, brightening. "Enough about my personal issues. Let's take some calls. Unless you need me to look at that paper cut of yours."

Eddy didn't answer right away, clearly unworried about filling two hundred-ish homes across the county with radio silence as he nodded slowly at Anna, eyes narrowed. His fingertips played along the side of his huge plastic mug. "*Kay den*," he said in one of the many Hawaiian pidgin phrases he had refused to give up. "We've got a couple of callers already waiting, so let's get started."

He looked at the microphone. "Welcome to *All of Us Animals* with Dr. Anna Dunlop from our own Milk River Veterinary Clinic. If you have a question for Dr. Dunlop about anything furred, feathered, or finned in your home, go ahead and dial in. You know the number. Suzanne? You still there?"

"Yup, I'm here, Eddy. Hi, Dr. Dunlop. Suzanne Heinz."

"Oh, hi, Suzanne. Is young Willie Lump-Lump up to his old tricks again?"

Eddy laughed at the cat's name. The sound worked like medicine on Anna, who stopped flicking through the chunky beads on her rosary and pulled her hand from her pocket.

"Well, that's why I'm calling," said Suzanne. "He's still so crazy to go outside all the time. We finally started letting him out some, just to see if that helps."

"You let him outside?" Anna bristled. "But—he's declawed, right?"

"Yeah, he is."

Anna let Eddy see her exasperation but kept it out of her voice. "Outside is a pretty dangerous place for an eight-pound creature with no street smarts, Suzanne."

"I know. I do worry about that. But he's still making that creepy, low meowing sound I told you about. And now he does this other thing. He jumps up, grabs the doorknob with his front paws, and just hangs there. It's really weird."

Eddy was clearly tickled by the mental image. "Wow, no kidding?"

"Yeah, and he's been peeing on the furniture a little bit too. When I catch him doing it I squirt him with water and yell at him. But nothing seems to help."

Anna leaned close to her microphone, and in a slow, conspiratorial voice said, "All right, Suzanne. Here's what you do, okay?"

Suzanne's voice took on Anna's same gravitas. "Okaaay..."

"The next time you catch Willie Lump-Lump urinating on your furniture…"

"Yes?"

"You roll up a section of newspaper—are you with me?"

"Yeah," said Suzanne, riveted.

"And you whack yourself across the nose with it for not bringing him in to get neutered, as I've asked you to do about five times now."

Suzanne giggled.

"Seriously though, Suzanne. I know I'm wearing out my soapbox on this one, but all of those problems might get a little better if you had him neutered."

"I believe you. But Carl won't even talk about it. He says it's cruel."

"Well, we're going to need another newspaper for Carl, then."

Anna was glad Eddy chuckled, softening the sarcasm she'd only thinly veiled. "Okay, let's sort this out. First of all, stop shooting Willie-Lump-Lump with the spray bottle. It's mean. And it's not going to work."

"Oh, really? Okay."

"Second, I'll examine him to make sure there's no medical reason he's peeing in the house. But Suzanne, I want you to do something for me. Take a moment to imagine what's going on inside of your cat's body right now."

"Menemene!" said Eddy.

"Excuse me?" Anna said, cocking her head. "May-nay-may-nay?"

"Yeah, menemene. It's a Hawaiian word for when you put yourself inside of someone else, to let their thoughts and wants be your thoughts and wants for a little while."

"Empathy," said Anna.

"Right. Like—I saw a squirrel once who was scratching himself, first with one back leg and then the other, which I thought was pretty dang cute. But then I started wondering why he was doing so much scratching and realized the poor guy probably had fleas. Using a little menemene, I pictured myself itching like that all day long, with no relief. Ever. I got a whole new respect for how hard it is to be a squirrel."

"Exactly! Menemene. I love that. So, Suzanne… if you take a moment to have a little menemene for Willie Lump-Lump—let yourself feel all of that testosterone pumping through your body, getting you totally riled up with crazy amounts of energy and sexual drive—do you think a squirt of water is likely to calm you down?

"Oh dear," said Suzanne.

"Don't feel bad. I'm not trying to *guilt* you into neutering him—I'm just pointing out something that may help all three of you get along better. How about if I talk to Carl? Can you put him on?"

"No, he's not here. He went to the bakery."

"Okay, then I'll call him later today. Keep the faith. And in the meantime, please don't let Mr. Lump-Lump out to go cattin' around until he's been fixed. Doctor's orders!"

Anna replayed that last line in her head. She'd been trying for a cheery tone but had landed somewhere between angry and odd.

Eddy thanked Suzanne and ended the call, never taking his eyes off of Anna. He knit his eyebrows into a sweet inquiring question, which she pretended not to understand. She fondled a rosary bead with her thumb before pushing it on and reaching for the next.

"Caller number two," said Eddy, "is from all the way over in Wanderoos." He touched a button on the control board. "Hi, William. You have a question?"

Someone on the line was talking, but just barely.

"Um, William? Can you speak up a little? We can't quite hear you."

"Oh. Sorry. Is this better?" William's voice, ragged with age, was also being held to a whisper.

"A little." Eddy and Anna cocked their heads at each other.

"I'm calling about a bird—my bird. A parrot." He said the word like he was hoping to get the pronunciation right. "What I want to know is—how do you—well—is there a way to erase his memory?"

"Excuse me?" said Anna.

William pushed a burst of air from his lungs. "Stupid question. I'm sorry. What I'm trying to ask is—I need to un-train this bird. He says things. Bad things. Not bad things, technically, but wrong things. Strange things at the wrong time."

Anna smiled. And the smile was genuine. Not the kind she'd been constructing for Eddy since she walked in. She squinted up at the speaker mounted on the wall as if it were William himself. "Okay, help me understand. So… your parrot says things you'd rather he didn't?"

"Yes. Exactly. At least not when I have people over."

Eddy's gesture to Anna requested permission to speak, which she granted.

"William? This is Eddy. Do you have a visitor over right now? Is that why you're whispering?"

"No, I'm alone."

"Okay…" said Anna again, stalling for time while her brain went hunting.

"I've only had Chi-Chi—that's his name—he's only been here for a few months. My sister had to go into assisted living in July, and she begged me to take him in. I had to say yes; Chi-Chi was her only child."

"That was nice of you," said Anna, resisting the urge to whisper along with William.

"He's a lovely bird, he really is. I'm retired, you know, and he's good company. He's fascinating to watch. And believe it or not, he actually likes to cuddle."

"I've heard that about parrots," said Anna. "So tell me more about what's going on."

"Sure, I'll try. And I'm sorry I have to talk so quietly. I don't want him to hear me. The sound of my voice seems to set him off."

"Oh, I getcha," said Eddy.

"What kinds of things does Chi-Chi say?" asked Anna.

"He imitates my sister. And I mean *perfectly* imitates." William's enthusiasm brought him to a near-normal speaking voice. He checked himself, dropping back to a murmur, mid-thought. "Sometimes if I close my eyes it feels like Millie's standing right here beside me."

"And that's a bad thing?"

"It is. Because my sister could be—pretty—I don't know—high spirited, I guess you'd say."

"I see," said Anna, not seeing.

"Millie loved her life. In a big, loud way. She still does. She's the person everyone wanted at their parties. The person you phoned when you needed to be cheered up." William's voice was on the rise again. "Most of us call her Auntie Mame, if you know who that is. She has about fifty different laughs, and I swear, any one of them could get you kicked out of a restaurant."

A woman's voice shrieked into the phone.

"Are you *kidding* me?" Chi-Chi screeched the question, ending with a long, belly-shaking laugh that started with the word *pah*.

Anna laughed too. She couldn't help it. And what a strange feeling it was. She realized, then, how long it had been since she'd tried one out. She looked over at Eddy, his shoulders bouncing in his signature silent chuckle, the lines around his eyes folding in like brown paper fans.

"Rats!" said William, no longer making the effort to be quiet. "That's it. He won't leave us alone, now. He'll start going through his whole repertoire, so get ready."

Still giggling, Anna said, "But she's—I mean he's—hilarious."

"The problem is," said William, his misery palpable, "laughter isn't always appropriate. In fact, in certain situations it can be rather appalling."

Anna and Eddy did their best to sober up.

Chi-Chi, on the other hand, sang out in a female smoker's voice, "Honey, you're a scream!" The bird's ensuing laugh was a single ear-splitting, "Ha!"

Anna fought hard to keep her laughter in check. Mostly because this man was suffering and wanted her help. But also because each time she laughed she felt a twinge of something less pleasant. Guilt, maybe. Or just incongruence, as if humor was out of place today. Like snoring in a movie theater, or a party dress at a root canal. It just felt wrong.

"So, William…" She paused a moment until she felt ready to go on. "I see how Chi-Chi's voice could interrupt your conversations. Have you ever tried putting him in another room when company comes over?"

"He *is* in another room. The laundry room. I move his perch there whenever I'm going to have an important conversation of some kind. He's as far away from the phone as I can get him. I've got a pretty tiny apartment."

"Really? He sounds like he's perched on your shoulder."

"I know. He's been blessed with good lungs."

"Okay. Here's what I'm thinking. Talking birds often imitate sounds that are delivered with a great deal of passion. So it makes sense that Chi-Chi would glom onto your sister's big laughs and funny phrases. It might be kind of tricky to get him to stop saying those things."

"Shuddup! Yer killin' me!"

The scream made Anna jump. And then titter.

"I'm so sorry," William said, horrified. "He's really wound up today."

Anna pressed her lips together, wrapping them around her front teeth. She clenched her throat, but a small snort made its way out her nose.

"I just don't know what I'm going to do," said William, plaintively. "I can't possibly give him away, but he really makes it hard for me to do my work." William's voice wobbled with pain.

"Shuddup! SHUDDUP! You did NOT just say that!" Chi-Chi punctuated his message with a series of short, airy sniggers that sounded like they were being squeezed out between the back teeth he didn't have.

Anna cleared her throat. Her cheeks felt hot. "Hang on a second, William. You say it's hard for you to work. But didn't you just tell us you were retired?"

"Yes, but certain people still come to see me when they have no one else to talk to. And lots of times they're telling me their most intimate thoughts, which is why Chi-Chi's abrasive vocabulary is such a problem. I guess I didn't mention—I'm a priest."

Anna let out with an explosive guffaw, making Eddy glance in her direction. She averted her eyes, working to shut some internal floodgate that had sprung its latch. Her hand shot to her mouth.

"Oh, William—Father—I'm so sorry." She could just squeak out the words. One more pinched noise escaped her, as she felt her face contort into a series of grim masks she couldn't hope to control.

"It's okay," said William softly. "It's not that I can't see the humor here. And Chi-Chi gets me laughing, too. But not when I have a person at my place who's hurting and looking for some kind of comfort—"

"Cripes, get over yourself, honey!" said Chi-Chi.

Anna's lungs pumped out the very last of her wind in a long string of wheezing snickers. Trying to catch her breath, she fumbled for her favorite rosary bead and squeezed it as hard as she could.

A single tear was halted halfway down her cheek by the swipe of a sweater sleeve. Her eyes prickled with more on the way. But she'd made a pact with herself. No more crying today. *Do not do this!* A memory of Tony throwing his head back to laugh flashed through her. Muscles around her ribcage tightened, trying to keep close to the heart what belonged to the heart.

When at last she could, she drew in a slow, deep breath. And then another. Just starting to compose herself, she didn't dare speak. Chi-Chi, luckily, was all too eager to fill the air time.

A high-pitch, porpoise-like laugh stuttered out at a decibel that made Eddy lift his headset from his ears.

"Same shit different day! Cripes!"

As the bird rolled on through a series of cackles and quips, making other radio chat impossible, Anna looked up, intending to signal Eddy to do the talking for a moment—but he wasn't in his chair. He was actually just crouching down beside her. Placing a hand on her back, he moved his kind look from her face to her fluttering sweater pocket. She stopped fidgeting.

Eddy reached back to the console to hit the mute button and grab her a tissue. "I was thinking how beautiful it felt to see you laugh today. But now I'm not so sure. How about I take over for awhile? You could get up and walk around or something, yeah? Check out the kitchen. I made you some microwave caramel corn."

Anna's smile was a grateful one. "Thanks, but I brought my own pacifier. I made it last night—but I don't think it's working."

She began slowly extracting the surrogate rosary from her sweater pocket. Evenly spaced along the chain of Tony's Navy dog tags, fastened with rings of crimped wire, were the items he'd had on him five years ago today when he'd left their short marriage and this earthly world behind: The key to his bike, a matchbook, a yellow guitar pick, a five-gallon blood donation lapel pin, the top to an ibuprofen bottle, and his wedding ring.

She drew it out, bead by bead, and handed it to Eddy. He studied the chain curiously, touching several of the mementos. Then she saw the revelation dawn on his face. Bowing his head, Eddy brought the rosary up to his chest in two hands. And as he pressed it back into both of hers, he leaned close to whisper a single word into her ear. "Menemene."

Three piercing whistles were the first bird-like sounds Chi-Chi had uttered. At last the parrot was slowing down.

Anna and Eddy locked eyes in a complex conversation.

With a twitch of a smile, Anna slipped the dog tags back into her pocket. She gestured for Eddy to unmute the microphone and then leaned in to talk. When she spoke her voice was calm.

"Okay, so, William?"

"Yes, I'm here."

"I've got a couple of suggestions for you. First, I know a really great bird expert down in New Richmond. I'll get you her number."

"Oh, good, thanks." His tone lightened a little.

"And in the meantime, you can work on rewarding Chi-Chi when he's quiet and completely ignoring him when he's loud, or when he's using phrases you'd rather he didn't.

"Reward him with food, you mean?"

"Right. Small treats that he really likes. And you have to stop laughing when he's cracking wise. He feeds on that. So make sure you don't—"

"Anna!" Eddy's tone drew her immediate attention. "I'm sorry to interrupt."

Eddy's assistant, Jenny, was just leaving the studio with a scowl on her face. Eddy was gripping a note she had slipped him.

"Something's going on at the clinic. They need you over there right away."

2

"Five newborn puppies. Hypothermic. In respiratory distress," said Katie above the din, as Anna crossed the threshold of the surgery.

"What? What are you saying?"

Drawers and cupboard doors banged in all corners of the clinic as her new employee, Noah, scurried about, grabbing for supplies. A shock of thick hair slapped his forehead as he moved. At full volume, three caged dogs expressed their ardent desire to break free of their kennels and join the action.

Katie, Anna's longtime vet tech, stood at the metal table picking newborn puppies from a laundry basket lined with newspaper. But what Anna found most difficult to absorb was why Bunny Hall, a diminutive seventy-something Georgia transplant, was shifting foot to foot in the middle of the room. Bunny's frizzy, grey hair was windblown and untethered. Her bare ankles and neon green slippers stuck out from under a cinched trench coat. Bunny vigorously rubbed a small puppy in an old flowered towel, offering a constant stream of encouragements in her thick southern drawl.

"Come on now, sweet baby, little girl. You can do it, sugar pie. I know you can."

Meanwhile, a longhaired white German shepherd with pleading eyes whined in steady, three-second bursts—over and over—a groove worn in a record. The young shepherd, whose flabby pink underside told Anna she'd recently whelped, paced the room back and forth between the lone puppy in Bunny's hands and the basketful of pups on the table.

Anna would feel shameful later that her first thought was to duck out. To come back when she had more to give this crisis, whatever it was. Her second thought was mostly a picture: Tony greeting her at the back door every night with a kiss and a question: *How did it go for the animals today?*

Anna entered the fray, closing the kennel room door to dampen the piercing barks, instantly bumping the stress level down a notch. Moving quickly toward Katie, she stopped to let the pacing shepherd pass. The dog was riveted on her puppies to the exclusion of everything else.

"We tried kenneling her," said Katie, "but she freaked out. Tying her up was worse."

Noah crossed into the surgery clutching an armload of supplies. He handed Katie the syringes clutched in his fist before bending stiffly from the waist to pile heating pads and blankets onto the counter. Straightening up, he received a small stack of thick, white towels right to the chest.

"Put them in the dryer, would you, please?" said Anna.

"Right." He turned full around, heading toward the door.

"And, Noah?" she said, more warmly.

He looked back.

"You're doing a great job."

He smiled. "I can't find the Dopram," he said, on his way from the room.

"Got it." Anna opened an upper cabinet to remove the small glass vial.

She checked back over her shoulder at Bunny, who was still rubbing her puppy with the towel.

"Bunny, go easy on that pup. She's got fragile skin. Try to use about the same amount of pressure her mother would when licking her."

Bunny softened her touch immediately, working a succession of heartfelt apologies into her doggie pep talk. Anna decided not to tell the old woman that newborn pups were entirely deaf.

She caught Katie's eye as they worked side by side at the metal table. "So, what the hell happened here?"

Katie pressed her lips together as she scanned Anna's face. Abruptly, she turned her attention back down to the wriggling, yellow puppy in her hands. Anna tried to peek around Katie's straight, blonde hair, which had fallen like a curtain between the two of them.

"Katie?" Anna lengthened the vowels.

"Buried."

Anna froze, one eyebrow twitching slightly, as the meaning of Katie's words began to take hold. "Buried."

"In that." Katie tipped her forehead toward a small wooden table.

Anna followed Katie's gaze, spotting a crumpled, brown paper bag caked in dirt. "I'm not sure what you're—" Anna closed her mouth. She let the commotion carry on without her for a moment.

She drew in a deep breath. Letting it go all at once, she dove for three pink Frisbee-shaped heating pads among the supplies Noah had delivered and handed them to Katie.

"Go."

Katie stepped into the adjoining treatment room to place the pads in the microwave, squeezing past Noah and his apology in the doorway.

Noah handed a heated towel to Bunny for the puppy she was trying to warm. He draped another towel across the newborns on the table. Anna drew a small amount of Dopram into a syringe, coaching Noah through the process.

"Usually the best way to prioritize when you have so many animals in trouble is to start with the biggest one first."

"Best chance of survival," Noah half asked, half stated. He was already reaching for the largest pup in the litter, a yellow male with a white chest, white legs and a white blaze down his face.

"Right. Now, here." She pulled the needle off the syringe, slipping it into the sharps container on the wall, then handed the rest of the syringe to Noah. "Put a couple drops under his tongue, like this." She administered the drug to the next puppy down in size, a male with classic black and tan German shepherd markings. "There. That'll help stimulate his respiration. Keep up the massage, too." She rubbed her hands together gently.

"I've got it," Noah said.

Anna watched him long enough to see that he had, before picking up her own pup. She rubbed the whelp gently with the palm of her hand, then grabbed a stethoscope to check his heart and lungs. His breaths were shallow but improving. And his heart sounded strong.

Katie came back with the first heating pad from the microwave, waving it toward Anna. In a rare move, she'd drawn her baby-fine hair back into a ponytail, revealing her entire face.

"Great, thanks," said Anna. "Try two to each one."

Katie placed a warm towel on the disc and carefully snuggled two of the three remaining puppies together on top of it, close enough to share body heat. She covered them with another warm towel before dashing back to the microwave for the next disc.

Anna lay her hand on the two pups, assuring herself they were breathing comfortably. As she felt their tiny chests moving in and out, she pictured the whole litter underground, stacked one on top of the other, struggling for oxygen.

She pulled her hand away, recalling her age-old mantra: *Fix the pain, don't* feel *the pain.*

Noah swept by her in his Hawaiian-print scrubs, on his way to help Bunny with her young charge. "Here, Mrs. Hall. Let me have her." He reached for the towel and its furry contents.

"Yes, of course, son, thank you." Bunny passed her bundle to Noah, her hands lingering longer on the pup than they had to. Her arms dropped to her sides, then, and she began a slow 360-degree turn where she stood, taking in the action all around her.

Anna glanced up, seeing the agony on the old woman's face. "Hey, Bunny, do you think you could jump in here and give us a hand with the rest of the family? They outnumber us, you know; we could use the help."

Anna placed the large yellow male on a heated disc and handed the whole lot to Bunny. "Could you see if this big ol' boy is hungry? I wonder if he'll take milk from Mom over there. He seems to be breathing pretty well, but if we don't get some food into him soon we could still lose him."

"The hell we will!" Bunny took the heating pad in both hands and lowered the grunting newborn into the path of his pacing mother who stopped short and began licking enthusiastically.

Bunny gingerly knelt down by the heated dog bed Noah had placed in a corner of the surgery. Clutching the puppy to her chest with one hand, she patted the bed with the other, cooing to the mother, encouraging her to lie down. Once the shepherd realized the puppy was part of the deal, she was happy to comply. Without taking her eyes from the yellow pup, the mother stepped onto the bed, let her legs buckle under her, and rolled onto her side with a loud *oof!*

"All right, Storm. Ready yourself. The children are coming for breakfast." Bunny dropped from her knees to her bottom, scooting in close.

She held the baby's head up to a likely nipple on his mother's sagging, pink underside.

"That's her name? Storm?" Katie asked over her shoulder.

"Yes, this is Storm. Isn't she the sweetest little girl?" Bunny took a moment to look into the dog's eyes. "She belongs to the—*person* who lives next door to me. One of those Ardeen boys. This poor animal has lived her entire life chained to a doghouse in his back yard."

"Seriously?" asked Anna, without turning around.

"Sometimes I sneak over to bring her extra food." Bunny ran a hand over the grimy white fur outlining Storm's conspicuous ribs.

Anna picked up the runt Bunny had been massaging, to continue the effort. She kept her touch gentle but let her voice go hard. "So let me get this straight. Some jerk buys a dog—who knows why, since he keeps her tied-up 24/7—doesn't give her enough food to live on, ignores her until she gets pregnant, then tries to kill the puppies because it's just too inconvenient to take them to a shelter."

Katie touched Anna's arm, her face urging caution.

"Are there really people like that?" Anna took the pulse of the deep golden puppy in her hands. "Noah, come here, please."

Noah jumped to her side. Anna picked up the male pup with shepherd markings, studied him for a moment, then handed him over.

"Do me a favor and bring this one to Bunny. His respiration is good and he should eat if he can. Bunny, how's the yellow one doing?"

"All right, I think. My, he's certainly going at it, anyway."

"Great. That's great." Anna concentrated on keeping her core temperature down.

Bunny took the next puppy from Noah, bathed him in sweet talk, and gently fended off Storm's licking while trying to hook the pup firmly to a teat. She sat back a little, shaking her head. "Anna, I have no idea if I'm doing this wrong or what, but this second one will simply not latch on. I keep moving him from spigot to spigot. He sucks for a bit, then just drops off."

Anna appealed to Katie. "You okay to go? I need to stick with this little one."

"Sure." Katie picked up another puppy. "I was just going to take number three over for a nosh, anyway. I'll see what's up."

She squatted down beside Bunny, nestling a grey and black female in amongst her littermates. Katie talked softly to Storm, petting her in slow, tender strokes. "Hi, Sweetheart. How 'bout if I check you out, would that be okay?" She ran her fingers through the dog's long, dingy fur.

The white German shepherd, who'd calmed considerably since she'd begun reclaiming her brood, included Katie's right hand in the line-up of things needing to be licked.

"I'm gonna take that as a yes."

She palpated Storm's mammary glands and tried to express each of the nipples. Katie took the black and tan male from Bunny, helping him suckle at a teat where milk flowed freely.

"Anna, she's only got two teats working like they should. A couple of others are producing a little bit, but not enough to do much good."

"Crap, I was afraid of that." Anna was attending her tiny pup with quick, practiced motions. "I'll take a look when I can. Storm probably hasn't had enough nutrition to—oh, damn it. No!"

Anna jammed the stethoscope into her ears and listened to the puppy's heart.

"What?" Katie rose to join Anna at the surgery table.

"She's stopped breathing. And she's in arrest. Watch me!" Anna snatched the stethoscope from her ears and put the puppy in her left palm with the head facing out. She placed her right thumb and forefinger on either side of the puppy's chest, directly behind the elbows. She began compressions.

"About ten times. Not too hard. Like this. Now you."

Katie let Anna put the puppy into her left hand and started compressing the motionless chest.

"A little faster. We need a heart rate between 120 and 180. Good."

After ten compressions, Anna lifted Katie's hand higher, to a plane even with her own face. She placed her lips over the puppy's nose and mouth, puffing three quick, shallow breaths into the new lungs.

"Again!"

Katie administered ten more compressions.

Anna fought to keep her voice steady; Noah and Katie would be taking their signals from her.

"More Dopram?" Katie asked.

"She's already had two doses. It's done what it's going to do. Noah, come watch this."

Anna began mouth-to-mouth again. Noah, just back from delivering a white and apricot pup to her mother, stepped in to study the procedure. Bunny, for her part, had become perfectly still, as if moving too suddenly might ruin the animal's chances. Head tucked low between her shoulders, her small, arthritic hands balled in fists in her lap, Bunny seemed to be willing the puppy to live.

During the few seconds it took Katie to complete her next ten compressions, Anna pulled off her stethoscope, thrusting it toward Noah.

"Is her heart beating yet?" she asked.

Noah listened to the puppy's chest and shook his head. Anna went back in for more resuscitation before letting Katie pump her next series of ten.

"Notice how small my breaths are?" she asked Noah. "Imagine the size of her lungs compared to mine. I could do some serious damage if I weren't careful." Anna and Katie continued CPR for a full minute before stopping for a heart check.

"It's beating!" said Noah. "But it's slow."

"Really?" Anna took the listless puppy into both hands.

As if summoning a genie from a lamp—and with about as much hope for success—Anna rubbed the pup's stunted body from dewlap to tail. A final circulatory boost was the last pitiful trick in her bag. She glanced at Katie.

"You guys should make up bottles for the other pups."

"I'll get the milk," said Noah, hooking the stethoscope around Anna's neck before heading off.

While Katie grabbed a couple of small baby bottles, she and Anna exchanged looks, Anna's begging for this puppy to survive, Katie's wishing she could help.

Katie showed Noah how to warm the milk replacer by holding the filled baby bottle under hot running water. She wondered out loud whether these weakened puppies would be able to feed themselves. Would their compromised bodies be strong enough to suck? If not, they'd have to move to plan B: Force-feeding the pups with a medicine dropper.

As Anna massaged the defenseless runt, she glanced over her shoulder. Noah stood extraordinarily close to Katie in conversation. His face only a foot from hers, his eyes riveted on her lips, he looked smitten. But Anna recognized the posture she herself had assumed with Katie early in their relationship, before she'd trained her ear to Katie's quiet voice. Noah was simply straining to hear the vet tech over the sound of the running water.

Anna looked down at the small female pup, who lay so still in her hands. The whelp's coloring was beautiful. A rich caramel, with a black muzzle and black-tipped tail. Anna's realization that she was about to lose this little one sent a sharp stab of pain through her chest, erupting in a small cough. She forced herself to breath slowly, trying to relax.

Though she hadn't experienced this type of physical reaction before, her depth of emotional attachment to animals had made her an oddball her entire life. She'd never been able to see the line that others could see so clearly. The one separating humans from *less important* living beings. People were smarter, no question. But dogs, for instance, were more loyal and forgiving than humans—and far less cruel—all of which seemed more significant to Anna. At this particular moment, in fact, she felt embarrassed for her own species that so often treated other creatures as if their lives had no meaning.

A tear fell onto the limp body of the pretty little puppy she wouldn't be able to save.

Katie turned each baby bottle upside down, testing to make sure that milk dripped from the nipple with only a gentle squeeze. She offered a bottle to Bunny, who was now sitting cross-legged on the floor with Storm's panting head in her lap.

"Here, Mrs. Hall. Care to do the honors? That fuzzy grey and black one is pretty hungry by now, I bet."

"Yes, yes, please!"

Katie focused her attention back onto her boss, who had fallen still, looking down at the pup in her hands. "Can I get anything for you, Anna? How's she doing?"

Anna could barely summon the strength to turn and face her three helpers. She felt heavy but hollow, like the widow at a funeral. But the news was good.

"I can't believe it. She's okay. I think she's going to be okay."

The spontaneous cheers made Storm's tail play the metal supply cabinet like a drum.

3

The story trapped inside of Bunny Hall was too terrible to tell. So, the other three waited. Bunny held the black and tan puppy face up, cradling him in the crux of her arm as a human mother might feed her infant. She brought the bottle down to the pup's mouth.

"Hang on a second," Katie said. "A puppy can't eat very well that way. Let him rest on his tummy, like he would be if Storm were feeding him."

"Oh, that makes sense, doesn't it?" She repositioned the pup, putting his stomach on her upturned palm. "Forgive me, little one."

Bunny pushed her wild grey hair back over her shoulder and reached for the baby bottle. Prying gently with the nipple, she encouraged the puppy to open his mouth. "I don't know. He just doesn't seem all that interested. I can't get him to open up."

Anna continued her examination of Storm without involving herself in Bunny's problem. She'd remained mostly silent since she saved the newborn with the black muzzle. The puppy, still stretched out along Anna's upturned arm, fed hungrily from a bottle held in the same hand. With her free hand, she felt along Storm's body, examining the dog's ears and checking her mammary glands one last time. By the dog's musky smell, Anna wondered if Storm had ever in her life had a bath.

"Come on, sugar pea, I know you're hungry," Bunny said, with a hint of a whine.

Noah slipped in beside Bunny, kneeling down, analyzing her technique. Normally the veterinary staff would have taken over by now, tending to the shepherd and her litter from here on out, but Bunny had not yet relinquished her duties. In fact, she was clinging to them.

"Try giving the bottle a little squeeze while you're moving the nipple," said Noah. "Let him taste the milk."

Bunny tried exactly that, depositing a large drop onto the puppy's unopened mouth, then working it in through his lips. The puppy's head began to wobble, overtaxing his brand new neck muscles, as he blindly groped for the source of the milk. He reflexively sucked the nipple into his mouth with a gratifying slurp.

"I'm in!"

Noah and Katie laughed. No one could see Anna's wan smile. She was up and tidying the surgery, showing only her back to the group.

"That," said Bunny, "was a very good idea, um—I'm sorry, son. What's your name again?"

"Noah. Noah Long."

"Long. I don't know any Longs."

"We just moved here from Sioux Falls, actually."

"From South Dakota to Wisconsin? Out of the frying pan, into a different frying pan, I suppose. So, Noah Long. What's in this milk exactly? It seems to suit his fancy."

"It's got all sorts of vitamins and minerals. And lots of digestible proteins."

"Mmmm, sounds delicious." Bunny's eyes twinkled. "If I live long enough, I'll learn everything, I suppose."

For a couple of minutes the only sounds were the occasional grunt of a puppy and Storm's soft, even snoring. Sitting crossed-legged, rocking forward and back, Bunny watched the puppy in her lap drink enthusiastically.

"He just—drove away," she said, her voice trailing off.

Every human head in the surgery turned in her direction. Katie and Noah looked briefly at each other, then back at Bunny, who was opening her trench coat to snuggle the puppy into the skirt of her pink flannel nightgown.

Anna held her breath. She wanted to hear what had happened out there this morning—needed to hear. But the cramping in her chest had returned; anger tightened every muscle in her body. "What did you say, Bunny?" To her own ears, she sounded calm.

"He buried these puppies, then just got in his car and drove away." Bunny spoke with total disbelief. She surveyed the faces watching her. Bracing her.

"You know, I think it might be best if I started at the beginning. At least the beginning of my part in this."

"That sounds good," said Anna, her voice steady, but not her heartbeat.

"I guess I slept kind of late today. Since Carson died, I don't sleep very well, so I'm up and down all night long. I think I officially got to sleep about five-thirty this morning. But something woke me up just a couple of hours later. It was the strangest sound. I couldn't quite figure out what it was, but it made me feel awful. Just awful. I wasn't sure if it was a child in some kind of trouble, or exactly what.

"I sat up in bed, groggy—I'm not my best when I haven't slept—and that noise, it got louder, and worse. Well, it finally got through all the stuffing in my sorry head, to the part where I keep my brains, I suppose, and I realized the sound must be coming from Storm.

"I jumped up and went to the laundry room to take a look. That's the window with the best view of her doghouse. She was chained up like usual, but oh, so terribly upset. She was—"

Bunny halted. She spoke again when she could.

"She was crying like I'd never heard her cry before. Long, loud cries. I suppose you shouldn't use a word like this with dogs, but to me, honestly, it sounded like *sobbing*. I don't know how else to describe it. She was yanking on her chain, trying to break free. That was another thing I couldn't understand. She had always seemed so resigned to that life she was given. I'd never seen her make a fuss about it before. At first I thought she was in pain. Caught in something, maybe. And I was about to run over there, but then I saw the man. That disgusting man."

Bunny's grey eyes darkened. Her face grew hard.

"He was outside. He was too far away to be beating her, but he was yelling at her, telling her to 'Shut the hell up!' I tried to get a better look, but it was impossible to see what was going on. He was bent over working, but I just never thought—well, who would ever think he—"

Bunny was giving in to tears. Katie placed her hand on the woman's back and began rubbing in slow circles.

"He wasn't facing me, so I couldn't see what he was up to. But Storm could. That was the most awful part. Storm saw everything."

This particular detail made Anna's stomach flip. She leaned her backside heavily against the surgery table. She clutched the dark golden puppy with both hands, pulling the newborn tight against her chest. She looked over at the sleeping Storm, now so peaceful, and tried to remember this story would have a happy ending.

Bunny continued, even more agitated. "But I didn't know. I couldn't see. I decided to go over there and find out what was making this lovely dog carry on like she was. Talking with him about Storm was going to end in an argument. It always does. But I was ready for a fight and was just throwing on my coat when I heard a sound I'll never forget, no matter how many years I am granted. It was our young dear here."

Bunny let her gaze move across Storm's head. "She began to—Lord, I don't know how to explain it. *Scream,* I guess. I flew out the door ready to punch or kick that man for whatever he was doing to her. But his rickety old car was just leaving the drive.

"As I ran toward Storm, she was so frantic, she was lunging with the full weight of her body against the chain. And wailing. Just—wailing. It all happened so fast, but before I could get to her, the chain snapped and she fell in a somersault, then kept on running. I mean, she sailed toward where that—*beast* had been working. There was a pile of fresh dirt and—and Storm started digging at it like crazy. Whining and digging. For the first time I got a good look at her. And that's when I realized she wasn't pregnant anymore.

"I looked over at her doghouse, saw no puppies, then looked back at Storm digging madly at the ground. I finally got it. So I dropped to my knees next to her and started clawing at the dirt with my hands. I think I let out a scream of my own somewhere in there, too."

Anna tried to disengage; she could feel herself being pulled too far into this nightmare. She forced her eyes around the room, as if barely noticing Bunny's presence. But her gaze soon landed on Noah and Katie, where the horror of the tale was reflected in their faces.

"And then I saw the shovel. Thank god, that person never puts anything away. I grabbed it and helped Storm find her—find her—"

It was getting harder to make out Bunny's words. She was weeping openly, talking in a pinched voice, gulping air in the middle of sentences, the middle of words.

"I got them out of the paper bag, and Storm started licking them, trying to get to them all at once. She was so upset, I was afraid she was going to stomp on them. I ran to my house for that old laundry basket. I knew I had to hurry and get here. But when I put the puppies in the basket, Storm started moving all around me, whining, and now I was the enemy, stealing her pups, and—it just broke my heart.

"When I'd almost made it to the car, she put herself between me and the door. She just stood there. Blocking my way. She had stopped crying by now and was staring me straight in the eyes. I thought she might attack me, to make me stop. And she would have had every right to, my poor, sweet love. But that's not her way. She finally just threw back her head and let out the most woeful howl. It sounded like—well, like *loss*."

Bunny, with one hand holding the bottle for the puppy in her lap, used the other to cover as much of her face as she could, because all she had left to add to this story was the hysterical sobs she had been holding in all day.

Katie leaned over to lift the pup from Bunny's nightgown. The grateful woman pushed herself into a standing position.

Still weeping, Bunny looked left and right before squealing, "Ohhh, I don't know where the powder room is!"

Noah sprang to his feet to guide her by an elbow out of the surgery.

Anna saw Katie wipe her eyes with a tissue and knew she should offer words of comfort to her friend. Or at least, words of wisdom to her employee. But she had nothing of substance to give. She'd been a wimpy veterinarian lately, and now a bad boss, too. And that's when it happened.

Pent-up pressure burst from her muscles, speeding out into her whole body, coursing through veins too small to carry it. It swirled in her chest, gathering energy for one final surge to her brain. Black spots popped in front of her eyes with every beat of her heart. She was breathing too hard. Her hearing was muffled. She turned to hide her face from Katie, who was sniffling and gently stroking Storm along the full length of her body. Anna bent over and, with trembling hands, placed her puppy alongside of the other four as a blade of pain sliced through her chest.

"I'll be in my office," she said too loudly, longing for the other side of a closed door.

4

Anna dropped into her desk chair and leaned forward, hands gripping her knees. She wondered if she were having a heart attack but thought it unlikely.

Waiting for her body to normalize, she let two minutes pass, then three. Her chest pain had ebbed, but everything else was in overdrive. Her vision was spotty, her pulse racing.

Katie would be wondering about her by now, wanting to knock on the door, sensing she shouldn't. But Anna stayed right where she was. Out there she would need calmness. And advice. And a plan.

She opened her desk drawer and reached all the way back to pull out the CD. She studied the cover on the collection of songs Tony had recorded for their third wedding anniversary. In his bold, graceful penmanship, he had titled the disk *Pieces of You.*

Anna had been slow to let Tony come to know the full extent of her odd self but had eventually offered every part of her being up to him—all except one absurd, mortifying fact. The affliction she'd actively hidden from everyone her whole life. It was her very worst habit. Her *poetry*. Actually, she thought that an extravagant term for what she wrote, but she was too poor of a wordsmith to come up with a better one.

She would compose rhyming lines of verse about nothing at all, extolling the virtues of Velveeta, turkeys, Weed Whackers, or knuckle cracking. It was her one creative endeavor in a lifetime of linear thinking. Anna would stare at the notebook paper until thoughts began to bump up against each other. She'd push the words around until they made her laugh, then rip the page out, tuck it into a bulging folder in her bottom desk drawer at home, and promptly forget about it.

But Tony had stumbled upon her stash, and as a studio musician by trade had felt moved to turn a few of the poems into songs. He had somehow transformed Anna's ridiculous scribblings into ten truly kick-ass tunes.

Tony. And his boundless ability to find new ways to love her.

She ran a trembling finger down the first few songs listed on the back of the CD.

1) "Ken Left Barbie for Gumby"
2) "I Peeked into Your Dream Last Night, and You're in Trouble"
3) "Praise Be, and Haul-It-To-Ya!"

That third cut—a spirited a cappella gospel tune about online shopping—was almost impossible to be sad to. Anna plugged her earbuds into the ancient CD player she kept just for this purpose. She cranked the volume and hoped the soulful voices would take her somewhere else.

"Praise be, and Haul-It-To-Ya, brothers and sisters! Haul-It-To-Ya!"

As the full choir kicked into Tony's joyful arrangement, Anna closed her eyes, watching him whirl through the house, belting out lyrics, tugging on her arms to get her gangly, way-too-tall body up and dancing. She was likely to oblige him if the drapes were pulled.

"Everybody clap your hands!

Ain't no need to change your plans.

Send an email, shout Amen!

Never leave your house again.

Praise be the internet credit line givers.

Stay home, 'cuz you know Jesus delivers!"

Remembering the day Tony had brought their stoic Rottweiler, Jackpot, up on his hind legs to dance—the two of them moving in unison with ridiculous grins on their faces—Anna's eyes popped open as she lunged for the eject button. She placed the disc reverently into its clear plastic case before pushing the cover closed with the finality of a coffin lid.

This was not helping. She needed to move. To pace or something. She stood so quickly that everything went grey, and she had to grab the back of her chair or fall over. She couldn't breathe, and her heart was still pounding. She wondered how long her body could run at this rate without incurring damage. With no conscious decision to do so, Anna reached for the cure she had relied on since she was seven years old.

Eddy.

She sat down at her computer, clicked on the bookmark for WLCM, and started the live stream. Eddy's understated voice came like a warm washcloth to her forehead. She exhaled deeply, forcing her shoulders to relax, clearing her mind of all puppies and people who would do them harm. She focused on Eddy, tilted back in his chair, playing with one of the small toys he kept on the console.

"—and one more thing about snails," he said. (She could hear him smiling.) "They have so much slime on their undersides they can crawl across the edge of a razor blade, no problem! That's wild, yeah?"

Anna felt her muscles begin to loosen. She closed her eyes, blocking out everything but the sound of her dearest friend. His voice was soft and slow, starting from somewhere deep in his chest. Mostly, he sounded like a guy from Wisconsin. But when he got excited or overly tired, she could hear shades of his Hawaiian accent, taking her right back to second grade when this brown, mystical kid had arrived at their school speaking English she could barely understand, his words missing all of their hard edges.

She leaned back in her chair. Amiable, readily delighted, Eddy was healing her from across town with one of his many amazing gifts: His tendency to feel at home wherever he went. He spoke without pretense or insecurity because he had none. This was the attribute she most admired in him. Coveted, even.

Anna ran both hands through her hair, gathering it into a thick wad behind her head, then releasing it. She stared at the wooden slatboard ceiling, searching for her inner Eddyness—a gentler, more tolerant outlook on her raw, rage-filled morning.

Eddy spoke to his listening audience about whatever intrigued him, and he was a man who took interest in pretty much everything. Eddy Kaimi Rivard (Kaimi being a Hawaiian name, meaning *The Seeker*) had created the perfect job for himself, talking to people in a twenty-mile radius—many of whom he knew by name—about local goings-on, helpful household hints, articles he'd read in the paper, funny things he'd heard on TV, card tricks that tickled him, quizzes he'd taken online, bumper stickers he'd driven behind, and cultural oddities from other countries.

"Okay, remember the other day when I admitted how much I liked the special sauce on the chicken sandwich over there at the Burger Boy in Cumberland? And I was wondering if it had a secret ingredient or something? Well, lots of you condiment connoisseurs emailed me your personal inside information on exactly what that magical ingredient is. And let me just say, if every one of you is right, and all those things are really in there, Burger Boy's special sauce is the most complex substance on Planet Earth since the invention of nuclear-grade boron carbide. So today we're going to—"

Anna clicked off the radio stream. Her racing heart and shaking hands had quieted some. She concentrated on breathing deeply for a minute or so longer, inhaling what she could of her normal self from the objects around the room. The photo of her brother Greggy as a kid, dressed as Oscar Wilde for Halloween. Jackpot's old collar hanging on the wall above her desk. A sketch her mom had made of two lopsided swans landing on the Milk River. Her WLCM coffee mug.

With her physical restoration came clarity of thought. Anna picked up her phone to make a couple of entries on her List of Things to Do: *Research panic attacks* and *Call Mom's shrink.*

Then she left for the police department on the slam of two doors.

5

"It's almost time for the news, and not all of it is good today, as you might have heard already. Some sad, sad happenings with a litter of puppies over on the west end of town. There are some humans in the story, too, of course. Most of whom were trying to do the right thing. One of whom probably could have tried a little harder. I'll get you the latest details at the top of the hour or thereabouts."

Eddy brought the front two legs of his chair down to earth as he reached for one of the framed photographs on his console.

"I don't want to let much more of today go by without thanking you all for my yesterday. As many of you know, it was my grandmother's birthday; she would have been eighty years old." His honeyed voice mellowed further as he brought the photograph close to his face, looking into her eyes.

"So many kind emails and voicemail messages and actual snail-mail cards have been coming my way from yours; I hope you know how much it means to me. The cockles of my heart couldn't get any warmer. And some of you sent me pictures again this year. Photos you took of her while she was reading to your kids, or serving hot lunch at the senior center, or sitting on your patio with a joke on her face and a cool drink in her hand. I wonder if I could ever describe the greatness of such a gift. Seeing my grandmother—my *tutu* is the Hawaiian word—on a particular day, caught in a particular moment that I never knew existed... it's like I open up your card or your email, and for one sweet second she's back here with me. Like she's dropped by my house from that timeless place where she is now; and when she comes to visit I never know how old she'll be, or what she'll be wearing, or what mood she'll be in. But I'm always crazy-happy to see her. And for that I thank you from the bottom of my full, full heart."

Eddy stopped talking, a small smile on his face, his eyes on the photograph. His mind meandered for the next thirty seconds or so, creating an equal amount of dead air, his listeners well accustomed to the phenomenon.

Until the reading of his grandmother's will, he'd had no idea that the reason she'd been scrimping and scratching her whole life, getting by on so little, denying herself so much, had been to help him realize his dream of someday owning a radio station. When she'd died, she left Eddy all of her worldly goods, including just enough money to help him start WLCM and keep it up and running (if he were frugal). Combining her money with his own savings, Eddy was able to afford his FCC licensing, electricity for the transmitter, and a small salary for himself—about half of what he paid his only employee, Jenny. Jenny was his DJ-Producer-Researcher-Production Assistant-Vacuumer. Eddy hated to vacuum.

As grateful as he was for his tutu's generous gift, he couldn't stand the thought of her having sacrificed this, too, for him, when she'd already given up so much.

His blessed grandmother, Leikili Rivard, had raised him from the time he was an infant. Eddy's own mother, lost in a world of poor choices and hallucinogenic drugs, had offered to trade her baby for a bag of groceries and a '62 Dodge. Leikili had taken the deal.

Eddy lived with his tutu on the Big Island for his first seven years, until their savings ran out, forcing them to leave the land they'd considered part of their own bodies, to begin life in a place Eddy's dead grandfather had abandoned long before: Milk River, Wisconsin. Leikili sent a letter to her husband's brother, who swiftly and without condition agreed to support her until she found a job. Though he'd thought that she and the child were probably uncivilized, they were family, and family was to be helped. So seven-year-old Eddy began grade school in a cold, prickly place with no salty-sweet air or colorful fish. And life got a little harder.

Being the only two people in town with brown skin was challenging for Eddy and his tutu at first. But the novelty eventually wore off, and with it, the cruelty.

Eddy set his tutu's photo back on the console with a silent thank you for raising him into a good, respectable man when no one else had seemed interested in the job.

He leaned back again, bringing the microphone with him.

"In any case, I know she changed many of you in one way or another, because that's the kind of person she was. And I do love to hear those stories. But if you have other photos I haven't seen yet, I'm going to ask you to hang onto them, maybe spread them out over time, so I can continue to find her unexpectedly at my door for as long as I live. Wouldn't that be something?

"All right. Onward! Remember last week how I told you that Shakespeare had actually come up with—or had been the first person to write down—a lot of common phrases we still use today? Like: *Good riddance, love is blind, foul play, too much of a good thing, what a piece of work, mum's the word,* and *as luck would have it.* And really, I could go on and on, 'cuz there are so many of them. But I just found out about another phrase he invented: *the live-long day*. Now I coulda sworn that *the live long day* came from *I've Been Working on the Railroad!* That's wild, yeah? *The live long day* was Shakespeare's? I looked it up, and sure enough, it's from a passage in a play he wrote about Julius Caesar.

"I don't read much Shakespeare, or any, really. But digging into it today was kinda fun. I gotta say, even though I didn't quite understand everything I was reading, I liked how it sounded. The phrase *the live-long day* appears during this guy's major rant about—something. But even anger sounds kinda sweet from old Shakespeare's pen. Let me read you a little of it. I'll go slow.

"'...Many a time and oft

Have you climb'd up to walls and battlements,

To towers and windows, yea, to chimney-tops,

Your infants in your arms, and there have sat

THE LIVE-LONG DAY *with patient expectation...'*

"Okay, so... maybe it doesn't *rhyme* as well as *I've Been Working on the Railroad* does, but it has some other cool stuff going for it, yeah? I like the way he pairs up words that sound nice together. *Patient expectation.* Try that out loud. *Patient expectation.* It's just fun to say, isn't it? But then again, so is *Fie, fi, fiddly i o.* So I guess they're both good."

Eddy never took this remarkable life for granted. Every day before his walk to the station he would sit still for five minutes to come up with at least one new way he could be of service on the air. In return, his listeners were few but devoted. People who switched on the radio just before six a.m. to hear Eddy sign-on in the morning mostly kept with him until his seven p.m. sign-off. So as it happened, Eddy's daily chores included helping people wash breakfast dishes, milk cows, putz around at the work bench, scrub toilets, tinker with cars, nap on the couch, drive to the market, organize closets, and clean up after supper. Also, as the story went, Eddy had proven instrumental in populating at least one Milk River family.

Try as they would, John and Bev Johnston had been unable to have children. But one morning, right during Eddy's helpful suggestion of removing a broken light bulb from the socket by pushing the sharp glass edges into a bar of soap and using the soap as a handle to unscrew the bulb, little Sandy Johnston had gotten her first start on the world. Bev swore it was a divine intervention of some kind, and Eddy's presence in their bedroom that morning had made all the difference. When Sandy Eddya Johnston was finally born, Bev decreed that from that point on, all procreating would take place only between the hours of six in the morning and seven at night, since anything else would be a pure waste of time.

This moved John Johnston to strike a deal with Eddy. If he would keep WLCM in business and on the air throughout Bev's childbearing years, John would mow the station's lawn for free all summer long. Eddy promised to do his best, and the men shook hands on it. They both stayed true to their word; Bev Johnston was now forty-four years old, the proud mother of five.

Of course, Eddy knew he hadn't actually helped Bev conceive any children. That had been his grandmother's doing. She was the person who'd made it possible for Eddy's words to hover above the Johnston's marital bed in the first place.

"I've got an email here I'm finally ready to answer, then it's on to today's news. This email's from Big Ben. Benny Steener. For the two or three of you out there who aren't acquainted with this particular character, he's the assistant manager over at the NAPA Auto Parts in Cumberland.

"He wrote: 'Dear Eddy, I've been working a lot of double shifts lately because I'm saving up for a motorcycle, and I want to buy new this time, and that takes a lot of money. Problem is, I'm not getting much sleep. How dangerous is that? Can I go another six months without frying my brain or something? Because I really gotta have that bike. Let me know. Signed, Big Ben. P.S. What's with that pile of junk in your front yard? I see it every time I drive by, and I think, nope, he still ain't hauled it away. Don't your neighbors get ticked-off?'"

The next sound WLCM listeners heard was a long, rolling laugh that began somewhere deep in Eddy's belly.

"Ho, brah! Very funny, Big B! He's been hassling me ever since I made a large sculpture out of some scrap metal I'd been saving. It's actually an eight-foot-high rooster, and lots of people tell me they think it's kinda cool. And either way, they *all* know what it is! So, Big Ben, even though your taste in art is a bit unsophisticated, I think your question is a valid one. What happens if you go without sleep for too long? I've done some research, and here's what I found out.

"It messes with your immune system, so you're more likely to get sick. And you've probably already noticed your memory and concentration getting worse. Oh—and your reaction time! That one might be a deal-buster, Big B. I hate to think of you out there driving your car with a slower reaction time. I mean, what if you were late flippin' that middle finger out your window?

"But seriously, Benny, you're risking a lot by working those double shifts. You ever thought about taking out a small loan for the bike? I know a guy over in Comstock, a banker who cares a lot about the little guy. His loans are based more on his gut than your credit report. Call me, Ben, if you're interested.

"And now let me get to the news. In case you just tuned in and haven't heard yet, something happened today that's going to be pretty hard to listen to, so if you have little kids in the room, you might want to ask them to leave. I'll wait."

And he did. Eddy said nothing for another thirty seconds. He could be heard sorting through papers, taking a drink of ice water, and scribbling something with a pencil. Then, careful not to editorialize, he reported on the story that most people had already caught wind of from a neighbor or chatty stranger.

"A twenty-six-year-old man named Brian Ardeen, who lives on Fourth Street, way over there by the hospital, was taken into custody a few-and-a-half hours ago, right around ten-thirty this morning."

Eddy picked up a furry beanbag cat he'd gotten from Anna. He closed his hand around the silky coat, taking a moment to appreciate the feel of it against the sensitive part of his palm.

"It seems Brian Ardeen's dog, a white German shepherd, gave birth to a litter of five pups sometime during the night. And this morning—well—he allegedly buried those puppies. Alive.

"Mr. Ardeen lives next door to Bunny Hall, who you probably know from around town here. As I understand it, Bunny got to the puppies, dug them up and brought them over to the veterinary clinic just in time. And according to Anna—Dr. Dunlop—two things worked in favor of the pups staying alive. First, it's autumn outside. Meaning, the ground was cold enough to lower their body temperature, slowing their metabolism. And second, they were buried in a paper bag with enough air for them to breathe a little while. Almost enough, anyway. Dr. Dunlop and her team had to work pretty hard to revive some of those puppies; but now all five of them are safe and sound with the mother dog down at the clinic.

"Chief of Police, Max Cotton, arrested Mr. Ardeen on five charges of cruelty to animals. The arrest happened out at the factory, which is where he works. And I've since learned some other details from employees out there who saw Max taking the man into custody. At first, Mr. Ardeen couldn't quite figure out why the law might be interested in him. But once he understood why he was being arrested, he was quoted as saying, 'I can do whatever I want to with my own (bleep)-ing property.'

"Well, those dogs aren't his property anymore. The mother and all five pups have been officially placed into the care of our own Milk River veterinarian, Anna Dunlop. And it looks like Mr. Ardeen will be spending the night in a cell, because he won't have the money for bail 'til tomorrow. That's all I know so far, but I'll keep you posted as things develop.

"So now the news is over, and I'm back to the editorial part of the program, which I guess is the whole program pretty much every day, except for the news, yeah? Apparently, requests are flooding in from people around the county interested in adopting those pups. That speaks to the character of our citizens, I believe. And our heartfelt thanks goes out to Bunny and the folks down at the vet clinic, that's for sure.

"Y'know, the reality of this story is pretty difficult for most of us to take in. We feel torn up by the shock of it all. I know I do, anyway. Personally, I can't imagine someone doing such a thing. And yet the thing got done, yeah? There are all sorts of people in this world, committing acts of cruelty—and acts of kindness, too—acts that most of us bumping around in the middle ground between Adolf Hitler and Mother Theresa would never even consider doing. It's strange, isn't it? I mean we're all made up of the same basic materials. Five or six quarts of blood, a bit of bone, a few pounds of flesh. So how is it we can turn out so completely different from one another? Did my little DNA ladder twist left where yours twisted right, and bang! I like fish sticks and you're a concert pianist? How does that happen?

"Anyway, it's a pretty mournful day for lots of us in town here. First, because of that mother dog and her puppies. I can't imagine anything scarier than to lose your babies. Unless it's to lose your mom, and be put into some cold place where you can't catch your breath. And then there's Dr. Dunlop, her staff, and Bunny. They probably didn't realize when they were brushing their teeth this morning that they'd be called upon to become heroes in about an hour.

"And I also believe it's a disturbing day for all of us here who call Milk River home, because of the way crime against innocent victims makes us feel. Personally, I get this sick sensation, from my stomach right up to somewhere behind my eyeballs.

"But what happened today to those animals is about to affect all of us in another way, too, because this has now become a national story. Watch for it on the five-thirty news. And if you miss it, just tune in at ten o'clock tonight, and probably tomorrow, too. It won't go away for awhile. So, this is how the world finds out about our little town, with all of its rich black soil, clean bathrooms and gracious, just-tell-me-what-you-need people. We're about to be known for one terrible deed. For one troubled soul. The man spending a night in jail with so much pain in his life that this awful act seemed like a good idea to him.

"I don't know how he got to that place in his thinking, but his other options must have seemed pretty darn grim. I close my eyes and try to imagine any situation that might make me choose what Brian Ardeen chose today. And I just can't find it. I think the ceiling must be lower in his world, yeah? Keeping him hunched over, not able to stand tall enough to see a few of the other options out there. I don't know why a person builds a house like that for himself, and I don't know how strong he has to be to break out of it. All I know is that what I feel mostly for Brian Ardeen right now is sorry. And I wish things were different. But until then, I want you to find somebody you love this afternoon, hug 'em close, and feel lucky for who you both are."

Eddy took a couple sips of water.

"I want to play you a song I can't seem to stop thinking about today. It was written and sung by another man who used to live in a house kinda like that but somehow found his way to the door. One of the Beach Boys, Brian Wilson. The name of the tune is "Love and Mercy."

6

Anna stood in the street looking up at the old firehouse, which would soon revert back to *being* the old firehouse. No one would ever refer to the building as *the old veterinary clinic* once the exam tables, centrifuge, and x-ray viewers were gone. Her fifteen years in residence had been a mere blip on the screen compared to the ninety-year firehouse history preceding her. The physical changes she'd made to the property would be absorbed with time—the sign would be taken down, flowerbeds would turn to weed, awnings would fade and fall away—leaving the reddish brick building to snuggle back into its proper place within Milk River's chronology.

She was aware that she should feel something right now, standing curbside on her decision to undo her business, her career, and the livelihoods of two faithful staff members. But both arms dangled slackly at her sides, her eyelids felt heavy, and she took a breath only when she seemed to need air. Fresh out of opinions, Anna Dunlop, DVM, headed toward the front door of her clinic for what she imagined to be one of the last few times.

She plodded up the four cement stairs she normally took two at a time, being longer on leg than patience most days. And the thick glass door weighed twice what it had this morning. Anna watched her feet drag themselves over the threshold onto the welcome mat, and stop. The schnauzer-shaped die-cut rug. Printed with a realistic canine image, it always looked as if the dog had been steamrolled—its face flattened into the permanently happy position. But she'd received it as a gift from a favorite client and had been waiting for it to wear out. She could never have guessed the rug would outlast her. She scraped wet leaves from her boots onto what she tried not to see as the dog's fluffy, grey throat.

A cat hissed. She looked up to realize there were other people in the world—several of whom seemed to be sitting in her waiting room, staring at her, smiling mostly, holding animals in laps and on leashes. Other sounds filtered through—the panting of dogs, nails skittering on hardwood floor, Noah on the phone, Katie's voice in one of the exam rooms.

"Oh," Anna heard herself say to the gathering. "Hi."

A roomful of faces wanted something from her. It took only a moment to riddle it out. She'd left the clinic hours ago, with no word to her staff. So these, then, would be her appointments for today. People who didn't know she wasn't a vet anymore.

"Anna, hi!" said an exuberant Noah, hanging up the phone, swooping out from behind the reception desk. "Great to see ya! You okay? We were worried."

"I'm good, thanks."

Crap. How's Noah going to pay rent on his new apartment now? Guilt was trying to wheedle its way in.

Anna kept staring in the direction she wanted to go until Noah stepped aside. She noticed his expression turn to confusion, or maybe disappointment.

On her way down the hall, she disturbed the three occupants of the first exam room by leaning in to pick up the cat carrier from under the counter. Katie was there, and a client whose name Anna could have recalled if she tried. And the third was a rotund Pekinese trembling on the metal table. All three creatures turned to look in Anna's direction, but only Katie was trying to send her a message with her face—something frantic and dark. Anna offered most of a wave and kept moving.

Entering the surgery, she squatted down by the spring-loaded baby gate penning Storm and her five puppies into a corner of the room. Anna hooked all ten fingers through the holes of the plastic mesh, and watched Storm lick the underside of a grunting pup. Lulled by the milky warmness of the air and the smell of wet newspaper, she let her eyes defocus.

A puppy squealed, jarring her back to the task. Anna removed the barrier, let the shepherd smell her hand, then gave the white dog's head a caress or two before standing up again. She turned around quickly, banging hard into Katie.

A moment passed before she realized she was expected to say something. "Hi."

"Hi? Really? Hi?" Katie's eyebrows were up by her hairline.

Her friend wanted to talk, but talking wasn't what Anna wanted. She mumbled an apology, stepping around Katie on her way to the linen cabinet. She opened the door, and for maybe the first time in fifteen years, felt zero pleasure from seeing the army of tightly rolled towels, ends out, color-coded by towel size, stacked four levels high on the shelf she'd built to precise towel dimensions. She selected a green one and, holding it by the end, let gravity unroll it.

"What's going on, Anna?"

Anna glanced over her shoulder at Katie, having almost forgotten she was there. She gave her friend's upper arm a little squeeze as she slipped by her again.

"What, you're not even going to talk to me?"

Anna paused, wondering if she had to, then decided she probably did. She turned around to face Katie, clasping her hands in front of her, the green towel drooping almost to the floor.

"I'm sorry. Sure, let's talk." Anna knew she was freaking Katie out and wished she had the reserves to give her what she needed. "How can I help you?"

Katie let out with a single sarcastic laugh. Anna looked down at the pups, their pudgy legs making swishing sounds against the newspaper. By the time she tuned back into Katie she had missed some of the verbal content but could see where they were headed. In keeping with the surreal nature of this whole day, Katie was speaking with more passion than Anna would have thought possible.

"—because you tear off outta here at ten o'clock in the morning, not a word about where you're going, then miss five hours of appointments without even checking in, which is something Dr. Spotless Queen of—of—Anal Retentia, Anna Dunlop, would never, ever do. So who the hell *are* you?"

Katie's head and shoulders jerked as she spoke, the ends of her long, blonde hair moving in counterpoint. She finally came to a stop, shoving her arms into the crossed position.

"Um, okay," said Anna. "You seem—upset."

Katie sucked in a quick rush of air, forcing it out all at once. After a moment, she placed a hand on each of Anna's shoulders.

"Look, are you even *in* there? Seriously, you sound really bizarre. So… you just need to tell me. Can I go on with my barrage of indignant demands, or should I be bundling you up into the station wagon for a ride to the emergency room?"

Anna examined Katie's words one at a time until they made sense.

"Is there an Option C?"

"Hey, okay. Great. Houston, we have contact." Katie dropped her hands back to her sides. "This is good. Now—can you come and sit down? Maybe tell me what's been happening?"

Anna turned back toward the table to begin folding her towel. “I really don’t have time to sit down.”

In the silence that followed, she pushed the small rectangle of towel into the cat carrier, saw it didn’t quite cover the bottom, and pulled it out for a do-over.

“You don’t have time?” Katie spoke slowly. “Where are you going? We’re pretty far behind on appointments out there. I sent a bunch of people home already, but I kept hoping you’d show up, so I didn’t call to cancel anyone. We’ve got clients who’ve been waiting over an hour for you—and more coming.”

On her third try, Anna found the fold she liked, fitted the cushion into place, and gave it a pat. A puppy chirping in mild distress drew her attention. The big yellow male was trying to swim his way back to the warmth of his family circle. Having somehow stranded himself, he wriggled and wobbled over slippery newspaper, making headway in fractions of inches. Anna scooped him up, plunked him onto the row of colorful siblings tucked within the U of Storm’s pink belly, jabbed a finger into the air in a *be right back* message for Katie, and left the room.

She returned with a load of supplies and a canvas bag she’d picked up at a veterinary trade show last summer. Dropping everything onto the table beside the cat carrier, she began to sort through it. She picked up the red plastic dog food dish. Crosshatched with scratches inside and out, the bowl had held water for several years of visiting canines, most of whom Anna had been able to help. The memory triggered something like melancholy. Not an actual sensation, but the threat of one. An understanding that pain waited in a dark corner of a room somewhere, ready to jump her when she passed. She jammed the dish into the canvas bag.

Katie’s heated exasperation rippled in waves against her back, but if Anna didn’t press on, she’d never make it out of there. Katie, however, would not be ignored. She came around to stand directly across the metal table from her, in the position she’d assumed during countless surgeries over the past decade.

Pushing sample packs of dog food into the bag, Anna sensed that when she looked up, Katie would be gaping at her. And when she did, she was.

She owed Katie an explanation, but that would mean putting words to a mash-up of gut feelings. She tried to think it through. After four long years of college, then four more years in veterinary school, and another fifteen in practice—twelve of which were spent trying to *pay off* veterinary school—she was yanking the plug on her whole career. After one hard day. That made no sense, no matter who you were, much less a person who had allowed herself maybe five snap decisions in her entire life; and those were on choices like firm or extra firm tofu.

"What's going on, Anna? What are you doing? What happened?"

"Happened?" Anna pushed a little air through her teeth in a grim laugh. "You know, that's the weird thing. Nothing really happened. I had a conversation with a guy, and now I'm quitting my job."

"You're qui—what? What are you talking about?"

"I don't want to do this anymore. I can't. I mean, I shouldn't. I need to stop doing this."

She lowered her head, grabbed the cat carrier, and went to sit on the floor beside the puppies, folding her praying-mantis legs into a lap formation. After a moment, Katie followed, seating herself on the newsprint beside Anna.

Anna couldn't look at her; she'd arrived here free of doubt and wouldn't let Katie jimmy the lock on her resolve.

She picked up the black and tan male. He squealed a little but quieted when she brought him up to her chest in the baby burping position, his head bobbing against her shoulder. She reached for the carrier, but Katie got there first, taking it into her lap and opening the door. Anna nodded a thank you as she put the puppy into the kennel, settling him with a few reassuring strokes.

Reaching for the next pup, she stopped and forced herself to survey Katie's face. Her eyes seemed puffy. Her cloud-white cheeks had been stained pink by the day she was having. The day Anna had just put her through.

"Dr. Spotless Queen of What?" asked Anna, eyes narrowing.

"Anal Retentia?"

Anna considered the title and nodded before returning to nestle puppies against each other inside of the carrier. She kept an eye on Storm who seemed keenly interested, though not worried. The small caramel colored runt—the one they'd almost lost—was last in. Anna set the whelp in place, let her hand linger over the puppy's back, then slipped a finger under a tiny front leg for a pulse. Satisfied, she shut the door to the kennel, continuing to stare at the pups through the metal bars. She listened only to their soft grunts, purposely tuning out siren calls from scattered rooms down the hall: Talking, barking, the occasional laugh.

Anna stood, lifting the carrier as she rose. She stepped high over Katie's lap on her way back to the surgery table, trailed by Storm, who cleared the same obstacle in a quick hop. From her still-seated position, Katie picked up sheets of soiled newspaper, rolling them into a ball. Meanwhile, Anna filled the last square inch of canvas bag with cartons of milk replacer. She looked down at her friend.

"I went to the cops," said Anna.

"Sorry?"

"When I left here this morning, I went to see the Chief of Police. Max Cotton."

"You did? To turn the guy in?"

"To turn him in, and to make sure Max knew every sickening detail of what this jerk had done."

"Okay.... And how'd that go?"

Anna took a deep breath, not wanting to get as worked up as she had at the police station.

"You're not going to believe this."

"What?"

"Mistreatment of an animal isn't even considered an actual crime. It's a Class A Misdemeanor—one step above a parking ticket. Technically, this pathetic creep *could* get up to nine months in jail and a ten thousand dollar fine, but, apparently, that won't happen. That never happens. Max says chances are he'll get a tiny fraction of that fine and no jail time."

"No jail time at all? That sounds—messed up." Katie seemed hesitant to react, afraid to feed the fire.

"Messed up? It's a total—" Anna didn't have a word for what it was.

A brief pause in their conversation gave her time to slip back into her dark imaginings, replays of individual moments that must have taken place at Storm's house that morning. She didn't know what Brian Ardeen looked like, so she pictured him from behind in every scene. Under his kitchen sink picking out just the right size of paper bag. Tamping down the dirt, then turning to bellow at Storm for making so damn much noise.

"I want him to *suffer*." She saw the shock on Katie's face, but didn't let it stop her. "He's a vile, malicious mistake of nature, and needs to be thrown in jail for a long time. But too bad, because the legal system can't be bothered. 'So, go ahead, dude, grab your shovel; kill as many dogs as you want, because, hey, nobody really cares.'"

She knew why Katie looked afraid. Anna was scaring *herself*. When the person who usually kept the peace was suddenly hungry for revenge, what else was likely to turn upside-down?

"So..." began Katie, picking her way along carefully. "I hear what you're saying. And, of course, I know how you feel about abuse, but—I'm not quite sure I'm getting it. What's the connection between this particular terrible thing and you quitting your job?"

Anna put both hands flat on the cold table. It was a valid question. One she should have asked herself before now. What was the connection? She'd reached extraordinary depths of sadness on this job over the years, working with animals in peril; what was it about this particular instance that was making her dump everything and run?

She looked down at the floor, holding very still, trying to get a solid picture from jelly-like impressions. She could hear her pounding heart.

Tony.

Was this about Tony? Her instinct was to reject the idea, but here she was, about to make the most end-it-all decision of her life on the anniversary of her greatest loss. Put that way, it didn't seem like much of a coincidence.

She closed her eyes and replayed her reaction to the puppy emergency. Pictured herself in her office clutching her chest. What it felt like, was that the world had handed her an armful of junk exactly five years ago and had been stacking the pile higher and higher ever since, until she'd become a staggering tower of ache and fury, ready to collapse if one final straw flitted in with the morning breeze—and then someone dropped a piano on her.

Loath to admit it, Anna was starting to see how Tony's death had been eating away layers of her well-being, leaving mostly exposed nerve. Which was how the unflinching, unflagging, unshakable Anna Dunlop had been brought down by a basket of newborn pups.

Nevertheless, this was still the right decision. She'd had no business becoming a veterinarian in the first place. She was ill-equipped to do the work the way the world wanted it done. For one thing, the number of incurable animals a vet was forced to euthanize was overwhelming. And every life she'd taken had sapped a little of her own. Someone had to do the humane procedure, yes, but she needed it to be someone else for awhile.

That, however, was only a fraction of the problem. Though most of her clients took good care of their animals, too many did not. The sheer number of people who used her clinic as an option of last resort was unbearable. They'd bring her pets too far gone to save, wanting miracles she couldn't offer.

Still other clients expected her to euthanize curable animals they couldn't afford to treat, which she simply refused to do. To their faces she'd agree to put their cat or dog down, but would then heal the creature by night, at her own expense, later smuggling it to a distant shelter for another chance. People would consider this strange, she realized, maybe illegal. But it was the only option she could imagine for herself.

Also, Milk River, Wisconsin, consisted primarily of working farmland—further exacerbating Anna's pain. Small animals were disposable on too many farms, a constant flow of cats and dogs breeding and dying off without much human notice. It was the main reason she'd chosen to practice small animal medicine only, unable to look a cow in those large, sweet-tempered eyes, knowing the beast would not be exiting this life from natural causes.

Katie had come to stand beside her. “Anna?”

There was pity, or concern, or caring in Katie’s voice that made Anna move away. In one graceless, long stride, she made it over to where Storm stood staring at the cat carrier, tail wagging slowly. Anna bent to remove the dog’s filthy collar, then gave her neck a good scratching.

“It feels like—like I’ve lived forty years trying to be a decent person, pouring my whole self into doing whatever I could do for animals. Trying to make things—better.”

“Yeah, I think that’s a pretty good description of you.”

“But it doesn’t work! Doing everything I can isn’t enough!” Her voice cracked. “At the police station, I stood there staring at Max’s mouth. Watching it form the words—that legally, these puppies were Ardeen’s *property*. That they had the same rights as the rest of the trash littering his backyard. And I realized it was we *people* who had made that decision. Back when the laws were being created, we had this choice—this chance—to either look at ourselves as part of a whole *group* of beings on the planet who deserved protection, or to decide we were the only ones who mattered. And we failed. We failed the Human Test. We used our really impressive, superior brains to prove what superior assholes we were.”

“Yeah, I see what you mean. Those laws are totally wrong.”

“The universe is wrong. And unchangeable. And I’m just—tired. I’m done.”

Anna snapped the price tag off a bright red nylon collar she’d taken from the hook of retail items in the reception area. She increased its length a few inches and clipped the collar around Storm’s neck.

“But—” Katie scraped flyaway hairs from her forehead with the heel of her hand. “Hang on. So. You decide to stop doing your part around here, and things become a lot worse for the animals in this town. You get that, right?”

Anna fastened a new purple leash to Storm’s collar, then stood to face Katie.

“Yeah, that’s what I used to think, too. Until I realized that pretty much everything I’ve always been so damn sure about is verifiably wrong.”

“Like?”

“Like being a veterinarian does *not* mean you can stop animals from suffering.”

“C’mon, that isn’t—”

"And just because a despicable act is technically against the law, doesn't mean the law is going to do anything about it."

"Okay, yeah, but—"

"And just because I said I'd be a vet fifteen years ago, does not mean I have to keep being a vet until the end of time."

Anna's throat clamped shut. Her next words creaked out feebly.

"Oh—and by the way—marriage is *not* forever. It actually lasts about three good years, then destroys everything else that comes after."

Katie took a moment to replay what she'd just heard. She studied Anna's face, which seemed to be disintegrating, breaking away into the raw sorrow Katie had known about for years but had never been allowed to see. Every part of Anna's body was crying, moving in waves, lurching with each tormented phrase.

"Something broke in me today, Katie. And that broken piece—I think it was really important—like maybe it kept other parts working—parts that aren't—working anymore. So, I've gotta go. And I hate that I'm quitting. I hate *me* that I'm quitting. God, I'm—pathetic!" Anna gritted her teeth so violently that her head shook.

Katie took Anna by both forearms. "Hey. Try to calm down."

"I'm sorry, I've gotta go." Anna pulled free of Katie's grasp. She fumbled for the bag of supplies and hooked it over her shoulder. Shaking her head, she whisked the cat carrier from the table, pulled Storm to her side, and fled the surgery through the back door.

Katie hadn't moved when Anna's wet face reappeared at the doorway, almost spoke, and then vanished again.

7

The panting Rottweiler lay stiffly on the exam table. Like a giant pipe cleaner, the dog would freeze and hold whatever position Anna bent him into as she worked. If she raised a limb into the air, or cocked his head at an odd angle, that became his new shape. She was just returning his hind leg to a more relaxed position when her hand brushed across something sharp.

She bent down for a closer look at one of his many injuries, extremely aware of her client's face peering into the gash with her. Annoyed, she opened her mouth to ask the man to step back when her forceps hit against a piece of twisted metal. She squinted at the fragment, trying to work it carefully out of the wound.

With this emergency patient arriving before clinic hours, she hadn't had time to pin up her unruly hair, which fell forward at precisely the wrong moment. One hand steady on the forceps, her face so close to the dog she could feel the heat of his skin, she used her free hand to jam the offending hair behind her ear.

"Um, I think that's mine." The voice came from inches away.

Anna turned, coming nose-to-nose with her client, now lashed to her head by a thick shank of his own hair. "Oh, my god," she said without standing up. She removed the wavy, brown locks, handing them back to the owner with a wince. "Right. Mine's the reddish stuff."

He stood and smiled down at her with an invitation to smile back, which she eventually did.

With the scrap metal extracted, she finally rose, realizing from her full six-foot-two perspective, she was still looking *up* into the man's eyes. She took her first long look at her client since he'd entered her clinic about half an hour earlier.

She'd just arrived for the day when he'd come through the front door carrying the limp, bloodied Rottweiler, and the dog had held her full attention ever since. She stared at the man's unusual face. Muscular, angular, a continent of hard ridges of varying elevations, engulfing eyes that sent messages of kindness and curiosity.

"Guess I was too close. Sorry 'bout that." He ran a hand through his hair. "Sort of." He said it with a grin and a shrug.

Good gawd, is he flirting with me?

The dog groaned softly, and that interesting face looked down at the animal, darkening.

"You can keep him alive, can't you? He looks pretty bad. Damn. I wish I would have found him sooner."

"I can't be sure yet, but as bad as he looks from the outside, I'm thinking his insides might be all right." She touched the sutures on the dog's neck. "I've stopped the bleeding and he's stable."

She bent over again, relaxing into the work which always soothed her. She flushed the injury with water, then gave it a good antiseptic wash.

"I'll be taking him into surgery as soon as Katie—my vet tech—gets here. Which should be any second." She reached for the electric clippers. "He's going to lose this eye though." She began to shave around it.

"Oh, no." The man reached out to touch the head of the panting Rottweiler. "Aw, the poor guy."

The animal's drool mixed with blood on the metal table in a small, pink pool.

"You know what?" She wanted to smooth some of the worry from the man's expression. "His other eye looks totally normal to me. He'll get around just fine."

Anna guessed her client to be somewhere in his mid thirties. In gym shorts and a blood-drenched T-shirt, he revealed an athletic body that would have had no trouble hefting a 130-pound dog.

"Were you out running this morning? Is that how you found him?" She assembled a smile. Chatting had never been her strong suit.

She squirted blue surgical solution onto a gauze pad and began gently cleansing the dog's skin. The fresh, soapy smell was a familiar sensation among others more unknown.

"Yeah. I was heading up that big hill in the woods behind the quarry. I like to run out there early. Lots of company that time of day."

"Really? I've been up there tons of times and haven't seen a single human being."

"Yeah, neither have I," he said, petting the dog's massive head. "But there's always some kind of interesting critter up there on the lookout for his breakfast. I even spotted a coyote once, which was odd because they're pretty nocturnal, aren't they?"

"Um, mostly—yes." Her voice cracked. This second smile, though sheepish, came easily.

"Until today, though," he said, looking into the wide eyes of the trembling dog, "all of the animals out there have been alive and well, not whining in a ditch by the road."

"I'm pretty sure he was hit by a car."

"You think so?" He blinked his eyes a few times. "You mean someone hit this dog and just kept driving?"

"You'd be surprised how often that happens."

"That—doesn't make any sense to me."

Anna studied his face for signs of a joke being played on her, as she listened to the dog's lungs through her stethoscope. She began moving about the room, gathering up instruments and supplies, feeling the client's magnet pulling on hers.

"So, what should I name him?" he asked, from a faraway planet.

She turned a one-eighty, accidentally kicking the IV stand. "You're going to keep him?"

"Well, yeah, if no one claims him. I don't think there's anything sadder than a dog with no one to take him in." He gently wrapped his hand around the Rottweiler's snout. "Everybody's got to belong somewhere."

Anna's breathing had become shallow.

"Call him anything but Cujo. I know way too many big dogs named Cujo."

"Ha! I bet." He ran a hand through his hair, his eyes narrowing. "No, I think an animal coming from a tragic place like this should have a name that lifts him up from here, don't you? Like… Apollo. Or Galahad. Some name that says he has—value, you know?"

She did know.

"What's *your* name?" she said, hearing the bold question, wondering who'd asked it. "I'm sorry; I know you told me when you came in, but I was distracted by our patient here."

"Yeah, of course. Tony. My name's Tony. Griffin."

"I'm Anna Dunlop." She offered him a hand but pulled it back when she noticed the amount of blood on her rubber glove.

Chuckling, he showed her his own red-smeared palms, then reached both of them out to take her right hand.

"Uh—wait," she said. "I've got a card." She jerked her hand away to fish around in the pocket of her white coat. "Here." She pushed it in his direction.

The puzzled look on Tony's face drew her attention down to the bloodied lottery ticket clutched in her fingers. Her whole body flinched. "Wow. Please be gone when I look up again." Anna held her gaze on the cartoon treasure chest overflowing with gold and the bold headline above the five scratch-off pads.

"Jackpot!" he said, brightly. "I like it." He gave her a playful nod. And then he grew solemn.

He squatted down to put his face by the black, triangular ear drooping against the dog's head. "Jackpot." The name was half whisper.

The texture of Tony's voice slid like a warm fingertip down the back of Anna's neck.

"You have to focus on getting strong again, Jackpot." As he spoke, his lips almost brushed the silky edge of the dog's ear. "You're not done here yet, you got that?" He rested the flat of his hand gently across Jackpot's forehead, and the animal stopped shivering.

Anna turned away from the private moment they were having, this dog and his man. She noticed the stainless wall cabinet a little to her left and leaned over to catch her reflection.

She wanted to see what love looked like.

8

As much as possible, Eddy Rivard lived his life one undivided thought at a time. He liked to give his full attention to whatever he was doing in that particular instant. After he'd thanked his ancestors and crawled into bed at night, he'd make a point of not lingering over things that had happened during the day, or what he might do with the next one. He thought about how soothing it felt to open his cotton clamshell, climb inside, and close it gently over himself.

Eddy never ate while watching TV or listened to music when he read. He did one thing, or he did the other. When he was on the radio, he spoke about what was in his heart at that very moment. And when he was out on a run, he liked to listen to the sound of his shoes patting the ground, watch faraway things grow closer, and—on a crisp late afternoon like this one—breathe in the revitalizing scent of fall. He knew they were actually the smells of death and decay, but there was no sadness in the cycle. Just color, crunch, and the cleaning of trees for a better look at what the birds were up to.

But today was different. Eddy was having trouble keeping his head and body in the same place. Despite efforts to give this run its due, his thoughts drifted uncontrollably toward Anna. By the time he'd learned about the puppy story and called the clinic, she'd already left, with no word to anyone on her whereabouts. Very un-Anna. He'd played more music than usual on the air today, using the free time to try to reach her by phone.

And then had come the call from Katie.

"It was Anna," she'd said, "like I've never seen her. Like nobody's ever seen her, maybe."

"What d'ya mean?" He'd stood reflexively at the alarm in Katie's voice.

"You know that white Arabian pony the Rudmans have, and how he got spooked that one summer, bolting right into a barbed wire fence where he got all tangled up? And how he took off running?"

"Yeah…?"

"I was the one who found him just south of town. He was standing with all four legs spread out at odd angles, his white coat smeared with blood, his saddle upside down, hanging loose against his belly, and his sides heaving with these deep raspy breaths."

"Jeez. And?"

"And that was Anna. Just standing there. Breathing."

"So what, she was scared? Mad? Bleeding?"

"Right. Well, no, she wasn't bleeding."

Eyes closed, trying to picture the scene, Eddy had listened to every word Katie told him about her conversation with Anna. Then he'd hung up the phone and begun the four-mile run to Anna's house, starting to trot before he'd left the building. Eddy wasn't a fast runner, and he owned a car he could have run home to fetch, but it would have required a moment or two of thought.

Leaving Ferry Street, he hopped up a curb onto the grassy boulevard, then headed into the woods. As a rule, he would take this path to Anna's house to let the beauty of the enormous trees recharge him. Today he took it because it was the fastest way. He knew this for a fact, because he'd created the trail himself, having used a compass to plot the route. He'd been ten years old. Exactly.

He and Anna had been friends for a few years already, playing at each other's houses, but Eddy had always been taken to hers by car. His tutu wouldn't allow him to walk to Anna's place by himself until he turned ten. Which had given Eddy plenty of time to think about how his first trek might go, and how he would blaze the trail.

For his tenth birthday he'd asked for a compass and gotten one. He'd torn open the package, kissed his tutu on the cheek, and begged for permission to go to Anna's. Eddy still remembered how he'd held that compass straight out in front of his body, shuffling his feet to begin the path, his eyes boring into the point of the needle. Nothing but a tree was going to deter him from the straight line between his house and Anna's. Even if it meant having to climb over gigantic rocks and tromp up steep hills that he could easily have walked around. (Judging by existing paths, the deer had chosen the flatter ground in most cases.) But a straight line, the shortest distance between two points, had been the plan, and he refused to vary from it. Actually, the concept had been Anna's, straight lines being far more important to her than to Eddy, who was, in spirit, more of a meanderer. But he'd always loved Anna's missions, seeing them through as speedily and perfectly as time—and tutu—would allow.

Thirty years later, Eddy tugged his thoughts back to the run, back to the path. The packed dirt, the straight line, the rocks he could now vault over. Almost to Anna's house, he kept pressing for speed where he normally would have slowed his pace. He was closing in on one of his favorite moments of the route, where the rushing Milk River bent itself close to his path, treating many of his senses all at once. He could listen to the water bubble over rocks and fallen logs, watch sparkles on the surface hurry out ahead of him as he ran, even smell its algae, trout, and muddy banks when the wind was just right. On a normal day, he would take a moment to appreciate how the river both lulled and stirred him at the same time. It made him watch for other experiences in life with that same dual nature. Tribal drumming, maybe, was invigorating yet soothing. And espresso with a shot of Bailey's.

A movement caught Eddy's eye, pulling his thoughts back to where they belonged. He recognized the silhouette instantly. It was that of his best, oldest, most remarkable friend. But he hadn't expected her to be outside. He'd pictured her in the house, tending to the puppies. Or, Anna being Anna, hard at work constructing the ultimate whelping pen from hypoallergenic, splinter-free, bamboo planks she just happened to have on hand.

But there she was, ambling along the river, hands in her jacket pockets, watching her feet. He wanted to avoid startling her, so Eddy made noises as he approached. He dragged his shoes through the dry leaves, hummed *I've Been Working on the Railroad*, and jingled the change in his pocket.

The mouth came out of nowhere. A set of barking jaws filled with white, pointy teeth demanded he stop that very instant. Eddy did as he was told. Anna came jogging up to where he stood entirely, absolutely, Statue-of-Liberty still.

"Storm, it's okay. It's okay. He's one of us." Anna smoothed the dog's downy head with both hands. "Eddy. What's—why are you—who's on the radio?"

She shifted her weight, looked up at the trees, tried different places for her hands. It was clear she didn't quite know how to be around him right now, which made him sad.

"Jenny is." He was panting as he spoke. "I think she might be reading the *Turtle Lake Times* again. She likes that. If I don't make it back to the station before she finishes the news of the week, she'll probably work her way through the obituaries and start on the want ads."

"Ah. Then we'd better make this quick. Here's the scoop: Today I brought five animals back from the dead, verbally assaulted a cop, had a nervous breakdown, adopted six dogs, and quit my job. Thanks for coming by, Eddy. See ya later."

He nodded slowly, considering. "No arson then? Public nudity?"

"Well… day ain't over yet."

It was one of their all-time favorite movie lines and gave them a chance to smile.

"Want to walk?" Anna headed back toward the river. Eddy waited a moment, watching her move, gauging her okay-ness before jogging to catch up.

Storm passed them by at a gentle trot.

"Sorry she scared you. I know you're not wild about German shepherds."

"Not true. I love them. I just prefer to love them from a distance. Until I know they didn't come to tear the flesh from my face." He reflexively fingered the scar below his right cheekbone. "Besides, she's so white and furry—and skinny—she doesn't really push that button for me. I'm kinda surprised she's not with her babies, though."

He watched the dog walk ahead of them, nose to the ground along the water's edge.

"She'll have to go back to them soon. But she needs a break once in awhile. Can you imagine having to deal with that much raw need, twenty-four hours a day?"

"No. I really can't. My guppies have their issues, but being too clingy isn't one of them."

Eddy let the sound of streaming water and snapping twigs fill the space for a long while as they eased back into the familiar shape of their friendship. She'd ventured so far out of her own character today, he thought she might need some time to remember where they'd left off.

"So, then," he began, "are you going to keep the whole canine family? Forever? Is that the plan?"

"Yeah, see, there's the problem. That pesky plan thing. So far my grand scheme consists of bulldozing my life and curling up in a little ball around these animals, hoping the whole world goes away. I haven't thought very far past that yet."

"Okay."

As they walked, Eddy bent down to pick up a leaf, studying its festive red, orange, and green pattern. "Well, from what I hear, there've been a bunch of people asking to adopt those puppies."

"Nope. Not gonna happen. I'm not going to give them away to people I don't know. People I can't trust."

"Really?"

"Yes, really. They deserve a good life. And I couldn't know for sure how strangers would treat them. So they'll have to live with me. Or people I trust."

"I see."

"Maybe you could take one when they're weaned."

"I don't think so. It's all I can do to walk my guppies and keep them groomed. So... how's Storm doing in her new role? She's a good mom?"

"She's doing a great job. It seems to come naturally to her."

"It's amazing how a dog just knows how to do that. First time out, no coaching or anything. I mean, these wet, squirming things pop out of her body, and somehow she knows she's got to use her mouth to clean everything up, and get each pup out of that sticky—uh—*da kine* it comes in. That baggie thing, yeah?"

"Birth sac." Anna never tired of how the Hawaiian pidgin phrase da kine could be substituted for any word you were having trouble remembering.

"I mean," said Eddy, "me personally, my first reaction to seeing that bloody mucous stuff all over the ground would *not* be to start eating it, y' know?"

Moving, joking, avoiding. He knew how to mend her.

Anna stopped and looked upriver at the sun closing in on the horizon as she spoke.

"I've been doing a little online surfing, trying to diagnose what the hell is going on with me."

"Oh?"

"Best I can figure is that I might be fairly seriously depressed."

"Y' know, I've been thinking of suggesting that to you lately. I guess I'm about one brash decision too late."

"I suppose I didn't realize I was in such a bad way, emotionally—and—I think I just snapped."

"That makes sense. But… now you've snapped back again?"

"I dunno." She turned to continue their walk. "I feel like I'm a little more me, anyway. I've made an appointment with a shrink in St. Paul, so I'll let you know after that if you should remove all the sharp implements from my kitchen drawers."

"Good. That's good, Anna. I'm glad you're going to talk to someone. But we can keep the pickle fork, right? I love that little pickle fork."

"We'll see."

They walked awhile longer without speaking. It was Anna who broke the silence.

"Seriously, though, you must be getting tired of all my whining. At least I know I'm boring myself."

"Well, I have a higher tolerance for you than you do. Besides, you're entitled to feel awful this time of year."

He took a roll of tropical LifeSavers out of his jacket pocket, opened it up and offered her first pick. There was a coconut on top; she pulled it out and gave it to him, helping herself to the tangerine underneath.

"I have a pretty good idea of what's going on," he said, with a gentle tap to her temple as they walked. He put on his thickest Hawaiian pidgin accent. "I know you, sistah, and what makes you tick, yeah?"

"Tick. Like the sound before a bomb goes off?"

Eddy sat down on a willow log. "Maybe you should take a little time off. Have a nice vacation."

Anna didn't sit. She talked to the river.

"Vacations are for people with jobs. And as I'm sure Katie has told you, I don't really have one of those anymore."

"Yeah, she told me. But I thought maybe you'd reconsider. You know. After your vacation."

"No. I'm closing the clinic. I've got Martin Hallsey coming in for a bit—he's a floating vet—until I can get things sorted out. But then it's over."

"Are you sure? Don't you think this is a bad day to decide something like that?"

"It's not just about Tony. And my depression, if that's what this is. And the disgusting waste-of-skin who buried those puppies. It's more than all of those things; I picked the wrong career. I finally get that. It's time to cut my losses and get out. I can't stand most of the things a vet is supposed to do. The whole job makes me feel crappy."

"Curing sick animals makes you feel crappy? Helping people take care of their pets makes you feel crappy? Spaying and neutering... crappy and crappy?"

She spun her shoulders around to almost face him, her voice severe. "You know there's more to it than that."

He nodded, making note of how fragile she was.

She turned back to the water. "You've watched me struggle all these years. Why would you want me to keep doing something so painful?"

"*Because* I've watched you struggle all these years. And you're strong enough to do this important job that needs doing. And though it's hard for you to see it today, you're making some pretty good progress. You're helping people around here. And their animals. They need you to stay at it."

"Even if that were true, that's what everyone else gets out of the deal. What's in it for me?" Anna turned all the way around to face him.

"Same answer. You live to help people and their animals, yeah? That's what makes you happy. And, yes, it's really hard. But I happen to know you even get something out of *that*. You like hard. Think about it, Anna. You totally downplay accomplishments that come easily to you, because if you can do them, they must not be worth very much. And please don't ask me to explain that any better, because it's your messed up logic, Doctor."

Eddy knew he was sounding frustrated. He wasn't very good at convincing people of things. But once in awhile the responsibility of an important argument fell to him because there was nobody else to take it on. Anna stared at him now, trying to make him uncomfortable enough to drop the subject, but though Eddy wasn't a great fighter, he was hard to scare off.

Anna sat herself down on the log beside Eddy.

"I'm not going back." She sounded wrung-out but certain.

"Anna May *Honoratus* Dunlop. Listen to me. You ignored my advice on picking a confirmation name, and look what happened. Do not make the same mistake twice. I'm telling you right now, you're about to become the old witch who lives out in the woods with a hundred mangy dogs. In the house that all the kids dare each other to run up and touch."

Anna placed her hand on Eddy's leg, offering him a sweet *fight's over* squeeze before loosely clasping her hands between her knees. The two of them sat this way for several minutes without a word.

Then quietly she said, "I'll have you know that Honoratus is the patron saint of cake makers."

"I know." He nodded slowly.

"I love cake."

"I know."

A two-tone whistle sounded from the other side of the water, and in unison they peered across, waiting. The answering call, slightly lower in pitch, came from a spot just downriver from the first.

Anna bumped her shoulder affectionately against his, a tentative smile emerging; the chickadee had always been *their* bird.

9

"Hey, look what the cat spit out!" said a pudgy young man in a roomy Packers sweatshirt. He slid onto the stool next to a muscley, twenty-something guy with hair shaped into an oncoming splash breaking just above the forehead.

"Hey, Toot," said Brian Ardeen into his beer bottle.

"You were in court today, weren'tcha?"

"Yeah." His response was nearly buried in laughing men, the clacking of pool balls, and Garth Brooks coming through cheap speakers.

"Thought so. Kind of surprised to see ya, Dawg." Toot was trying to position his wide yellowish smile in front of Brian's face.

"Do me a favor." Brian had his attention focused on the Budweiser coaster in his hand. "Don't ever say 'dog' to me again."

After a beat Toot laughed, and Brian smiled. Toot Monson punched his buddy's upper arm. Then he called to the bartender, loudly enough to make other drinkers glance in his direction. "Mikey! Pull me a Leinie." He turned back to look at Brian. "Need another one?"

"Not yet."

"I figured they might keep you locked up for awhile or somethin'."

"No way. I mean, I guess they could have, but they hardly ever do that with something this lame-ass. I just have to pay some bullshit fine."

Toot Monson could see Brian's anger. What he didn't notice was the tremble in his friend's jaw as he ground his teeth back and forth, or how he shifted constantly on his stool. Or the fact that even after three-and-a-half bottles of ice cold righteous, Brian still wasn't looking him in the eye.

"You gotta pay a fine? That's seriously messed up, dude. For what you did with your own dog? And they kept the dog too, didn't they? The mother dog?"

Brian nodded, smirking.

"Like you said. Bullshit. That's bullshit. Ya ever gonna get it back?"

"No. They say I can't own any animals for five years, now. Whatever. I've been spanked and put to bed without supper, I guess."

"Yeah." Toot nodded and pushed a stream of air from his lungs. "Good one."

"I don't give a rat's ass about having that dog. It was a major hassle, anyways. I only got the thing for Maggie since she was home alone all the time."

Brian took a drink ending in a long exhale and a small burp. "Not exactly an issue anymore."

"No kidding. And why didn't she take the stupid mutt with her, anyways? She took everything else, right?"

"Y' got that right. But I'm done talking about this shit. You seen Bo?"

"No. He said he'd be comin' down tonight, though. Hey, get him to tell you about this guy he knows who can put a whole tennis ball in his mouth. It's freakin' hilarious to watch Bo imitate him."

"So what's been goin' on at work? Denny say anything about me these last couple of days? I know he's been waiting to hear how stuff turned out in court. He gonna fire my ass?"

"I dunno. I can't really tell about him." Toot squeezed one eye shut. "He makes jokes all the time about you being arrested and stuff. But he hasn't said anything about firing you or not."

Brian took a long pull on his beer.

Toot, scratching his belly, took his hand out from under his sweatshirt to point at the door. "There he is. Bo."

Even backlit by the neon beer signs on the front window, Bo was easy to spot by the glowing red tip of his perma-cigarette. Pissed off by the law making it illegal to smoke in bars, he always made a point to walk in with a lit one, then crush it under his boot on the floor.

Wherever it was legal, Bo was smoking. He would light one up, put it between his lips, and leave it there until all he had left to suck on was the burning filter. He could talk around it and drink around it. When people asked him why he didn't hold the cigarette between his fingers like the rest of the goddamn world, he'd say that smoking was a disgusting habit, and he refused to touch the filthy things.

Toot half got up, half slipped off his stool, as the small, wiry man approached them. "Mr. Bo! Over here!"

Dewayne "Bo" Beaudry showed no sign that he'd been waved over to the bar, moving there on his own timeline. Silent. Bored. Freshly-buzzed hair, a shiny shirt pasted to his jockey-sized body, a face carved into planes and sharp intersections, Bo said *mean* no matter where a person looked.

Swaggering up to stand by the invisible Toot, he shot Brian a vicious smile; a cat with its paw on the rat's tail.

"Ardeen. I was just thinking about you."

"Hey, Bo. How ya doin'?" asked Brian without waiting for an answer. "Thinking about me again, huh? Kind of lonely down there in your mom's basement, I guess."

"Big talk for a guy who was almost made prettiest girl on the cell block." Bo caught the bartender's attention, then picked up Toot's beer glass and pointed to himself. "But the thing is... I wasn't in the basement thinking about you. I was right out there on the street. Just a few minutes ago. Talking with that lady vet. The one who has all your dogs."

"What's that?" said Brian, having trouble keeping his face in the disinterested position. "You're babbling again, Bo. You having a stroke or something?"

"No, but you're about to, douchebag. You might wanna take a deep breath, Ardeen. You're not gonna like this. I, on the other hand, am enjoying the hell out of it."

Bo pulled a bright orange piece of paper out from under the leather jacket he had draped over his arm.

Toot, seeing what was printed on the page, stepped back like he'd been stung.

"Gimme that, limpdick," said Ardeen, snatching the paper from Bo's hand, which made Bo laugh. Brian mumbled as he read the flier. "What the hell?"

The top third of the page was filled with a blurry photo of his own face. There was a large headline under the picture and a short paragraph below it.

> *PUBLIC NOTICE:*
> *This Man Buries Puppies Alive*
>
> *BRIAN MICHAEL ARDEEN of 208 Fourth Street, Milk River, WI, has been found guilty of burying a litter of live puppies. He did so while the mother dog watched. He has been sentenced to pay only a $2400 fine, with no jail time.*

"Where did you get this?" It wasn't a question, it was a demand. Brian crumpled the bright orange sheet, jamming it into the pocket of his windbreaker.

"Like I said. Your doggies' new mommy. That vet chick who saved the poor puppies you tried to murder." Bo pulled the lid off a tin of chewing tobacco. "She was handing those out just up the road, so I stopped to talk. She's hot, by the way. Kinda tall, but a nice ass and a good story. Don't get no better." He tucked a pinch of chew between his cheek and gum.

Brian hit the bar with a ten dollar bill and began shoving his way through the crowd.

He burst out onto the sidewalk before Bo had finished laughing. He glanced west toward the residential area that began just past the bar, then turned to walk as fast as he could in the opposite direction.

When he reached the end of the full five blocks of downtown Milk River, he stopped to scope things out. Panting, gnashing his teeth, he turned in a deliberate circle, narrowing his eyes in search of his prey.

What he saw across the street, stuck to a telephone pole, made him wheeze like he'd been kicked. A bright orange piece of paper. He shot a look up the block and onto the next. One on every third post. He bolted toward the flier across the street. He ripped it off the pole, tearing it into a few pieces with both fists. He clawed at an orange shred of paper caught under one staple, ramming a splinter of wood under his nail. Harder and harder he kicked the telephone pole as he grunted through clenched teeth, his lower lip wet with spit.

10

Eddy switched on the front porch light and, without checking to see who might come calling at three in the morning, opened the door.

"Anna." He'd never realized how easy it was to yawn her name.

"Hi." She stood hunched in the long, black wool coat she'd bought—if memory served—in ninth grade. In folded arms she clutched a carton of soy milk to her chest. Someone seemed to have etched ten years into her skin with a thick lead pencil.

"You okay?" He was scratching the back of his head.

"I'm good. Why do you ask?"

He smiled. "Come in."

"Thanks." She walked by him into the living room, flumping onto his overstuffed couch.

Still standing, he reached over her to pull the chain on an old floor lamp.

Staring at a fixed point about ten feet beneath his grass rug, she held the milk carton straight up over her head. "I'm really sorry to show up here like this, unannounced and everything. But it was way too late to call." She tried a grin.

"Oh, that's okay. He took the milk carton and studied it. "Can I get you some—Cocoa Puffs?"

"I wanted to bring red wine. I didn't have any."

"No worries, I've got red wine. But it's lousy on Cocoa Puffs."

"In a glass, then. A big one."

By the time he'd come back with the wine, she'd taken off her coat, revealing pink flannel pants dotted with purple monkeys, and her faded red sweatshirt with the big white peace sign on the front. The sweatshirt he knew well. The monkeys were new.

"Pretty." He handed her a glass and sat down beside her.

"Well, I figured you'd be in your jammies, and I didn't want you to feel underdressed."

Eddy readjusted his white terrycloth robe over his T-shirt and grey sweatpants. "Considerate, thanks."

"So, I need you to understand why I'm abandoning my practice. I've got a really good reason, but until you think it's good, it's not officially good, you know? So I need to have you listen to it, and affirm it, because I could really use some sleep."

"Ah, that's why we're here. *Kay den.* Let me have it. And I've got some good news, by the way. Burger Boy is hiring."

"That is good news."

She closed her eyes and took a large swallow of wine. When she opened them again, Eddy noticed her sea green irises sway slightly for a moment, each independently of the other. The rest of her muscles, too, seemed to be giving up on trying to hold her face in its awake position. As Eddy reached out his hand, she closed her eyes again, letting him put the tip of his pointer finger softly on one lid, and his thumb against the other, just as his tutu would do for him as a kid, when he was too sleepy to stay awake and too afraid he'd miss something to go to bed.

"Oh, that feels good. Thank you, tutu."

He thought he could feel her pulse, but might have just imagined one for her as he watched her breathe. Then, either his elderly refrigerator or a Sopwith Camel came alive in the kitchen, causing Anna to twitch, making him wonder if she'd fallen asleep for a moment. She wrapped long fingers around his hand, giving it a quick squeeze before placing it back onto the couch between them.

"Okay. Here's the simple truth of it." She brought her purple monkeys up into the cross-legged position. "I've had a lot of time to poke around on the internet lately, and you wouldn't believe how many people out there think it's perfectly okay to kill puppies. Animals of any kind, actually. No guilt about it at all." The evenness of her tone surprised him and proved how tired she was. "Apparently, Ardeen just happened to get noticed."

"That's not a big shock to you though, yeah?"

"It shouldn't be, but I guess I've been pretty good at repressing that kind of stuff. The point is, that's how Ardeen and his ilk view—and will always view—the world. I can't change people like him. And they're everywhere. Doing damage faster than other people could ever undo it. So that's why I might as well get out."

"But hang on a sec. You do make a difference on the animal population around here, Anna. I know for a fact you've bullied a lot of your clients into spaying and neutering."

"Yeah, but big deal. Cats like Willie-Lump-Lump are allowed to roam the streets at night, where people swerve their cars to try to hit them. For sport."

She stared hard at Eddy through the bottom of her emptying wine glass.

He folded his arms across his chest and looked down at his lap. "I don't think you're going to get what you need from me tonight."

"What, are you out of booze?"

"Booze I've got," he said, picking up the bottle from the rattan end table. "Affirmation, not so much."

He poured her more wine, deciding to skimp a little on a full glass. "I know you're hoping I'll tell you to quit your job—and say that only you know what's best for you. But the thing is, you're not *you* right now."

"I am too. I'm the disconsolate, horrified, furious me. But I'm in here."

"The double-whammy of your Tony anniversary and this puppy thing—I just think you'd be in a much better place to make a major life decision a few weeks from now."

He knew he was right, but when her shoulders slumped into an *Et tu, Brute?* sigh, he found himself wishing he wasn't. She'd come over here tonight hoping to be made better. But he was pretty sure they'd both feel worse when she left.

11

Anna opened an inside section of the St. Paul *Pioneer Press*, bending from the waist to spread it onto the floor. She looked at Storm lying in the corner of the makeshift whelping pen. Two puppies sucked hungrily on the shepherd; three others yipped and grunted, swimming clumsily along the newspaper.

"Okay. You guys did a great job of soiling that bigot on the editorial page. This morning, your mission is a half-page ad for shotgun shells. Give it your worst. Good dogs."

Clutching warm bottles of milk replacer, she stepped over one of the two pine planks defining the pen. Nailed together into a V, butted up against an empty corner of her kitchen, the boards were six-feet long and a foot high, tall enough to keep puppies inside, and low enough to let momma out for sanity breaks. Anna sat down on the ammo ad, tucking one leg under herself.

"Soup's on!" She shook a bottle. "Come and get it while it's body temperature!" She picked up the grey female with the black circle around her ear. Holding the animal's face up to her nose, she inhaled deeply, letting puppy breath work its magic on a few seconds of her gloomy morning.

Anna offered a bottle to the youngster, who seemed delighted to oblige. Storm was watching the transaction with mild interest. Anna looked into the dog's large brown eyes, viewing for certain what she'd been hoping she had *not* been seeing. The animal's soul. She felt a connection with Storm she couldn't explain. They knew each other, she and this animal, and they were probably meant to be together. But how could she live with a dog again? She cringed inwardly, remembering Jackpot's passing. He had gone peacefully in his sleep, at a ripe old age.

And still the pain of his loss had been one of those unbearable events a person somehow bears. From then on, whenever she'd needed a doggie fix, she would seek out a patient at the clinic to cuddle with. No more dogs in the family.

While the puppy fed, Anna let her mind drift. She and the shepherd were definitely linked in some way—as if they had some ancient life force in common. Maybe some small mammal, like an eohippus in the Cenozoic Era, had died, leaving its decaying molecules to disperse. Some were eaten by scavenger animals, others evaporated and were breathed in by birds, or washed to the ocean to be snapped up by fish. These minute particles, distributed to points across the globe, were passed down, some through Storm's ancestry, others through Anna's. And now the two of them shared a genetic sameness they could both sense. Whatever the explanation, the bond was real. She felt it in her chest and saw it on the dog's face. No. She wouldn't let her stay. But she couldn't let her go.

Anna had to do some puppy and bottle juggling to reach the phone in her pocket. It was her mother, calling way too early for a simple chat. She answered anyway.

"Hi, Mom. What's up?"

"Good morning, dear. Am I interrupting anything?"

"No, I'm good. Just feeding the puppies."

"A-ha."

It was a common expression of her mother's, which, to the untrained ear, could sound like an affirmation. But recipients in the inner circle knew it to be the exact opposite.

"Anna, I'm calling to see if you're ready for some company yet. It's been a few days now, and I'm still not quite sure what's going on. With you, I mean. And of course I realize that the whole thing happened on—well, I'm aware of what day it was. And I want you to know—I'm here for you."

Her mother had never acknowledged the anniversary of Tony's death before, not that she'd actually spoken the unpleasant nouns this time, either. But the effort was endearing.

"I know you are. And I really appreciate that, Mom. Maybe over the weekend. How about Saturday night? I'll make dinner."

"Saturday night?"

Anna could picture her mother sifting through strategies over in her townhome, sitting straight as an L, the hand not holding the phone splayed flat on her kitchen table, manicured fingers tapping lightly, one at a time, thumb to pinky and back again. She had an agenda; Anna was sure of that. The topic had yet to be revealed.

"Right," said Anna. "Doesn't Saturday work for you?"

"It's just that Saturday night is typically—you know—date night."

And there it was. The topic.

"I don't want to be the person standing in the way of your love life."

"Actually, Mom, the person standing in the way is the guy who isn't asking me out."

"Which guy?"

"The universal guy. Guy with a capital G. Mr. Right. Or even Mr. Doesn't-Scare-Me."

"Now wait one minute, Daughter. I know for a fact you have no problem asking men out. Remember, I knew you when you were in high school."

"There were no men in high school. Only frisky little boys, unless you count Wheezy the janitor. But the closest I ever came to asking Wheezy out was that time I vomited in homeroom, and Sister Magdalena made me go confess to him what I had done, and ask him to come wash up my evil filth, and bring a little scrubbing powder for my unclean soul while he was at it."

"Anna, she never said that." Her mom was trying not to laugh.

"How do you know what she said? You weren't there."

"No, but Sister Magdalena called me in the next morning. She wanted me to know how you'd stood outside of that poor man's janitor closet, hands folded, head bowed, bellowing at the top of your lungs, 'Bless me, Wheezy, for I have puked! My last stomach flu was three months ago!'"

Anna let out a single cackle, the sound strange in her house.

"It's not funny. It's sacrilege!" Her mother was giggling.

"And for my penance, as I recall, he made me sing ten times through the Marvel the Mustang jingle."

"All right, Anna. That's enough."

"Wheezy wasn't a religious man, but he knew what he liked."

"You've always been such a master deflector, child. Don't think I haven't noticed that we're not talking about dating anymore."

Anna gave the puppy she was holding a kiss on her head, and traded her out for another who hadn't eaten yet.

"Okay, Mom. Dating. You don't have to worry. I've lured plenty of men into my tangled web this year."

"I didn't know this. Why are you keeping it a secret from me?"

"I'm not keeping anything secret. I've seen a couple of guys one time each. No big deal."

"So, tell me. Who are these men? Do I know them?"

"Jeez, I can't believe we're even discussing this. Okay, I went out with Mike Esau. The owner of that little hardware store in Amery."

"Oh, him! The one who wears shorts all year 'round. He's a looker."

"Did you really just say that?"

"Why only the one date? Did he try something?"

"Try something? Like what? Second base? I'm not even sure what second base is. French kissing? That can't be right—what would first base be? Making goo-goo eyes at each other? A particularly firm handshake?"

"Deflecting!"

"He talked along with the movie."

"Pardon me?"

"Mike. He kept reciting lines along with the actors in the film. We went to a late-night screening of *Deliverance*. You know how I love that flick.

"Yes, and I've never understood why. It's perfectly gruesome."

"It's perfectly classic. And has a lot of classic lines we polite moviegoers wanted to hear. But we were treated to Mike's version instead, each line just a fraction ahead of the actor so we could all be amazed by how well he knew it."

"He was trying to impress you. That's sweet."

"It wasn't sweet, Mom. One guy threw a bag of popcorn at his head. And anyway, he's at least four inches shorter than I am."

"Not this again. A lot of men are going to be shorter than you. And by the way, my magazines say that tall women are status symbols for men."

"Right."

"I know you don't accept this, Anna, but you're a stunning beauty, and your height is part of the package."

"I know a mother has to say things like that to her hulking Amazon daughter, but let me relieve you of that duty, okay, Mom? Next topic."

"Fine. So, what about mystery date number two? Who was he?"

"His name is Brad Wayson. An organic farmer outside of Connorsville."

"An organic farmer… he sounds *tall*."

"Wow, hey, look at the time! I've gotta fly."

It was unheard of for Anna's mom to drill this deeply into her personal life. Joey Dunlop's M.O. with her children had always been to ask one broad sweeping question, make a few disapproving clucks, and move on before she inadvertently triggered an emotion she was unequipped to handle.

"All right," said her mom. "I'm sorry. I'm just wondering, what was wrong with Brad?"

"Nothing was wrong with him. He's a good guy. I wouldn't mind hanging out with him as a friend, I guess. But I have enough friends. He's just not what I'm looking for in a—" She struggled to find a term she was willing to use. "Significant other."

"Ah-ha."

Anna was able to end the call by promising the interrogation could continue on Saturday night. But if she'd needed any more proof that it was time to get her life in order, this had been it: Joey Dunlop sacrificing herself to venture this far afield of her usual don't-ask-don't-cry zone.

Anna picked up the last puppy and studied him until the cute little sucking sounds began. Then she leaned back against the wall, closing her eyes. When she opened them again, her gaze fell on the 8x10 photo hanging by the kitchen window. It depicted Tony and herself from behind, arms draped around each other, looking out over a dramatic run of rapids on the Wolf River. She'd long ago packed away all other photographs of him, allowing herself only this one, because it mercifully hid his kind, asymmetrical face with its hundred thousand ways to make her feel.

"What should I do? I don't know what to do." She asked it out loud to the photo and instantly felt stupid.

But Tony didn't answer. He didn't do anything. He just stood there with his arm casually around her waist, with that beautiful hand grazing her hip as if both of them would be fine forever.

12

"Thir—teen," said Tony, completing the push-up with a grunt and a smile.

"This is just plain sad," said Anna, as cynically as her mirth would allow. She sat cross-legged on his upper back, looking down over the top of his head. "*Thir—teen* is a long way from twenty, my friend, and you're already feeling the pain. In fact, twenty is so very far up the road, I think I'll write it a letter and tell it we're not coming."

Tony lowered himself and his passenger quickly to the blue tarp.

"No fair making me laugh!" He began his push into number fourteen.

"Give it up, Mister." Anna pulled her freezing hands out from under her armpits to gather up the long, curly hair falling into his face. She split the locks in two, gripping them like reins. Pulling gently back, she straightened herself until her head brushed the ceiling of the tent. "Whoa, Flicka!"

"Flicka? That was a girl horse!" The next word rasped in his throat. "Fifteen."

"Was? What do you mean *was*? I'll have you know Flicka is alive and well, romping around in some pasture with her friends, Mr. Ed, Fury, Pi from *National Velvet*, and the lesser-known Cochise—Little Joe's pinto on *Bonanza*."

"Right." He dropped to his belly so abruptly she needed the reins to steady herself. "Ow! Sixteen. In fact," he said, into the blue tarp, "I think the word *flicka* actually means *girl* in Swedish, doesn't it?"

"All I know is both you and Flicka have long, pretty ponytails."

She gathered his curls together again, smoothing them with both hands. As Tony hit the ground after push up number seventeen, she nuzzled her face into his hair and inhaled deeply. She smelled campfire and river water—souvenirs of their trip. But she could also catch hints of his familiar body scent, where clove met baking bread. Tony's smell, even after days with no shower, seemed programmed to attract her. Like a glance at his wedding ring, it was a reminder that he was for her and she for him.

Anna snapped back into position. "Now giddy-up!"

Lips to tarp, he said, "Look, you copper-headed wench. Admit it. Your little challenge to my manhood isn't going to pay off. I'll make it to twenty, no problem, so find your woolly socks 'cuz your tall, sultry self is on its way out into this thirty-degree night to rustle me up some piping hot chocolate. Extra chocolate."

"We'll see who's making whom what kind of chocolate, cowboy. Now come on, you're at the bottom of seventeen and stalling. In fact, hey! You're trying to rest! For that, you shall be punished." She wiggled herself around until she was facing Tony's feet.

"Yow! Easy up there."

She clapped her hands. "C'mere, Jackpot."

The huge Rottweiller by the door raised his head from his front paws.

"No way!" said Tony. "Not part of the deal."

Anna patted Tony's butt several times and raised her voice an octave or so.

"C'mon, Jack. Here, boy. Wanna go for a ride?"

Jackpot, excited by something he couldn't quite grasp, made his way through the jumble of bunched-up sleeping bags, backpacks, and other soft bundles. He stood beside Anna, his head almost even with hers. With his one good eye, the dog looked from her face to her hand that again patted Tony's rump.

"Come on, boy, jump up."

Jackpot placed one massive paw onto Tony's backside and tested it, seeming to wonder if he could balance up there.

"Anna," said Tony, her name a chuckle. "That's another 130 pounds."

"Conservatively."

"Okay, okay, I'm going. Here I go." He pushed up into a shaky number eighteen.

"Stand down, big guy." Anna pulled Jack's foot off Tony, scratching both sides of his squishy face. She could never get enough of the dog's baggy cheek skin. Jackpot lowered his head until she could reach behind his ears.

As Tony slammed to the ground, Anna let go of Jackpot, grabbing for her husband's butt with both hands to keep from falling off. She squeezed him playfully, appreciating, as always, his muscled body.

"Come to think of it, maybe you should stop before you damage something I might want later."

"No, ma'am! You can forget about that right now. I'm onto you. You trick me into stopping with your girlish wiles, then suddenly I'm out there pumping up the camp stove and looking for marshmallows. Huh-uh. Not gonna happen. Oof! Ninteen."

"Oh-my-god-oh-my-god-oh-my-god!" said Anna, falling to her knees through the slit in the tent, then turning full around to reach back outside through the portal. "It's freezing out there!"

From the bumpy ground she drew two mugs into their flickering orange lair, warmed by lantern, husband, and dog. Whiffs of cocoa blended with the earthy universal camping smell. It was a mystery, that sour tent smell. Why did her new, hi-tech nylon mountain tent smell exactly the same as the gargantuan canvas version of her youth? Could it be that it wasn't the cloth that emitted the odor, but the conglomeration of camping objects *inside* the tent? Maybe a nasty composite of sleeping bag dander, mosquito carcass, and water-soaked map? Whatever the origin, it was the scent of her childhood—the good parts—of forest, and camping, and summer vacation. And now, hot chocolate.

"Brrrr!" She knee-walked toward the tall, dark, and gorgeous males in her life. Tony and Jackpot sat snuggled together, huddled inside of a double-wide sleeping bag, with just their heads poking out.

"Oh, no you don't!" Anna laughed at the massive, slobbery head beside Tony's. "One of us has to stay out from under the covers to fight off the bears, and I vote for the big guard dog."

Jackpot seemed to miss her meaning, distracted as he was by the steaming chocolate passing just below his nose. Anna handed one of the tin mugs to Tony.

"Oh, my Sweetheartedness," he said, accepting his beverage. "Have I told you lately how beautiful you are? How good and kind? How nurturing and perfect for me in every way?"

"Just save it. Here's your blood money. I only hope you can sleep tonight, knowing how cold I was out there."

He paused to consider. "Yup. I'll be good, thanks."

Teeth chattering, Anna took a sip, wondering for a moment if this much chocolate might bring on a morning migraine. She put down the mug and sat on the cold floor to dig through her backpack.

"Dang. I was sure I'd brought one more sweatshirt to throw on. The big red one with the white peace sign?"

"Huh. You know… I think you did bring it, honey. I feel like I've seen it somewhere on this trip."

Glancing around the tent, she closed her pack and used her feet to shove it back into the corner.

"Well, you'll have to snuggle with me, then." She pivoted to face him. "You think you could encourage His Royal Jackpotedness to relinquish his position?"

"I think so. He's getting kind of hot, anyway."

Tony opened the sleeping bag, and there sat Jackpot leaning against him, wearing a red hoodie with a huge, white peace sign across the front. Anna laughed so hard she spilled half of her cocoa.

Food of any kind outranking warmth in Jackpot's world, the dog bustled over to lap it up off the floor. Anna took one more chilly moment to pull the hood up over the dog's neck, down to his eyes. "Your head is your chimney."

She slipped in beside Tony with what was left of her cocoa. He put an arm around her shoulder, pulling her hard against him. They sat that way for awhile, sipping their drinks, listening to the wind. It was Anna who spoke first.

"My nose is cold, my arms are killing me from paddling that ancient canoe, and I totally stink."

"Me too." He licked a drip from the side of the metal mug.

"I couldn't be happier."

"Me neither."

Anna reached out with her free hand to pick up the lantern. She held it high between them, the candlelight bouncing and lurching as if trying to get somewhere. When Tony saw what she was up to, he rolled his dark eyes.

They'd been married three full years, but she had never tired of looking at his face. In fact, she craved it. She started on a cheekbone this time, following the thick, angular line from the outside, inward. Then his jaw, square and chiseled, his mouth, not quite horizontal like other people's, slanting up on the right, his eye on that side slightly higher. The two halves of Tony's face were noticeably different from one another, yet together they formed one of her very favorite views. She mostly studied it when he wasn't looking—while he was sleeping or busy—because Tony rarely indulged her.

Neither of them could imagine why she felt such a need. Not back then. Later, she would come to realize that some part of her had known that this face would be taken from her early, and she'd needed to etch the outline into her brain.

Tony set down his cocoa and gently took the lantern from her fingers, placing it beside him on the floor. He took her hand, turned it over, and pulled back a few layers of sleeves to softly kiss the inside of her wrist. She shivered.

"Anna." He slowly pulled the wool cap from her head. He slipped his hand, warmed from the cocoa, around the back of her neck, under her hair. He kissed her temple, then her ear as he spoke. "I wonder if you could possibly understand how much I love you."

She could. Tony spoke often, and with great passion, about the immensity of his love for her, both emotional and physical. And though this would have been a perfect opening to express the depth of her own feelings—and she ached to do so—the words would stay lodged in her throat. It was one of her many failings. The language of love had been unspoken in the Dunlop family household when Anna was growing up, and she'd never learned to speak it as an adult. Attempts to put words to her most intimate feelings had the stilted, laughable sound of a traveler with a foreign phrasebook. Even with Tony. So she rarely tried.

She turned to look into his eyes, hoping her expression would say what she could not: That she was surprised every day such a man could exist. That he colored in all the places where she had been settling for grey and beige. That he made her believe she could be someone's favorite person—and she had no idea how to thank him for that.

Tony wrapped his arms around her body and whispered the words. "I know."

She leaned her head back onto his shoulder, letting herself relax into his chest. She pictured his cheekbone. She begged the universe for a million more years of him.

Tony would be gone before the same time tomorrow.

13

Anna was having the dream again.

Perched on the roof of her farmhouse, she watched, horrified, as the river wound itself into a thundering whirlpool, sucking everything around her into its churning center. The trees, the dirt, and chunks of her house flew toward the water. The screaming gale-force wind battered her ear drums. Clinging to the chimney, Anna understood she was living her final few seconds. And just as her fingers were losing their grip—she was awake.

She was in her own bed, her own room, solid and intact. But the insane screeching of the wind hadn't stopped. She slapped her alarm clock to see if it would make the noise quit, which it didn't. Heart pounding, she grabbed her phone, pushed the talk button, and pulled it to her face. She had another responsibility too, but wasn't sure what it was. Squeezing her eyes closed, she rubbed them with her free hand.

"Anna? Anna?"

It was Katie. This was a phone call. She was on Planet Earth. Okay.

"Katie." Anna, checking the clock, was fairly certain this wasn't the 2:30 that came in the afternoon. "Are you all right?"

"Yeah, I'm fine. It's so good to hear your voice," she said, warmly.

"You too." Anna was slurring her words. "But, um—maybe we could chat a little later?"

"Wait! Don't hang up. Snorky's got a blockage."

"Snore key Scot habla kej? That's not English, is it? Because if it is, what's this I'm speaking right now?"

"Sorry." Katie slowed her cadence. "Snorky. The Greenlee's Siamese. He's swallowed something again, and they might have waited too long this time. He seems pretty bad."

"Oh, jeez." Anna propped herself up on an elbow. "Is Martin coming in?"

"No, he's out of town. He's got a dachshund delivery over in Fox Creek. I've called everybody else, but no go."

"Yes... and...?" Of course, she already knew what followed *and* in Katie's mind.

A profound silence wobbled between them.

"Katie, I—I don't think—I just—hmmm."

"I know. I wouldn't have called if I didn't have to."

"I believe that, but—oh, man."

Anna had made a pact with herself a couple of months back. No longer a vet, she would find a job where the only suffering creatures were the disgruntled employees. So far, though, she had made little progress; it turned out there weren't many jobs in Milk River for a person with steady hands, a strong stomach, and a thorough knowledge of the oxidative capacity of guinea pig skeletal muscles.

Besides raising five puppies, her only other occupation lately had been keeping Brian Ardeen's egregious act in the public eye. But publicizing his misdeed was never going to change him—only shame him—which was precisely the pathetic revenge she'd been seeking. It was time to stop the campaign.

Besides, the truth was she'd been thinking about the clinic constantly since she'd left. Her staff, her clients, and her chance to turn sick animals into healthy ones. That said, the job had forced her into some kind of mental breakdown; could she be sure it wouldn't happen again?

Such was the circular argument she'd been sorting through with her therapist for eight weeks now. She tried to imagine what her shrink would say about this middle-of-the-night dilemma and decided it would probably be: *Baby steps.*

So all right, then. She didn't have to decide her whole life tonight. She could help the cat's digestion problems and worry about her own blockage later. She pulled on the thick green booties her mother had knit for her.

"I tried Andrew from the Turtle Lake clinic too, but no answer," said Katie. "It's just for tonight, Anna. Martin will be back in tomorrow morning."

"Yeah, of course. I'll get dressed and meet you down there in fifteen minutes. First one there starts the coffee."

Anna lifted a section of Snorky's small intestine, placing it onto the sterile towel draped across his belly. "Let's see what we've got here."

She drew in a deep breath and silently recited her pre-surgery mantra: *Focus, precision, decision, completion.* And then she began.

Palpating gingerly along the intestine, she felt for anything harder than the waste material she'd expect to find. Anna took a moment to glance over her shoulder at the x-ray again. "There's obviously something in here. Maybe two somethings."

It could be difficult to get an accurate picture when the intestine doubled—or even tripled—over on itself, right where the obstruction seemed to reside. She might have been seeing one large object, or two smaller problems layered together. She wouldn't know the full extent of Snorky's poor gastronomical choices until her rubber-coated fingers had felt along the entire length of his small intestine.

"This part seems vital and pink. How's he doing?" Anna asked, with a glance at Snorkey's broad, ivory face and dark brown ears. Even with the trach tube down his throat, and his tongue lolling to one side, this was a handsome cat.

"Everything looks good," said Katie, jotting down the animal's temperature, blood pressure, heart rate, respiration, and oxygen level on the stats sheet.

Anna nodded.

"So...," Katie said, tentatively. "Martin mentioned yesterday that when he agreed to help us out, he hadn't really been looking for a full-time job. Which, of course, is what it's been for two months now. He was kind of joking, but only kind of, you know? I think he's wondering if you're ever coming back, or what."

"I know. I've been as non-committal with poor Martin as I have with you and Noah. And myself, for that matter. I'm sure I'm quitting, maybe I'm coming back, I'll never come back, I might come back part time... I'm a mess."

"Don't feel bad. I know how it's been for you. It's just that—Noah and I have been wondering—thinking—we should be looking for other jobs if you're going to shut down the clinic." Katie looked up from the blood pressure gauge to search Anna's face.

"I know. It's not just *my* career I'm dangling over this deep canyon by a single fraying suture strand. In fact, that's the most convincing argument for returning. I can't stand the idea of letting you guys go. That would be awful. For so many reasons."

"I'm sure. But just so you know… even if you close the clinic down, you can't fire me as your friend."

It was a joke and also not a joke. Katie would have every reason to believe that this new, unreliable Anna might slip out of her life by dark of night, never to return.

"I'm really sorry, Katie. I know you guys have had to take on a lot of extra work around here, since I slunk into my dank little corner to lick my wounds."

"It's okay. We're okay."

Anna thought about touching Katie in some way, but didn't. Instead, she reached her hand back into Snorky, replacing the segment of his intestine she'd been evaluating, and pulling out another five inches or so. She began to explore along the smooth sheathing, her movement fluid, her mind visualizing what was inside. She felt at home here in Snorky's body cavity. Anna had always loved surgery. It was a part of the job where she could actually change things that needed changing. And she was good at it. She couldn't help but realize how much she'd been missing this.

"I almost called you about a million times," said Anna. "I could have used some insight from Katie-my-friend, but I was worried that Katie-my-employee might—I guess it just seemed like it was something I needed to work through by myself."

"Without my wailing sobs imploring you to come back to us, you mean?"

They both worked without speaking for another several minutes. *Focus, precision, decision, completion.* Anna always liked the mood of the clinic at night, with no ringing phones and only blackness coming in through the wood-framed windows of the old firehouse. It lent the patient's emergency a special significance. A respectful hush in deference to the fragile life in play.

"Oh, here we go," said Anna, studying the delicate organ in the palm of her hand. The section she held was an angry red color and swollen to half again its normal size. "We're getting closer."

Carefully bringing out the next portion of intestine, she followed it along, pressing just hard enough to find something that didn't belong inside of a cat. She spied the problem before her hands had quite reached the spot.

"Ha! Here it is."

Anna knew she had found the foreign body by the deep crimson color and the odd shape of the intestinal wall. Her touch confirmed it. As she'd suspected, the bulge contained a hard object that had gotten hung up on its way to the large intestine.

"Jeez, it's huge!" She used her fingertips to define the obstruction.

"Can you move it to a less inflamed area?"

"No way; I don't want to risk a tear. I'll go in right here."

She could feel a collection of digestive fluids in the area—the liquid remains of kibble and kitty snacks that Snorky's body had busily been processing until the whole works had shut down. She gently squeezed the organ between her first and second fingers to move the content upstream, milking it away from where she would be working.

Anna picked up a scalpel to begin the enterotomy. She made an incision directly over the object the cat had swallowed, releasing a small amount of brown liquid ooze from the cut—and by the fetid smell, he'd been blocked for quite awhile now. Anna used a small forceps to tease the object out through the incision.

"Ah, look at that. I don't believe it."

"What? What is it?" Katie tried for a better view of the object, but it was covered in a layer of greenish-brown slime and smeared blood.

"It's another one!" said Anna, chuckling.

"Another letter? No way!"

Both women looked toward the refrigerator door in the next room; it bore the last unwelcome item to get yanked out of poor Snorky: A baby blue letter *h* from a child's magnetic alphabet set.

"Yup. That's what it is." Anna dropped the letter *n* into a metal basin.

"You'd think the little Greenlees would have learned to pick up their toys after the last major surgery."

"Or at least switched to capital letters. Harder to swallow."

But that had been only half the obstruction. The women fell silent again as Anna coaxed another letter out of Snorky's intestine. *Focus, precision, decision, completion.*

"We've got ourselves a *u*!" said Anna, holding it up for her vet tech to see.

Shaking her head, Katie took notes on the cat's vital signs. After a short pause, she asked a question, clearly keeping her voice as casual as possible. "So, you've made a decision then? About what you're going to do?"

"Well..."

"Wouldn't giving up this job mean giving up on the little beasties who need your help?"

"Like you and Noah?"

"Exactly."

"Actually, we should probably talk."

Katie looked up. When their eyes met, Anna lowered hers again and started to suture the intestinal incision.

"Over the last couple months," said Anna, "I've done enough soul searching to know that I'm not very good at soul-searching, for one thing. But I was also able to figure out that being a vet isn't exactly the perfect job for me." From the corner of her eye, she noticed Katie droop slightly. "I'm not what people want in a vet. I don't see their animals the way they do. The way most people in this country do. So that makes me a freak. I'm the freak vet."

"But, Anna." Katie set down her clipboard. "You've always been a freak."

"Your point is?"

"You can be a freak with a job or a freak without one. What's it gonna be?"

Since Anna's breakdown, she'd been envisioning herself swathed in a special grief wrap, given the *handle-with-care* status granted to survivors of house fires or random shootings. The grace period, however, was limited; Katie was letting her know that the pussyfoot phase had come to an end.

"Well… if I come back," said Anna, "can I still boss the two of you around?"

"I guess so. If I can still boss Noah around when you're not bossing him."

"Deal. I'm in."

"Really? Anna—I'd give you a big hug if you weren't totally covered in cat guts."

Anna hesitated for only a moment before snapping open a clean towel and holding it in front of her body. "Lay one on me."

The squeeze made Anna feel better than she had in a long time.

She bathed the distressed section of Snorky's small intestine in warm saline and checked his other organs for problems before carefully tucking all of the kitty's insides back where he'd prefer them. "Instead of suturing him up, we should probably just pull the two pieces of skin together, roll them down, and use a chip clip for easier access."

Anna froze, making Katie stop laughing.

"What? What's wrong?"

"I know why Snorky keeps eating these letters."

"Because he likes chewy things? That soft plastic probably appeals to him."

"No, I don't think that's it. I think he's malnourished," said Anna.

Katie scanned the length of the animal and ran her fingers down his side.

"You do? His fur looks good, his gums are pink. His weight's a little low, but the Greenlees said he hadn't eaten very well for the last few days. What makes you think he's malnourished?"

Before Katie finished the question, Anna had grabbed the debris tray, rushing it to the sink. She washed the plastic letters as she spoke.

"Katie, we've talked about this. You have to learn to be more observant. Obviously, Snorky is trying to send us a message. Look."

She snapped the two new letters alongside the first on the refrigerator. They now spelled out: *h-u-n*.

"He's just a couple surgeries away from telling us he's *hungry*!"

Putting on a fresh pair of surgical gloves, Anna tried to relax herself into the idea that maybe this wasn't the wrong job for her after all. Maybe it was just a stinking hard job. And lots of people had hard jobs.

14

“We could have guessed she’d pull something like this,” said Russ, pushing his blue U.S. Postal Service jacket closed with a fist in each pocket. “Getting everybody in here, then not showing up herself. And cripes, would it kill her to turn on the heat? Those of us with only two feet have no fur coats, you know!”

As would be expected, the man wasn’t whispering quietly to his neighbor in the next metal folding chair. Trapped in any group situation, Russ Pioske commonly took it upon himself to speak for everyone in the room. At the doctor’s office, at high school plays, and in line at the GreedyAss Markup (his name for the SpeedyGas Market down the block). Everyone who knew him—which was most people on this side of town, since he was their mailman—referred to him as Bitter Russ. It was a moniker he bore proudly, since it reflected an important service he provided: The bold reporting of what everyone else was too wimpy to say out loud.

Katie smiled as she watched Bitter Russ in his full acerbic glory, because she was privy to his most guarded secret. He would take offence, should she ever accuse him of it, but he was—for the most part—a pretty good guy. However, like musk from a skunk, or ink from an octopus, words could be spewed to keep predators from getting too close, which was Katie’s take on Russ’ rants. The act was a defensive maneuver cultivated by a scared little kid, who had eventually grown into a scared little fifty-eight-year-old man. A man who had just lost his mother. Katie had seen her obituary only a few months before, and the word around town was that Russ and his mom had been pretty close.

Try as he might to convince people otherwise, Russ betrayed his crusty façade with too many kindhearted acts. He was a person with his finger on the pulse of Milk River, often literally. He made it a point to keep his CPR training current, having saved with those skills, to date, three of the town's senior citizens.

Lots of people out in the country relied heavily on Russ Pioske. For some, his was the only human contact they'd have for weeks at a time. And not everybody owned a reliable car. So, unknown to the federal government (which had a few rules about that kind of thing), along with the mail, Bitter Russ frequently delivered non-postal items in his old beater Chevy, such as groceries, gossip, and other Milk Riverans. In return, a number of his postal patrons regularly brought him inside for a cup of coffee, a slice of cake, or a little hotdish, fully expecting to be reproved for weak coffee, dry cake, and a hotdish that should be tossed into the woods as a salt lick for the deer. It was all part of the Bitter Russ experience.

Katie listened to the small man's litany from her position behind the old metal desk at the front of the dog training ring. This concrete walk-out basement below the clinic had been the truck garage when the building was still the old firehouse. Truth was, the space was too chilly and stark to make a good meeting hall. But it was big enough to hold all the people who'd expressed an interest in adopting a puppy. And Katie hadn't wanted to waste any more time searching for the perfect gathering place, afraid Anna would change her mind again and keep all six animals herself—instead of just the one.

After a long internal debate, Anna had decided she wouldn't be able to part with Storm, and had officially declared herself the dog's human caretaker. Katie was relieved to know there would be another living creature bumping around in that big old farmhouse with her friend.

Public interest in these puppies had never let up. Maybe it was seeing them on TV that did it—putting actual faces to the innocents who needed help. On a couple of occasions over the past two-and-a-half months, Anna had allowed news teams into her home. Her discomfort with the intrusion had been outweighed by her desire to raise awareness of animal cruelty. (And, suspected Katie, Anna had wanted to keep Brian Ardeen's foul doings on public display.) But the scope of the ensuing media blitz had taken everyone in Milk River by surprise. As a byproduct of national attention, kind souls all over the country had been reaching out to offer these unfortunate dogs a safe place to live.

Anna's very specific plan for these puppies, however, meant limiting potential adopters to local people only, so that's who had been invited to the gathering. Actually, Katie was a little worried for Anna, who'd thrown her whole self into devising only one single fate for these puppies, with no backup plan, and was hinging everything on the success of a peculiar deal she would try to strike with some of the people here tonight. But what if it didn't work? When she'd asked Anna that question, the two of them had stood there staring and squinting, in one of their Tower of Babel moments; they would be friends forever, but sometimes she and Anna could make no sense at all of what the other was saying.

An attractive man, probably in his late twenties, opened the thick red door for his wife and small son, a biting January wind entering with them. The boy hesitated at the threshold, shocked by the size of the crowd.

"Hey!" Bitter Russ yelled at the three newcomers. "This handbasket ain't quite reached Hell yet, so it's still kinda nippy in here. Close the door, would ya? Cry-eye!"

The little boy used his mother's leg to hide his face from the mailman, prompting his dad to pick him up and move the family to seats in the back row. Katie glided over to greet the latest of Russ' casualties, offering them a heartfelt apology, an adoption application, and a pen. She realized she was down to her last few forms, meaning there were almost thirty families represented here. She suddenly worried that—like the little boy—Anna would find herself overwhelmed by the number of people crammed into her building, all trying to abscond with her puppies.

Katie checked her watch. Seven-fifteen. Why wasn't Anna down here yet? Considering the particular items on the docket, this was liable to be one bizarre meeting, and Katie was looking to get it over with.

"Come on, already!" said Bitter Russ in a bellow. "How much longer do I have to stare at the back of Kuball-the-Cue-Ball's shiny pink head here—which, by the way, had thick curly hair on it when I first sat down!"

About half of the room laughed, the other half gasped, and Bill Kuball slipped a little lower in his seat.

At last, Anna's newest staff member, Noah Long, came down the stairs carrying a wooden slatted playpen which he set-up in the front of the room. The group hummed with anticipation. A few people even clapped their hands for the empty structure, prompting Noah to look up and wave.

A moment later, Anna appeared with Storm on a leash. The energy in the room swelled considerably, with most everyone having something to say, a few *ah*s and *oh, wow*s rising up over the general hubbub.

And then, down the stairs came Eddy and Bunny, both with a ten-week-old puppy tucked under each arm. The crowd exploded into applause, startling Storm, who jumped back about a foot. Katie moved to the front of the room, helping Anna use hand gestures to quiet the audience as Bunny went back up for puppy number five.

As soon as all of the pups were placed in the pen, they began tumbling over each other, pushing their faces through the cracks between the slats, vying for the best possible view of the audience. From time to time, one would stand on its hind legs to investigate the possibility of escaping over the top. The dark gold runt with the black muzzle and black-tipped tail stuck her chubby leg through the slats, reaching out toward the crowd. Unfulfilled, she let out with a tiny bark of frustration, forcing the eruption of more applause.

"Look!" said a woman in the front row. "They're all different!"

Which indeed they were. Along with the broad-headed, caramelized-sugar-colored runt, the other four pups presented an assortment pack of shades, textures, sizes, and shapes. The black and tan puppy developing classic shepherd markings was also decidedly shepherd-like in shape. Both the grey- and black-spotted puppy, and her similarly patterned white and apricot sister had become wads of fluff with narrow heads, foretelling a collie-type future. And the yellow male with white on his chest and legs, and forming a stripe down the center of his face, was still by far the biggest of the lot, with massive feet and long, droopy ears.

"It's a friggin' variety pack," said Bitter Russ, at his usual volume.

"Excuse me," said the same woman from the front row, looking right at Anna. "Why is that? How can they all be so different?"

Not expecting questions so soon, Anna tensed, but then turned to address the room.

"Actually there's no way to tell for sure without a DNA test, but since the mother was kept outside, unsupervised, she might have bred with more than one male. So, it's possible that the litter has multiple fathers."

This theory caused small pockets of surprise in the room, but nothing Bitter Russ couldn't talk above.

"Huh! So what's the mother's name? *Sleazy*?"

A round of laughs followed, impelling Anna to gain control of her audience. She moved to a center position by the puppy pen and cleared her throat.

"Actually, this is Storm." She petted the white German shepherd's head as she spoke. "The mother of these five pups. And I should probably tell you I've decided to keep her for myself."

A few people in the group moaned, but most of them had come for a puppy and hadn't hoped to go home with a full-grown dog. Anna took one last look over at her support team. Bunny, Noah, Eddy, and Katie had all lined up against the wall about halfway back, each wearing their best *go get 'em* face. Anna pressed on.

"Hello. I'd like to introduce myself to those of you who don't know me. I'm Anna Dunlop, and this is my clinic. But as it turns out, I'm afraid, I'm not a very good host." Anna looked down into the pen of puppies then back at her guests. "I didn't bring enough for everybody."

She got the laugh she was hoping for and relaxed a little more.

"I want to thank you all for coming. Just by showing up here tonight you've already demonstrated more respect for these puppies than they were given by the first human in their lives."

A big round of applause.

"Anyway, I know it's a little odd to have gathered you here all at once instead of having you drop off an application for a puppy. I'd like to explain my thinking. I'm guessing that you already know the story of how these pups came into the world."

Anna paused to take a deep breath.

"And because you're here, I'm guessing that their plight has touched you in some way. Well, me too. And because of that, I'm proposing a very special kind of adoption contract for these puppies. As a lot of you know, it was difficult for me—well, I had a very strong reaction to the abuse that these little guys suffered."

"Yeah, first you lost your marbles, and then you picked 'em up and went home," said Bitter Russ, to mixed reactions.

"Aptly put, Russ." Anna noticed he'd positioned himself dead-center of the room, where he could be heard by the greatest number of attendees. "But if it's okay with you, I've got a lot of details to get through, so I'm going to ask you to please hold your comments until the end."

"Hey, sure, it's your picnic. Don't mind us annoying little ants."

"Thank you. I just wanted to explain that like all of you, I've been moved by what happened to these dogs. To Storm, who spent the first nine months of her life on a three-foot chain, and to these puppies who were born to become one man's garbage."

She paused and squared her shoulders, wanting to stay one step removed from her own words. Dwelling too long on the history of Storm and the pups could make her lose her composure—and with it, her credibility.

"I've been thinking it would be great if those of us humans who know better could offer a little payback to these animals. To even things out a bit by making sure the rest of their years have more meaning. And I think I've figured out a way to make that happen. I'll say straight out, though, that once you hear what I've got to say, I'm pretty sure some of you will feel like you've been right about me all along: That I've banged my head on too many low doorways."

Their laughter seemed natural, like they were joining her side.

"I'll totally understand if this arrangement isn't for you, and you want to take a pass."

A wave of chatter swept through the room, then died down.

"But those of you who wish to continue with the adoption process, once you know the terms, can hand in your applications. We'll read them carefully to find the best possible homes for these puppies and then call you within the next few days to let you know if you've been approved. Again, thanks so much for coming in."

She could stand still no longer. She began to pace the front of the room.

"All right. Here's my proposal. I'm not selling these puppies. Whoever takes one home, does so free of charge."

This part of the arrangement met with enthusiastic endorsement from the entire group. Heads were bobbing and smiling.

"And in addition to that, I'll give your puppy free medical care for the rest of his or her entire life. Or the rest of mine, whichever comes first."

People weren't sure if they were supposed to laugh at that or not, but they seemed thrilled with the notion of free veterinary service.

"And here's what I need in return."

Anna stopped walking, took another deep breath, and glanced at her friends against the wall, all wordlessly cheering her on.

"As you may or may not know, I do a one-hour radio show with Eddy Rivard on WLCM every Monday morning. It's called *All of Us Animals*, and people call in to have me answer questions about the animals they live with."

She looked at Eddy, helping herself to some of his serenity before dropping the bomb.

"Anyway, since these puppies were treated as if their lives had no meaning, every month I'll expect you to come onto *All of Us Animals* and report on what you've done to make your dog's life meaningful since the last show. Something little that you and your dog have done together. You tell us about an experience that made your puppy particularly happy that month, and—"

She stopped herself, not because of an outburst of sound from the crowd, but the pull of their deadly silence. Did so many jaws dropping open at once change the air pressure in a room? People grabbed the person beside them and turned to make faces at each other; a few tried to stare Anna down. But not a word made its way to her ears. Until Russ poked a hole in the dam.

"You gotta be kidding!" He leaned back in his chair. "Lady, have you been smoking your own catnip?"

The room felt electrically charged, as one person then another began whispering to people on all sides. Anna waited about thirty seconds to let them burn off some energy.

"All right. If I could have your attention please?" Her words drew faces in her direction, but they weren't what she would call *what-a-great-idea!* faces. "I know this is an unusual contract, but it's actually a simple request. You're planning on giving your puppy a great life anyway. So, just come in and tell us a little about it. That's all. This way, the whole county becomes part of your dog's life. These puppies go from having no one care about them to having *everyone* care about them. It'll help balance things out a little, don't you think?"

Clearly, that was not what they thought.

"I don't get it," said a disembodied voice. "Are you giving the puppies away or not?"

"Sure, I am. They'll be your dogs. It's just that I want you to share some of their life stories with us as they grow up. Isn't that what gives our lives meaning? People taking an interest in how we are and who we are? These puppies will—"

"And do you give us their food, too? Collars and beds and stuff?" asked a man about halfway back.

"No, no," said Anna, her calm trying to escape her. "I'm providing the healthcare, but this will be your dog, with all of the other responsibilities that go along with that."

"How would this even work?" said a woman, who sounded more judgmental than interested.

"Good question. Let me talk about the process a little more."

But before she could, other questions arose—not angry questions so much as fearful ones.

"Why should we have to tell the whole world about our business, anyway?"

"Is this even legal?"

"I heard your radio show once. I thought it was—I'm sorry, but kind of lame. And now I have to be on it?"

The crowd had turned. Anna stammered through her answers, feeling the solid support she had started to build crumbling beneath her. She tried to remember she'd had a lot of time to process this concept. But maybe the disparity between what this crowd had expected and what they had just gotten was too great.

"Do you have any other questions?" she asked.

They had many questions, but mostly for each other. They talked amongst themselves, some making jokes, others expressing disbelief. Anna's momentary lack of action as she assessed the phenomenon gave them blanket permission to misbehave. She was no longer leading a meeting; she was watching a discussion group where circles of strangers felt comfortable talking to each other, bound by a common issue—her kooky idea.

"Well, anyway, that's my offer," Anna said, needing to speak loudly. "Take it or leave it."

She didn't mean to sound unreasonable, but truth was truth. *Take it or leave it.* She meant to hold firm on what she'd set out to do, even though she was fighting the urge to get the hell out of this place with all six dogs in tow. She flashed back on her recurring dream; she was back on the rooftop; the chimney, the pull.

A couple of people rose and began to walk out. Then a few more, many with a sad smile for Anna, but others ignoring her completely. A few people made rude comments as they passed, pretending they didn't want to be heard, but making sure they were. Someone actually balled-up his application and lobbed it toward the front and accidentally—she assumed—hit her in the chin. She stooped, picked it up, and smoothed it out.

In a sing-song voice, stronger than she felt, she called after the offender. "I'm sorry, Mister—" she glanced at the application. "Hayden!"

The departure of these lead sheep prompted the rest of the flock to follow, and the training ring began to empty. Anna, having had her idea literally thrown back in her face, was overcome by the scope of the mass exodus. She'd expected to lose a few applicants who wouldn't want to abide by her contract, but she hadn't quite imagined such resounding condemnation of the idea. She felt herself pale.

The room had emptied entirely now, with the exception of three applicants. In a far back corner stood a rough-looking man in his mid-thirties, wearing a one-tooth-shy-of-a-full smile, frizzy, bright red hair pulled back into a ponytail, a patchy, red beard, a long tattoo of some kind around his neck, and a Harley T-shirt that read: *My bike eats your bike for breakfast.*

In the other back corner sat the nice looking couple with their young son.

And smack-dab in the middle of the room, his arm slung casually over the back of the chair next to him, Bitter Russ stared Anna straight in the eyes. There wasn't a sound to be heard. Even the four-year-old seemed to understand that something bad had just happened and kept himself still. Noah, Bunny, Katie, and Eddy moved in to group around Anna. Bunny took her hand.

Bitter Russ broke the silence with his slow, sarcastic applause, one staccato clap at a time bouncing off the unforgiving cement walls. The act affected even the biker guy; his smile waned into an expression of concern for Anna who probably looked like she might fall down. The young child slid off his mom's lap and walked toward the silent contingent of sad grown-ups at the front of the room. The boy stood only as tall as the top of Anna's thigh. He handed her his family's adoption application.

"Can I have a puppy?" He had the pure, trusting voice of a child who had been spared a disappointing family.

Even Anna, usually a little frightened by kids, was captivated by this one. In fact, his fearlessness helped her find her own.

"Hmmm, let's see," she said quietly, squatting down by the boy. "What's your name?"

"John Henry McCoy."

"Well, John Henry McCoy, we might be able to give you a puppy. But I'll have to talk to your mom and dad about it first. While I'm doing that, would you like to play with the pups for a little while? They look kind of lonely."

"Yes, please!" He broke into a grin that could have warmed the most trounced-on heart.

Anna stood, sweeping him up to deposit him into the middle of the doggie pen. The puppies used their whole bodies to welcome their new playmate, who promptly fell to his bottom and giggled uncontrollably under their enthusiastic attention. Anna, a bit revitalized by the Kodak moment, turned and stood tall to address her few remaining guests.

"So. You guys are just hanging around for the cake and coffee, then?"

Soft laughter from John Henry's parents.

The biker guy pointed to the mountain of treats, then gestured out over the empty room. "Looks like you brought enough of *this* for everybody." His voice was far deeper than Anna would have expected.

All of them, even Bitter Russ, had a little laugh.

"Right!" said Anna. "On to Plan B. But first, a question. Am I to assume that everybody here is still interested in adopting a puppy—under the terms I've just laid out?"

The family and the biker guy nodded. Russ didn't move.

"Good!" She exhaled in relief. "Glad to hear it."

Enough takers to keep her from feeling insane for cooking up the scheme. But what kind of human guardians would these people make for her puppies? She took another long, speculative look at the biker guy.

"And you know," she continued, "maybe it's okay that so many people have weeded themselves out. Instead of having to spend the next several days poring over a whole pile of applications, I can read all three of them right now. Then I can have a private little chat with each of you upstairs to find out which of these puppies might be best for you. And I'll call everybody tomorrow to let you know if I think this is a good match, okay?"

Her potential adopters seemed to like their new odds of receiving a puppy.

"But let's have a short group discussion first. I can answer any questions you might have about how it's all going to work. Maybe you'd like to move up front with me, though, so we can talk more easily? I think there's been enough shouting here tonight."

"Good night, Russ. Thanks for staying," said Anna, letting him out into the freezing night through the front entrance of the clinic.

"Right," he said over his shoulder. "And don't be calling me before suppertime tomorrow. I've got a day job, you know."

"Of course."

She locked the door behind him, watching through the glass to make sure his old car would start. All in all, she felt okay with how the evening had turned out. Clearly, the grand plan hadn't gone as she'd expected, but she could say that about a lot of things lately. It was right to do this—the thought came like knowledge, not opinion.

Bitter Russ' car protested a little but finally agreed to head toward home. Anna turned to find Katie and Eddy sweeping into the waiting room, parking themselves in chairs along the rust-colored wall.

"Spill it, sister!" said Katie.

"Yeah, give!" Eddy said.

Her pals jiggled anxiously, brimming with anticipation.

"Where's Bunny?" asked Anna, unable not to smile.

"I gave her a ride home a little while ago," said Katie. "Now talk."

"Who are you two, and what have you done with my gentler, more mind-their-own-business friends?"

"We want to know stuff! What's that Harley guy like?" Katie asked.

"That family sure looked nice. They gonna get a puppy?" asked Eddy.

"And, oh, my god," said Katie. "What was it like having to interview Bitter Russ? Come on, start talking."

"Okay, okay, you guys."

Anna lowered herself into the third of three 1950s vintage chairs in the clinic waiting room. She slipped off her shoes and brought her knees up under her chin. Rubbing her feet through thick, orange chenille socks, she said, "First, the McCoy family. Could they be any cuter?"

"No," said Eddy. "They couldn't. That kid is so polite. He called me 'sir.' He'd be fun to have on the show, yeah?"

"And they're going to be perfect puppy people," said Anna. "They've got a fenced-in yard, she's a stay-at-home mom. Cleo and Jeffrey are their names. And, of course, we all know John Henry."

"What does he do?" asked Katie.

"Well, he finger-paints, and plays outside, I guess."

"Very funny. I mean Jeffrey."

"Oh. He owns a frame shop in Turtle Lake. John Henry's been begging for a puppy, and they told him he could have one when he turned four, which he just did last week." She looked at Eddy. "Cleo said that when she heard you talking about the puppies on the radio, something just clicked. She knew that John Henry was meant to have one. And I think he is, by the way. I'm fine with that." She had realized it just then.

"One down, four to go," said Katie. "Now what's up with Mr. Harley Man? He looks a little—I don't know—dangerous."

"Jake Ellertson. Yeah, he looks kind of scruffy, and he's definitely a free spirit. But you know, I really like him. Wow, what a voice, huh?"

"I know!" said Katie. "The Barry White of the biker world."

"Apparently, he lives in some dome home out on County Rd I, just north of Bunyan."

"Ho, brah! I know that house!" said Eddy. "It's in beautiful shape, with tons of space and all sorts of interesting landscaping out front. He has these funky-looking sculptures made out of old metal oil barrels along the driveway. In fact, that yard was the inspiration for my scrap metal rooster."

"Ah, he's the guy your neighbors should thank," said Anna.

"Hardy-har." Eddy tried to look sarcastic, which he could never pull off.

"And, yeah, he's a sculptor and a freelance welder. Apparently, behind his house he's got a motorcycle bone yard. He builds and fixes bikes and snowmobiles."

"So we like this guy. But is he puppy-worthy?" Eddy asked, speaking her thoughts aloud.

Anna shrugged. "He makes more money than I do, so I know he's financially sound. And he seems to truly love dogs. He went on and on about the Newfie he and his girlfriend had raised together. But she got custody when they split up last year, so he's been waiting for the right dog to come along ever since. He's installed invisible fence around two acres of his land, which sounds great to me."

"So, how did he seem?" asked Katie. "Is he responsible enough?"

"His looks make you wonder about that, don't they? But really, he seems incredibly grounded. He's a bit of a philosopher, methinks. He's got a pretty intriguing outlook on life. Really artsy, but—serene, you know?"

"And he's funny, from what I could tell," said Katie. "You like funny."

"I feel good about him. He lives the kind of life a dog would love."

"So, two down?" asked Eddy.

"Yup. Two down. But then… there's Bitter Russ." Anna shook her head slowly in consternation. "He's a riddle, wrapped in a mystery, inside of a—a—"

"Porcupine?" offered Eddy.

"Bucket of glass shards?" Katie asked.

"Yeah, those'll do," said Anna. "I don't know. Bitter Russ with one of these dogs? I kind of don't think so."

"You know, Anna," said Katie. "I was shocked to see him come to the meeting. Russ doesn't normally put himself into situations where he has to ask somebody for something. I think he must want one pretty badly. I sat down there tonight watching him lash out at people. Controlling the room, you know? His usual grumpy old man act. But if you remember, he's a totally different person around animals. I keep thinking about how he was with Cricket."

"Oh, he lived for that dog," Anna said, suddenly finding a warmer spot for Bitter Russ. "He had her in here every time she'd skip a meal. Or if her eyes didn't look right to him."

"That was his old Springer Spaniel, yeah?" asked Eddy.

"Right," said Katie. "He got her as a puppy. I think she was with him pretty much every minute from then on."

"I'd see her on the mail route with him," said Eddy, "riding in the car whenever he did, then hopping out to follow him when he took to foot.

"That's right! She always rode along," said Anna.

"And did ya ever notice?" asked Eddy. "As she got older, she couldn't get around as well but wouldn't stay in his car. So, like it was the most natural thing in the world, Russ would walk as slowly as she needed him to. The both of them shuffling their way across town."

"I saw him carrying her back to the car once," said Katie. All three fell silent.

"And you know," said Anna, "his voice would change whenever he talked to Cricket. He was—sweet," Anna remembered.

"Maybe he saved up whatever kind words he hadn't spent on anyone else that day and gave them all to her," said Eddy.

Anna realized she had fallen into Russ' trap. She'd been focusing on his abrasive demeanor instead of the other parts of his personality that should matter. She'd do well to remember that these were not auditions for friends, but for doggie guardians.

"He never married, did he?" asked Eddy.

"In order to get a girl to marry you, I think you'd probably have to pay her a compliment, or smile or something," said Anna.

"Yeah. It's very sad how he lives," Eddy said.

After a short pause for the three of them to have their own private think about what it must be like to be Bitter Russ, Anna sighed. "You know, if he wasn't petting Cricket, it was because he didn't have a free hand."

"I always wondered why he didn't get another dog after she died," said Katie. "One day, a couple years after her death, I came right out and asked him. I think I caught him off guard, because I got a pretty straight answer. He said it wouldn't be right to replace Cricket."

"Oh, that's sad," said Anna.

"Then he got kind of choked up and said something rude about my shoes."

Anna and Eddy laughed.

"I guess he must be ready to try again," said Eddy.

"Yeah. I think I know how he feels," Anna said, looking over at Storm who was curled up in a tight ball on the rag rug, her pink nose hidden under her back leg.

"Of course, it's your decision to make," said Katie. "But if you gave Bitter Russ a puppy, you'd only have two puppies left to find homes for."

"And," said Eddy, "you'd be doing the whole town a service."

"How so?" asked Anna.

"Well, a guy can't sweet-talk a dog and hurl insults at people at the same time, yeah?"

"You should have stopped at that story about him shuffling along his mail route. It was a much stronger finish," said Anna. "Okay. Let's give Russ a puppy."

"Yes!" said Katie.

"But if he names the dog some four-letter word, the deal's off."

15

He had to suck a couple of times on the beer can to get everything he'd paid for. But he hardly took his eyes off of her. The vet stood there posing for him behind the glass door while she watched the mailman rev the engine on that '82 Chevy Rustbucket.

He turned his back on her just long enough to drop the last beer can onto the toe of his boot and kick it into the woods, slamming it into a tree he couldn't see.

The mailman heard the noise and glanced in his direction. But Brian Ardeen knew how to use the dark. He'd been standing out in the open, right across the street this whole time, unable to see the meeting taking place in the basement, but snapping to alert whenever anyone came upstairs. He'd seen the people trickle in, then leave again all at once about an hour later. Everybody except a few stragglers. The Hawaiian radio guy and a blonde chick were taking their time. They were laughing with the vet behind the glass door, not even putting their coats on yet. He clenched the muscles in every part of his body, including his throat, squeezing a long exhale into a low moan.

Brian took off his gloves, stretched his fingers, and pushed his hands deep into his parka pockets. He flexed one bicep and held it, then the other. He tilted his head as far as he could to the left, then to the right, making his thick neck crackle.

And he watched her.

Her big-ass Hawaiian bodyguard lifted the kennel onto the open tailgate. Already up and waiting in the bed of the truck, the veterinarian slid the huge kennel into place and started to strap it down. Brian watched her say goodbye to her helpers, who wanted to stay until she got safely behind the wheel. And when he heard her tell them she'd be okay, he had to be careful not to laugh. He watched as she sent her friends off to their cars, out of the small parking lot, out of the way. She took a few seconds to cover the crate with a Mexican blanket, making a big deal of leaving some air holes on one side.

The dog—*his* dog—already in the cab, watched the vet through the back window. The tall woman—Jesus, she was tall—jumped to the ground and closed the tailgate. Starting toward the front of the truck, she looked down to button her coat. But she wouldn't get the chance.

"So, how'd it go?" asked Brian.

He stood with legs apart, hands in his parka pockets, blocking her path to the driver's door. He was ready for the dog when it lunged at the side window, but the vet wasn't. Either he or the mutt scared the shit out of the woman, and she jerked so far back, she almost fell over. The dog kept barking and snarling at him, throwing itself against the door, smearing spit across the window. Brian pounded the glass with his fist, making the animal even madder. Through the window he bellowed into the dog's face. "Shut the hell up, you stupid bitch!"

He saw the dog recognize him. It dropped to its belly with a whimper. It sprung up again with a nasty bark, then silenced itself, and lowered its head when he purposely met its eyes. It wasn't until he finally looked away that the dog sat up straight and began a steady, deep-chested growl. Its eyes darted back and forth between him and the woman.

Brian could see the fear in the vet's face. He smiled and unsmiled. He took a step closer. But she lifted her chin and held her ground. He wondered if this was going to be harder than he thought, until he saw her glance in the direction her friends had gone.

He made sure to keep his lips pressed together. Tight. Like he was barely able to keep from going ape shit all over her. "Hey, come on. I just wanna know if you had fun at your little party tonight, *Anna*."

He slid his jaw to one side and blinked slowly. She stayed quiet but was breathing kind of hard, puffing quick frozen clouds between them.

"Really? Nothin' to say to me? Would ya rather write it down and staple it to a telephone pole?" He'd thought of that line while he was out here waiting for her.

He gave her about ten seconds of silence to worry about. Then, in a rattlesnake strike, he snatched the blanket from the top of the kennel, making one of the pups give out with a yipe.

"No!" Anna said, lurching toward him. She froze when he whipped his head back in her direction.

Stay quiet, then move fast and hard. He had decided that would be scariest. He slowly turned his attention back to the mound of puppies visible through the bars of the kennel door. A couple of them stood. All of them looked.

"Ain't they cute?" He slid his hand sideways into the cage. "And they've gotten so big!" A yellow puppy gave his wiggling fingers a lick. "The hole is gonna have to be a lot deeper this time."

When she flinched, it aroused him. Not in a sexual way, but with the same kind of full-body prickling. He took another step forward. But still she didn't step back, and now he stood so close he had to tilt his head up to keep hold of her eyes.

He turned to lean his backside against the truck, getting some space between him and the giant. Touching the vehicle made the dog freak out again. It started barking and pawing at the window. Brian stretched one shoulder, then the other, never taking his eyes off of her. She looked away first, scanning the area, probably for help.

"You're kind of a chicken shit when it comes down to it." He looked over at Storm and then back at her. "A chicken shit with *my* dogs."

He noticed her take a breath.

"And that doesn't seem right."

He was pretty sure he saw her hands shaking before she pulled them inside the sleeves of her coat. She seemed like she wanted to say something. Again, that tingly feeling, hair all over his body coming to attention.

"What? What is it? What're you trying to say? Come on, I really want to hear it." And he did. He wanted to hear her apologize. He wanted her to make excuses. To beg.

She finally said something.

"Are you…okay?" Anna asked, her voice sounding worried.

Brian's vision felt jumpy as he struggled to keep his eyes on her.

"I mean," she continued, "you didn't lose your job or anything over this dog problem, did you?"

"What the hell are you talking about?" He stood up straight to face her. He clenched his hands into iron balls at his sides.

"I—I don't mean to make you mad. It's just that—I've been thinking about you, and—I know I've had some pretty bad days because of what's happened, and I just want to say that—I'm sure this must be really hard for you too."

Brian crunched his face together. His lip was twitching.

He made himself remember all those people at the meeting who thought they could do better with his dogs than he could. And those goddamn fliers. His mug shot on TV.

He shifted his weight, hard, from one leg to another, pushing a disgusted laugh through his lips. He looked down at the ground for a second, smiling, shaking his head. But when he brought his attention back to those bright green eyes, he felt his jaw clamp shut and his face get hot. She was staring down at him like she wanted to cry. Not because she was scared, but because she felt sorry for him. Like he was a little kid or something.

Brian rushed at her, grabbing the front of her open coat in both fists, yanking her shoulders down to his level, goddamn it. The smell of peppermint surprised him.

He felt the heft of the hunting knife in his back pocket. But that would be too much. Too far. Wouldn't it?

He stood there, shaking her, watching her face, when a sickening thought squeezed itself in between the folds of his brain, tightening his bowels before he could squash it. He was scared—and she wasn't. *Jesus!* A hot, white blast exploded around him, plowing him toward her.

He shoved his hands inside her coat and ripped open her shirt, popping the buttons all the way down. She yelped. Her skin, her bra, her waist. *Holy shit.*

He wanted to slam her to the pavement. But some part of him was keeping the brakes on. Before he could get it sorted out she was opening her mouth to talk again. He had to shut her up. He thought he should punch her in the gut to get her to shut up, so he cocked his arm back—but there was all that skin.

"Brian," she said quietly. "Everything's okay. You're all right. We're both all right. It's over. You can just go. It's okay. You can go." She was almost whispering.

She placed a soft hand across the back of his, the one still clutching her shirt. She wasn't trying to pull him away. She was just—holding him.

He stepped outside of his body to watch a slow motion version of what was happening here. He felt tears on his cheeks, but the face wasn't his.

He turned and bolted as fast as he could toward the trees, forcing the dark to take him back in.

16

"Is he asleep?" asked Jeffrey, as Cleo joined him on the sofa.

"I don't think he'll ever sleep again. Not 'til we bring that little puppy home. He's way too excited."

Cleo's deep, breathy voice cracked like it always did when she spoke with any enthusiasm—which was most of the time—because she was always either happy, or trying to get herself happy. *Make a joyful noise unto the Lord, or hush up.* Her mom, a self-confessed Spunky Christian, had invented a storehouse of memorable proverbs to keep her children on the right path.

Cleo took Jeffrey's hand, using it to pull his arm up and over her shoulder. She nestled in, resting her head against his chest.

"You think we'll get him, right?" Jeffrey asked, with more worry than Cleo would have expected. "I mean, the one we want?"

"I'm not sure, sweetie. Any one of 'em would be good if you ask me. That vet seemed pretty particular though, so I don't know. I hope she liked us. But y'know what? If not, we could maybe get a puppy somewhere else."

Jeffrey shook his head. "I keep thinking about that big black and tan male. That's the one I want."

"I know you do, honey. You only said that about a million times so far. You're so funny." Cleo began to play mindlessly with the zipper on Jeffrey's dark green cardigan. "John Henry, he doesn't care which one, that's for sure. As long as it's a real puppy. Hey, maybe now I'll be able to pry BippetyDog away from him long enough to throw it in the wash."

"Yeah, really," Jeffrey said, in that distracted tone a person uses when they've listened only well enough to sense it was time to make an agreeing sound of some kind. He lowered his head to kiss her hair, letting his lips rest there.

Cleo loved it when he did that. It was so romantic. She knew he was probably thinking about something that had nothing to do with his lips in her hair, but that was fine. He was a deep thinker; she'd always known that.

In fact, his complicated mind had been one of the reasons she'd zoomed in on him in the first place—jeez—eight years ago now, at Carlson Community College. A person who knew as much about as many things as Jeffrey did usually ended up at an actual four-year school. So, he'd really stuck out on campus, and she'd noticed him right away. She would ask him questions just to listen to him talk about facts she never tried to remember. Places, and dates, and science facts had never been quite interesting enough for her to want to memorize, but she liked to listen to them. Which was probably why she'd always had boyfriends who were interested in stuff like that.

She knew she wasn't the brainiest person ever born, but she'd been smart enough to know the kind of man she would settle down with. *A wise, prayerful husband is a gift from God—and a good lookin' one's a bonus!* Jeffrey had been all three. She'd recognized him instantly as her perfect match and had spent every day after that waiting for him to see it, too.

It wasn't like Cleo was trapping Jeffrey or anything. She believed she had a lot to offer a man. She was good with a checkbook and liked to take care of people. She'd also been told her whole life that she had perfect skin, whatever that meant. And her dark brown eyes were big, and supposedly gentle, like the eyes of a deer. Which was why Jeffrey had nicknamed her Faline, after Bambi's wife. And by that, he'd said he meant Faline from the Disney film—not from the original book—because in the book, Bambi and Faline separated right after they mated, like real living deer did. But the two of them were going to stay together forever.

Anyway, knowing she'd had good skin and good eyes to work with, she'd learned to highlight those features with make-up and never went without it. Even around the house. Even when she was alone.

People liked her body too, though it hardly stood five-foot-one—and that was at her tallest, first thing in the morning. Of course, her limited height meant she would never be beautiful, just cute, but that never bothered her.

And then there was her voice. For some reason it had developed a kind of Marlo Thomas hoarseness in her teens and never smoothed itself out. To Cleo, it sounded like laryngitis, but her voice seemed to make people smile, so she considered it one of her positive qualities. Her mother had reassured her that since it came from God it had to be good.

"I like that he looks so much like a German shepherd," said Jeffrey, after they'd swum a little while in their own thoughts. "And as his coloring changes, he'll look more and more like one."

"Why do you say that, sweetie? Are you wishing you could own a designer dog instead of a mutt?"

"No, it's not that. We can't afford a purebred. And anyway, I like the idea of giving a home to a rescued dog. I just think a German shepherd sends a certain kind of message to people. Like, 'Don't mess with us,' you know?"

"Oh. Is that our message to people?"

"You know what I mean. Like when you and John Henry are out alone with the dog. He can stand guard over you guys."

"Huh," said Cleo, sitting up straight to look him in the eyes.

"What?"

"I *knew* I'd be the one walking the dog!"

Jeffrey smiled, squeezing her tightly, his arm still around her shoulder. Cleo lived from kiss to squeeze, like Tarzan, vine to vine. She reveled in Jeffrey's affection, which he offered generously and without hesitation. They held hands in the car, kissed in the movie theater, and took ten minutes every night when he first got home from work to lie together on the sofa, telling each other everything that had happened in the past nine hours.

But Cleo's need for still more physical contact was a steady, low-grade buzz in her day. Not that she'd ever complain about it to Jeffrey. He was so much sweeter than most men were to their wives. Her girlfriends told her all the time how jealous they were of her marriage, so she knew the problem was all hers. But honestly, being close to him like this put her in such a good mood, and a good mood made her want to touch him all the more. And more and more.

Cleo turned to swing her leg across Jeffrey's body, putting herself in a loose straddle over his lap. She massaged his shoulders as she spoke eagerly about life with the new puppy. She watched her husband close his eyes and roll his head back, totally relaxed, his lips in the most beautiful smile.

"And what do you think we should name him?" she asked. "I mean, I was thinking about how it might be best to let John Henry name him, but then again, that's how we ended up with BippetyDog, y' know? He has a way of making up those nonsense names which are kinda funny when it doesn't matter, but this is a real animal now, and it should have a real name, don't you think?"

Without opening his eyes or lifting his head, Jeffrey said, "Yeah, I can just hear myself calling out to our big, tough German shepherd at the top of my lungs. 'Poopy-Dingle-Cha-Cha, come here, boy! Here Poopy-Dingle-Cha-Chaaaaaaaaaa!'"

Cleo's laughter shook her whole body, which rubbed her private parts accidentally over Jeffrey's, setting off a series of events as much a part of their marriage as their morning kiss. It took only an instant for the electricity to shoot through Cleo, causing a quick little movement of her hips before she could gain control, which in turn, triggered a hardly noticeable reaction in Jeffrey. This time she felt it in the muscles over his collar bone—a tightening where her fingertips were. Barely more than a twitch, really, but a definite pulling away.

As always, Cleo stopped what she was doing and did something else. She casually retreated to where she'd sat before, beside him on the sofa. She folded her arms across her chest and tilted her head until it leaned gently against his.

"So. Seriously. Do you have a good name in mind?" she asked cheerily.

"Not off the top of my head. Let me think about it for a second."

And both of them set to thinking about dog names, without reflecting for even one moment on the other conversation they'd just had. This was how things were.

A couple of years ago, Cleo, feeling brave, had asked Jeffrey why he thought they didn't make love more often. And to her terrible surprise, he'd looked down at her with a face more miserable than she'd ever seen on a person—and she had caused it. Before she could take the question back, he covered his face and exploded into tears. Little boy tears. She knew, then, that something awful had happened to poor Jeffrey in his past, something that would make it hard for him to love her in that particular way very often.

She never asked him for any details and would never again suggest he give her more than he was able to. Because even though Cleo loved, loved, loved having physical relations with her husband, she understood that the specific act should be only a small part of what made a good marriage work.

So she was fine.

17

The beams from her headlights bounced crazily through the trees as Anna took the sharp turn into her driveway. The light dived and jerked upward as it swept sideways, illuminating only fragments of the scene at a time. As she spun the truck in the direction of the garage and its safety, shafts of light swooped across the expanse of rushing white slats—and a flicker of a human form. The moment the image registered, Anna slammed on her brakes, her hi-beams now pointing toward the river.

She twisted her head and shoulders toward where she'd seen the figure, though that part of the world was again black with night. She threw the truck into reverse and wheeled madly back, repositioning the headlights to bring the intruder into view. Storm sprang to her feet, snarling fiercely.

The woman trapped in the hi-beams had been frightened by the vehicle crashing up the drive and now shielded her eyes from the blinding light. She could just make out the truck door bursting open, someone half jumping, half falling out, then slamming the door closed, trapping a barking dog inside. The driver was Anna, recognizable only by silhouette.

The woman's daughter dashed toward her, bent at a run, arms thrust forward, long legs devouring the ground between them. Joey dropped her purse, preparing for the impact.

A split second before Anna's body hit hers—without slowing down—it had blocked enough light for Joey to get a good look. Anna's unbuttoned coat revealed her shirt, open to the waist, awakening the fear a mother harbored for her daughter her entire life.

They clung there together, touching in a way they hadn't for maybe thirty years. And though Joey wasn't sure where to put her hands, or how much pressure was appropriate, she wanted to hang on a little longer.

After telling her mother what had happened, after telling the police the same thing, after showering, and then changing into sweat pants and a thick fleece turtleneck, Anna sat hunched over a mug of cocoa at the kitchen table.

She glanced up to find her mom studying her face, one fingertip with its blush-colored nail circling the rim of her teacup. The gesture seemed inherently ladylike, as did most everything about her mother. Her hair, though professionally enhanced over the past couple decades, still matched Anna's own light auburn—both babies having come into the world with a full, curly head of it.

Baby gates in both doorways of the kitchen kept five squishy puppies tussling and knocking about Anna's feet, offering a welcome counterbalance to being shoved around in a parking lot. Storm lay on her side, eyes open, half under Anna's chair.

"Hot chocolate, Mom? That's so nice of you." She bent down to smell the steam, which sent her instantly back to her last night with Tony. The tent. The wager. She rejoined her mother in the kitchen, and concentrated on holding a strong curve to her smile—until something odd occurred to her. "But, um, I don't actually have any hot chocolate makings here in the house, so… do you carry the stuff with you at all times, just in case you might come upon someone who was almost assaulted and might need a little comforting?"

Her mother took a sip of her tea, silently returning Anna's only china cup to its saucer before responding.

"First of all, I carry a little packet in my purse, yes. I've been trying to cut down on caffeine, and some restaurants don't offer cocoa, so I ask them for a cup of hot water. And second of all—"

"Wait, don't tell me." Anna peered down into her mug. "You tuck the marshmallows into your sock."

"They come in the cocoa packet as little pebbles that swell up into real marshmallows once they get wet. And second of all, you weren't *almost* assaulted, daughter. You *were* assaulted. There's no almost about it."

"Ohhh, I wouldn't say that. He didn't actually hurt me."

Her mother leaned forward. "Anna, he tore open your shirt!"

Anna leaned back. "So, really then, my shirt was assaulted."

"I don't understand you. Why are you insisting on downplaying this? My god, I had to bully you into calling the police. You were obviously terrified when you got home tonight, and that criminal is the person who made you feel that way. So, why are you protecting him?"

"I'm not protecting him, Mom. Really, I'm not. Obviously, he didn't have a right to do what he did. And I was totally scared out there. Probably the only reason I didn't break down was that I could see, when he ripped my shirt open, how shocked he was. And not just by the haunting beauty of my perfect breasts and porcelain skin, you know? He could tell he'd gone too far."

"Ah-ha." Her mother nodded once, eyes wide, and Anna realized how insane this newfound empathy must seem after all the loathing she'd expressed for *that Ardeen creature.*

"Don't get me wrong," said Anna. "I still have an incredible amount of hatred for the weasel. If I had my way, he'd go to jail for a long time for what he did to those puppies. But after a nice hot shower and a little time to think, I don't believe I was in any real danger out there tonight. He was just trying to make me feel like I was. This guy is the grade school bully who terrorizes kids who don't have the nerve to back him down. Call him on his bluff and he folds."

It felt foreign, but kind of good, to share personal thoughts with her mother. Of course, it was only a certain portion of her personal thoughts. She had no intention of explaining how she'd arrived at her current wisdom on Ardeen.

She had had a *menemene* revelation in the shower. Twenty minutes of pounding hot water had given her the clarity to see inside of Ardeen's head. In a flash of intuition, she'd come to understand his behavior tonight—because it had been so much like her own. The epiphany had jolted her, making her almost lose her balance in the slippery claw foot tub.

Ardeen's mounting anger at her—however misguided—had brought him to the clinic tonight, most likely to deal with his problems as he always had, with some tough guy talk and empty threats. But when she'd thrown him off guard by speaking kindly to him—an idea she'd bumbled into with no real plan—he'd become so furious that he'd acted from another, more primal place.

She had seen her own self undergo a similar transformation on the day the puppies were buried. Sudden, intense anger could turn you into a person you were not. And if you were lucky, something came along to deliver you back to yourself before you were forever lost.

It would be an exaggeration to say she felt compassion for Ardeen, but she was forced to identify with him. So, she would call the police tomorrow morning to let them know she wouldn't be pressing charges. On one condition: That Ardeen leave her the hell alone. She wanted to die an old lady, never having heard him speak her name again.

"I don't care what his intentions were, Anna. What if he'd accidentally hurt you before he realized what he was doing?"

"I really don't think he's got the guts, Mom. That's what I'm saying. It feels to me like he couldn't have made it to that point. I think anyone more threatening than a large bunny could back him down. And besides, I'm just sick of playing the victim lately, you know? This isn't who I am. So, my husband's dead, I'm stuck in a tough job, some puppies were almost killed by a really bad man, and now that man has succeeded in scaring the crap out of me. Well, boo-hoo. Get over it, you know? I mean, I'm sick of my bellyaching. I can only imagine how everybody else must feel."

"Well, as the person who's known you longer than anyone else, I can tell you what I'm feeling. You're one of the strongest people I know, and—"

"Then you've gotta get out more, Mom."

Joey took a deep breath and looked up at the deco ceiling light for several seconds before beginning again.

"May I finish?"

Anna pressed her lips together and gestured for her mom to continue.

"Thank you. What I was trying to say was that you're one of the strongest people I know—who's been going through an incredibly difficult time. Believe me, honey, this too shall pass. You've got to admit, you've stored-up a lot of compassion chits over your lifetime. And all right, yes, you've been cashing a few of them in lately. Big deal. I believe that's how the friends and family system is supposed to work, is it not?"

"I suppose so."

"None of us are worried that this is the new you, forever and always. We know you'll get out from under the dark cloud pretty soon. In fact, it seems to me you almost have."

"Really? I hope so."

"Frankly, it feels good to be able to help *you* for a change. I think your friends would agree with me. You're what the world considers a Giver. You're terrible at the Taker role, Anna, and you know it. Maybe you believe that always giving and never taking is something to strive for, but you're wrong about that. People like to give. And you continually deny us the chance. Clearly, you know how good it feels to give, or you wouldn't be hogging it all for yourself. Shame on you."

"Wow. I don't know which seems more surreal to me at this moment," said Anna, looking off to the side as she spoke. "The fact that what you're saying is actually making me feel better, or my sudden wish that I could have been eloquent enough to deliver this same homily to you on any number of occasions."

Joey sat back and gave one quick tug on the bottom of her blazer. "Point taken." She punctuated her words with a controlled nod. "All right, so the Dunlops are woefully inadequate at letting their loved ones bear the burden once in awhile. Perhaps we suffer a genetic flaw of some sort. In that case, maybe we can both commit to doing a little better from now on—in spite of what evolution hath wrought."

"Okay. It's a pact." Anna poked at a sticky rehydrated marshmallow and then licked her finger.

The two women sat with their warm beverages and each other, in this hundred-year-old home where they'd both grown up. Anna would give Storm a scratch behind the ear or sweet-talk the puppies nearest her once in awhile. The night's terror was fading into pudgy tummies, furry faces, and floppy ears.

Without comment, Joey bent down to pick up the caramel-colored pup with the black muzzle. This was the puppy Anna thought of as Five, all of them numbered by size. She'd purposely given them only digits for names, hoping—foolhardily—that this might keep her from growing too attached. Her mom lifted the puppy from under its front legs as if picking up a baby. She held the dog's nose up by her own, front legs sticking straight out, back legs dangling mid-air. Far from distressed by her vulnerable position, the puppy seemed in immediate danger of falling asleep.

"That's the one who almost didn't—the one I was most worried about when they first came in," said Anna. "She's the runt of the litter."

"She's very sweet." Her mom set the puppy in her lap, placing the animal's two front feet onto the kitchen table. The puppy looked around casually, appearing for all the world to be wondering when dinner might be served.

"I'm trying not to get too emotionally involved," said Anna. "But I do have a soft spot for this one. She seems to wait and think, when all the others are just—doing, you know?"

"Hmmm. She's just like you then."

"Not just like me. I've never fallen asleep with my head in my food dish."

"Maybe not. But you were always my thinker. When you were a kid—well, still today—I'm continually humbled by your ability to think things through."

"Only because I'm afraid to make the wrong choice. Wrong is failure. Must. Be. Perfect. It's a weakness, Mom."

"It's not a weakness. If you ask me, it's an excellent survival skill. Think about what happened out there tonight with that Ardeen animal."

"Do I have to?"

"I'm only saying that I've heard you tell the story three times now, once to me and to two different policemen. With all the horror I feel as you tell it, I'm also left with this strong sense of—wonder, I guess you'd call it."

Anna cocked her head, lowering her eyebrows.

"There you were, facing who-knew-what-kind of danger, and in a split second you hatched the absurd, highly effective idea of being *nice* to this guy. I mean really, Anna. I hear that part of the story, and all I can think about is—Denny Fitch."

"Denny Fitch?"

"Denny Fitch. He was the off-duty airline pilot who just happened to be a passenger on that plane that crashed in Iowa in the late eighties. You know the one. You saw the footage a million times on T.V. You're looking through a chain link fence, the plane comes in and somersaults as it hits the ground."

"Oh, right. I remember. That was awful."

"Yes. The plane had lost all of its hydraulics, and I don't know much about planes, but from what I understand, on a DC10 that was considered a death sentence for everyone onboard."

"Jeez. Scary."

"Exactly. But this Denny Fitch offered his services to help out in the cockpit and came up with a complex set of maneuvers to land the plane."

"But the plane did crash, didn't it?"

"Yes, of course. You can't land a big plane without hydraulics, Anna. Are you listening, dear? The point is, keeping his wits about him, using his intuition to work the throttle, he was able to bring the plane down in such a way that he saved the lives of about half the people onboard. People who should have, by rights, died that day."

"Really? I don't remember that part of the story."

"Well, it's true. And there's something else, too. While Denny Fitch was recovering from his injuries, unable to report how he'd done it, professional flight trainers tried to recreate his landing but couldn't make it happen. They put their virtual plane, or whatever it was, into the same mechanical condition as his and tried to come up with some kind of landing procedure—any kind—that would save even a single person onboard. They couldn't do it. They crashed it twenty-eight times with no survivors.

"Seriously?" Anna had always appreciated her mother's gift for telling a story.

"With all those brains working on the problem, over that whole length of time, nobody could do what Denny Fitch had done right there in the moment, under all of that life-and-death pressure. Instead of letting go, instead of bowing to what he knew to be true—that a DC10 couldn't land without hydraulics—he pushed himself to find a way to make it happen."

"Wow. I had no idea. That feels like some kind of divine intervention to me."

"Maybe it was and maybe it wasn't. I'm just saying that what you did tonight—coming up with your own idea to calm your attacker when most people would have screamed, or tried to run away, or just stood there and let him do whatever he had in mind—it was brilliant."

"Mom, you're being really nice, and I know you're trying to make me feel better. But believe me, I'm no Denny Fitch."

"Don't miss my point, Anna. I'm not saying this to make you feel better, though I hope it does."

Joey reached over the head of the puppy now sleeping in her lap to take her daughter's hand; the rarity of such an act drew Anna's full attention.

Her mother's voice softened and slowed. "I'm trying to tell you something. I want you to know that because of your incredible mind, and your bravery, I am very, very proud of you. No, that's not right. I am in awe of you."

Anna started to reply. Twice. In the end, she held to the pact she had made, letting her mother give these kind words to her, accepting them as graciously as she could.

"Thank you," she said to the table. "That's really—thank you." She wasn't sure if her face wore the right expression.

"You're welcome." Her mother cleared her throat, bringing her hand back to play with the loose skin around the puppy's neck.

"Here's the weird thing," said Anna. "When Ardeen confronted me like that, yeah, I started sorting through my options. If things had been different, I probably would have decided to outrun him, which I'm sure I could have, unless he'd had a gun or something."

"Don't even say that."

"But it wasn't just me out there. Running away would have meant leaving him alone with Storm and the puppies."

"Yes, you would never leave the dogs. I do know this."

"So, what I ended up saying to him—all of that fake concern stuff? A couple of minutes in, pretending to care about his life and telling him how worried I was about how he was doing, I started to really listen to myself. And I began to wonder if I should have actually been feeling some of those things, instead of lying about them. I mean, I don't know anything about this jackass; maybe he had some horrible life before all of this happened."

"Even so, that doesn't excuse him for what he did."

"True. But just maybe, besides hating him and disparaging him all over town, I should have been feeling a little sorry for the guy. When I saw how freaked out he was, I stopped being scared of him and felt mostly pity. So really, it wasn't bravery I was showing out there, Mom. It was more like—arrogance."

"Huh. I should have known. When will I learn?" Her mom folded her arms across her chest.

"What?"

"I figured that somehow you'd try to find a way to tell this assault story with you as the bad guy. But I honestly didn't think you could do it. I just should have known better, is all."

Anna grinned, closed her eyes, and dropped her head to her chest. There was something so maddening—and so reassuring—about having people on the planet who knew her this well. Tony had been one such person. Her mother, and probably Eddy, were now the only two.

Anna was unexpectedly overcome with love for her mom. She felt the urge to jump out of her chair and give her a big squeeze, as she had earlier this evening when tragedy had bent the rules.

"Another cup of tea?" asked Anna, cordially.

"Sure. Thanks."

Her mom picked up the caramel-colored pup, snuggling it tightly to her chest, and made kissing sounds into the dog's ear.

18

"It was this funny little picture frame, maybe four inches square, yeah?" Eddy sounded delighted, almost winded. He was careful to keep his lips a little farther from the microphone than usual, knowing that when he got worked up he tended to pop his Ps.

"And there was no back to the frame, y' know? You could see right through it. But—the frame wasn't exactly empty, either. Wait, I've gotta think a second about how to explain this."

Eddy ran his hand through his hair. He blew short bursts of air through his front teeth, making the pondering sound he used almost every day but hardly ever heard.

"Okay. There was some colored cellophane—Saran Wrap, yeah? Stretched between the sides of this little frame. Light blue was the main color. Then right in the middle of all that blue, go ahead and picture a vertical rectangle made out of *red* cellophane. And then, dead center of that rectangle was a vertical oval of *yellow* cellophane. And that was it. A yellow oval, in a red rectangle, on a field of blue. In a teeny, tiny picture frame. And then get this. It looked like somebody had straightened out a few paper clips and somehow engineered 'em to perfectly outline the rectangle and the oval. It was the darnedest thing.

"Anyway, whatever it was, it was just sitting there on this eight-foot table with all the other typical estate sale stuff—toasters, coasters, probably a few other things that rhymed with that. And there I was with a big old question mark in my head. So I picked up the little frame and said, 'What is it?' to the nice Mrs. Osborn, who looked at me like I was crazy, which I've been accused of before, by the way.

"In a voice that—even with all of its politeness—couldn't hide its *Well, duh!* quality, Mrs. Osborn said, 'It's a stained glass window for a hamster cage.'

"That made me happy. I held the little window up to the sun coming into her walk-in basement, and told her I thought it was really pretty, and that it reminded me of a painting, maybe by an artist who tended to use those geometric shapes. Like Mondrian or somebody like that. And right as the words left my tongue I wished I could have reeled them back in, because I was afraid she might think I was trying to talk big. But the truth was, I'd just gotten a book out of the library on twentieth-century painters, and that's the only reason I knew anything about anything.

"Good ol' Mrs. Osborn, though, just gave me one of her many sweet smiles, drew in a deep breath of fresh patience and said, 'Eddy, Mondrian is about *non*-representational geometric abstraction. This is *rep*resentational.'

"Go, Mrs. O! I'd totally forgotten that she'd majored in Art History or something like that. So… snug in my proper place—where I'd just been put—I asked her if she could please tell me what the design in the hamster's stained glass window was representational *of*, 'cuz I was obviously too thick to see it. She pointed to the yellow oval and said slowly enough so that even I could understand, 'This is the Baby Jesus.' Of course it was! And the long, red rectangle was the manger! Brilliant, yeah? Right then I knew I had to own it. So I slipped her a Washington and told her to keep the change, again acting The Big Man, I guess.

"But here's why I wanted to make sure to include this story in my weekend update. I wanted to tell you what I took away from this exchange—besides a fine piece of art from the Rodentine Period, that is. It reminded me again of how cool it is to be human, with our intricate communication skills. My conversation with Mrs. O. fascinated me—fascinates me still—because it's a perfect example of human language flexing its powerful muscles, yeah? Here's what I mean.

"You're standing around, watching a group of Japanese people talking together, and they all break into laughter at the same time. And you realize that somehow their conversation must have been real, not gibberish, or they wouldn't all have known to laugh at exactly the same time. But how can they make sense of those random sounds? It's so cool. And I'm sure non-English-speakers feel the same way about us. Heck, *I* feel the same way about us. I mean, it seems like almost a miracle to me that right now, I can call you on the phone and just sit here uttering some strung-together syllables at you, syllables that come to mind as quickly as I need them, without having to consciously figure out how to put them together. And then you, without having to concentrate at all, understand this really complex thought that I'm trying to tell you. And, in fact, you understand it so well that you can turn around and throw a bunch of other syllables at me that are specifically positioned in relation to each other to get me to agree with you, or learn something I didn't know, or feel supported, or confirm a meeting date, or feel shocked, or take a particular action. And I do it! Just because some specific combination of sounds came out of your mouth in a certain order.

"This is a pretty amazing skill we humans have but mostly ignore, yeah? And I think we should step back once in awhile to appreciate it, that's all. I mean, in just one short minute of Mrs. Osborn's life, she had spoken the words: 'A stained glass window for a hamster cage,' 'non-representational geometric abstraction,' and, 'Baby Jesus.' Now come on, ya gotta love that. Who else but humans communicate by flinging themselves to such drastic verbal destinations within sixty seconds' time? Not dogs. I know that.

"I mean, sure, dogs are way better than us at reading body language, and with their own bodies can express some pretty detailed information such as: 'Hey, it's been a long time since that tiny cup of kibble this morning, and I happen to know that this cupboard is where we keep the Piggy Twist Rolls, and if you don't come over here right now and open it up and make me sit for one, I'm going to continue to blink my wet brown eyes very slowly in your direction, and eventually fall to the floor right here with a big heavy sigh, and I'm not kidding.'

"So, yeah, they've got some ways to communicate. But mostly, on simple topics like food, lovin', and ride-in-the-car. Truly though, very few dogs think about deep concepts like the Baby Jesus—except maybe that it's the most tempting chew toy in the Christmas crèche.

"And okay, so I also know that humpback whales have a complex half-hour song that's constantly changing, though no matter when you tune in, no matter what part of the ocean, somehow all of the humpbacks are singing the same updated version of that song. Yeah, yeah, yeah, mysterious creatures. But, hey, think about it. They're all singing the same dang song! Sounds kind of limited to me. I'm no expert, but I just don't see how that can possibly come close to the vast breadth of the human language, do you?"

One single, "Oh, please!" groaned within audible range of Eddy's microphone.

Anna had poked her head into the studio. With a huge smirk on her face she went on to say, "If humans are such great communicators, why do you sound like such a doofus?" She closed the door again, laughing her way out.

And there it was.

He'd been wondering how far he'd have to venture into this Them versus Us, animal-human rant before getting a rise out of Anna, and now he could move on.

He never tired of inventing new ways to razz his old friend. The humorous parry and thrust of their relationship had felt important to him since they were kids. It spoke of an extra effort they made—not only to enjoy each other's laughter but to work for it. This personal way they'd just touched each other had always warmed Eddy's insides. Being reminded of her friendship was like picturing his cozy living room on a long plane ride home.

"That was veterinarian Dr. Anna Dunlop, protesting apparently for humpbacks everywhere who couldn't join us here today for their own rebuttal. Which is just as well, because square footage is tight here in our modest little WLCM space. In fact, we've already had to do some remodeling to expand our studio into what used to be our walk-in equipment closet. Extravagant as a closet, the space seems kind of cramped as a studio wing, but we'll see how it goes.

"We needed the extra room to accommodate all the bodies involved in our new monthly feature, which in case you haven't heard, will air the first Monday of every month, starting today. Instead of following the usual format of our *All of Us Animals* program where Dr. Dunlop takes your questions on the air, we'll be chatting live in our studio with the adopters of the five puppies who almost left this big bright world before hardly getting out into it."

Eddy looked through his large studio window, out into the hallway where humans and canines were gathering, only one species of which making any effort to keep the noise level down. People stomped snow from their boots and shook it from their long, winter coats, while yipping puppies slipped around on the wet floor.

"I think all of us remember that sorry day about twelve weeks ago, and I bet you still feel as bad as I do about what happened to these pups. But I'm here to tell ya, if the amount of fluffy frivolity out in our hallway is any indication, you'll be comforted to know that these little guys do not appear to be dwelling on the bad times. In fact, I'd say life looks pretty good.

"And now… it's time to wedge a whole bunch of unsuspecting people and playful puppies into my old storage closet. Since that's likely to take a little doing and a few unpleasant sounds, I think I'll let you listen to some uplifting music instead for the next two minutes and seventeen seconds. Do you remember that one-hit-wonder group back in the '70s—a choir of dogs barking out their rendition of *Jingle Bells*? Well, here, from the flip side of that forty-five… please enjoy the very same group of vocal artists performing, *Oh! Susanna.* And as always, feel free to bark along."

19

The canine version of *Oh! Susanna* coming to its inspired finale prompted Eddy to lunge for the microphone, laughing. His studio was no longer a serene, soundproof space with only one man's voice to break the silence. Hands flailed in wild directions as humans tried to bring order to chaos as noiselessly as possible, over the rustling, whining, and squealing that seven extra people and six dogs couldn't help but make.

"Okay! Let me try to describe what we've got going here. First of all, I'm gonna use my limited elbow room to raise my arm, to toot my own horn a little. I'm pleased to announce that the old equipment closet seems spacious enough to accommodate the whole gang after all. Our puppy adopters are seated in chairs, in what I'm now proudly referring to as the studio *alcove*. Their newest family members are being held on laps or on leashes, depending upon the squiggly factor."

Eddy turned his head off mic to talk to his many guests. "Is everybody ready? Anybody need a quick walk on the grass? No? Then let's do this thing!"

He turned back to the microphone. "It's a little after eight o'clock, and if you've just tuned in, we're about to begin our weekly *All of Us Animals* show—as always—with local veterinarian Dr. Anna Dunlop. Hiya, Dr. D."

"Good morning, Eddy."

And no sooner had she finished speaking, but the puppy she'd been referring to as Three, gave out with a mightier sneeze than an animal of its size should have been able to muster.

"Bless you!" said Eddy, adjusting the volume on Anna's microphone. "So, Dr. Dunlop, why don't you give us a little background on the show today? Explain why we've got so many sneezers in the studio."

"Sure."

This was it. The day that Anna had been anticipating for so long. It would mark the beginning of a convoluted plan that either would or would not work. She'd tried to prepare, to go over the program in her head, to play out the various scenarios of how it might unfold. But it had been no good. She couldn't visualize the show, since it was entirely dependent upon a bunch of dissimilar people she barely knew. Exactly how was she supposed to lead a coherent discussion in a group this size? Luckily, she was an old hand at big meetings, as long as her goal was to have the entire audience get up and walk out—maybe throw something at her.

She talked for a few minutes, recapping the traumatic story of the puppies' first day in this world.

"...And everybody survived. We were incredibly lucky."

"Um, yeah," said Eddy. "Luck was a part of it. But I also happen to know that if it weren't for what you personally did, Anna, some of these puppies wouldn't have made it."

"My staff, Katie Larson, and Noah Long—and Bunny, too—we all jumped in. Anyway, three months later, everybody's healthy and in safe homes."

She'd noticed a recurring phenomenon in her conversations with Eddy on the radio: The constant push and pull of him wanting her to shine, and her wanting a more comfortable, dark place. Anna felt less of a star and more of a mushroom. She glanced over at Eddy. He was doing nothing in particular, fiddling with a knob on the control board, when she experienced what she had termed as a child: A *Brain Bridge*.

A Brain Bridge zapped her to a mental perspective she'd never had before. The crossing of a gap. The first Brain Bridge she could remember took place when she was five years old. Until then, she hadn't thought of her body as being different from that of anyone else; in fact, she hadn't thought about her body much at all. But at the doctor's office for a check-up, the nurse measured her height and exclaimed, *My, you're a big one!* And that was the precise moment Anna had *Brain Bridged* from being a regular kid to a mutant behemoth who towered over her friends. Until then, she'd had no idea she was such an aberration.

And now, watching Eddy work, watching how his shiny black hair fell along his collar, she had Brain Bridged to a feeling she'd never had for him during their three decades of friendship—something more vital, more knife-edge.

But before there was time to examine that feeling, or shame herself for having had it, it was gone. The Brain Bridge had collapsed. Eddy was just lovely Eddy again. The shift had occurred and un-occurred so quickly, it was easy to imagine it had never happened. So that's what she did.

After a pause brief enough to have been mistaken for a breath between words, she was back to talking about puppies.

"But here's the thing. What really gets to me—gets to the whole town—the whole country, really—is that these animals were born alive, with their own ideas and emotions, and would have grown up to play ball in the yard, or save a kid's life, or give a person someone to walk with. But that didn't seem to matter very much to the man who had the power to give them that chance. And that's why I wanted to figure out some way to bring a little extra meaning to their lives from now on."

"So here we are, to do exactly that," said Eddy, smiling at his many wiggling guests.

"Right," said Anna, watching one of the pups chew on Storm's leg. "So, let's meet everybody."

Anna sat at an angle to the tight little alcove line-up with Storm lying quietly beside her. She started from the left of the assembly with Bitter Russ. He was trying to look bored with the experience but not doing a very good job. Too much throat clearing and a series of vague facial ticks he couldn't quite hide.

"First up is Bitt—is Russ Pioske," Anna said. "A mailman from right here in Milk River. Russ, why don't you tell us about your puppy."

"Uh, let's see. Two ears, a tail and one, two, three—" Russ lifted up the pup's tail for a quick peek. "Yup, four feet. Oh, and she likes Chubby Hubby ice cream."

Russ, trying to be his usual ornery self, was sitting there holding his puppy as if he were burping a baby. And a person could only seem so gruff doing that. Anna smiled, feeling better and better about Russ raising one of these dogs.

"Check. All parts accounted for," she said. "But now, for the benefit of those experiencing this over the radio, maybe you could describe your puppy in a little more detail, and tell us her name."

Russ rolled his eyes and shook his head.

"She's, uh, kind of the color of mustard, I guess. The good dark German stuff, not that cheap, bright yellow crap. But she has some black on her too. Her snout, her ears, the tip of her tail. Like that."

"She's beautiful," said Anna. "I think she'll have a nice broad head and muzzle. And huge brown eyes. What's her name?"

Ignoring Anna's question, Russ scanned the full line of puppies. "And by the looks of it, she's littler than everybody else."

"Yeah, she was the smallest one in the litter. We almost lost her. Right now, by the size of her, I'm guessing she might grow up to be maybe fifty-five, sixty pounds. But it's just a guess. So, have you named her, Russ?"

"Cripes, whaddaya think? We've lived together for two weeks. 'Hey you' was kinda cumbersome."

"Oh, good," said Anna, studying Russ and his resistance. "So, what should we call this little lady?"

"Her name is—" Russ hesitated, then stretched his lips and licked them. He coughed into his hand. "I named her after my mother."

"You did? That's sweet. What was your mother's name?"

Another lengthy pause, making Anna wonder if Russ would become a problem on the radio.

"Kitty. My mother's name was Kitty."

The studio walls inhaled. Perhaps it had actually been the *people* in the studio, but if so, they reacted in one shared, startled breath.

The man sitting next to Russ—Jake Ellertson, the stringy biker guy with the incongruously deep voice—ended his own inhale with a loud, single laugh. "Ha! Man, let me get this straight! You named your dog—Kitty!"

Russ nodded once, crisply, not looking up. Others in the room looked at Jake, worried about how far a guy dressed in a T-shirt that said *This is not a T-shirt!* might go to make Russ feel foolish. Jake's smile broadened to touch both ears.

"That just couldn't be cooler, man," Jake said, his throat a bassoon. His face beamed as he patted Russ on the back, then put a massive hand on his shoulder and shook it. "A dog named Kitty. That's bitchin'."

The studio exhaled.

"Thanks, Russ and Kitty," said Anna. "And you've just heard the melodious tones of our next puppy's human, Jake Ellertson. He lives in a dome home that you might have seen just outside of Bunyan, with a series of sculptures out front. Jake's a sculptor, a motorcycle repairman, and a welder. That's right, isn't it, Jake?"

"And a dog lover. You got it."

"So tell us about your friend here."

Jake was holding the puppy in his lap, facing out. He stroked and played with the dog's front legs, unconsciously using them to gesture with as he spoke.

"Okay. Well, he's a boy. Kind of a big boy, I think. 'Cuz jeez, look at the size of his paws! And he's the only one with these long, droopy ears. Mostly he's sort of a light, powdery yellow color. But he's got a cool white blaze running down the center of his face, like—kinda like Trigger, I guess! Roy Rogers' horse, y' know? Same color, same stripe. That's funny."

Jake looked down at the puppy's leg he held in his hand. "And he's got these white socks, I guess you'd call them, on his front legs. Hey, didn't Trigger have those too? I've got me a freakin' palomino!" He laughed and others laughed with him. "Anyways, I named him Fritos."

"Fritos? That's fun," said Anna.

Young John Henry squealed the word. "Fritos!"

Cleo, holding the four-year-old on her lap, pressed her lips against his ear, whispered a little something, then left with a kiss. If the boy had just gotten a suggestion to keep his voice down, he either hadn't heard it or couldn't help himself.

"Mommy, that puppy's name is Fritos."

"I know, honey. That's funny isn't it? But we've gotta stay quiet until it's our turn, okay?"

Anna knew that Eddy had taken special care to position microphones strategically, so everyone could be heard at once. To *capture the festivity*, he'd said. And by the look on his face, he had achieved festive. Eddy's peaceful smile and lion-in-the-sun sleepy eyes caused a flicker of a Brain Bridge, but she forced herself back to focus on the non-Eddy creatures in this room.

"Friiiiiitos!" said John Henry, in that four-year-old, screeching voice.

"I'm with ya, John Henry," said Eddy, smiling over at the boy. "I really like that name, too." Then to Jake he said, "I, for one, and John Henry, for two, would be interested in knowing why that little puppy was named for a snack food."

"Fritos," said John Henry.

"Hey, John Henry," said Jake, leaning around the silent Jeffrey to look at the child. "You ever smelled a dog's feet?"

John Henry smiled shyly, looked away, and sank a little lower into his mom's lap.

"I'm not kidding," said Jake. He turned the puppy around and picked up his paw, burying his nose between the pads. He took a deep, long sniff.

The animal took the opportunity to paw at Jake's head with his other front foot while biting his red, frizzy hair. John Henry's eyes filled with something like wonder, watching this grown man smell a dog's foot.

"Okay, so maybe as a puppy they don't smell so much yet. But just wait. Really, wait 'til your dog grows up. His feet will smell just like Fritos. It's the funniest damn—" he glanced apologetically at Jeffrey. "It's the funniest thing." Jake turned back toward Eddy and Anna. "I love that about dogs. So I thought it would make a good name."

"Yeah," said Russ. "I know what you mean. I was gonna name mine, Eat-My-Own-Poop Breath, but I worried it might have been taken."

"Well, I like Fritos," said Eddy.

"I like Fritos," said John Henry, using Eddy's same inflection.

"So, welcome, Fritos," said Anna. "And, Jake, do you want to know where that smell comes from?"

"Sure. Why wait 'til you're dead to learn all the mysteries of the universe?"

"It's a combination of things, actually. Dogs have sweat glands on the pads of their feet. The moisture mixes with the action of some micro-organisms living between the layers of the skin and creates a certain smell. Voilà—Fritos!"

The puppy on Jake's lap looked up at Anna expectantly.

"I see he already knows his name," she said.

"Yup. He's a puppy prodigy."

The dog licked the green and black Celtic snake that wrapped halfway around Jake's neck. Anna realized she barely saw the tattooed skin, chains on his boots, or leather wrist bands anymore. Only Jake's amiable core.

"Okay, let's move on," said Anna. "So much to get to. Or should I say 'so many?' We've only met two of our five puppies so far. That little voice you've heard a few times already belongs to Master John Henry McCoy. His parents are here too. Cleo and Jeffrey."

Their black and tan puppy was lying between Jeffrey's feet in the Sphinx position, trying to stay awake. Jeffrey was bent at the waist, an elbow on each knee, petting the pup with one hand, clutching one end of a thin, purple leash in the other.

"Hello, McCoys," said Anna.

Jeffrey straightened up. Cleo took his petting hand, squeezing it gently. They offered a couple of quiet *hi's*.

"Cleo, Jeffrey, and John Henry live in Turtle Lake," said Anna. "Cleo works part time at Simple Pleasures, a candy and popcorn store."

"And candles," added Cleo, nodding her head and smiling as she spoke, which was her way.

"Sounds like a store that covers all of *my* simple pleasures, except maybe a warm dog on a cold night," said Anna. "And, Jeffrey, you own a frame shop in Turtle Lake, right?"

"Yeah, yes, that's right," he said. "I do. We do."

"And you have a male puppy. The second largest of the litter, Fritos being the first. Tell us about your newest family member."

Jeffrey and Cleo looked at each other, talking with their faces about who should answer the question. They soundlessly decided Cleo would speak first.

"Well," she began with her husky voice, nodding to emphasize certain words. "He's really pretty. Black and brown—he looks like a German shepherd, right, Jeffrey?"

"I think he does, yeah—yes. We've looked online at German shepherd puppies, and they seem to look just like our Patton here. The black and tan ones, anyway."

"Right," said Cleo. "He must've gotten all the German shepherd genes from his mom, but a lot more color."

"So, his name is Patton?" asked Anna.

"Right. He's gonna be a tough guy," said Jeffrey, bending over to give his pup a fast scratch on the chest. Patton flattened his ears to his head, looking more sweet than tough.

"Nice to meet you, Patton."

"All right, then," said Eddy. "If you've been keeping score at home, we've got three down with two to go in the cuddly canine countdown. Where to next, Dr. Dunlop?"

"In an interesting twist to our story," said Anna, "it seems fitting that the adopter is none other than the woman who gave all these dogs a second chance. Bunny Hall. Hi there, Bunny. It's good to see you."

"Good morning, Anna. Pleased to be here."

"And don't let that smooth southern drawl fool you, folks," said Anna. Bunny's from right here in Milk River. At least she has been for the past twenty years or so. You know, I've never really asked, Bunny—why did you move here, anyway?"

"Lately I've been wondering if it wasn't to save these puppies."

"Good answer. Do you think there may be some element of destiny to all of this?" asked Anna, reaching down to play with Fritos, who'd strayed over.

"Well sugar, I've never been a one to believe in destiny per se. I've always thought that things happened more as a result of free choice and nature's grace, you know what I mean? But this particular turn of events has set me to thinking along slightly different lines. I wonder if these puppies were chosen to be saved for some reason, and I was the tool for the job. And as a little extra gravy, I've received a great gift of my own. In this long, long life I'm living, I can now point to at least one moment where I know I did somebody some good."

"I know you've done a lot of good for several somebodies in this room."

"Oh, anyone would have done what I did. I just happened to be there when someone needed me to be, and I'm eternally thankful for that. An old woman needs a purpose, you know."

"Now, come on. I know young women who are a lot older than you."

"I'll give you that, darlin'. I do have healthy genes. You'd better believe I gave a long thought to my life expectancy before adopting these pups. But the timeline works out. You see, my people have always been long-lived. We stay spry to the very end, and the end is usually three numerals long. My momma lived to one-hundred-and-two. Her momma to one-hundred-and-four. I did have an aunt who only lived to be ninety-eight, but she died in a river rafting accident; I don't think that should count."

Giggles all around.

"Let's meet the reason you're here today," said Anna. "Would you care to do the introductions?"

"Absolutely. But first, I have to tell you, I am so honored—" Bunny's voice squeaked and stopped. She began again. "I feel a special connection to this litter. And I wanted badly to bring a couple of the pups home where I could cuddle them raw. But I was afraid. You see—I still lived next door to—I still lived—where I did. Where bad things could happen. And I just—I knew I wouldn't get a moment's sleep, what with worrying about the babies and all. And if I don't get my usual three-hours-a-night, I'm a wreck.

"Then one day Anna appeared on my doorstep asking if I would be interested in adopting a puppy. I told her no! I wanted *two* puppies. But when I explained why my geography made that impossible, she solved my problem in one simple word: 'Move!' And honest to Pete, I had never considered it. So, perhaps I'm too stupid to raise puppies into dogs. But Anna trusted me for the job. And trusted me to live in her mother's neighborhood. A couple weeks later, I found myself the proud renter of a townhouse unit and keeper of two of Storm's children."

Bunny looked down at the furry pups wrestling by her feet. Her contented expression faded into something more wistful. "You know, I would never have suspected this, but it feels good to be out of the home where Carson and I had lived for so long. I think I was trapped by all those memories. Worried about abandoning them. But you know what? It turns out they come right along with you." Bunny turned her head slightly, her eyes fixed on some decade Anna couldn't see.

In the brief silence that followed, puppies were hugged more tightly, John Henry was rocked slowly, and a heavy sigh escaped from over by the control board. It was Bitter Russ who broke the stillness.

"So, how much do you want for your house?"

Groans and at least one gasp were probably audible to Eddy's listeners. Most everyone in the studio gazed at Russ, the horrible but fascinating beetle under pins at the science museum. It was difficult, though, to tell if Russ was surprised by the group's disfavor or if he'd been fishing for it.

"Hey, I'm just sayin'. It's a nice place. I like to keep my options open."

"Okay, great!" said Anna. "That concludes this episode of *All of Us Realtors.* We now resume our previously scheduled broadcast of *All of Us Animals*, already in progress. So, Bunny, let's talk about your two animals, shall we?"

"Absolutely. I am ever so proud of my girls. It's just perfect that these were the two littermates left for me. Not only did I feel an instant connection to them both, but I believe they look like two dogs who should stay together. A matched set, wouldn't you say?"

"You know, that's true," said Anna. "They don't look anything like the other pups, but they bear a striking resemblance to each other."

"That's right. They're both ridiculously furry, with collie-type ears, where the tips fall forward."

"Semiprick ears, they're called."

"Cute as little bugs. And their coloring is the same—but opposite. One of the girls is mostly white, with the cutest dark apricot circle around one ear and some apricot dots on her face and legs too. The other darling is the most beautiful shade of grey all over, with the same circle, dots, and patches, but the markings are in black. Two different color schemes."

"And tell us their names."

"I wanted to name them after Storm in some way. And when I thought about their colors, one white and one grey, I had the perfect answer. Two different kinds of storms!" She bent to hug the sitting puppies, one under each arm. "So these are my girls. The white one is Snow, and the grey one is Rain."

A roomful of smiles and nods made Anna think this crazy solution seemed a little less crazy and more like a solution with every tick of the studio clock.

20

The hour-long radio show seemed only half that, and damage was limited to one puddle on the floor and a few outbreaks of puppy mayhem, sparked by Snow barking at Fritos. It made Rain lunge at Patton, scaring John Henry, who started to cry, which made Snow bark more and Storm begin whining as she tried to tend to everyone all at once. Anna shot a look at Eddy, who seemed pleased with his choice to put a microphone on everybody in the studio. Relative calm was soon restored, and the show pressed on.

"We're a little short on time today," Anna said to the group, "since we had to introduce man, woman, child, and dog at this first gathering. But I want to make sure we get a chance to do what we came for. To tell everybody listening what a great life your puppy is living. I want to go right down the line and have everybody describe a single moment when they realized their puppy was happy to be alive. Bunny?"

Bunny thought for only a beat before answering.

"Thursday night. Late. As usual, I could not sleep, so I was reading in bed, one dog on either side of me. And yes, I am one of those people who lets dogs climb into bed with them. I finished my book and set it on the nightstand, wondering what I should do next. Without thinking, I let a hand fall to either side of me and began petting. I kid you not, like I was Esther Williams and this was our synchronized swim team, both girls, at precisely the same moment, rolled over onto their backs for me to pet their bellies. Which, of course, I did. And upside down as they were, their top lips fell open, showing me their big, toothy grins. It felt like—the three of us were part of a single unit, you know? Perhaps the unit was only a petting machine, but these two critters could not have looked happier."

"Excellent!" Anna turned to address the whole group. "That's exactly the kind of story I'm looking for. It doesn't have to be huge. Your dog's life is going to be made up of a long series of individual moments. Just give us a peek into one of them. McCoys, how about you? Can you think of a joyful snapshot in Patton's life?"

Cleo and Jeffrey looked at each other, trying to come up with an example. But John Henry beat them to it. He turned to his dad.

"*Ring Around the Rosie*!"

His parents smiled.

"John Henry and Patton have invented a game," said Jeffrey. "I guess it's called *Ring Around the Rosie*, because that's what John Henry sings over and over as they play it."

"And over, and over, and over," said Cleo, nodding.

"The rooms in our house are laid out so you can walk in a circle," said Jeffrey. "From the kitchen, to the dining room, to the living room, and back to the kitchen. John Henry starts running in that circle, singing *Ring Around the Rosie* as loud as he can—"

"Not the whole song," said Cleo. "Just that one line, in that one tune. Over and over."

"And Patton follows right behind John Henry, pushing him with his nose," said Jeffrey. "But yesterday something happened, and they bumped into each other so hard they landed in a heap on the floor."

"Ashes, ashes, they all fell down?" asked Eddy.

"Right!" said Jeffrey, chuckling. "Then Patton climbed on top of John Henry, licking him all over. I think it qualifies as the highlight of his week so far."

"Love it!' said Anna. "A very sweet story, and another great example of puppy Nirvana." She got a little more serious. "But—um—Jeffrey and Cleo? I hate to say this—I feel like I should let you know—that game actually feeds into Patton's instinct to chase after things you'll want him to ignore when he's bigger. Like passing cars and running kids, you know?" Anna felt like a giant boot coming down on John Henry's fun.

"Oh, I totally get that," said Cleo, nodding her head so expansively the motion took an almost a circular path. "We just won't play that one anymore. But that still leaves about a million other games you guys can play together, dontcha think, Tweedle?" The bear hug Cleo gave John Henry squeezed a new smile onto his face.

"And Jake?" Anna said, shifting focus to the tall, sun-weathered man. "How about you? Was there a time this week when it seemed Fritos had found some particular meaning to his relatively new existence?"

"Yeah, wow." Jake's voice was a rumble. Scratching patches of red beard, he said, "There've been so many. I mean, it seems like he's only got two states. Happy and asleep. But I did think of something. Every time we go outside I try to get him interested in fetching, y' know? I keep a bunch of sticks by the door so I can grab one and give it a toss. But I don't think he's got the concept yet. I throw the stick, he runs to grab it, and then just keeps on running. He won't bring it back.

"He'd rather play Keep Away," said Eddy.

"Right. On Saturday morning, though, after the big snowstorm, he was in a pretty peppy mood, running full throttle, scooping up snow with his face. I threw a stick for him, but it sank down into the snow where he couldn't find it. After awhile, here came Fritos, proud as all get-out, carrying this enormous icicle in his mouth. Seriously, it was about twice as long as he was. Freakin' hilarious. He just brung it right up to me and set it down with this 'Wanna play icicle?' look on his face. I guess I've just been throwing the wrong thing."

"Yeah, dogs do have a way of training a person," said Anna. "Of course, you might have trouble keeping a supply of icicles on hand, come spring."

"Right. I've been thinking about that too. Anyways, that icicle morning. That was a good day to be Fritos."

"I agree!" said Anna. "Thanks, Jake."

She looked over at Bitter Russ, apparently the next man up for the firing squad. His face had paled, his brow had furrowed, and his lips had all but disappeared. Russ was jiggling his legs frenetically, bouncing his whole lap up and down at about four reps per second. Curiously, Kitty, stretched across his lap and clamped in place by Russ' small, dry hands, was sound asleep. How could the lightweight creature possibly nap through such motion? Anna had barely formed the question in her mind when the answer took its place. The puppy was *fitting into him.* And he into her. They were learning each other's peculiar ways and adapting. Need had the tendency to make an unworkable situation—work.

The scene triggered a revelation for Anna. She had focused on carving out a good life for these puppies, struggling to get them into families who would protect and nurture them. But it had honestly never occurred to her what the *people* might derive from the arrangement.

She could see now that Russ needed Kitty. Not someone who would forgive him his quirky nature, but someone who didn't notice it. Kitty would shape herself around him, seeking his company whenever he'd allow it. Russ was unable to earn such devotion from another person, resisting, as he did, all human kindness. Without a dog there was no one.

In fact, as a condition of this adoption, she was requiring him to do the one thing he'd spent an entire lifetime avoiding. He was going to have to talk about himself. Maybe even his emotions. At the very least he'd have to talk about his dog's emotions, and weren't they inexorably linked? Anna had just realized the great sacrifice Russ was making to keep this animal.

"So, Russ," she began, gingerly.

His jiggling halted for a split second as he shifted his attention over to her. Anna spoke slowly, casually, showing him a caring smile she genuinely felt.

"Let's talk about Kitty. What was her week like? Did anything stand out to you as particularly meaningful?"

"Well, let's see," he said, a distinct edge to his voice. "What kind of meaning are you looking for? She hasn't invented anything yet, if that's what you're asking. And the poetry she writes is for crap."

Anna tried not to join in the group laughter.

"Seriously, Russ. You know what I'm asking. We want to hear a little story about your puppy. A taste of what her life is like, now that she's with you. I'm sure you've discovered some interesting parts of her personality."

"Not really. She internalizes a lot. I think she might be Norwegian."

Anna used the time it took for laughs to die down to plan her strategy. What if she were to call Bitter Russ on his resistance? Had anybody ever done that? Was it mean? Or could it help him get to a place where he felt invited to talk more openly?

"You're a funny guy, Russ. I like that in a person. But here's the situation," said Anna, gently, bending forward to get physically closer to him. "Your problem with me is that I harbor the same feelings of discomfort around people that you do. And my defense mechanism of choice is humor—just like yours. So you see, I don't shrivel up and blow away when you poke me with the Funny Stick. It's an old friend. Like my Smokey Bear toothbrush. So I'll tell you what. I promise to respect your tremendously large personal space and ask only questions about your puppy. But you need to try to answer them. Okay? Does that sound like an arrangement you can live with?"

"That wasn't a puppy question." He was smirking.

"You're absolutely right. Try this. If you were to think back over the past couple of weeks since Kitty came to your house, would there be any one moment when she had a big emotional reaction to something in her world?"

A memory popped into Russ' head. Anna read it in his expression, just as clearly as his hesitancy to share it. She leaned slightly back in her chair, took a sip of coffee, set the mug down. She clasped her hands together, placed them into her lap, and looked over at Russ, smiling calmly. Actually, he folded sooner than she'd expected.

"Yesterday. I was—she was asleep in the kitchen," he said, pushing each word from his throat. "And I'd gone into the den to—I was—playing the accordion." He finished the last words and did a quick sweep of the room to survey faces.

Anna used every fiber of her being to show no reaction.

"And suddenly she—Kitty—came running into the den, making the strangest sound. When she got there, she started to—howl. Really howl. Like a wolf. It made me stop playing."

Anna was trying her best to focus on his story when most of her brain was still stuck on the word *accordion*.

"And when I stopped playing, she quit howling and just sat down, looking me over. I tried to play again, but she threw her head back and started to howl."

"Oh, that's so great!" said Anna, laughing. She wanted to pelt him with questions about his musical skills and the other million true things she couldn't possibly imagine about him.

"So you think it's great," he said, uneasy. "Because when I heard her do that—I thought there was something wrong, y' know? It seemed woeful. Deep in the bones, woeful. I wondered if I was hurting her ears. But then watching her, it didn't really look like she was in pain. It sounded more—I dunno—like she was trying to get me to do something. I didn't know what to do." He rubbed his mouth hard with the palm of his hand.

"So what *did* you do?" asked Cleo.

Bitter Russ, startled, whipped his head around to stare at her, then the others, his face like crumpled paper.

"I yelled, 'Everybody sing!' and stomped my foot to another rousing chorus of *Lady of Spain*—whaddaya think?"

Cleo lowered her chin to John Henry's shoulder, staring into his lap.

"You weren't hurting her ears, Russ," said Anna. "And it's fascinating you thought it sounded like she was trying to get you to do something. Because she was. Sort of. The howling thing that domestic dogs do is leftover from their ancestors. Wolves howl for various reasons, but we think the biggie is to gather the pack. To say, 'Hey, come on over.'"

"I don't see how that applies at all. She was sitting right there with me and howling."

"Right. But your accordion somehow triggered her instinctive response to howl. In some way, she thought your music sounded like another howling dog."

Anna and Russ locked eyes, both of them afraid Anna would make the obvious joke. She compelled herself onward.

"It's hard to say why that happens. Why particular sounds affect certain dogs that way. You're just kindling some vestige impulse. You're right though, it sounds kind of significant, doesn't it? Thanks for your story, Russ. It was great. And I'm so glad you came." She turned to face the group. "I'm glad *everybody* came to our first show, here because—"

Bitter Russ muttered something under his breath, which she could just make out: *Maybe I came, but I ain't coming anymore.*

"What did you say?" she asked, turning to face him, feeling her face get red. He was silent. From the beginning, she'd worried about his willingness to comply with the arrangement, and now here he was, planning to pull out. She kept her voice calm, though her stomach churned. She glanced at Kitty, wondering if this was her last time on the radio. And if other puppies would follow suit. "Come on, Russ. Let's talk about this."

He said nothing. He was looking down at his puppy's back, running his ragged fingernails through the golden fur.

"I know what you said, Russ. You said, 'Maybe I came, but I ain't coming anymore.'"

"Geez, get a Q-tip! I said '*Lady of Spain* ain't in my repertoire.' I don't want people here thinking I actually play that corny song. Hell, I don't want people here thinking anything about anything."

And one more time that day, the two of them looked into each other's eyes, frozen solid.

Laughter splattered everywhere around them. Anna looked over at Eddy, who was leaning back in his plain wooden chair, bouncing against the wall with every *hyuk, hyuk, hyuk.* His sparkling almond-shaped eyes reached out to tickle her until she couldn't help but laugh. And for just five seconds of the thirty-three years she'd known him, Anna wondered what it would be like to give Eddy Rivard a good long kiss.

21

Anna sat in a soft, red chair in the *river room*, an area of the living room so-named by her at age five, when her mother had placed a green, oval rug at the river end of the living room, and two comfortable chairs facing out toward the water instead of into the room. Decades later, once Anna had taken full possession of their family home, she'd added a low table between the two chairs where a person could set drinks and snacks previously forbidden in that part of the house. It wasn't so much a table, actually, as an old wooden Victrola cabinet, etched on the front with the RCA fox terrier, head cocked, listening to *His Master's Voice*. The piece of furniture was one in a long line of vintage additions Anna had purchased that dismayed her mother, who had modernized whenever possible.

Legs fully extended, stockinged toes gripping and ungripping the edge of the windowsill, Anna peered out at the river through the last few moments of viable sunlight. She bent one knee, bringing her leg up to her chest, holding it there with both hands. Repeating the action with the other leg felt more pleasurable than it should have, reminding her how inactive she'd been all day.

She dropped to the floor on her back, heaving both straight legs up and over her head, touching toes to hardwood, supporting her hips with her hands. Storm, in her belief that anything on the floor was fair game, trotted over, wagging her feathery white tail. She pushed her head into Anna's neck. She pawed at her shoulder.

"Hey," said Anna, giggling. "Knock it off."

When she rolled onto her side and began doing leg lifts, Storm barked in single syllables, evenly spaced, and pawed at the black turtleneck Anna had known she'd regret putting on that morning. Living with a white, longhaired dog was challenging from a wardrobe perspective; lying on the floor with one was insane.

Anna stopped and outstretched her arms toward the excited shepherd. "Get over here, goofy."

Storm threw herself against Anna, rolling immediately onto her back. Anna, instead of scratching the tummy being presented, wrapped her arms around the deep chest of the dog.

"Lesson number—let's see, where were we?—twenty-six, I think. Yes, lesson number twenty-six on *Adapting to Life as an Inside Dog*: At any given moment, I'm likely to hit the floor to stretch these gargantuan appendages of mine. And though I appreciate your willingness to assist, it's really better if you just watch silently, maybe with a look of awe on your face at my Olympic precision and amazing stamina."

Anna lay there holding Storm for a minute or so.

"Okay, lesson's over. Time for push-ups."

She was counting out loud and had gotten to push up number three before remembering the tent wager with Tony. She lowered herself to the floor, feeling the aged wood against one cheek. Storm twisted around to put a cold, damp nose against the other one.

22

Though it was free to buck and roll wherever it wanted, the old maple floor in the former firehouse complained anyway. Grunts, groans, clucks, and caws made up the soundscape in Anna's office. The walls took olive green down as far as it could go before hitting brown; photos of prairie flowers, trumpeter swans, and her beloved Milk River added to the serenity. Indirect northern exposure light sifting through massive oaks on its way in made dusk and dawn seem like the only two settings in her office, which everyone called *The Burrow*.

The heavy junk store desk—a collection of stories told in smooth scratches and divots in the wood—gave Anna a place to huddle up early mornings at the clinic. More naturally a nocturnal creature, she forced herself to come in an hour ahead of everyone else, so she could gather her thoughts before taking on a full day of other creatures' problems.

She pushed the button on her Mac for her daily buzz (getting the start-up chime and watching the screen come to life). Fresh computer, new day, infinite everything. Her favorite part of the boot-up was being greeted by her randomly selected desktop image—today a white-on-white photo of Storm lying in the snow—and then three folders popping on in a perfectly straight line.

She opened the last folder, her puppy project folder, for a quick double check of the health maintenance schedule she'd created for the five canine siblings. As she'd thought, Bunny and the girls would be in first thing today for their second DHLPP vaccination. Good. That would give her just enough time to check her email, which she hadn't done since yesterday morning.

There was one from her mother with nothing at all in the body of the email; the entire message was contained in the subject line.

Reminder—Greggy's birthday Friday.

The only other email in her box was from an address she didn't recognize. The subject read:

URGENT: mesage for health.

Misspellings in spam always made her smile. In this case, were they trying to sell her a massage or send her a health message?

She couldn't resist—she opened the email and whispered the word *What?* several times as she read.

Hello.

Your that vet on the radio today. I need you to get a mesage to Jake. I think that's the name. The guy whose puppy eats icicles? Lots of people don't think about this but it's not healthy to eat icicles. The water ran down the dirty roof and started in the sky with its pollution. Really, this is serious. Tell him to put an icicle in a coffee filter once and let it melt. He'll see what's in there. Yuk! Hope this helps.

Mrs. Gena Brent

Anna read it again. Then one more time, getting happier and happier. She rarely heard from radio listeners, and never via email. She might get a phone call from a client whose pet had a problem like one discussed on the show. This was different. A listener she didn't know was interested enough in Jake—and Fritos—to want to get involved. Beautiful. She printed out the email and left The Burrow at a trot.

"Noah, hey! Guess what I got."

Noah was stepping out from behind the reception desk.

"Hi. I was just coming to get you." He gestured toward the commotion in the waiting room. Bunny had arrived and was being tugged in two separate directions. Rain was pulling on the leash to get to the bowl of treats on the reception counter, and Snow was lunging for the door, wanting no part of this place.

"Bunny!"

Anna squatted down by the grey Rain, who body-slammed her with total abandon. The puppy jumped repeatedly, her tongue hot on the trail of Anna's dodging face. "Jeez, she's so aloof. I hope you can get her to come out of her shell a little—oh, man, I think she just Frenched me!" Anna made a spitting sound.

"Yes, she is brash, that one," Bunny said with a grunt, still fighting with Snow's leash. "Luckily, her sister here makes up for it with her calm, passive disposition."

Snow was yipping wildly at the door now, trying to propel herself through it but spending most of her time splayed out on the slippery wood floor. Anna took Rain's leash, gesturing Bunny toward Exam Room One.

"Come on, let's duck in here."

On her way past the desk she handed Noah the email, mugging a big *you won't believe this* look.

She turned her head toward the surgery and called, "Katie… Rain and Snow are here."

"Be right there," said Katie.

Bunny carried the white, fluffy Snow into the exam room, setting her onto the metal table. Anna petted the panting pup to calm her.

"Hmm, she doesn't seem to like it here very much. I'll try not to take that personally. Why don't you stand around in front of her so she can see you. Katie will be here in a second with the vaccine."

"You're just fine, punkin' pie." Bunny was murmuring a full octave above normal, her forehead pressed against Snow's. "You're all right. Just hang on, darlin'. You'll be fine." Bunny abruptly stood upright to look Anna in the eyes. "Oh, my stars."

"What?"

"A flashback! Just three months ago, in this very building, I was saying these very same words to these very same puppies." Bunny turned her wrists to look at her creased, pink palms. "Back when I could almost hide them in my two hands. Oh, honey, look at you!"

She stroked both sides of Snow's head, smoothing the downy fur, which feathered right back into the *out* position. The pup was trembling inconsolably.

"She seems so awfully fretful," said Bunny. Do you think she remembers that day?"

"Huh. That's a good question. I hadn't thought about that, but puppies do perceive smell from the day they're born—before birth, actually. It's possible she could remember the smell of this place, I suppose. Then again, a lot of people think puppies haven't developed well enough by the first couple of weeks to be affected psychologically, good or bad."

"That sounds merciful, with the first day they had."

"Hi, Bunny," said Katie, stepping in beside Anna with a couple of syringes.

"Hello, Katie. Lovely to see you."

"You too." Katie was already focused on the puppies. "These two furballs look great. How's life around your house these days?"

"Good. Real good. Always something happening."

"I bet. Oh, Anna!" she said, touching her boss on the forearm. "Noah showed me that email. What a hoot! Fan mail!"

"Well, she didn't actually say she liked the show, but at least she cared enough to write in."

"And what email is this exactly?" asked Bunny.

"Someone I don't even know wrote me about yesterday's show. A lady who didn't like the idea of Jake's puppy eating so many icicles."

"No. Seriously? Oh, that is so funny."

"I know!" Anna laughed. "Okay, I know icicles aren't clean, but they're probably not going to—"

"No," said Bunny, shaking her head. "I find your letter funny because I had a stranger talk to *me* about the show, too."

"You're kidding!" said both Katie and Anna at the same time.

Anna and Katie had spent so much time together, they'd developed a similar speech pattern, often speaking in unison. Usually, when Anna realized she and Katie were about to complete the same sentence, she'd choose other words on the fly, or at least slow down to let her sentence stream out a beat behind Katie's. But lost in the joy of the moment, she played her role in the Greek chorus.

"I kid you not," said Bunny. "Out on our walk yesterday. Someone from behind me said my name. Kind of tentative, like. Truly, I wasn't even sure I heard it. So I turned around to see this pleasant young woman, probably in her late twenties, looking from me to my girls. And she said, 'Are you Bunny from Eddy's show?' which made me stop to think for a moment, until I realized that yes, I probably was. The giveaway was the old broad with one white and one grey puppy, I imagine."

Katie smiled, giving the orangey spot surrounding Snow's left ear a good rub.

Anna laughed, shaking her head. "No way!"

"Way indeed," said Bunny. "Melanie Wagner, her name was, and she wore a perfume I hadn't smelled in years. *Ambush.* I so loved that scent, but I have no idea where she got it, since it disappeared in the 1970s. They recreated the perfume recently, but I tell you, it's not the same at all. Ghastly.

"Anyway, Melanie crouched down to play with Snow and Rain, stalling for time, I believe now. She seemed shy as I watched her, which struck me as odd for someone fearless enough to flag me down like she did. But she eventually looked up at me and said, 'So—your husband—Carson. Did he die?'

Anna reared her head back. "She did not say that!"

"She did. And I'm here to tell you that Carson's name in this stranger's mouth sucked all the air from my lungs. Because again, I had forgotten that I'd mentioned his name on the radio. At first—well, it just seemed otherworldly to me. Here I was, walking down Water Street, approached by someone I had never laid eyes on who knows my dogs and my dead husband. I felt like—like I was standing there in my underwear. All I could do was stare at this woman. She did have the kindest eyes. I could tell that she meant me no ill will. She seemed—sad. And after a moment she said, 'I was wondering…'" Bunny was now impersonating Melanie Wagner. Her voice was quiet, her eyebrows knit together into a plead.

"'Could you tell me how long ago he—died?' And you know, it did not even occur to me to tell her to mind her own business. I simply answered. 'Seven years.' She nodded. She thought. She spoke again, this time with the most tortured expression. She said, 'How is it? I mean—to live this long without him?'

"As you can imagine, I had no idea what this poor girl wanted from me. So I just told her the truth. I said, 'There are days when I do not consciously think of Carson at all. Lots of days. But even on those days there's a distinct portion of my body which seems to start under my armpit on the right hand side and run down to just under my ribcage that houses a certain sensation. Not pain, exactly. Not emptiness. More like an awareness of something warm. It radiates, sort of. And I can't actually tell if it's a good warm like a source of energy, or a bad warm like a mild infection. So I don't know if this is where he lived in me while he was here, and what I'm feeling is his absence, or if this is where he moved to once he left, and this is his warmth I carry. All I know is I noticed the heat only after he was gone. One way or another, it seems it's my *memory* of him burning there.' So, anyway, that's what I told her."

Anna wanted the sadness welling up inside of her to be entirely for Bunny. This was Bunny's story. Bunny's grief. But she felt tangled up with it somehow, hurting bodily for Tony, like he'd died just moments ago.

"I truly have no idea," continued Bunny, "why I told that woman what I had never told any other live human being. But I needed to, I believe. Not for me but for her. And as I was talking to her about my physical oddity, her eyes became watery. When it was her turn to speak again, she didn't. And then I saw her make the decision to come out and tell me what she wanted. She said, 'I just need to know if the suffering ever stops.'

"While I was trying to figure out how best to answer that question, she told me that her husband died a year ago, and that the pain felt exactly as strong today as it had the night he killed himself. And I could see that it did, the poor, poor dear. I told her that I was sorry, but I could not know exactly how things go when someone ends their own life, since Carson did not *choose* to go."

As an aside to Anna she added, "My god, quite the opposite. The man went kicking and screaming."

Katie looked as alarmed as Anna felt.

"Hell, ladies," Bunny said, seeing the looks on their faces. "Not literally. His was a peaceful, trickle-out-then-slip-away kind of death. But I'm telling you, he surely did not want to go. He told me so almost every day when he was first diagnosed—hoping, I think, that someone would tell him he didn't have to. And I swear, he fought it to the end. During those last months, he would grip the wooden slats in his headboard so hard his hands would turn white. And when I'd ask him if he were in pain he'd say 'no,' and look surprised by the question. Luckily, we were able to keep him comfortable with morphine and such.

"So I suppose it was just some drug-induced reflex, but it always looked to me like he was trying to rivet himself here on terra firma. When he fell asleep I would lift his arms and place them down by his sides. And the minute he awoke, they would move right back to the headboard. The next time you visit your momma, Anna, come on by. I'll show you where the wood is darkened. The oil from his hands, I imagine." Bunny looked off into nowhere for a moment. "I touch it every night before I sleep."

"Oh, look at me." Bunny huffed. "Here I was trying to tell you about poor Melanie Wagner, and suddenly we're trudging through my own gloomy past. Aren't I the Sorry Sue!"

Which made Anna think herself a sorrier person still, for stealing Melanie's story, folding it into Bunny's, and using the whole mess to feed her own pathetic desolation. Especially when there was a woman out there in such a bad way she was approaching strangers on the street, hoping to squeeze from them a drop of relief.

"So what I told Melanie," said Bunny, "is that I was sorry, I didn't know much about suicide. I did, however, know a little something about death. And for me, the first year was the very worst. It lessened after that, a mite less every year for several years. And now I believe the feeling has finally diminished as far as it plans to. Sometimes it bobs up closer to the surface for another go 'round, like when I'm eating dinner and happen to notice our wedding photo above the kitchen table. But mostly we've come to an arrangement: The pain gets to stay—and I try not to resist it. It's curious, but the hurt itself has become my companion in a way. A reminder of what I had and how lucky I was to have it."

Out of the corner of her eye Anna saw Katie glance her way. Anna knew her friend was wishing her the same kind of peace. And actually, Anna considered herself on the road to that peaceful place, as if she could see it from where she was, but couldn't quite get there before the next lonely nightfall.

"And what did Melanie say?" asked Katie, tears in her eyes.

"Now that was the most interesting part. 'Thank you.' Just that. She rubbed my arm from shoulder to elbow a few times and said it again. Just, 'Thank you.' And she turned and walked back in the direction from where she had come. What she said—it seemed like a big, *broad* thank you, you know? Thank you for telling her something so personal, maybe, and for sharing some particular insight she thought I possessed. But I also got the sense—and do not ask me to explain this any further because I cannot—but she was also saying 'thank you for going on the radio,' I think."

"Isn't that the damnedest thing," said Anna.

"No, I don't think that it is," Bunny answered with a penetrating look. "I suppose a woman who drops a pebble in the water might not see everywhere the ripple goes, but that does not keep the little waves from reaching people."

The abrupt shift of attention caught Anna off guard.

Bunny touched the tip of the vet's nose. "Thank you for having me on the radio, Anna."

"Um… you're welcome?"

Bunny gathered the ends of both leashes. "Well. If I ever see Mrs. Wagner again, I shall pass that sentiment along. Now. Are we through here?"

In the time it had taken Bunny to recount her strange story, Katie had vaccinated the puppies and fed them both two doggie treats each.

"I guess we are," said Anna. "I suppose I'll see you next month on the radio, if not before, right?"

"Yes, indeedy. Let's go, girls. Bye, you two."

"Bye, you three," said Katie.

And off they went. Katie shot Anna a look of sympathy she didn't deserve. Anna shook her head and waved her hand, but left the exam room so deep in thoughts of Tony, she missed the first several words of what Noah was trying to tell her in the hallway. But even without the preamble, she understood that her next appointment awaited her in Exam Room Three. Seth Robb and his killer cat, Brutus.

Brutus, a classic grey tabby, had, once upon a time, weighed in at a stalwart fourteen pounds. But struggling with diabetes over the past several years, he'd lost a considerable amount of both fat and muscle mass. At a svelte nine pounds, his skin hung loosely in folds, lending him a deceiving aura of feebleness.

The mighty Brutus, however, maintained his substantial height, his speed, most of his teeth, a full set of functional claws and the will to use them—making him a formidable opponent. Especially to the object of his utmost fear and loathing. The dreaded veterinarian.

Anna, still feverish from her conversation with Bunny, made the conscious effort she renewed several times a week—to push thoughts of Tony far enough down to be able to step over them and keep on moving.

"Very well," said Anna to Noah, dramatically placing a firm hand on his shoulder, righting her posture, puffing out her chest. "We who are about to die, salute you!"

"Hey, I get it. Brutus. The whole Caesar thing. You're quick." He handed her a long, faux-leather glove.

"Thanks." She tugged it on until the open end cupped her elbow. "I'm given to moments of great clarity before a good blood-letting."

Seth Robb had placed his cat carrier on the table. He stood nearby, hands behind his back, an apology as a face. The sound emulating from the box was the standard cat-in-the-car protest, a deep-throated growl opening to a clear, gradual verbalization of the word, *Wow.*

"Hiya, Seth," said Anna. "Noah, I don't think you've met Seth and Brutus yet."

"Nope. But I've heard the legend." Noah shook Seth's hand.

"Yeah, I bet," said Seth. "Sorry in advance."

Seth was one of Anna's favorite clients, mostly because of the tenderness he showed his cat. And the world at large, really. He was a pudgy, good-humored man in his thirties. Evidenced by his ten-year-old fleece jacket and messy hair, Seth spent far more money and attention on Brutus than on himself.

"Okay, let's do it," said Anna.

"Should I open the gate?" asked Noah, his fingers on the latch of the carrier door, the last bastion of peace between man and beast.

"Nope. Physics means nothing to ol' Brutus. You could tip that box all the way on end and shake it like a maraca, but he'd stay glued to the back wall. It's easier just to remove the top."

Seth was already unscrewing the bolts when Noah joined him. Brutus, familiar with the routine, upped his resistance. His growl rose significantly in pitch and urgency as Anna reached into a cabinet for a thick towel, drawing pleasure from the color-coded line-up of perfectly rolled linen. She set the brown towel on the table, then widened her stance and squared her shoulders.

"Ready?" Noah asked.

"Let 'er rip!"

Noah cracked the top open along the front of the carrier, allowing Anna a few inches to slip inside. Brutus was not amused. He used his back legs to skitter himself into the far corner, intensifying his commentary on their plan. His complaints made Anna feel a little bad, and Seth worse, by the look of him.

"Got him!" said Anna. "Get ready with the towel, Noah."

Anna held Brutus' spitting head in place with her gloved hand just long enough to grab his scruff with her other one. She lifted him from the carrier and brought him—howling—up against her midsection. He twisted and lashed out with every pointed implement at his command, trying to keep Noah from half-placing, half-tossing the towel over his head and body. Within seconds, though, the cat's cries faded to a stuttering, warning sound. Easier on the heartstrings and all exposed flesh, thought Anna. She held him against her, wanting him to feel protected and getting him used to her touch.

"So he's having trouble standing?"

"Yeah. You know, I've been wondering for a few days if he seemed a little weak in the back legs. Once in awhile I'd think I was noticing something, but then he would seem okay again.

Seth's demeanor downshifted from fear to something more like grief. Anna joined him there, thoughts of her own sorrow still close to the surface.

"Is it from his diabetes?" asked Seth. "Is he dying?" His voice begged Anna for the right answer.

She looked down at the cat-shaped towel. "Well, I haven't exactly gotten a good look at him yet. But no, I don't think he's dying." She was careful to keep a cautionary tone. "Let's see what we can see. Okay, kitty cat… nice and slow…"

She lowered him to the table, holding him there as she spoke. In a flash he curled his body around her glove, gnawing it through the towel, clawing at it with his back feet.

When she tried to rearrange Brutus into a more comfortable position, she got her bare arm too close to one of his front legs. With a high-pitched snarl that sounded like a woman shrieking the word *There!*—as in *Take that!*—Brutus slashed the skin across the back of her wrist. A red beaded bracelet emerged, then smeared against the cat's twitching tail.

"Whoo-hoo! We're oh-for-one."

She looked into Seth's troubled eyes. "There are all sorts of conditions that can make a cat walk on his hocks. Lots of them can be fixed. But we just don't know what we're dealing with yet. It could be something with his thyroid, or a potassium level issue, maybe renal failure, pancreatitis or—really, any number of things. I'd like to do a full blood panel and a cystocentesis, meaning I use a needle to get some urine from his bladder. I want to see if there's any glucose in it so we can—"

"Should I go pull all that together?" asked Noah, already on his way out the door.

"Hey!" said Anna. She raised her gloved fist chest high, elbow jutting sideways. "Either get me out of this thing, or send in the falcon!"

Seth's hearty laugh filled the time it took for Noah to study Anna's face, cock his head, and then smile. As the vet tech tugged the glove east, Anna pulled her arm west, letting her thoughts dash in a third direction. She was musing on Noah's scientific approach to jocularity. He seemed to appreciate a good wisecrack but not for its entertainment value. He preferred, instead, to dissect it. To see what made it run. She'd never known anyone so entirely humorless. And more, she was surprised to thoroughly enjoy the company of such a person.

Noah did, however, broaden his grin when he saw Seth loosen up enough to laugh. The mood in the room had lifted, bringing Noah's smile along with it. So, her assistant was not without joy—he simply siphoned it from available third parties. It was this same empathy, she imagined, that made him brilliantly adept at offering just the right words to a troubled client. She'd been honing that skill in herself for months now, watching him in action.

"This'll just take a few minutes," said Noah with a bolstering nod to Seth on his way from the room.

Brutus, on the table and under the towel, had frozen in place. But Anna kept hold of his scruff. Unwilling to trust him not to bolt, she slowly removed the towel. Registering no recognition whatsoever that he'd been unveiled, the cat lay on the table exactly as he'd been placed, moving only the muscles necessary to pant. His mouth hung open, displaying an impressive set of bright white teeth for such an old guy; his tongue held the stiff contour of ribbon candy.

Anna bent over to look into his mouth, checking inside for sores which could indicate renal failure. None. She pressed her fingertip against his gums and released, watching the capillaries refill to a nice rosy pink in about one second's time.

"He's not dehydrated, so that's good." She checked the tissues lining his eyelids. "Has he been at all lethargic lately?"

"No, not really. Yesterday he unwound an entire roll of toilet paper."

"Let's see if we can get him up."

Anna put a hand on Brutus' abdomen, gently lifting him into a standing position. The animal began a fierce gallop that would have propelled him off the table into a wall were it not for her firm grip on his scruff. He stopped then, as abruptly as he'd begun. He was supporting his weight, but as she'd anticipated, instead of standing up straight on all four feet, his back legs rested on the table up to his hocks. She repositioned him a few times, each test ending the same way.

Anna kept one hand loosely on Brutus' side as she pivoted to look at a laptop on a shoulder-high shelf. Before every appointment, Noah or Katie would bring up the patient's history on a screen in whichever exam room they were using.

You've still got him on one-and-a-half units of insulin, right? The Vetsulin?"

"Yup."

"Twice a day?"

"Yup."

"And no problems with the injections? That goes fine?"

"Seems to. He's pretty used to it by now."

As Anna palpated Brutus' abdomen, she worked through possible options for his muscle weakness. She loved this part of her job. Solving the riddle.

"Did you happen to bring his insulin supplies with you?'

"Yeah, I did." He began to dig in his small backpack. "I always bring the stuff with me whenever I take him somewhere. Just in case." He came up with a glass vial and a new syringe in its paper package.

"Great." Anna took the insulin vial, looking it over. "I know you've been giving him shots for years now, so don't be offended. But I was wondering if you'd mind showing me exactly how you inject him—hang on a second." Anna took the syringe from Seth's hand, then whipped around to double-check the computer screen as Noah entered the room.

She turned back to Seth, neglecting to keep the unease from her voice. "Is this the syringe you've been using?"

Seth didn't answer. His lips parted but froze. Anna consciously summoned a more relaxed approach, softening her voice and her physical bearing.

"So… is Brutus getting his insulin from one of these?"

"Um. Yeah." Seth confessed to the blunder before knowing what it was. "A friend of mine—his cat died. His cat was diabetic too, so he gave me a ton of syringes he had left over. He didn't want them to go to waste, and it seemed kind of important to him, like it would be something good to come from her death. And when I saw that the needle was smaller than mine, I thought it might be easier on Brutus. So I've been using these for a couple of months now, I guess."

Anna paused, searching for the most caring way to break the news. Noah, on the other hand, responded instantly and naturally. He placed an open palm on Seth's back, letting his eyes say how sorry he was. Seth's face went into pre-panic mode.

Anna spoke kindly. "Seth, your friend must have been using a different insulin. Maybe Humulin?"

"Yeah." He sounded a little defensive. "That's why I didn't take his insulin, only the syringes. They've got units marked on them just like mine. And a unit of insulin is a unit of insulin, right?"

"Right, but what you give Brutus is a *solution*—one-and-a-half units of insulin suspended in liquid. And his solution had a different concentration than yours—a different amount of fluid. So actually, you've been giving Brutus about two-and-a-half times less insulin than he should have been getting."

Seth breathed out his words. "Oh, my god. Oh, my god."

"So now I'm thinking neuropathy, brought on by long-term hyperglycemia. In other words, if I'm right, his blood sugar has been too high for awhile now, and it's done some nerve damage."

"So he's going to walk like that forever?"

"If it's neuropathy, and we can get his blood sugar back under control and keep it there, chances are pretty good that in a month or two he'll be up on all fours again."

Seth looked sick. His eyes moistened.

With purpose, Anna shifted her position to face her client, catching his eyes and holding them.

"Seth. I want you to take just a minute here to think about everything you've done for Brutus over the years. If he'd been living with someone else he might have died a long time ago. A lot of people wouldn't do what you've been doing. You've always been there to give him whatever he needed, no matter how much it cost, or how much time it took. You've been giving him two shots a day—every single day—for over five years now. You need to feel good about the life you've given Brutus. You've done the very best you could, all along the way. It was an accident, what went wrong here. No matter what happens, your cat is better off for having lived with you. Okay?"

No answer.

"Okay, Seth?"

Seth nodded weakly. He swallowed hard.

"Now let's just get some blood, take a look at his urine to see what's going on here. And I'd like to keep him 'til the end of the day so we can check his blood glucose every hour. Is that okay?"

Seth only mouthed the word. "Okay."

When lunchtime finally came, Anna let herself drop the last several inches into her cushy desk chair, much to the delight of every muscle in her body. A good chair was one of her few sanctioned luxuries since it was where she napped when animals needed overnight attention. She opened her old, pink *Waiting for Guffman* lunchbox, noticing the yogurt container filled with stir-fry leftovers. She'd meant to microwave her meal but forgot, and the hassle of uprooting herself to traipse back to the kitchen outweighed her aversion to cold, slippery vegetables. She scooped up a forkful, took a bite, reconsidered a trek to the microwave, then swiveled over to her computer.

With a reflexive glance toward the door, she opened her *Poems* folder, then a document entitled *Ideas*. She made the following notation.

CONCEPT: Slimy Food

POSSIBLE RHYMES:

stir-fry from the night before - unfit for a prisoner of war

Squinting her eyes at the computer screen, she used her teeth to scrape the skin from a pear. She set the fruit back into her lunchbox and wrote:

pan fried okra / tapioca
oysters, eggplant, half-cooked eggs / french press coffee's bitter dregs
sautéed mushrooms, cookie dough / fancy olives, escargot

She heard a sound out in the hall and clicked the document closed. Listening for a moment, she heard the person continue on without knocking, but Anna didn't reopen the file. She would barely have time to check her email and update Seth on Brutus' good news before her next appointment.

Anna bent closer to her screen and counted. Her inbox contained eight messages, considerably more than her usual zero this time of day, and none of them were from her mother or Eddy. She skimmed the subject lines.

You're doing the right thing for dogs
too late to get a puppy?
All of Us Animals? All of You Hilarious!
My Dog is the Puppies' Father
PUT PIX OF PUPPIES ONLINE FOR US TO SEE?
Tape those German shepherd's ears!
can't wait for next week
Let the mailman talk more

Anna sat very still. She felt her face get hot. A laugh, a whoop, a squeal—they all seemed like good ideas. Instead, without opening any of the emails, she began a new one of her own, to eddy@wclmfm.com. Her subject line read: *Dinner?* And into the body of her email she typed:

Hiya Eddy.

I'll make chili. You bring the chocolate. You won't believe this.
-a

23

On her way to the stove with his empty bowl, she offered Eddy seconds—the question only a formality. Over his shoulder, he tossed her a query of his own.

"You wanna know my favorite thing about your chili?"

"Sure. What?"

"Your corn muffins!" He licked his finger clean of butter.

"Oh, you sweet talker."

With great gusto, Eddy opened his mouth for the remains of muffin number two, just as Anna plopped ladle number two into his bowl. She noted the likeness in sounds.

"No, really, Anna, these are delicious. *Brok da mout!"* It was one of the Hawaiian pidgin phrases he'd never lost, much to his grandmother's chagrin. (His tutu had considered pidgin a bastardization of the beautiful Hawaiian language.) *Brok da mout* was one of Anna's favorites, the phrase describing food so delectable it broke the mouth.

"One more time," said Anna. "Come on, please?"

Eddy groaned.

"Okay, you don't have to read them all," she said. "Just my favorite one."

"Anna, these are your emails. You've had them all day. You've read them a hundred times. Why do you want to hear me read them?"

"I don't know, it's just so thrilling to hear them actually spoken. These are real people writing to us about the puppies, Eddy. Can you believe it?"

Shaking his head, Eddy wiped his hands on the cotton napkin in his lap, his skin color stunning against the white. He began to paw through the stack of printed emails beside his salad plate.

"All right." He sighed, playfully. "But this is absolutely the last time, yeah?" Eddy found the page he was looking for and began to read as Anna set his bowl of chili in front of him. "His salutation reads, *Dr. Dunlop, you'd better take me seriously."*

"Oooo, a threat. The perfect opening," said Anna, plunking down into her chair. "Sorry. Go ahead."

Eddy read the words with a haughty, pompous attitude, doing his best to recreate the spirit of the letter.

"He says, *I am a retired executive of a Fortune 500 company, and I know whereof I speak. I live in the same neighborhood as the pathetic man who had those puppies; approximately three blocks east. I often walked my dog down the alley behind his house. Norman (my intact Chesapeake Bay Retriever) would see that white German shepherd and try to get at her. He'd pull on the leash, but I always kept him from getting too close. However, Norman does get loose upon occasion, and I suspect that when the female was ready and open for business, he went to that house and had his way with her."*

"Had his way with her! Too good!" Anna was unable to contain herself, even the third time through. "I bet when he was done with her he sat up and begged for a cigarette!"

"Here's the reason I am contacting you," continued Eddy in the writer's pretentious tone. *"Norman's coloring might also be considered dark mustard, just as the puppy of the rude mailman. So I believe he may be the father.*

"Norman or the rude mailman?"

Eddy laughed and read on. *"You are a veterinarian, correct? Certainly there must be a blood test we can do?"*

"A paternity test!" She interrupted one last time. "Hey, I know. Let's bring Norman onto the *Jerry Springer* Spaniel *Show!"*

Her joke made Eddy laugh his way through the final few words of the email.

"Because if he is, I'm clearly entitled to a cut of the considerable profit you're certainly gleaning from your radio program, and you know that I am. Contact me soon, and let's see if we can do this without having to get our lawyers involved. Sincerely, Robert J. Winters."

Eddy sprinkled cheddar cheese onto his chili. Anna swallowed a big mouthful of red wine, then made a show of placing the stemmed glass on the table with a particularly loud thunk. She jerked her head forward toward Eddy, slapping the table with both hands.

"Dear Mr. Eddy Kaimi Rivard." Her voice, too, was affected. "It's recently come to my attention that I should surely be gleaning a considerable profit from my radio program, and I am patiently awaiting same. You had best take me seriously, because my lawyer can beat up your lawyer, and—"

"This is so *you.* Out of all the emails you got—what—eight of them?"

"Nine, if you count the icicle lady. I forgot to bring that one home."

"Okay, nine. And almost all of them are supporting you and the people who got puppies, and thanking you for doing what you're doing. Or at least they're writing to try to help in some way. But the letter you spend all your time thinking about is the one where somebody actually threatens you, yeah? You ignore the praise and dwell on the negative stuff."

"Really. I do?"

He nodded. She kept her eyes trained on Eddy, loving how he savored his dinner, one large spoonful at a time.

"You're right, that's exactly what I do."

"Mm-hm. Classic Dunlopian behavior." His words bounced around the inside of his wine glass.

"So, okay," she said, settling back into her chair. "If I look inward here, I guess I'd say that I tend to disregard people who say nice things because I have trouble believing them to be true. But the judgmental people seem to jibe more with how I talk to myself, so those are the *real* emails. Right? What you're saying is I'm one seriously messed-up individual."

"No. You're not messed-up. You're humble. And self-conscious. And probably a little insecure."

"A little insecure? Thanks for the polite understatement. Like, *World War Two... what a shame.*"

They sat a few long minutes without speaking. Anna tried to recall the thoughtful sentiments people had expressed in those emails, and in the four phone calls Eddy had said he'd gotten at the station, and in the two phone calls of her own she'd fielded at the clinic that day. Not just overwhelming, their appreciation of her actions felt wholly undeserved. She honestly didn't believe she was doing anything out of the ordinary.

Wasn't it right there in the human job description? *Help all kinds of creatures if you possibly can.* But maybe the *possibly can* part was open to interpretation. How far out of your way were you expected to go to help another creature? If you possibly can without inconveniencing yourself? If you possibly can without destroying yourself? It seemed a matter of degrees. Anna knew where she registered on the Possibly Can Scale. Closer to one end than the other, but nowhere near the people who gave up everything to move to some burning hot country to feed starving children, or study elephants in the wild. Those were Anna's heroes.

And where was Brian Ardeen on this scale of human generosity? Would he go out of his way to help *anybody*? Though dogs seemed below his radar, were there any creatures he would lend a hand to? His family? Friends? Anna had to believe there was some part of his being, though shrunken and peach-pit-hard, still capable of compassion. She knew for a fact he could feel at least one emotion besides rage. She had seen him cry.

More so than the violent act itself, it was the image of those tears that had haunted her first few days after their clash in the parking lot. She'd wanted to believe he was one thing only, but now he was at least one other. Her picture of him running away into the park, a scared little boy, was fiddling with her clear-cut contempt.

"Eddy?" She crossed her arms in a deliberate fashion. "Do you believe that absolutely everybody has some inherent goodness in them? Even people like Ardeen?"

Eddy pushed his empty bowl out of the way, making room for his elbows. He laced his thick fingers together as a shelf for his chin, considering how best to answer. She could always count on him to deliberate thoughtfully on an opinion before offering it.

"People *like* Ardeen, or Ardeen? Just so I know exactly what we're talking about here."

"Okay, then. Ardeen. We don't know much about him except for some pretty bad stuff. But would you guess he's also got some good stuff in him somewhere, because all humans are basically good?"

For another extended time Eddy looked at Anna without moving. Long accustomed to his tempo, she felt no impatience. She folded her napkin, finished her last sip of wine and sunk comfortably into her chair. She watched Eddy's face, admiring its beauty. The history of the Hawaiian people had sculpted its exotic shape, and with every passing year, his own kindness and serenity had textured it further, adding lines in all the right places. She'd been friends with this face and its landlord since she was seven, and she wondered how other people got by without his presence in their lives or his view of the world to draw from.

"I'm struggling a little," said Eddy. "Not with the answer, but with the question, yeah?"

"You are?"

"I am. I guess I don't really look at people like that. In terms of good and bad."

"Well, then, what do you think drives Ardeen to act the way he does, if not some lack of inborn decency, or generosity, or whatever?"

"All right, I'm going to tell you. But warning—I'm about to 'go all Hawaiian on you,' as you would say."

She laughed but settled herself to listen intently to his wisdom. Eddy's heart and mind approached life in Wisconsin from an island perspective he'd been forced to leave geographically but never in spirit.

"Okay, I'm ready. Lay some ancient wisdom on me."

Eddy smiled. "I guess the way I've been thinking about Brian Ardeen is more in terms of how far out of *pono* he seems."

"Pono. I know you've told me about that before, but I'm sorry. What is it again?"

"Literally, it means *right*. Rightness with everything else. It's like—how to explain this? The ancients never made a distinction between people and water and land and other animals, stars, spirit forces—whatever. It was all part of one big thing. So if you believe like they believed, which my tutu did, and I guess I do too, you spend your whole life trying to remember how awesome it is to be connected to this enormous world full of things, and you work hard to stay in balance with them. And by that, I mean you have to view all of the other parts with love and compassion. That's when you get that good feeling of harmony in your life. And that calm, harmony feeling is called *pono*."

Anna had put water on for tea when she'd gotten Eddy more chili and was now being whistled to the stove. "Decaf okay?" She got the nod. "So Pono is the peacefulness you get from connecting yourself to everything else. I like that."

"You pretty much live that, Anna. I mean, without knowing the actual philosophy, you seem to come by it kind of naturally. This whole Brian Ardeen thing has knocked you out of pono lately, but you're mostly back to loving the stars and rocks and slimy lizard things now."

"So instead of seeing Ardeen as good or bad, you think he's out of synch in some way."

"Yeah. My guess is that Brian Ardeen doesn't appreciate all the other cool things in the universe besides himself. He's out of balance, so he falls out of the pono canoe and starts splashing around in the whole ocean of negative stuff around him. His job, money, whatever. We all do that sometimes. And the way you get yourself free is to just relax. Stop struggling. Float for awhile."

"Get back into the canoe."

"You've got to try, or you'll get pulled under, yeah? I think maybe Brian Ardeen can't even see the canoe from where he is. Doesn't think to look for it. He's too busy trying to get back at the people who hurt him, or feeling jealous of people with more than he has, or—"

"Or taking his crappy life out on a litter of puppies."

"Huh. Yeah. I don't know why he did that. But mistreating parts of the universe can upset the balance. I do know that."

"So, you think that what he did to those puppies could lead to more trouble for him?"

"I dunno. Who am I to say, yeah? But if you look at the trouble he's had since he did what he did, you kinda wonder. He's spent a night in jail, been publicly embarrassed, which seems to make him crazy, and by next week he has to pay the court a whole lot of money he doesn't have."

Anna, carrying a tray holding a small teapot, two cups, a spoon and a jar of sage honey, motioned with her head for Eddy to follow her to the living room. He did, and they sat on either end of the mid-century, overstuffed couch. As she pushed herself back, she relished the nubby feel of the dark green, '50s-style upholstery fabric she'd found at a flea market. Her mom couldn't understand why she hadn't modernized the old couch, while Anna couldn't imagine why she would.

"So, by next week he's got to pay that fine, huh?" Anna turned sideways to face Eddy, curling her legs up under herself. "Last I heard, he'd been given sixty days to pay. And when it was up, he asked for an extension and got it."

"And now the extension's up. Word on the street is he still won't be able to pay it."

"And what'll happen to him?" Anna realized she was hoping for the worst. She'd come to pity the guy, yes. But his act was unforgivable, and in her mind, the punishment hadn't come close to fitting the crime.

"Hard to know what'll happen. Max says he might get jail time if he can't pay."

"Love it. Sounds like justice to me. I think they should have thrown that guy in jail a long time ago."

Eddy's voice was quiet. "I know. I know you do."

"What?" The word was a challenge; she heard herself sound more irritated than she meant to. "You think the punishment he got for that crime—that *misdemeanor*—seems fair to you?"

Eddy kept his composure, as usual, though the critical eye had turned toward him.

"It's not for me to decide what's fair or not. I don't have—"

Anna interrupted with a reflexive burst of air from her lungs, clearing the way for an onslaught of words to pelt Eddy with. How could he take such a passive approach to even this? Something so personal to her. She couldn't believe he wasn't taking her side. Her incredulity caused just a moment's hesitation—enough for Eddy to slip in and head off the barrage.

"Wait a minute, Anna. I don't think you know what I was going to say." He smiled then, for a reason she had yet to understand. "In fact I'm sure you don't know what I was going to say. Because if you did, you'd be a whole lot madder than this."

"Oh, great." She lightened up a hair.

"What I was trying to say was that I have no control over legal matters. But if I did, I would have stiffened Brian Ardeen's sentence quite a lot, since this one didn't send much of a message to him."

"Okay, that was a very good sentence. I'm not madder at you yet. What else've you got?" She narrowed her eyes.

"I've been thinking about something lately." He spoke slowly and cautiously, a barefoot man tip-toeing his way through broken crystal. "Remember when you came over to my house, when the puppies were just a few days old?"

"Yeah…?"

"That night, do you remember what you said? The thing that upset you the most? In fact, it was the reason you gave me for wanting to give up your practice."

"Oh. Um, let me think. That was a pretty grim time."

"I know." Eddy had a face full of understanding. He reached out and held her ankle for just a moment.

"Well… I know I'd finally realized—or thought I had—that I wasn't going to be able to make much of a difference of any kind. So why stick with it? There'd always be horrible people out there like Ardeen. People who would purposely hurt animals for all sorts of stupid reasons, and nothing could ever change that."

"Specifically, you said '*him.*' You said nothing you could do would ever change people like *him*."

"Right. Okay." She still had no idea what they were talking about, but she began to feel mildly nauseated. She didn't want Eddy to finish his thought.

"But what if you could change him? Or at least you had a chance to try."

"What are you getting at, Eddy?" She sounded severe, fighting to keep her mounting unease in check.

"I've been talking to Max Cotton. And it turns out that if a person can't pay his fine, the judge can rule to have him work it off. Do community service, yeah?"

Anna paused to process. "You think I should hire that waste of skin? You are not saying this to me."

"Wait. Hear me out. This is me. I know everything about you. Including how panicky I'm making you feel."

"Ya got that right. You just capsized my pono canoe, *brah.*"

"Hang on a second. Try to do this. Try to put your anger somewhere else, just for a few minutes. Then you can bring it out again, and I promise to join you and get really ticked off at Brian Ardeen, okay? For as long as you want. I might even swear a little."

"Okay. I'll try. But it's gonna have to be some truly foul word."

"Deal." He offered his hand and got it firmly shaken. "Okay. I'm telling you, Anna, if you could find a way to cope with the fact that you hate this guy's guts, you might have an opportunity here to do what you've always wanted to do. To reach someone who doesn't understand the value of animals and help him—force him—to see it.

"And just how do you propose I do that?"

"By having him work at the clinic and mentoring him a little bit. But also, by making him hang around tons of people who love animals. Some of it's got to rub off on him, and before you know it, he'll be inside of your head, seeing what you see." Eddy nudged her with his elbow and shifted to a thick Hawaiian accent. "You teach him the *menemene*, yeah?"

She shot him a look. "I don't know what to say."

"That's a start. You're not saying 'no.'"

"You actually think a person so far gone that he could bury a litter of puppies might be changed into a—a decent human being?"

"Look at it this way. He wasn't torturing the puppies to watch them suffer. He didn't even necessarily want them dead. He just wanted them gone and didn't care one way or the other if it killed them."

Shaking her head, Anna let loose with another puff of air in Eddy's direction.

"It's a slim difference in meaning, I know. But it's a difference. So yeah, I'm letting myself think there could be some hope for a change."

"How? I wouldn't even know where to start with a puppy killer."

"Puppy *almost* killer." Eddy offered an innocent smile as an olive branch.

"It would cost me a lot of money, too. I'd have to get more insurance just to keep a liability like him at the clinic."

"Probably true. But when would you ever get another chance like this? No one else with his attitude would ever sit still to be preached to. And this guy would be a captive audience; the judge would make him stay."

"That's another thing. Doesn't community service have to be done at a nonprofit place? I don't make much money, but technically, it's a profit. So, I don't think the court would even allow it." She was groping for a loophole in Eddy's plan.

“Max says community service can be at a private business. And he’s pretty sure the clinic would qualify.”

“I’m so glad you and Max got this whole thing all worked out. Now which one of you is going to talk me down off the water tower after a few months in close quarters with this joker?”

“Uh, that would be Max. You know I’m afraid of heights.”

The two of them looked at each other. Measuring.

“You were supposed to bring chocolate tonight.” She crossed her arms.

“Oh! I did. Brownies. I guess I left them in the car.”

“Well go and get them. And when you come back we’re going to do some real Ardeen trashing, and I’d better hear you cuss like a sailor.”

24

Anna, her hair piled high on her head, a sharp pencil holding it in place, had shape-changed into the woman who had ruled her first grade class with chalk and awe—the stern Miss Bobis. She looked out over her sea of students this Monday morning in its habitual state: mostly silent except for that one annoying girl who always had to be the expert on everything.

"Please, oh, please, pick me. *Please!*"

But this time it wasn't the six-year-old Anna Dunlop waving her straight arm in a metronomic arc at Miss Bobis. It was Bunny. And in lieu of the customary eye roll from the aggravated Miss Bobis, this young girl would receive the instructor's full attention and an appreciative laugh to boot.

"Bunny! Gee… you wouldn't be at all interested in going first, would you?" The other adopters tittered.

"No, I don't think so," said Bunny, dropping her arm to gaze introspectively at her fingernails.

Once she got her laugh, Bunny continued, more rapidly than Anna had ever heard her speak.

"I've been waiting and waiting to tell all y'all." She swept her hand across the whole room. "The very best moment in the past month for my girls—I think the best moment in their lives so far—came a little over two weeks ago. It was so marvelous that right after it happened I went to my computer to write it all down in my journal. I wanted to describe every detail while it was still fresh."

Bunny opened a red folder, removing several typewritten pages. "I know this is a little unusual Anna, but would you mind awfully if I just read the darn thing? It truly does capture the essence."

"You're going to read to us?" Anna sent a cursory glance around the room to spot potential objectors. "Funny. Sure, why not?"

"Thank you, sweetness. You see, I write the interesting parts of my life down, trying to capture the full emotion. That way, whenever a day becomes too dull I can slip into another, more vivid one."

Anna walked over to Bunny's chair, collecting the woman's two puppies who were currently engaged in the sumo belly bump game, which, if history served, would soon escalate into a barking contest. And Bunny would need both hands to manage her journal pages. Storm welcomed her two daughters with several licks each as Anna returned to her own chair. She wondered if the older woman wrote like she spoke, with a thick drawl and a rapier wit.

"And this is nothing but the truth." Bunny cleared her throat, perched her leopard print reading glasses on the end of her nose, and settled herself to read. "On this particular Saturday afternoon I was preparing for my bridge club and was about to whip up the topping for my nationally acclaimed cardamom meringue cake."

She lowered her script and peered over the top of her glasses for an aside to the room. "Truth be told, it is not yet nationally-acclaimed, but it should be. Sour cream, that's the secret. Anyway."

She straightened her papers and went back to reading. "I turned to my darling Rain, who at this moment in my story was lying under the kitchen table, pretty as you please. I told her that her momma was about to whip up a meringue cake that would put those Pillsbury Bake-Off Bozos to shame! This, by the way, was to prove my undoing—pride cometh-ing before a fall and all that.

"My bridge gang was due over in about an hour, so I got the raspberries out of the fridge to rest awhile, then put the whipping cream, some sugar and a little almond extract into the biggest metal bowl I own, before going at it with the electric hand mixer. A few minutes later the gorgeous cream was just short of ready, so, I stopped the mixer and grabbed a whisk."

Bunny removed her glasses for another aside. "I like to do the last of the whipping with a whisk to make sure I've gotten all the liquid from the very bottom." She replaced her specs, returning to her journal.

"Well. I picked up my whisk and the metal bowl, but unbeknownst to me, a large dollop of cream which I could not see and would live to regret had dripped down the far side of the bowl. I lifted the enormous bowl to begin whisking but gripped it in exactly the wrong place, so it slid through my slippery fingers and plopped to the floor. Now, this little bit of pastry paradise called for an entire pint of heavy cream, which whipped up to approximately—well, half a bucket full. Splat. Right onto the Congoleum. And frankly, I was relieved to see that the mess had contained itself to an area of only about four feet square, nothing I couldn't handle. Then, as you might guess, over trotted my doggie, Rain, who could scarcely believe her great luck. I ran to the sink to wet down a sponge, trying with my most authoritative voice to discourage the dog from her mission, but—and I did not know this until just then—the poor darling is apparently stone deaf!"

The group laughed heartily.

Bunny flopped her papers to her lap, looking straight at Anna with a sly grin. "I have been meaning to talk to you about her deficiency, Dr. Dunlop. It is the strangest condition. The hearing comes and goes, though the symptoms seem particularly acute when food or fun of any kind are in the air."

"Yeah, tough break. I got nothin'." Anna looked down at Rain's exposed tummy and gave it a scratch.

Once again, Bunny took to her journal, her voice rising in volume and vigor.

"Meanwhile, down the stairs and into the fray came my other puppy, Snow. (By the way, this dog is colored as the name implies, which I mention so that anyone reading this journal years from now can get the full impression of what's about to play out in its furry, alabaster glory.) Snow had heard the commotion, and from several yards away spotted the sweet, white bonanza her sister had no right to deprive her of, and headed in at maximum momentum. Tragically, Snow miscalculated the necessary braking speed, slipped to her belly when she hit the pile of whipped cream, and skidded smoothly along my kitchen floor, halted only by my guaranteed-dog-proof trash can, which—buyer beware—is not. At least not in a high-speed Dairy Luge situation.

"Garbage spewed out over the slippery tile, intermingling with the whipped cream in a tantalizing canine ambrosia. By this time I was back from the sink but could now see a simple sponge would do me no good, and besides, the floor show was a hoot. So I leaned against the counter to observe.

"The two of them were beside themselves wondering what to eat first: yesterday's tuna, a bleu cheese wrapper, or the dirt from an old potted plant. But the question was pointless, because neither of them could keep their footing in so much butterfat long enough to consume a single thing. They slipped repeatedly into each other and slammed uncontrollably down to their chins in the muck, sometimes holding that prone position to lick whatever the tongue could reach.

"It was only the sound of my hysterical cackling that finally caught their attention. The two of them, never having heard such a thing—I myself had not heard it in years—did their very best to get up and stand, cocking their heads as my guffaws aroused the last of their five senses to be tickled in this savory, stunning, stinky, sticky escapade. They both looked me over with the most amazing faces, covered in coffee grounds and good fortune. And it was that picture. That moment when their lives could not possibly have gotten any better that I thought, *I will be talking about this on the radio soon.* And I guess I just did."

The studio broke into spontaneous applause. Anna, her heart a song, felt the moment she was living right then was absolutely *her* most meaningful in the past month. She had studied the faces of everyone in this room as Bunny regaled them with her story. The young family, consisting of Jeffrey, Cleo, and John Henry McCoy; the artist/biker dude, Jake Ellertson; Bitter Russ, the mailman; and of course, Eddy. Every single one of them had interacted during the telling of the tale with head shakes and wide, can-you-believe-it eyes. They'd each connected with Bunny as well, urging the older woman on with their smiles, their laughs, and now their clapping.

What occurred to Anna just then was that this was no longer an aggregate of dissimilar people with nothing in common—it was an official group. A *clan* actually, bound not by marriage nor by ownership (Anna never considered the human/animal relationship to be one of owner/property), but by blood and love, through the wet-nosed siblings of a single family. She liked that concept. A clan.

And through her relationship with Storm, the matriarch of the canine family, Anna could count herself among its bona fide members. By that definition, Eddy would be the only non-related clan member, though he was clearly part of the magic happening here. So Anna decided right on the spot to think of him as the kooky uncle, which she couldn't wait to tell him. In the meantime, though, she had the remainder of this radio hour to fill and needed to get at it.

She stroked Storm's immense paw, which had been unceremoniously plopped onto her thigh when the clapping began. But the longhaired white German shepherd had not been the only creature in the studio moved by the unexpected swell of energy. As the applause ended, John Henry, feeling the mood of the room, pierced the brief radio silence with his shrill request.

"Mommy, I wanna talk!"

He sat on his own chair between his mother and father, playing with the buttons on his mother's shirt. Cleo shrugged at Anna, mouthing the word *sorry*.

"Hey, John Henry," said Anna. "What would you like to say? Do you have a story you want to tell about Patton? Something really fun he got to do lately?"

As soon as John Henry had drawn the rapt attention of everyone in the room, he wanted to give it back. He stared at Anna, possum in the headlights, until his mom leaned over to whisper something in his ear.

And there was that trait again, which Anna found decidedly engaging. As was so often true, Cleo nodded her head as she spoke. The action piqued Anna's curiosity. When you spoke to her, the nod seemed an affirmation that yes, you were saying something she willingly embraced. But why did she nod as *she* spoke to *you*? Perhaps as a constant reminder that whatever her message, she meant it in only the most supportive way? Or was the nod a candy coating for her words, an added incentive for you to accept them? Maybe it was a reminder to herself to keep her thoughts pleasant and undemanding. Or could the nod be an avowal in advance to welcome your answer, no matter how you should choose to respond? Whatever her motivation, the gesture seemed hopeful and positive.

"Puppy class!" John Henry shouted, after receiving a lengthy message and several affirming bobs.

And that was it. Neither Cleo nor Anna could coax John Henry to say another word about Patton's puppy class. But no surprise, Eddy could; kids always loved Eddy. So with only minor prompting from the kooky uncle, John Henry told a long, meandering story about Patton's first day at class, and how it ended with all of the puppies being taken off leash and set free. They ran instantly to the center, smashing into one another, breaking into a number of hilarious, slobbering, bumbling brawls. Much to the delight of John Henry.

Cleo picked up where John Henry left off. "He jumped up and down and screamed and just kept screaming. In a good way." She looked at Jeffrey for corroboration, reaching across John Henry to take her husband's hand.

"Yeah," Jeffrey said, smiling. "It was pretty neat. Nothing's better than seeing him that happy."

Anna thought Jeffrey seemed quiet today, even more so than last time. Not sullen or depressed. Just quiet. Pensive.

"Tell everyone what you've been checking into, Jeffrey," said Cleo. "He's been so excited about this. Do you feel like talking about it here, sweetie?"

It was a good thing he did, because she'd left him little room to say *no,* what with the pressure of several towns listening in. Jeffrey's face lit up at once.

"Oh, yeah, this is so great. What I really want is for Patton to become a good guard dog when he grows up. You know, a trained attack dog. So I've been looking online for a school to train him. It took me awhile, but I finally found a school in Tennessee. They've accepted him already, and it's not even as expensive as I thought it would be. They do everything, like bite training where the dog attacks but stops biting right away if you tell him to. You know, with a secret code word, so only you can call him off."

Anna couldn't believe what she was hearing. The whole idea of training Patton as an attack dog was absurd for a plethora of reasons. But more disquieting than that, Anna couldn't reconcile this new information with what she thought she'd understood about Jeffrey. She'd pegged him for a patient, peaceful individual who wanted little more than a simple routine to his day and a family to come home to at the end of it. Yet here he was, all fired-up at the prospect of his dog viciously attacking another human being. Perhaps killing one, if Jeffrey forgot the secret code word.

A little too late, Anna remembered why it was such a bad idea to take five seconds to think before speaking. Bitter Russ only needed three.

"Jeez, McCoy, just what kind of whack job are you?"

"Hey, Russ, come on," said Anna.

"No, really, I wanna know. What kind?"

Jeffrey looked wounded. Cleo, worried. But the lilt in Russ' voice told Anna his intention was not to be cruel. He was trying to be funny. The man made conversation in the only way he knew how—each word a plunge of the dentist's drill. And either he was unaware of hurting people's feelings or chose to press on anyway.

"Are you the harmless-enough-year-'round nutball who wakes up every morning wondering what brand of crazy to try on?" He chuckled his way into the next sentence. "Or are you more of the silent, repressed type who everybody loves until you show up at work one day with a festering grudge and a sawed-off shotgun?"

No one anticipated Jeffrey's response. "I think that's usually the *mailman*, isn't it?"

Jake Ellertson's booming bass laugh was loud and relaxed. He casually slapped Jeffrey's upper arm with the back of his hand, grinning so widely Anna noticed a second missing tooth she hadn't seen before. Was Jake unable to sense the tension in the room or refusing to engage in it?

And then it occurred to her—Jake Ellertson was simply paddling merrily along in his pono canoe. Actually, the guy was a pono master. His serenity was probably difficult to capsize, no matter what was happening around him.

Russ, however, had trouble staying in his boat. He turned on Jeffrey. "What'd you say?"

"Whoah-kay! That's enough." Anna tried to channel the stern Miss Bobis. "Time out. Let's get back to the topic at hand here."

Physically turning her back on Russ, she leaned forward to give her whole self to Jeffrey.

"So, Jeffrey, let's talk about this a little. I can see you're interested in having Patton protect your family, which makes a lot of sense to me. But what I'm not clear on is why you feel the need to take it so far. Training him to attack? Really, I don't think you want any of that, do you?"

Jeffrey blinked his eyes several times. "Um, I think I do," he said, seeming unsure that he did. "I really want Patton to be able to keep them safe." He gestured toward Cleo and John Henry.

He seemed agitated. Anna was trying to run off with something he needed. Cleo, uncharacteristically, wasn't looking at Jeffrey as he spoke. She'd brought the napping Patton up into the sitting position and was now intent on giving his back a good scratch. The black and tan puppy liked the attention, wiggling himself into a stand. He nuzzled his head between her knees, his wagging tail giving sway to his whole backside.

"The thing is, Jeffrey, I don't know what kind of school has agreed to train Patton, sight unseen, but right there, that's a red flag. Bad training can mess with your dog's head, and it puts your whole family in danger."

Hearing that, Cleo stood up, lifted John Henry from his seat and sat on that chair herself, setting the boy on her lap. She stared open-mouthed at Jeffrey with what Anna interpreted as a *See? Please don't do this!* expression. Apparently, Jeffrey was the only person in this little family who wanted to send Patton off to doggy boot camp.

"I need him to be tough." Jeffrey's tone was adamant.

And once again, it was aggression from the wrong man. This stoic, educated person, so quick to offer affection and slow to anger, simply did not fit Anna's stereotype of people who went in for attack dogs.

"But you know what, Jeffrey?" she said, pointing at Patton. "This little guy is going to do a great job of protecting your family all on his own. Believe me. Guard dog training is overkill."

"Pun intended," said Russ, though barely anyone noticed.

"Really?" Jeffrey brightened. "You think he can do the job without the school?"

"Sure I do. He's only four months old, but I bet anything he's already barking at strangers."

"He is!" said Cleo, a condemned woman getting the call from the governor. "So that's it, right? He won't need the training?"

"He seems like a confident, happy dog to me, which is good. And he's going to be big—and look like a German shepherd. Good and good. I can also give you a few tips on pumping up the protection factor, if you want."

She did that. Anna told them to stick with obedience training because a well-trained dog sent the message that, *This is one tough, smart animal, so look out!* And she suggested they invent a few fake commands to make Patton look like he knew more than he did. For instance, before heading into a store, they could order him to *Watch the car!* The dog wouldn't know what that meant, but bad guys didn't know that.

"Just send the message that this is one serious canine dude not to be messed with. His own natural instinct to protect you is going to do the rest. You'll see."

She'd gotten Jeffrey to nod along with Cleo, so hopefully her work here was done. Patton had been snatched from the jaws of—well—snatching people in his jaws.

"So, who wants to go next—Jake or Russ?"

A giant nothing on the ceiling demanded Russ' close scrutiny.

"So, Jake. Fritos. How's tricks?"

"Ah, things are so great!" As Jake talked, he rubbed his palomino pup briskly on both sides of his neck, making his long, droopy ears flop every which way. "Aren't they buddy? Huh? Yeah."

How curious that this grungy motorhead with his frizzy red hair, scruffy beard, and tattoos snaking along most visible body parts, would be the person among all of these adopters to make her feel most at ease. She thoroughly enjoyed Bunny, of course, but Jake required very little upkeep. She never had to worry about hurting his feelings or wondering if his needs were being tended to.

"So? I'm guessing you have any number of fascinating tales to tell, Jake. Is it even possible to pick out the single most elated moment in Fritos' life last month?"

"I've got a goodie."

"Let's hear it."

"We got that decent snowfall last week, which rocked. 'Cuz we got to have our first toboggan ride!"

As the image began to sink in, the room filled with surprised sounds, from everyone except Russ, who tightened the fold of his arms.

Eddy's broad smile forced his eyes closed as he leaned back in his chair, a quiet *"Ho, brah!"* on his breath.

"You guys went tobogganing?" asked Anna. "Help me out here, Jake—how does that work exactly?"

"Well, safety first," he said in that mellow, basement voice of his. "I crafted a cushy puppy seat. Adjustable, so it can become a mammoth dog seat for next winter. And I just bolted it to the toboggan. Then I found this seat belt for dogs in some catalog. Who knew, right? We took the whole rig up to Cracker Hill, and down we went. Whooshhh!" His arm mimicked the trajectory of the speeding toboggan.

"Oh, wait! One more thing." He fished around in his jacket pocket. "Doggie goggles!" He brandished them high above his head.

At the sight of the goggles, his yellow dog went insane. He sprang into the air repeatedly, his head hitting an easy six feet, as he yodeled for the race to begin.

The sudden show of their brother's *joie de vivre* stirred the other four pups, three of whom began yapping and straining against their leashes. Storm, too, got into the spirit, her deep bark piercing the high-pitched puppy merriment. In fact, the only *yin* amongst all that *yang* was the white pup, Snow, who whined and flattened herself to the ground, sliding farther under Bunny's chair.

The vocalizing of the pack—including humans adding to the din, trying to shush the others—had reached its peak when Anna glanced over at Eddy. With his hands cupped over his headphones he was leaning forward, elbows on the table. Listening. Grinning. Anna imagined the cacophony blaring through radios twenty miles in every direction and envisioned her own mother jumping up to switch it off. She motioned for Jake to put the goggles back into his pocket, and the tumult gradually died down. "Well. That was stimulating."

"Nothing like a little sing-along once in awhile," said Jake. "Hey, Russ, next time bring the accordion."

Anna headed off the vile response already on the mailman's lips.

"So, Jake. Fritos kinda likes tobogganing, I guess."

"Yeah. But what's cool is how much he likes to pull the thing back up the hill too. I'm a lucky man."

"Thanks, Jake. And hey, Fritos—you hang loose, baby." Anna rotated her wrist in the Hawaiian surfers' shaka sign, thumb and pinky finger up. Eddy got a big kick out of that, as she'd hoped he would. They shared a look as Jenny entered the studio to hand Eddy a note. He read it and nodded.

"All right," said Anna. "There's one puppy left to hear from. But Kitty doesn't seem to be much of a talker. So….Russ?"

"What."

She was going to have to work for it. She chose her perkiest, most pleasant voice for the occasion. "I'm just wondering how you and Kitty got on this week. Any highlights you can tell us about?"

Russ' scowl, though intense, couldn't keep Anna from reading the thoughts behind his face. He had a story all right. And some part of him wanted desperately to share it. But a bigger part resented the breach of privacy. Anna felt the same tenderness she harbored for any wounded animal.

After half a minute of silence, which would have seemed interminably long to any radio listener outside of Eddy's audience, Russ acquiesced.

He said nothing. He just reached down and picked up his puppy. Kitty was the smallest of the litter, and at four months old still fit comfortably in his lap. She seemed content there, enjoying the higher vantage point. She looked both ways at the line of creatures in Eddy's alcove. Once she had settled, Russ rubbed his hands up and down her front legs, then addressed her in a sugary-soft voice. "Kitty? You know what? I just love being here on the radio with so many fascinating people. All their compelling life stories and riveting conversations. I just couldn't be more excited, could you? Huh? Could you?"

And right on cue Kitty opened her mouth into a lengthy yawn so dramatic, her head all but disappeared behind her gaping maw.

The humans in the clan burst out laughing, startling Kitty. Russ wrapped his arms around her, clutching her to his chest as he and his girl received their well-earned round of applause. Anna chuckled herself deep into her chair, impressed by Russ' skirting of her requirement to *speak* on the radio. "Wow, Russ. I mean—wow. That was cool for so many reasons."

With a hard push from both feet, Eddy pitched his chair back against the studio wall and began bouncing from his shoulder blades, eyes closed, swinging the microphone on its long arm close to his face as he recounted every detail of the visual trick for his listeners. At story's end, he stopped bouncing. Stopped speaking. The back of his head nestled in the foam rubber wall, feet dangling, he stared up at the soundproofed ceiling for a good long while before bringing himself square to the floor and pivoting ninety degrees on the slippery wood seat to address the studio gang.

"Anna? Is it okay if I ask the group something?"

"Please."

"Y' know, here at WLCM-FM, you've probably noticed, we don't have any real advertisers. I guess I plug a lot of stuff unofficially, like the Cajun breakfast down at Mom's Kitchen. And I'm not kidding, I could eat that meal every day. Brok da mout, yeah? But I don't have any advertisers that actually pay me, so I'm not required to track who-all is listening out there. Which is good, 'cuz there's no real way to do it without a bunch of technology and financial resources I currently have tied up in other capital investments—like food and shelter.

"Anyway, I've always guessed our listening audience to stand at somewhere around a couple hundred people at peak times, give or take. But I've based those numbers on some pretty soft statistics, like how many people call in or email me. I keep track of names, and do some bad math, and two hundred or thereabouts is where I usually come out. Until recently.

"For awhile now, ever since you nice folks joined us here in the studio last month, things have been changing. I've gotten a bunch more calls and emails in the past thirty days from people I've never heard of, and most of them have mentioned this show.

"The reason I'm bringing it up is that Jenny just slipped me a note that we've gotten seventeen calls in our first twelve minutes on-the-air today. Which is about fifteen more than I'd expect. And I even said at the beginning of the program, if you remember, not to call in 'cuz this is the special monthly *All of Us Animals*, and we don't take calls." He glanced down at a flashing green light on his control board. Hello, Mr. Eighteen!

"Even with my bad math, I can see that things are changing. And it's got me wondering. So here's my question. Have you heard anyone mention that they've become listeners because of you guys? I'm trying to chart my latest dubious guess at how many ears we've got, yeah?"

Eddy stopped talking and looked from one person to another. Cleo McCoy was first to chime in.

"I don't know if this helps, but we've been hearing some things, huh, Jeffrey?"

Jeffrey agreed and Cleo carried on. "I was at the grocery store—Hungry Pete's. And this one woman kept looking at me kind of funny. I saw her first in Produce, then again in Frozen Foods, and then she ended up right behind me at the checkouts. Later I figured out it was prob'ly on purpose, because I swear she was following me around. As the boy was ringing me up, this lady kept staring at me. So I finally looked right at her and smiled, hoping she'd either look away or say something, y' know? And she did. She said, 'Aren't you Cleo? Cleo McCoy?' And I'm really bad with names and faces, so I couldn't quite figure out where I knew her from, or even if I did. Then she told me she was Tim Labno's mom, Claire. Tim Labno is one of John Henry's friends from Montessori school. And I think I remember seeing her there once.

"Anyway, she told me that right during our show last time she got a call from Jillie Stark's mom, saying that I was on the radio and she should listen in. So she did. And you know what, Eddy? She said she's been listening a lot ever since, because she got hooked on hearing about all the interesting stuff you get into. Especially when you talk about what you did over the weekend. She loves that part. And you know what else, Eddy?"

"No, what else?"

"She asked me what you looked like, because she said she thought you sounded—hot."

When the laughs quieted enough for Eddy to be heard, he said, "Please don't tell me what you said to her. I want to keep the dream alive."

"Oh. Okay, I won't." Cleo seemed a little unsure of what Eddy meant. "But anyways, I'll just say that she thinks you're so interesting and funny that she's been telling all her friends to listen to your station and to call in if they want to."

"Is that right?"

"Yes, it is. And she has an unmarried sister she wants you to meet."

Again, more laughs.

"Okay, so lemme figure this out." Eddy picked up a pencil to make notes. "I'm going to guess that Tim Labno's mom has, oh, maybe seven friends she might have talked us up to. And maybe two of them might actually tune-in from time to time, so I'll add two more listeners to my databank. And there we go. Bad math in the making."

"Eddy?" said Bunny. "I might have something to figure into your stats."

Eddy assumed that Bunny was going to tell him about Melanie Wagner, the grieving woman who'd approached her on the street. Anna had told him all about it. But Bunny had a different story in mind.

"A week ago Saturday, I took the dogs down to the river at Mitchell's Landing, where it doesn't ice up, even in the winter. It was too cold for the girls to swim, of course, but they love to run along the rushing water just the same. Well, that day there were three high school boys up on the bridge over the landing. They apparently recognized me by my dogs, and being more bold than Tim Labno's mother, called down to find out if I was the lady from the radio. When I said I was, they said how much they liked my dogs and got back to talking amongst themselves. What nice kids, I thought. For about thirty seconds.

"The boys apparently suffered under the misconception that strolling a few steps to hang over the far side of the bridge would keep me from hearing them. Unfortunately for all of us, the combination of my keen aural faculties and a brisk, northerly wind brought every word down with a hammer.

"I heard one of the boys say, 'Cripes, I didn't know she was so damn old!' Then another one said, 'God, no kidding. And she takes two of those puppies? How long does a dog live, anyway? She's gonna kick way before those dogs do.'"

Eddy wondered if the lighting in the studio had darkened right then, or just the mood of its inhabitants. He found himself wondering about the wisdom of taking the group down this path. But Bunny pressed on.

"Then the first boy said, 'Hey, maybe when she croaks, someone will bury *her* in a paper bag.' They had a good laugh—the kind that high school boys employ to give a mean joke a sharper edge. And the third kid said, 'Yeah, maybe the puppies will dig *her* up this time.' And that seemed pretty funny to all of them, too."

Bunny repositioned herself in her chair. She uncrossed her legs, crossing them again the other way. "I thought about ignoring them; it would have been the prudent thing to do. But no one has ever accused me of being prudent. I picked up a rock and chucked it against the metal railing of the bridge, scaring the snot out of those boys. And then I yelled, 'Hey! You three dorks skip school just to listen to some Podunk radio station? No wonder you're here without girlfriends!'

"Then the pups and I turned around, walked up the beach, and had a perfectly lovely morning. Sorry about the Podunk crack, Eddy."

"No offense taken."

"I guess the point to my story is that—well—I might have lost you a few listeners last weekend, so you should probably subtract them from your equation."

"Hard to say. A lot of dorky kids relate to me. I'm like their dork king. So just in case those boys are tuned in today..." Eddy curled his torso down until his beautiful full lips (shaped like an archer's-bow, thought Anna) almost touched the microphone. His shiny black hair fell forward along his jaw line, covering both sides of his face. He deepened his voice and spoke slowly. "Hello, Boys. I'll do my best to pick up where the school system has failed you. So please take out your number two pencils, because coming up right after *All of Us Animals,* I'm launching a little show called *The Gross National Product and You.*"

Contributing to Eddy's tally, Anna described the rush of emails and phone calls she'd received right after the last show, as well as the smattering of questions and comments that had trickled in all month.

Eddy thanked Anna and then changed course. He shifted his interest to Jake Ellertson. Fritos sat with the side of his head against his human, one long ear draped across the man's thigh. Over and over, Jake drew his fingertips along the length of the silky, yellow ear, lost in thought.

"Hey, Jake," said Eddy. "You okay, brah?"

"Yeah, man, I'm good. I'm just sittin' here thinking about a guy I know. A customer of mine from Turtle Lake. Chad Kippel."

"I know Chad!" said Cleo. "He's a vendor at our store. A candy distributor."

"That's the dude," said Jake. "He came out to my place to pick up his snowmobile. I'd been working on it. He saw Fritos and really took to him, y' know? He kept petting him, telling him what a good boy he was, stuff like that."

Jake paused for a moment to mime a message for the studio gang only, not the outside world. With his two index fingers to his cheeks, he indicated that Chad had been crying.

"I asked him if he wanted to come in for a beer, but he didn't. Then when we were getting his machine on the trailer, he said he'd heard about the puppies when the story first went down but didn't know any more than that. So I told him 'bout what Anna had done, and how all of us were now doing the radio show. He wanted to know about your station, Eddy. The call letters, how to find it on the dial and stuff. And then he left. So—I dunno. He might be listening to you these days. At least maybe this show."

Cleo waved her hand to grab Jake's attention. She held up a deposit slip with the note she'd just scribbled. The message read, *His dog = MISSING. Very sad!* With a complex series of gestures and mouthing of words, she conveyed that she knew everything about Chad Kippel and would fill Jake in later when the radio audience wasn't sticking its big nose in.

Eddy said, "Um… by any chance, does Chad Kippel work for SweetBite Industries?"

Cleo and Jake answered simultaneously, and yes, he did.

"Mystery solved. I was going to wait until after the show to share the wealth, but—"

He reached under his control board and slid out an enormous cardboard box with the word SweetBite stamped on all sides.

"A couple days ago I found a case of microwave popcorn on the front steps of our building here. It's a major smorgasbord of corn. Hey, that's a fun phrase. Smorgasbord of corn. Try saying it."

"Smorgasbord of corn," said all of the adults, much to John Henry's amusement.

"Anyway, we've got regular popcorn, kettle corn, cheese corn, even parmesan popcorn—"

"Caramel corn?" asked Anna, made of hope.

"About four boxes worth. Well, Chad, if this is from you, I hope you're listening today, brah, 'cuz I wanna thank you for your kindness. From all of us. Think about stopping by after the show today—or any first Monday you can—we'll pop some up special."

Even John Henry yelled, "Thanks, Chad!" hearing everyone else do so.

"Okay, then," said Eddy. "Anybody else have other listener stories you want to share before I turn things back over to the good doctor?"

Aware Russ was the only person without a story to tell, Eddy made a point to keep his eyes off of him. The guy seemed wound pretty tightly today and could maybe do without the pressure. But just in case the mailman wanted to contribute, Eddy gave him a little space. He shuffled some papers, pushed a couple buttons on the board, took a sip of ice water.

"Okay," said Eddy to his public. "I sure appreciate any information on numbers I can get, so if you've just recently decided to let a few of our airwaves into your life and you happen to be sitting at your computer some day with nothing else to do, shoot me an email and tell me so: eddy@wlcmfm.com. Oh, and hey, if you write me, I'll forward you something I got the other day. A photo of this guy stuffing a whole tennis ball into his mouth. Ya gotta see it.

"And by the way, big news. We've been thinking it might be fun to take some of your questions for our little group here if you want to email them to me. I wish we could let you call in, but we just don't have the time since we've got so many peeps and pups to chat with. But if you send us your questions before next month's show, we can toss a few to our guests that day.

"All right. I'm hogging too much of your air time, Anna. So why don't you go ahead and—"

"Thanks the Shanks!" Russ blurted out the words with the red skin of his forehead stretched over a long, bent twig of a vein.

Eddy checked Anna's response to the frantic non sequitur and thought he saw at least three things in her expression. One, she was flabbergasted to hear Bitter Russ offer a thought so freely—no picks or shovels required. Two, she wished she could do a better job of hiding how flabbergasted she felt. And three, whatever it meant, the phrase *Thanks the Shanks* was hilarious, and she'd be making fun of it later with him in private.

Eddy, on the other hand, just hoped the guy was okay. Russ had looked more tense than usual this morning and now seemed like he'd swallowed a thought too big for even him to repress.

"Sorry?" Eddy asked. "What was that, Russ? Thanks the Shanks?"

"Thanks *to the* Shanks." Russ was mumbling. "That's what I meant."

"Oh, you wanna thank someone? Cool. Go ahead."

"I want—they are these people who—awhile ago I—cripes, just forget it."

"Sure, okay. That's cool. No worries."

Eddy took a silent moment to ask his tutu, if she wasn't busy, to please help Russ relax a little. And Eddy did his part to help as well. He got Anna to quit staring at the man.

"Hey, Anna, didn't you have a shout-out you wanted to make?"

"Oh. Right." She dragged her unwilling gaze toward Eddy. "I want to take a second to thank all the people out there who are offering comments and asking questions about these puppies—and about Storm too—bringing them into the circle of creatures they care about." She visualized the clan expanding, with branches of distant relatives stretching as far as the radio signal could reach. "Really. It's so touching."

"They're city people!" said Russ, snapping all heads back in his direction.

"Excuse me?" said Anna.

"Ron and Nancy Shank. They moved up here from the Twin Cities and built a mammoth place out there on the river, thinking, 'Oh, wouldn't it be so *perfect* to build it to look like an old farmhouse?'" His resentment oozed into a snigger.

"Russ?" Anna was unclear as to where this was leading but sensed a rant on the build. "Maybe you could take a deep breath and give us a hint of what you're talking about."

The barn sour horse let himself get reined back in. Scowling at Anna, apparently still under the impression it had some effect on her, Bitter Russ began his tale from the beginning.

"These people get exactly what you think they would in the mail. *New Yorker* magazine, cutesy postcards from Oo-la-la France, and lots of questions from the IRS. Ah, cripes, I shouldn't have said that on the radio. Anyway, they live on this stupidly steep, dead end street that bottoms out at the river, and the only thing scarier than trying to ease a car down that ice-covered road is trying to coax it back up. So on the days when they don't get any mail, I grab my binoculars and check to see if by some wild chance they've put the flag up on their mailbox, because otherwise I'm not going down there. They never do put it up, by the way, making me wonder if they even have that system down there in the big city, or if it's just a quaint rural custom." These last words seemed to taste particularly bad.

"There was a day about a week ago that I had nothing for them, so I did my obligatory binocular check. And wouldn't you know it, the flag was up. I gave my St. Christopher statue a quick rub and started down to see what kind of letter wasn't worth *a grand drive into town for a trip to that sweet little post office.* I looked in the box and saw there was just one envelope, which I could tell didn't have proper postage on it. No postage at all. And no address. Just one name dead center. Spelled wrong. Mine.

"I opened it up, wondering how they knew my name, and what kind of unholy request this would be, like maybe could I please tip-toe down the hill instead of drive, because the sound of my engine disturbed their Asiatic parakeet or some damn thing. But—it wasn't that." Russ' voice quieted. "It wasn't anything like that."

He pulled his hand out of his U.S. Postal Service pants pocket, clutching the envelope in question. It was folded in half and had been un- and re-folded so many times, the wooly crease had become a perforation across the crinkled, coffee-stained envelope. He placed it into Anna's hand.

"I—I don't understand." She looked down at the missive, then back at his face. "You want me to read this? Out loud?"

Russ' steady stare said yes, that was exactly what he wanted.

Anna scanned the adopters who waited, riveted. No question in their minds what they thought she should do. She looked for Eddy's advice, which he gave with a twitch of a smile and a subtle raise of the chin; signals she might have missed had she not been desperate for an answer.

She slipped her thumb and index finger into an envelope so fragile it threatened to fall apart in her hands. She slowly removed two folded sheets torn from a yellow legal pad. The letter was printed in blue ballpoint pen, the handwriting a woman's, though unembellished. Utilitarian. Anna cleared her throat with a tiny cough and then began to read.

Dear Mr. Peoski,

Please forgive me if I've misspelled your name. I've only heard it spoken, and I suspect I've gotten it wrong. My name is Nancy Shank, and my husband is Ron, but of course you know that already, don't you? One of the few people in town so far who does, I believe. It's not that I'm anti-social. In fact, I love it here and wish I had people to invite over for dinner, or sit by the river with, but our schedules don't seem to allow it. Ron commutes to the Cities and I work six days a week, upstairs, here in my home office.

I listen to WLCM while I work, which helps me feel less lonely. Eddy keeps me up-to-date on what's happening around town. I know this sounds odd, but he might be my best friend here, though I've never met him. And you, Mr. Peoski, are my second best friend. I see you come, and I see you go, somewhere between 1:30 and 1:50 every weekday afternoon. I always raise my coffee cup to the window and say "Hello, Mr. Mailman!" because until today I didn't know your name.

I listened to All of Us Animals *a couple of weeks ago, the day you and the others were on, and I was crying through most of it, if you want to know the truth. It was so horrible how those poor puppies almost died, and hearing about the wonderful lives they now live felt like a fairytale ending to me. As I listened to the show, I wondered if the mailman they were talking to could possibly have been my mailman but thought it unlikely.*

Then today when you pulled up, as I raised my coffee cup to you, I saw her. Kitty. Sitting on the seat beside you. So now I know, the mailman who gave that dear little puppy a second chance was my mailman. My second best friend. Russ Peoski.

And now, at long last, I finally get to the point of my letter. To thank you for the kick in the proverbial derriere.

It's said that we take our very first breath as we enter this world and expel it with one final sigh on our last day. And then our time in this body is over. So I can't help but picture all of my other breaths in between as marking off the choices I make on my way to the Great Exhale.

And that's where you shine. You made a choice to get outside of your everyday self and do something for someone else. You changed Kitty's life. And you keep that promise—breath to breath—by helping her LOVE the life she almost missed out on.

And then there's me. I do most of my breathing in motions that don't really matter very much. I've made elaborate plans for a long list of charitable acts I mean to "get to" some day. But when I stop to look at what I'm actually doing with my time—having already plowed through half of my given allotment—I see very little of substance. Cleaning house, cooking, and working, of course, so I can have a house to clean and cook in. What's the point in such a circle?

I'm going to try to do a little better because of you, Mr. Peoski. Breath to breath. From now on, every day when you arrive I'll raise my coffee cup and say, "Hello, Mr. Peoski!" and then tell you what I did yesterday to bring a little meaning to someone's life. Even if it was just my own. I feel so lucky to have you as my friend.

I hope some day we meet.

Upstairs, Second Window from the Right,
Nancy Shank

Anna tenderly refolded the letter, using the time to absorb the words she'd just read. She looked at Russ. He was bent over, watching his hand move down along Kitty's side as she slept next to his chair.

"So… Russ… have you gone up to her door to talk to her?"

No response.

"Nancy, how 'bout if you email me with a date that's good for you, and we'll both play hooky from work and go on a nice lengthy walk along the river. And I want to say one more thing, Nancy. Your letter was so—what you've written is just the most lovely—" She clamped her lips together, trying to plan a whole sentence.

"I think Russ put it just right," said Eddy, watching the man hover over his dog, face down. "And I hope the Shanks accept our thanks."

25

If it was possible for a pickup truck to sneak, this one did exactly that on its way up the snowy alley behind Brian Ardeen's house. Anna rolled her window down to survey the backyard. Air was leaving her body in billows of mist.

The reconnaissance revealed exactly what she'd expected. The place was a dump, leaving no doubt that she'd found the right address. Stacks of paper and trash hid the lower fifth of his house. Small sections of decrepit wooden fencing stood intermittently along the borders of the lot, like teeth in a rotting mouth. Fast food bags, broken furniture, car parts, aerosol cans and rusty appliances peeked out from under the melting snow in every corner of the property.

Anna brought the creeping truck to a halt, transfixed by Ardeen's disordered world. Black plastic bags lined one side of the yard, flapping with the sound of tiny flags. A metal garbage can on its side rolled noisily back and forth in the plowed alley.

Anna spotted the doghouse where Storm had been chained for the first nine months of her life and felt a new wave of disgust for this creature. She tried to imagine where Ardeen had dug the hole.

"This man is a pig," said Joey Dunlop from the passenger seat.

Anna got the truck rolling again, the sound of crunching snow fading as she rolled up her window. "I know. I've been lying in bed for the last several nights, trying to picture what we'd see when we got here. We just saw it. Almost exactly."

"Doesn't that make my point? He's a despicable human being. How can anything you do possibly fix him?"

"Yeah, I've had all those same thoughts myself. But I think about a lot of other stuff, too. Like how I should put up or shut up, you know? My whole life I've wanted to do something meaningful for animals."

"Like dedicating your entire career to them?" Her mother used one Dusty Rose fingernail to scrape a smudge from her sensible purse.

"I'm really struggling in this job, Mom. I don't know how much longer I can stay with it if being a vet is all I do. It's really getting to me."

"You mean the euthanasia?"

"That's part of it, yeah. But there's a lot more to it than that. And meanwhile, I'm doing nothing to open the eyes of people who feel so unconnected to nature that other creatures hardly register."

"Oh, Anna—"

"I know, don't worry. I'm not trying to convert the whole world. Not yet." She offered half a smile. "But what if I could reach some of the people who do the most damage, like this guy? What if I could help him realize that humans aren't the only animals with thoughts and feelings?"

"You honestly picture him someday stopping to help every stray dog he sees, like you do?"

"Probably not. But maybe he can get to the point where he notices a dog along the road, and instead of ignoring her, at least he wonders if she's lost and freaked out because she can't find her home or even a drink of water. That would be a huge step. I mean, one of the coolest things about our species is that we're smart enough to imagine another animal's suffering, right? What if that could make Ardeen at least stop *causing* the suffering?"

"I just don't see how you can force a person to care."

"Yeah, I'm not exactly sure about that myself yet. But Eddy thinks it's possible. And I'm a total hypocrite if I don't try."

"Ah-ha." Her mother looked to the ceiling of the truck for guidance.

Anna had agreed to let the court make arrangements for Ardeen to perform his community service at the Milk River Veterinary Clinic. He'd work off the twenty-four hundred dollars he owed in fines at six dollars an hour, twenty hours a week, keeping him in Anna's life for a total of five months. One part of her brain felt she could tolerate anything for only twenty weeks. Another part thought she was crazy. The latter had her mother's full endorsement.

"Anna. I want to say something. I know we've had this talk before, but—"

"Oh, here we go…"

"Yes, and I hope today will be the day you actually listen. The animal thing, Anna. Your blindness about them."

"I'd argue that I actually see something you don't, but go on."

"I remember finding you in the back yard when you were little, trying to wrap a garter snake in yarn because it felt cold to you. And remember the day you hid in Mr. Van Buskirk's stable and said, 'Good morning!' as he walked in, thinking he might not eat the new lamb if he thought it could talk?"

"And your point is?"

"My point is it doesn't work! You can't equate animals with people and then live your life based on that false assumption." Anna inhaled to respond, but her mother charged on. "I know! I know! You don't equate them, they have their own magical qualities. I like animals too, dear, but animals are animals and people are people."

"Actually, people are animals."

"Pull over, Anna."

Though she felt compelled to keep moving, she did what she was told. She'd been on her way around the block and now stopped just out-of-sight of Ardeen's house.

"Do you know why I begged to come with you today?"

"Yeah, you said you couldn't stand the idea of me being alone with him."

"That's right. And can you imagine why that might be?"

"Sure. He's evil incarnate."

"Don't be flip, daughter. I'm going to take one last stab at reason here. I've always known about your need to change the world. But do you have to start in his particular corner of it? I know what you're going to say. You're not afraid of him. And I believe you. But I'm afraid of him *for* you. He's a terrible person, Anna."

"Agreed."

"So come on, then. Change your mind. We can drive right past his house and continue on to a neighborhood where the garbage is kept in cans."

"I just don't consider him dangerous like you do, Mom—not to humans, anyway. Believe me, I despise him, too. I'm fighting to keep my breakfast down. But this is a done deal."

"Oh, Anna!" She didn't brush but slapped the white dog hair from her wool skirt. "This is so—*you*!"

"Yeah, sorry about that. I've tried to wish me away before, but it doesn't work."

"You know what I mean, honey." Joey softened. "You get an idea in your head and there's no convincing you otherwise, no matter how misguided. It's the finger in the hair all over again."

"Uh… beg your pardon?"

"I've told you that story before. About you learning to walk?"

"I don't know that you have. Humor me."

"I can't believe I haven't told you this. You had just turned ten months old. You'd already been trying to walk for about a month or so, long before you were supposed to be able to, according to people who knew those things. You could pull yourself up to a stand and did so all the time. You'd get that look on your face that said, *Outta my way, Ma, I'm doin' this!* You've had that same look on your face all morning, by the way."

"Mom."

"So you'd get the look and throw one of your feet forward, but it would just stick to the ground. You'd stand there, rocking back and forth until you fell down. You couldn't seem to pull off step number two. And as you can imagine, you being you, this was highly unacceptable. You'd get so frustrated sometimes. You'd fall on your bum, then slap the carpet with your little hand like it had pulled you down. So one day you stood there looking out the front hall window, sucking your thumb. You were also doing this cute little thing I'd never seen you do before. Sort of absent-mindedly, twirling that downy, reddish hair of yours around the pointer finger of your other hand. And when you turned away from the window, you *walked* away from the window, taking about five fast steps before you went down. You were so proud of yourself! You'd finally figured out the secret. For weeks after that, whenever you wanted to walk, you'd stick your finger into your hair, coil up a chunk of it nice and tight, and off you'd go."

"No way!" Anna laughed. "That's so—wrong."

"To you it made perfect sense. I'd try to show you it wasn't necessary by pulling your hand away, but when I did, you'd lose your concentration and fall over, which only proved your theory. No finger, no hair, no walkies."

"I love that story."

"To you it's a story. To me it was *Mother Beware*. This one will not listen. She knows better than you."

"You know, I've logged over thirty-nine years of life experience since then. Any chance I've made two or three good decisions along the way?"

"Of course, sweetheart. Mostly good, I'd say."

"Thank you."

"But not this one."

"I'm sorry you feel so strongly about this. I really am. And it means a lot to me that you barged your way in here this morning, even though I told you I was fine by myself. I'm really grateful you're here. I hope you know that. But—outta my way, Ma, I'm doin' this!"

She checked over her shoulder for traffic and pulled back onto the road. The greatest sacrifice for Anna in this deal she'd struck with Ardeen had been her agreement to provide transportation for him to and from the clinic. He'd lost his drivers license for Operating While Intoxicated (surprise, surprise), and she'd agreed to pick him up from his house in the morning, bring him the three miles to the clinic, and then drop him off at the factory at noon to work the middle shift. Apparently, some friend named "Toot," of all things, had agreed to bring him home from the plant.

Brian Ardeen sat by his dirty front room window, arms and legs spread wide, his body taking the same shape as the tattered wingback chair he sat in. The cartoon channel blared a few feet away.

He picked at the frayed arm of the chair.

One after the other, he conjured up the faces of the assholes who'd put him here. The weasel of a judge who wouldn't give him another extension on the fine. The Chief of Police Brutality, Max Cotton, who'd come up with the goddamn community service idea in the first place.

He jammed two fingers into a hole in the armrest.

And the vet. That goddamn vet. Thinking about her made him throw up a little in his mouth.

The front door swung open, exposing each to the other. Both of them had rehearsed what to say, but neither of them could say it. He was cleaner than she'd expected. She was better looking than he'd remembered. She purposely blocked his way. He acted like it wasn't driving him ape-shit.

"You ready?" she asked.

"Not really."

The only sound after that was the squeaking of the unshoveled snow under their feet. By the time they'd made their way to the truck, Joey had slid to the center of the seat, arms folded across her chest. She watched Ardeen, hawk-eyed from her perch. Anna paused when the realization hit her. Her mother had come this morning to place herself exactly there—in harm's way—between her child and potential danger.

Anna got in and gritted her teeth as he climbed in on the passenger side. It was dreamlike, this moment. Her arch enemy welcomed into her truck—Tony's truck—invited to sit beside her mother. He acted as if he saw no Joey Dunlop. He faced forward until the door was closed and then looked out his side window. Anna knew, for her mother's sake, that she should mumble an introduction of some kind, but the English language seemed ill-equipped.

"Turn around and look at me, young man," her mom said to Ardeen's hair.

Stock-still for several seconds, he eventually rotated his head in a slow, deliberate move, using the full one-hundred-eighty degrees to make his point.

"I'm Mrs. Dunlop. This woman's mother. I am vengeful and resourceful. I want you to remember that."

No one could face the Joey Dunlop Auger Stare for long, so after a moment, Ardeen shifted his gaze to look out the front window with a disgusted snort, as if he didn't have a deep, icy hole between his eyes.

Her mom turned to smile brightly at Anna, smoothed her coat, and readjusted the pink faux cashmere scarf around her neck. "Okay, honey. Let's go."

As they crossed the Potts Road Bridge, Anna gazed down into the depths of the Milk River. She'd been so distracted this morning, she'd forgotten to look out her kitchen window to check the color of the water, a daily ritual. She'd grown used to the phenomenon of how often the river's mood reflected her own, along its spectrum from muck-brown to steely grey. She was never clear on whether the river played thermostat to her emotional state or if it was she who affected the color of the water as it passed by her house, but the two usually intermixed. On their muck-brown days Anna felt sluggish, slow to react. At their steeliest grey, she was too high strung and easily agitated.

A good, blackish-blue found Anna in her most open, comfortable mindset, and here below the Potts Road Bridge the water was running precisely that shade today. The color was exactly wrong, but the river ran deeper here and always had a different tint than on her property—so, it wasn't a reliable forecast. She felt certain the water was flowing a metallic, shiny silver back at her house today. And, my, she thought, what a fruitcake she was.

As it happened, Ardeen's place was out in the boonies west of town, though not as far west as Anna's. It put him directly on her route into the clinic at the far east end, almost as if her taxi service had been pre-ordained. But for what purpose? The closer they got, the greater her self-doubt. How was she supposed to change this guy into an animal lover? *See the pretty kitty? Want to pet it?*

They rode without talking during the trip, with only three exceptions. One reproachful clearing of her mother's throat when Ardeen produced a pack of cigarettes, one closed-mouth grunt from their passenger as the butts again disappeared. And one spoken word about halfway through town. Anna and her mom abruptly broke the silence in chorus.

"Sorry!" they said together, Anna sounding truly remorseful, her mother less so.

Anna noticed Ardeen glance in their direction, reminding her that not everyone apologized to dead animals in the road. Both she and her mother had spotted the flattened rabbit at the same time and reacted as Anna had always done. As her loved ones had learned to do out of deference.

Since she'd been a child, the sight of a run-over animal had triggered a gruesome scene in Anna's head. Her imagination of the poor creature's final moments: trying to cross the road, seeing the oncoming car, feeling confused, trying to double back, or worse, freezing in terror, eyes wide at the approaching doom. And that's why Anna offered a 'sorry' now for every dead animal on the road. *Sorry we've taken over your habitat. Sorry you had to die violently because we want to live conveniently. And I'm very, very sorry if you had a mate or some babies who depended on you to return today.* It was her one-word prayer.

Anna pulled into the small asphalt lot in front of her clinic. She avoided her normal parking spot where she'd last seen this joker. No need to start the day with a flashback.

As they piled out of the truck, Anna looked to the road. Max Cotton's cruiser passed slowly by, and she waved at the rugged man inside. Ardeen noticed him and shot Anna a scathing look. Anna said her goodbyes to her mom before gesturing for her new employee to follow her inside.

"Just wait a minute," said Ardeen gruffly, his hands evident as balled fists in the pockets of his khaki polyester pants.

"What?"

"We haven't talked about what's gonna happen in there. What I'll be doing."

"Whatever I tell you to do."

"But what kind of stuff? I ain't doing jobs that involve shit."

"Yes, you are. That's not all you'll be doing, but animals—especially sick animals—excrete all sorts of bodily fluids, and the humans clean it up. That's part of the glamour of the veterinary business. Maybe you should have thought that through before agreeing to do this gig."

"I didn't have much choice, thank you very much. You and that shit-head judge."

"Watch your mouth. That's rule number one. This is my place of business."

Everything about him bothered her. His purposely-messed-up hair, gelled into a frozen topknot near the front of his perfectly round head. He looked like—*an onion.* She had to repress a laugh. To be fair, his face wasn't unattractive. It was what he did with it that annoyed her. Constantly squinting his eyes, tightening his lips over his teeth, like he was scrutinizing everything around him and finding it lacking. He soured her stomach. But no matter how repugnant she found her little Onionhead, she'd have to trick herself into relaxing around him. She couldn't live the next five months wanting to hiss at him every time he opened his mouth.

Maybe it would help her to remember the goal. She didn't have to like him; she just had to enlighten him. Find a way to change his perception of the creatures farther down the food chain than himself.

But first she had to get him through the door of the place. At the moment, he seemed ready to bolt.

"And just so you know," she said, with less venom, "Katie and Noah, the two people on my staff, were your supporters. They had to talk a long time to convince me to take you in. *Them* you'll get along with just fine."

Anna had been surprised by that, in fact. She'd brought Eddy's idea to her staff, half expecting—hoping—that at least Katie would push back hard enough to induce her to abandon the plan. An impassioned resistance would have given Anna a graceful way out. But no such luck. Katie, after careful thought, had come warily to the conclusion that it needed to be done. Noah, on the other hand, had embraced the scheme before Anna had finished laying it out. He'd had trouble even understanding her hesitation.

"So really," she said, eyeing Ardeen calmly, "I'm your biggest problem."

"And I can handle *you.*"

Anna searched his face for malice, finding something more impish.

"There will be no more handling of me. That's rule number two." She volleyed back without smiling, pulling her quilted coat closed with both hands. She was unaccustomed to being the second person to try humor in a tense situation.

"Come on, let's go in—" She turned away, mumbling the next word into the wind. "Onionhead."

Ardeen trailed Anna through the clinic door, into the waiting room. Scraping his feet on the welcome mat about five times too many, he watched Katie finish her phone call behind the reception desk. She set down the receiver and stood.

"Katie," said Anna. "This, as you already know, is Brian Ardeen. Brian, this is Katie Larson. She pretty much runs the place."

Katie chose not to walk the few steps out and around the counter but offered him a timid grin.

"Hello," she said, in her naturally creamy voice. She picked up a clipboard and without looking at it put it down again a few inches south. She gathered her yellow hair, pulling it back behind her neck.

"Hi." Ardeen swallowed the word as he dropped his head to supervise his feet giving the mat another couple of scuffs.

The door to the surgery flew open pouring Noah forth, his hand outstretched toward Ardeen. The newcomer had decided too late to respond, his arm raised only halfway before Noah pulled it into position by both hands clamped around his one.

"Hi. I'm Noah. Long. And you're Brian." He was beaming.

"Yup."

"Awright! Good to see ya. I think what you did was really sucky, by the way. But, hey, you're doing the right thing now, so welcome!" Noah released Ardeen's hand.

Anna tried to memorize exactly what Noah had just said, studying his precise inflection. She would practice it later, in an attempt to drive a little of his effortlessness into her own cells.

"Okay!" Anna said, with broad exaggeration, clapping her hands and rubbing them together. "This is fun. Ardeen—Brian, I mean—sorry." She was thankful she hadn't called him *Onionhead*. "Take off your coat. Noah, maybe you could show him the closet?"

"Sure. You want me to give him the grand tour while I'm at it?"

"You know, that would be great, thanks. Then bring him to The Burrow and wait there with him until I get there, if you would."

"You got it." And then to Brian he said, "C'mon. I'll show you the digs and introduce you to a few of our current residents." They headed down the hallway toward the closet. "Wait, hang on a sec."

Noah dashed back to fetch Anna's coat. He met her eyes in a question. Was it okay if he showed Ardeen the animals? She raised her eyebrows with intent, hooked her two index fingers together and tugged, a reminder of the instructions she'd delivered to him and Katie *ad nauseam*—to stick with the guy constantly. He was never to be left alone with an animal. Without missing a beat, Noah spun back around and began the tour.

Anna flung herself with dramatic flair into one of the three bent plywood Danish Modern chairs in the waiting room. She'd grown up with two of these chairs and had found the matching third on eBay. She looked at Katie and patted the aqua cloth seat beside her.

"How're you doing?"

Katie sat. "Good. I'm good."

"Not freakin' out on me?"

"Not at all. I think it's nice you've brought home a pet for Noah."

"Oh, my god, no kidding! Can you believe our man?" Anna, adept at impersonation, put on her best Noah expression and adopted his loose-shouldered posture. She mimicked his sing-song voice, exaggerating it. "I think shoving puppies into a used Pump 'n' Munch bag and kicking enough dirt over them to stop their little hearts is like, kind of sucky, dude."

"Whatever you're paying Noah, it's worth it. We just pull his string and he says all the right things."

"Yeah, he's a keeper."

"What must it be like to be so well-adjusted?" asked Katie, shaking her head.

"You're asking me? Anyway, let's talk about Brian's day. Just so you know, I'm thinking I'll have him shadow Noah for awhile, and then you. If you see something appropriate for him to do, go ahead and have him do it. Otherwise, he can watch and learn."

"He'll be great at holding down big, angry dogs. Did you check out those arm muscles? Jeez."

"I know. But, hey, I'm not sure if you've noticed. I've got a pretty good bicep goin' on here myself." Anna curled her arm, raising a respectable rock-hard lump.

Katie clamped her hand around Anna's muscle.

"Nice! Weight lifting?"

"Nope. Snooze alarm. It's just on one side, see?" She patted the underside of her other un-flexed arm, hoping to make it jiggle, but not quite having the flab to pull it off.

"So, what do you want Brian to wear? A scrub top? We've probably got one around here that'll fit him."

"I guess so. See if you can find one with a big scarlet A on it.

Katie cocked her head.

"*Abuser*. Duh."

After the tour, Noah escorted Brian to The Burrow and remained there with him until Anna arrived. He closed the door on his way out, leaving Anna and Ardeen to peer at each other.

Anna opened her middle drawer, pulled out an employee application, then looked up to see Ardeen running a ragged fingernail back and forth through one of the hundreds of gouges in her prehistoric desktop. She felt her eyes narrow.

"I need your address."

He gave it to her.

"Now your Social Security number."

Brian stilled his hand, keeping his fingernail where it was. "So this is how it's gonna be? You barking out commands, expecting me to jump?"

In order to clear some space she didn't need, Anna gently slid a three-ring notebook in his direction, nudging his hand from her desk. "You know, I'm not sure how it's going to be. You tell me. Can I trust you?"

"You mean… do I plan on killing anything while I'm here?" He raised his head a little. "I ain't decided yet."

Her answer bubbled up like a bodily function. "Yeah, I can see why you'd be tempted—all those weakened animals trapped in cages. Helpless. Your specialty."

She saw—or maybe sensed—him stop breathing.

With a short groan she pushed back from her desk and went to stand by the window. It was snowing the fakey, fat soap flakes from movies. She brought her face close enough to the glass to feel the heat from her skin ripple against the cold draft.

What would Noah do? For one thing, he wouldn't view the conversation as a competition he was afraid of losing. She needed to gear down. And, she decided, Noah would be respectful, but preposterously straightforward.

"All right, wait. I'm sorry I said that. Give me a minute." She came and sat down again. "Okay. Here's a topic I think you'll like. How about if you tell me why it is that you can't stand me. Just straight out. I promise not to get mad. It'll be good for you to say it and for me to hear it. Then I'll say why I can't stand you."

"What? You're nuts."

"I'm not nuts. Wait—unless you were offering that up as something you can't stand about me."

Brian averted his eyes and wagged the tip of his tongue along his bottom lip.

"Look." She focused on keeping her voice even. "We're going to be locked in this tiny building together five days a week for the next five months. In order to get by, we're going to have to pretend we don't hate each other. Maybe even actually *stop* hating each other. And I don't know about you, but that's going to be really hard for me. So I'm thinking that if we both get the truth out in the open, right here, and say how we really feel, maybe we won't be dying to scream it at each other all the time."

He grunted, mistrustful.

"Okay? Good." She repositioned herself in her chair and lay her hands flat on the desk. "You get to go first."

He took a deep breath, letting it out through his pinched throat as he traced another groove with the nail of his thumb.

"Come on. You can do this. *What I don't like about you is…*"

"Okay." He pushed until his thumbnail turned white. "What I don't like about you—is that—you think you're so much better than me."

Anna wanted to react. "Go on."

"Just what I said. You think 'cuz you have a good job, and you're rich, and everybody likes you, that you're a better person than I am. But you're not."

"Um… okay. Well—help me understand that." She made a point not to sound defensive. "What do I do to send the message that I'm better than you?"

His cheeks were reddening. "C'mon. Get real. You turned me into the cops, making you a good citizen and me some kind of criminal. You think that you and a bunch of strangers know how to deal with my dogs better than me. You're even on the goddamn radio every month showing the world how good you're doing it. And now you're my freakin' boss—who thinks she gets to tell me when I can take a shit and when I can't. Little things like that."

After a brief pause she asked, "Is that it? Anything else you hate about me?"

"No."

"Okay, then."

"But I don't know you very well yet."

Her mouth clamped shut, but too late. The short, dark laugh was already dissipating over her desk. "All right, it's my turn to say what I can't stand about you."

"Did I ask?"

"It doesn't matter. I get to say it."

She surprised herself with how at peace she felt, on the cusp of saying directly to his face what she'd been thinking about him for months. Her voice was relaxed.

"I believe people should be helpful and merciful, but you're self-absorbed and cruel. You'd rather kill than go the least bit out of your way to save. We humans have the physical strength and mental capacity to improve the world for all the other creatures who live here, but from what I can tell, you use those gifts to arm wrestle in the bar and see who can burp the loudest. Basically, you're the opposite of what I think a human being should be."

They looked at each other. Blinking.

"So...," he said. "You *do* think you're better than me."

After one meaningless syllable, she stopped herself. She slid her jaw to one side and returned his steady gaze. "I—guess I do."

She leaned back forcefully in her chair, folding her arms across her chest. She glanced up at the clock. 8:15 a.m. The earliest she could ever remember needing a nap.

26

Brian stood staring into the toilet, his hand flat against the dark red wall. He couldn't squeeze out a single drop. And that was because he'd already offloaded about twenty minutes ago—and twenty minutes before that—since using the can was the only excuse he could think of to get away. Not that they were hassling him, really. In fact they were treating him pretty good. Not joking with him or nothing, but at least talking to him like he was supposed to be there.

Out of habit, he shook his dick and pushed it back into his pants. He flushed, hawked up what he could, and spit into the swirling water. Only Dr. Giant would paint a wall red.

He closed the seat cover and sat down. She was so damn weird, trying to act like this whole deal was normal or something. It was like he'd gotten himself dumped onto some planet where nobody would tell him the rules that everybody else was playing by. It was the kind of situation his dad would call a *pig screw*.

But messed up as it was, being here also made him feel kind of amped. Like the buzz he felt after lifting weights. He had to admit that what had happened in the exam room a few minutes ago was pretty cool. He replayed the scene in his head.

He'd been standing in the back corner of the room where all the nobodies had to stay, watching her work on that Chihuahua or whatever it was. Supposedly it had a limp, but it seemed to be getting around pretty good if you asked him, spinning and snapping with that mouthful of rice-for-teeth.

Dr. Giant sent Katie to get the mini muzzle, probably from the box of Cracker Jacks or wherever they kept it. Damn, that was one scrawny mutt. When he first saw the dog, Brian had said to the owner, *Whoa! What is it? Some kind of bait?* Which he'd thought was pretty funny.

But the woman got all bent out of shape, and Dr. Giant looked at him, disapproving and shit, but he could tell she was trying not to smile, too. Actually, he'd made her laugh two or three times that day, and she'd looked surprised every time, like he was too stupid to be funny. Shit, one time he'd gotten Toot laughing so hard the guy had blown beer through his nose. And Brian had learned long ago that being a wise ass was the best way to deal with Bo. *Keep a guy laughing and he forgets to kill you.* It was the advice his dad had given him on his first day of high school.

Anyways, Katie was off getting the muzzle, so it was just Dr. Giant holding the Mexican jumping bean. The vet asked the dog's owner if the bean had ever been tested for Lyme disease, because that could make its joints hurt. But the lady wasn't sure.

So trying not to get bit, the vet looked all the way back to the bad-little-boy corner and asked him to bring her the dog's chart, since the computer wasn't working. He picked up the piece of paper from the open folder on the desk and held it with both hands so she could read it.

He'd watched her eyes as she looked through all that technical crap on the chart, seeming to understand it. And suddenly, he saw the whole thing—the whole picture. Himself there, Brian Michael Ardeen, wearing a hospital shirt, holding a goddamn medical chart for a goddamn doctor because she needed his help. For one quick second he felt like one of the clean people. Working in a place with thank yous, and sun coming in, and employees calling each other by their first names.

He almost smiled, thinking about himself in that exam room—until he remembered how his hands had been shaking, jiggling the chart all over hell while she was trying to read it. *Jesus, she'd probably noticed that.* Still on the toilet, he used the heel of one boot to grind on the toe of the other until it hurt.

Three hard knocks jumped him to his feet.

"Brian! Hey, you okay in there, dude?"

Brian didn't answer. Noah. Probably not a bad guy, but tough to be around. Brian didn't trust guys who smiled all the time.

He checked himself in the round mirror above the sink, liking how his neck sloped to his shoulders instead of coming straight down in an L-shape like regular people. He realized he could beat the shit out of anyone in this building, which relaxed him a little. He opened the door.

"Hey, hi," said Noah. "Man, it's none of my business, but you've been in here a lot today. You okay? Are you hungover or something?"

"No." Brian brushed past him.

He figured he should go find Katie since he was supposed to be following her around, but, damn, the girl was quiet. He could hardly ever hear what she was saying and never tell what she was thinking. She did, though, manage to spit out enough words to keep him running. And after every appointment she had him squirt this skanky green liquid onto the metal tabletop and get after it with a paper towel to clean up the smears and clumps that had come off of—and out of—the last animal to be scared shitless up there. Mostly, it wasn't too bad except when a dog was getting its nails clipped. There was something about dead toenails that had always made him gag. He clipped his own nails right into the trashcan so he didn't have to touch them.

And thanks to Katie, he was now a certified operator of the pooper scooper, or, as he called it, the shit picker. Of course, he couldn't be trusted to actually touch an animal around here. So the *professionals* would bring the dogs outside to take a dump, and he was invited to take care of the dukers they left behind.

He was pretty sure these assholes were throwing the worst stuff at him, maybe hoping he'd get mad and go away. But they had no idea how much abuse he could take. And besides, there couldn't be that many disgusting jobs left in this place. Unless some sticky kitten needed a tongue bath or something.

Anna ran the backs of four fingers along Bart's soft muzzle, watching his eyelids flicker as he dreamed the secret dreams of dogs. The big chocolate lab had been too jumpy to lie still for the x-ray, so she'd had to sedate him. And though she'd already given him naloxone to reverse the effect of the narcotic, he was still sleeping soundly, maybe physically exhausted from the string of seizures he'd had yesterday. Wanting to ensure he woke up safely, she'd laid him on the floor in The Burrow, on top of the patchwork quilt she herself often dozed with during all-night vigils. She'd taken instantly to the gregarious lab when her old high school chum, Debbie, had brought him in for his first puppy check-up, probably nine years ago, now.

Kneeling beside him, she studied his sweet face, expressive even in sleep. She tenderly touched the scar she'd given him just above his right eyebrow when he was still an adolescent. Three stitches after a run-in with a forgotten piece of rebar in the tall grass behind Debbie's barn.

She let her hand trace the side of his square head. Between the length of her first two fingers, she gently squeezed his lips together, smiling at the feel of the soft, saggy flaps. It had always been her favorite part of a dog, and she couldn't resist. With her thumb, she lightly rubbed the bristly patch of fur on his chin, one of many white spots on the once-solid brown of his face. She leaned in closer, pressing her nose against the top of his head and took in a deep, warm breath of doggie smell.

"It's been a long road, hasn't it, puppy?"

She drifted back to the day she'd first heard about his illness, three months earlier. She'd been at Mom's Diner when she overheard Debbie Stuber and her sister yucking it up about Bart, and how he kept tilting his head to one side. Debbie said it looked like he was trying to figure something out—like maybe what he would have to do to get her to bring him a steak. Laughing, her mouth full of blueberry pancake, Debbie's sister suggested that maybe Bart was tilting his head to listen for something—like whether or not somebody was on their way to bring him that damn steak!

On most occasions, Anna would have gotten a kick out of these two high school chums of hers, and maybe even asked if she could sit with them. But on that particular day, she'd found herself wrestling with a familiar dilemma: should she butt in to offer unasked for, unwelcome veterinary advice? Or should she ignore the suffering of an animal who could benefit from her help? As she religiously did in such situations, she'd chosen the former.

She interrupted Debbie's breakfast to tell her that Bart's head tilt might be a symptom of something incredibly easy to treat, like an ear infection or mites. But that it could also indicate a more serious condition.

Anna had offered to stop by Debbie's farm for a quick look at old Bart, fabricating plans to be out that direction later in the day. But when she'd gotten to Debbie's place, she couldn't immediately spot the source of the problem. And Debbie wasn't willing to pay for an appointment at the clinic. Anna offered to examine Bart at no cost—she'd known this sweet dog for a long time. She understood Debbie's financial concerns, but what she was unable to understand was Debbie's refusal of free treatment. Was her pride more important than helping her dog feel better?

Debbie had preferred to ride it out. To have Bart ride it out. And in that peaceful way dogs have, he did so with no complaints, walking around with his head tipping to the left, and on rare occasions taking a spill in that same direction. No encouragement from Anna had been sufficient to get Bart further medical attention. And now here he was. In crisis. She'd made contact with Debbie several times on the topic, always gingerly, but hadn't been able to convince her. Where was the line on this kind of stuff? She wanted to respect a person's privacy, but doing so in this case had led to Bart's collapse.

Anna learned yesterday that Bart had had two or three seizures over the past few months, but since they'd been so infrequent, Debbie hadn't wanted to bring him in. Yesterday morning, however, he'd suffered four seizures in quick succession, earning him a trip to the vet. And he'd had three more since arriving.

Phenobarbital and Diazepam IV had stopped the seizures, but whatever had been wrong with the poor guy was still wrong. Anna's exam had also turned up symptoms of neurological damage.

She watched the whiskers above Bart's eyebrows bounce as he twitched slightly, not yet free of his drug-induced slumber. Letting herself imagine what his life had been like over the past many months, Anna mixed herself a familiar cocktail of guilt and empathy.

She stroked the short, dry fur on the dog's shoulder with the flat of her palm. Then, lightly wrapping her hand around his elbow, slid it down toward his foot, liking the familiar knobs and ridges of his bones, muscles, and veins against her skin.

She ached to help him, this gentle beast. She'd ruled out conditions he didn't have but couldn't spot the one he did. The x-ray was her final hope, though she was keeping her expectations low. Taking quick mental stock of her checking account, she wondered if she could afford to send Bart to the U of M animal hospital on her own nickel if Debbie would accept such an offer. Anna had suggested Debbie take him there, but the idea was a non-starter: too long of a drive, too much money, and too old of a dog. Anna didn't argue but knew Bart could have several good years left if they could find his problem. Debbie had at last consented to the head x-ray at half price, for which Anna was grateful. And now they just had to wait for the film to develop.

Bart opened his heavy lids for a moment, rolling his eyes down into their normal position before giving in again to the great escape. Anna smoothed a floppy ear against his head, then curled down to kiss his face and whisper his name.

"Anna?" Katie stood in the doorway, an x-ray in one hand, her own throat in the other.

Ardeen's head and thick neck were visible over Katie's shoulder. *Oh, right. He's still here.* Though Anna had been making progress this morning in her resolution to imagine him as part of her team, she'd had to recommit to the pledge at every interaction.

She rose to take the x-ray from Katie, who looked a little shocky; Anna prepared herself. She slipped the film onto the viewbox hanging beside the door. Flipping the light switch brought Bart's brain into full clarity, with everything she was supposed to be seeing—and something she was not.

Deep in his thalamic region lay a dot of solid white, where nature had seen fit to issue only shades of grey. Whatever the small, round foreign object was, it read as metallic. As the startling truth took hold, Anna gave voice to what Katie had apparently figured out already.

"It's a bullet."

"Yeah. Well, a shotgun pellet, I'm guessing," said Katie. "Too small for a bullet."

"Right, that's what I meant." Anna pored over the film.

"Debbie's husband is a pretty big hunter, isn't he?"

"He is," said Anna, still studying the image, trying to put the story together. She looked away, deep in thought, then turned to her tech. "And you know what? Bart's symptoms started right around the same time as pheasant season."

"Wow."

"I'll bet anything he took Bart out for the opener, the dog flushed a bird, and when Chuck fired…"

"He shot his own dog!" said Brian. "Holy crap!"

Anna and Katie both turned to scrutinize Ardeen's expression. Luckily for him, it showed no hint of amusement.

Anna walked quickly to where Bart lay and squatted behind his head. With both hands she parted the fur at the base of the dog's skull, then worked her way up. Seeing nothing, she used all five fingertips to feel his whole head for any sign of an entrance wound she might have missed in previous exams. Nothing. Not that she had a right to expect a scar from such an old injury, and such a small projectile.

Looking over Anna's shoulder, Katie said, "Surgery's not an option, right?"

"No, but we can control his seizures with drugs. And I can tell by the x-ray it's steel, not lead, so we don't have to add lead poisoning to his list of troubles." Pushing her fingers deep into the flesh of Bart's neck, she could feel at least one, maybe two, other pieces of shot. "Yeah. That's what it is. Buckshot. There's more in here."

"Jeez, this is so cool!"

Brian brought the wrath of both women his way. But before either of them could shape a response, he continued on, never sensing he'd been in danger.

"I mean it's shitty for the dog. Sucks to be him, right? Just out there doing his job, and he takes one in the head. But it's so awesome an animal can live through that kind of thing. And right now he's got buckshot in his head, but he still eats and drinks and does his business and stuff. Is the shot tucked in some part of his brain he doesn't need or something? Christ, I mean, come on, the brain is way cool, ain't it?"

As surprised as Anna had been by Bart's medical diagnosis, she was just as surprised by Ardeen's apparent interest in the biology of the dog's anatomy. And to further complicate the moment, she and the puppy-almost-killer had actually just agreed on something: the brain was, indeed, way cool.

So she was giving him a ride to the plant. But that was all she was giving him. Though the judge could make her haul him around, he couldn't make her talk, and she was shoving that in his face. Whatever. Brian stared out his window at the acres of snow-covered nothing and tried to avoid thoughts of his past four hours.

A lot had happened. Most of it was annoying, and half of it smelled like ass, but it had turned out way better than he'd thought it would. For one thing, he'd never worked anywhere that you didn't know how your day was gonna go. Every job he'd ever had had involved standing in one place, doing the same thing he'd done all day the day before—except for that one short bartending gig down at Fuzzy's, where at least the customers were different every night. But working in a bar was a bad idea for him, and he knew it. Too many jerkwads looking for fights, and him wanting to give them what they came in for. The customer was always right, after all. Which was what he'd tried to tell Fuzzy the night he'd gotten fired, but that rat bastard had been too stupid to get Brian's sense of humor and always had it in for him anyways.

The vet job was different. You spent your day solving problems—like a car shop for animals. This one needed a lube job, this one better have its blood checked. You did for people what they were too ignorant to do for themselves, and you came out the other side a goddamn hero. It was the kind of job he could get used to.

But then he remembered. This was nothing, this job. It wasn't even a job. A job paid you money. He was working for free until some made-up-dollar-amount-per-hour paid off his bullshit fine to the court. Through the leg of his pants Brian grabbed a piece of skin and pinched it until his eyes watered. Besides, what had he been doing all morning? The nasty work no one else wanted to do. He was the same as Abdi now, and the other Somali guys who emptied bedpans down at the hospital for fifty bucks a day 'cuz that was the only job they could get.

He was no one at the vet's office. Less than no one.

The real people did the cool stuff. Like that cat that came in to have its nuts cut off. He would have killed to be part of that surgery. It seemed so weird that you could get inside of an animal, find what you were looking for, grab it and get out again, then close up the skin with hardly any proof you'd been there at all. And the thing lived. That was awesome.

Brian looked over at his driver. She hadn't said a word to him since they'd left the parking lot. *What the hell was her problem?* She was giving him the same damn attitude he'd gotten on the ride in this morning, but without the Nazi mother to double the fun. Actually, there was one major difference between that trip and this one—the kind of fact that would roll around inside his skull until his eyes wanted to bleed. The truth was, on the morning ride in, all he could think about was how to get out of this lame job. Now he was wondering how to keep it. Christ, what a pussy he was.

Seriously, though, what were the chances he could stay working at Dr. Giant's Shit Shop for the whole five months? Somewhere between *none* and *zip* he figured. Pretty soon he'd have to let loose with a personal opinion or two, which in their frilly-white world would make him about as welcome as a turd on toast.

He shifted his weight in the seat, exaggerating his movement more than he had to. But nothing caught her eye.

Maybe she wanted to dump his ass and was over there trying to figure out how. He stared at his fists in his lap, stiffening his lower lip, planning what to say to her, just in case. For one thing, they had a legal contract, so she'd have to talk to the judge if she wanted out—and good luck with that sorry prick.

"So," she finally said, still not looking at him, but with a tone of voice he hadn't expected. "Today went better than I'd thought it would. A lot better, actually, since neither of us is bleeding, wouldn't you say?"

He couldn't answer.

"Don't you think?" She nodded her head once.

"Guess so." He sounded pissier than he meant to.

He took a much bigger handful from the side of his thigh, on the door side, squeezing it as hard as he could between his fingernails and the heel of his hand. When the pain made him yelp she looked over at him, so he jumped into the first topic he could think of.

"I liked how you tested that dog's brain. When you turned its feet under to see if it would put them back in the right position. That's what you were doing, right? Seeing if its brain was working okay?"

She stared at him again, this time with a weird smile.

"Bart? Yeah, that's what I was doing. Checking his brain. Actually, checking his CPs, we call them. It stands for conscious proprioception."

"Oh, uh-huh." He sounded like a total numb-nuts.

"It's part of a neurological exam. You tuck the foot under to see if the signals from the outside world are getting through to the brain. You know—can he feel the sensation of his foot being upside down? You're also testing for the signal coming *from* the brain. Can he initiate the motor activity to move his foot back to where it belongs?"

"Two of his feet could do it pretty good, right? But not the others."

"Yeah, exactly. You saw that? Both feet on his left side showed no CPs at all. He kept them right where I put them. And when I tested the paws on his right side, the reaction was slower than I like to see, but he did move them back. So I knew there was something wrong with his nervous system, and maybe it was a problem on the right side of his brain.

"No shit."

"Nope. None." She gave him a longer look. "But, Brian, I meant what I said this morning. You've really got to watch your language around the clinic. I know it's going to be a tough habit to break, but I need to impress upon you how non-negotiable that is."

He felt an opinion pop to the surface—the kind that could get him into trouble. He tried not to say it, but not very hard.

"Jeez, you really think your shit don't stink."

"Excuse me?"

"I'm just sayin'. I could bring up lots of mistakes I saw *you* make today."

"What are you talking about?" She tried to watch both him and the road.

"You. You're what I'm talking about. You think you're some kind of animal savior or something, but half the time you have no goddamn idea what you're doing."

"Brian, come on. Let's not be this way. I'm sorry I said what I said. It was an okay day we just had. Can we just try to get through the last five minutes of it without going at each other?"

"I'm just sayin'. You screw up, too."

"Of course I do! I mean, is that really what you thought? That I never made mistakes? This sounds like your issue, not mine."

They rode the last mile to the factory with no more words between them until Dr. Giant pulled into the visitors' lot in front of the main building of the plant. She turned off the engine, then sucked in and released about half the available air in the cab. Her face said she had a pronouncement to make.

"I go in around back," he said, turning to look out his side window.

She started up the motor again and drove slowly around the building to the large parking lot in the rear, pulling up to the employee entrance. The truck still running, she made a big deal of putting it into park before turning her whole body to face him.

"Okay. Tell me."

"What?"

"I want to hear it. Really. All the mistakes I made today." She checked her watch. "You've got five minutes before you have to punch in. If that's not enough time to enumerate them all, you can call me with the rest on your first break."

Maybe she was trying to be funny. But either way, he was a clock-punching factory rat and she wasn't.

"Well, you got three things wrong, right off the top of my head."

"Only three? That's a pretty good day for me. Let's hear them."

"That little stomp dog with the limp. You never did figure out what was wrong with it. You sent it home to get better on its own—telling the lady to give it an aspirin."

"Coated aspirin. Yes. Our next options seemed too extreme at this point, until we see what some rest can do. He may have just twisted something. So you're right. I wasn't smart enough to figure out what was wrong with little Pepe. Guilty."

"And then there's the big brown dog. You keep it here like two days, pissing around with ideas like poisoning, or a bad thyroid, whatever that is, and even low blood sugar for chrissake. When the dog had taken buckshot to the brain."

"Again, you're right. It took me a long time to figure out what was wrong with Bart. Guilty as charged."

"And then that cat. For a few bucks you pop the cojones out of him, no worries. But when the guy asks you to pull its claws out too, while you have it under, you tell him he has to go somewhere else for that. You weren't *comfortable* declawing a cat. But de-balling him—yeah, bring it!"

"Not guilty. I'd make that choice again tomorrow. The pain involved in neutering is a necessary evil. Declawing, on the other hand, is an incredibly agonizing procedure that people do to protect their furniture. That, to me, is torture for our own convenience. I used to do it, but I won't anymore."

"What about the people who wouldn't get a cat if they couldn't have it declawed? A lot fewer cats would have homes to go to."

Dr. Giant didn't have an answer for that.

"You and I just don't see it the same way," she said. "We'll probably never agree on how animals should be treated."

"Bullshit."

"What?"

"Bullshit. You don't believe that. You think you're gonna change me, or I wouldn't be here."

Again, no answer from her.

"I'm gonna be late." He climbed out of the truck. Through the crack of the closing door he muttered, "See you tomorrow."

27

Packing provisions for a cup of tea, Bess Korhonen took the used teabag from the upside-down peanut butter lid, wrapped it in a paper napkin, and slipped it into the right side pocket of her housecoat. Into the left pocket she stuffed her teacup, to keep her hands free for catching herself—because though the Corelle cup was unbreakable, she was not.

The water in her electric tea kettle would boil and whistle for almost a full minute before she could get to it. She'd use fifteen seconds of that minute to stand and be certain she could stay standing, before letting go of the tabletop. She'd spend the next forty-five seconds in the senior shuffle, sliding one red Naugahyde mule ahead of the other, six inches at a time.

It made sense to her, at her age, that her body would start to shut down. But it complicated things. So far she'd been able to adapt to each new rebellion of deteriorating parts and felt she could continue doing so as long as she kept everything above the earlobes firing on all cylinders. Which was why Bess began every day with a Sudoku puzzle from one of her workbooks and a Gingko biloba capsule dissolved in her first cup of decaf tea.

She was embarking upon cup number two. Over the years, it had crossed her mind to plug the kettle into an outlet closer to the table, but the trips back and forth were key to her exercise regimen. She finally made her way to the contraption and would have shut it off if the switch hadn't broken a year or two ago. She took hold of the cord with both hands, turned her head away to avoid the sparks, and pulled as hard as she could. It wouldn't budge. She spread her feet wider to put her full body weight into the heave-ho, before stopping to think better of it. *I'm just one bad idea away from an ambulance ride,* she thought, picturing her hip smacking the floor in a splash of boiling water. She scratched her sandpaper scalp through thinning hair while scanning the kitchen for tools.

She opened the drawer she'd been leaning her stomach against and took out a wooden spoon. Wrapping the cord around the length of it, she leveraged the bowl of the spoon under the edge of the counter and pulled down with a hard steady pressure. More sparks than usual, but the plug jerked free.

She let two sugar cubes clink into the empty cup and pulled a pencil from the same drawer that had housed the wooden spoon. (For efficiency, she had long ago organized her kitchen by process, not category. For instance, she kept canned tuna, onion powder and a can opener in the fridge by the Miracle Whip, and potatoes and a peeler out on the counter by the cutting board.)

She opened the wet napkin and used the pencil to make a second hash mark on the paper tab of the herbal teabag. She filled the cup about two-thirds of the way, leaving room for slosh, since the senior shuffle was about as smooth a gait as it was speedy.

She reached into the cupboard above her head for another Corelle cup and the canister of instant coffee. She pushed her face into the metal tin as far as her forehead and chin would allow, taking a deep, rich breath and holding it as long as she could. A decade back, her doctor had told her to stop drinking coffee, which she had done that very day, extinguishing her last human vice and one of her few earthly pleasures. But she kept it around to offer company.

Having forgotten to swing by the built-in on her way to the kettle, she would have to make do without a teaspoon. She sprinkled a reasonable amount of dark flakes into the cup and dribbled hot bubbling water over the mound, while stirring with the wrong end of the wooden spoon.

Hesitating only a moment, she slipped the wet wooden stick into her mouth. Her tongue twitched at the bitter taste and began scouring the spoon for more, while memories flickered from Fredrik at the breakfast table, to neighbors stopping by for butter buns, to the smell of metal and Folgers puffing from her old percolator.

She turned around to get her body pointed in the right direction before twisting back to pick up the cups. She shambled past the table, dropped off her own teacup, and continued on with the coffee, heading down the long hallway, her eyes on the door at the far end.

She pushed it open a good minute-and-a-half later. The young dog raised its head, blinked heavily, and went back to its nap. The mailman was kneeling on the bathmat, wincing, hanging over the side of the tub, digging around in the drain. He pulled a wire hanger from the hole, and with it, a swollen clump of grey, matted hair. He'd worked the wad only halfway free when he spotted her in the doorway.

"Stay out! You don't wanna see this. There's a whole 'nother old lady down here!"

She knew enough to ignore the foul things he said, since they usually had nothing to do with what he meant. She scuffed her way toward him, keeping her eyes fixed on his, having learned that watching the cup only increased the height of the waves. Russ studied her laborious process for longer than she would have thought possible without a rude comment.

Lifting half of his upper lip into a sneer, he finally said, "It's okay. Iced coffee is good too. Take your time."

28

Russ let Kitty into the front seat from the driver's side door. He knocked the snow off his boots and climbed in beside her, still thinking about Mrs. Korhonen. Where were her damn kids? Obviously, she wanted them to think everything was hunky-dory around here, and they wanted to believe it, so the arrangement was working out swell. Except for the fact that the old woman would probably be dead by the end of the year if nobody took an interest. She'd already abandoned the upstairs of her house and half of her downstairs. The bottom half. Anything that required a bend or a crouch was gone to her now. And her world would keep getting smaller until it squeezed her right out of it.

Doing little things around the house for Mrs. Korhonen made him think about his own mother. And how he'd never gotten the chance to drop by her place and fix what needed fixing. Or have a normal conversation about the people next door or a hotdish she'd made the night before.

As always, Russ suffered a mild headache when he thought about his mom for too long.

He pulled six blocks up the road before stopping again. He put on his gloves, grabbed his mailbag, found the end of Kitty's leash, and got out. Walking up the north side of the next five blocks and down the south, pushing mail into icy boxes, he talked to his friend about things he knew she couldn't understand.

"This is the Jaraks' house. Have I told you about them before? He's a neurosurgeon, and she's a professional alcoholic. I think he's from Croatia or Kosovo, or some damn place where they still use leeches.

"Jeez, look at this next place, will ya? Correct me if I'm wrong, but I do believe that according to the Gregorian calendar, Christmas was two months ago. These people still have Santa's Workshop set up in their front yard. Why don't those elves just use their tiny little hammers to build themselves a helicopter and airlift outta here?"

Russ and Kitty walked a couple of minutes more, silently watching the neighborhood.

"I dunno… maybe we should put a tree up next year. Would you like that? Wait. Look what I've got." He tugged off a glove and reached into his coat pocket, pulling out a plastic sandwich bag. "I have no idea what else they do, but the Girl Scouts make a mean cookie. And we've got a freezer full. Here. One for you, one for me."

Kitty gently took the treat from his fingers and ate it, tail wagging.

"You like that, huh? Yeah, you're nothing like your namesake. Mom hated the Thin Mints. Said mint was for toothpaste and chewing gum, and that's it. But I think they're yummy, don't you? Don't you, puppy?" He sang the question, bringing his nose down by hers for a quick lick.

"Cripes, it's freezing out here. Let's pick up the pace."

The five-block circuit would end at Glory Finch's place. Kitty had started to get excited when they were still several houses away. She'd become accustomed to being asked in at Glory's, and if dogs were anything, thought Russ, they were hopeful.

The young woman in her late twenties, maybe, came bare-footed out onto the stoop of the biggest house on the block, where apparently it wasn't two degrees above zero like it was everywhere else. She waved wildly as they approached, like she was in danger of not being spotted, which was highly unlikely, since, as usual, her outfit could best be described as *Exploded Gypsy*. Strange clothes worn strangely, with lots of gold and spangles and colors not found in nature. He wrapped the leash a couple of times around his hand, bringing Kitty a little closer, to whisper a warning.

"Don't look at that vest too long. You'll go blind."

"Hey. Come in!" she yelled, still waving. "I made caramel rolls!"

"Well, there goes my girlish figure." He grabbed his belt to pull up his pants as he crossed into her yard.

Glory Finch was married to a man about fifteen years her senior who spent most of his time out of town, leaving her alone a lot with no one to talk to. And this was one girl who needed to talk. Her friends all had jobs, so they were never around to play with her during the day. Glory didn't work, which was how both she and her husband, Buck, liked things—he because he wanted to be the breadwinner, and she because she needed more time for her *art*. Supposedly, she painted pictures and made things out of clay, but Russ had never caught her at it. Far as he could tell, she busied herself mostly by concocting recipes for food nobody was there to eat, surfing the internet for weird facts she had no one to tell, and scoping out injustices to fret about because someone had to.

On his typical morning route, Russ made it to her house somewhere around ten o'clock, give or take, depending on who needed what from him before that. Glory had been awake for hours by then, half crazy with concerns and revelations, needing to talk to someone in the worst way. She'd lure Russ in with a promise of pastries or exotic hors d'oeuvres. Her house smelled like heaven's kitchen, but he'd still have to say that her food wasn't quite as good as his mother's. At least his memory of his mother's. Though he might have been remembering that wrong, since his mom had stopped cooking by the time he was ten.

"And so," Glory was saying, mid-story by the time Russ fully tuned-in. "'I said, 'Don't come crying to me about it, Bucko.' I love calling him that, since his name is actually Buck. Bucko, get it?" She had a high-pitched voice, like her throat was too skinny for an adult. "Anyway, then I said, 'I'll tell you why you've got swollen ankles. It's because you take too many laxatives!' And don't ask me what that's about. I'm not sure why he even needs so many laxatives, but I told him he should eat more prunes for that problem. And maybe for the swollen ankles he could walk on his hands once in awhile; get all that fluid heading the other way—"

After about ten minutes and maybe thirty-two hundred words, Russ needed to turn off the tap and get back to work.

"—because I think I can still do a handstand; at least I'm pretty sure I can. I haven't really tried for years. I know I can do a headstand though. I was always really good at headstands. Oh, my gawd, should I do one for you right now?" She whipped the purple fedora off her head.

"Gee, I don't know," he said. "Does the mouth stop running when it's turned upside-down?"

She put a hand to her chest. "Am I talking too much again?"

"Well, someone is, and I personally haven't said word one since, 'Here's your mail, lady.'"

"Gawd, I'm so sorry."

She looked genuinely embarrassed, so Russ smiled a little and used his hand to brush away her worry. He had a soft spot for this one. Having been relieved of most of life's little annoyances at an early age (by Buck, Bucko, Bucky, Buckaroo), she'd bypassed the hard knocks other folks generally took. It kept her sweet, but also meant she hadn't built up any callouses for protection. Her fresh-from-the-cabbage-patch condition made Glory Finch the world's tallest five-year-old. Everything was possible. She was an information sponge, sucking up truth—whole or partial—to dribble over whoever came 'round, without a single thought as to the poor shmuck's interest level. And she was completely unable to edit before speaking.

But perhaps her most childlike trait was a desperate need to please the genuine grownups in her life. And in one of fate's little screw-ups, Russ' mail route had put him somewhere on that list. In her presence, he felt a certain duty to be the kind of adult she could look up to. It was an awkward role for him, and he slipped up pretty regularly. Sometimes he'd try to smooth things over.

"Look, no big deal. You wanna see something Kitty and I have been working on?"

"Yeah, I'd love to!" Her eyebrows shot upwards, her hands hitting the table with a slap of pink flesh and clacking jewels.

He took a third caramel roll from the colorful plate, revealing enough of the design to confirm his suspicions. A bright green lizard with a tail so long it circled the rim of the plate stared up at him with only one of its bulbous eyes. The other peeper watched its tongue curl around a shiny blue fly.

"Hmm. Appetizing." His muttered words were lost in the gluey mixture of brown sugar and corn syrup he sucked from his thumb.

He couldn't help but notice the toes on the lizard. They were huge, bright yellow, and splayed out wide. What actually caught his attention, though, was the ring the creature wore. It was a bright orange human silhouette, wrapped around the lizard's toe. Russ glanced at the many rings on Glory's hands. As he'd remembered, a bright orange lizard clung to her middle finger in exactly the same position. Of course. She'd made the plate herself. So it was true; she did do something besides cook and surf the World Wide Wasteland. Though Russ wasn't sure he would call it art.

He cut the caramel roll in half, then swiveled on his chair to show the treat to Kitty. She padded over instantly, stopping when Russ put a hand against her chest to block her advance. He pushed her gently into the lying down position. The dog's eyes switched back and forth between Russ and the caramel roll. He kept his hand lightly on her withers, reminding her not to lunge for the food. She was still in training.

"Well, Kitty." He was cooing. "This looks pretty tasty, doesn't it? I've had a couple already, and I'm tellin' ya, you should try one if you get the chance."

The dog and Glory were equally rapt.

"Okay, I'll give it to you. But I want you to take your time with this, and really enjoy it, okay? No bolting it down like those other, less genteel dogs, all right? Okay. Now... *eat like a lady!"*

Kitty looked confused. Russ reminded her with light pressure to her side with his flat hand. "*Eat like a lady,* Kitty!"

She happily rolled over and exposed her belly, shooting her front legs into the air. Russ set the roll between her paws, then pressed his hands gently on her sides to remind her to stay on her back. Wiggling with excitement, Kitty brought the treat down to her mouth and bit it in half. Eyes widened far enough to show the white, she brought the roll to her mouth for two more chomps. When the last vestige of caramel roll was a couple of sticky paws, Kitty snapped back onto her tummy to begin cleaning up.

The twenty-something woman was beside herself with glee and responded as any tall five-year-old might.

"Again!"

"Naw, I've gotta get back to my route."

Russ petted his pooch, then reached for her leash, mumbling words he hoped Glory could just make out.

"I s'pose someday I should teach the mutt to sit or stay or something."

Russ and Kitty hit the mail trail again for another hour before heading to GreedyAss Markup. After delivering a small handful of junk mail and buying food for lunch, Russ pulled around behind the building to park by the dumpsters.

He'd forgotten it was Wednesday. Church night. And he had to show up. Without his accompaniment, the choir would be singing a cappella, in four-part pathetic. The only admirable trait about this pitiful group was that the voices were feeble enough to be drowned out by the piano. They needed him.

He knelt on the front seat, digging through the considerable collection of stuff in the back, coming away empty-handed. He stepped out to search the trunk and extracted what a casual observer might describe as a yellow plaid rag. He restored the rest of the clothing, gadgets, and papers deep enough into the trunk for him to close it by the third try.

He leaned against the car, glancing nonchalantly this way and that, hunching his shoulders against the cold. When he was sure only Kitty could see him, he slipped into the men's room, locking the heavy metal door behind him. The bar of soap was so filthy, he had to wash it before he could use it. He uncrumpled the shirt, held it under running water, lay it across the edge of the sink, and started scrubbing under the sleeves.

Back at his car he tossed the wet shirt into the seat behind him and drove to Riverbend Park, where he pulled into a spot at the far side facing the river, ass-end to any nosy onlookers. He draped the shirt over the front of the dashboard, cranked the heater to hot, and directed the fan through the front vents on what he'd always called the *blow-to-the-head* setting.

His copilot curled up on the passenger seat, tucking her nose under the tip of her tail. He stroked her slowly along her dark blonde fur, watching her eyes until she fell soundly asleep.

"Yeah, you nap for awhile. I'll keep the engine running, nice and warm."

Slightly nauseated from the pain in his head, he wondered if eating a little something might help. He opened the plastic SpeedyGas bag, stared in at the loaf of white bread and package of hard salami. He drew in a sudden breath of air and squeaked out a single word.

"Momma..."

Though only his dog had ever heard him talk about his recently dead mother, Katherine (Kitty) Pioske was still the most significant person in his life. And not just because thoughts of her would consume him on certain days. Like today. But also because she was central to how he'd turned out as a person. His mother had given him life—and had taken from him the will to love.

As an only child he'd been lucky to have the full attention of both parents, with something special to share with each one.

What his dad had lacked in affection, he'd made up for in years of accordion lessons. Russ had loved the sound of the instrument. Or maybe he'd loved the sound of his dad telling him what a great musician he was. But they played together every night.

And though his dad considered humor to be a silly waste of perfectly good breath, both Russ and his mother used it as their own secret language, speaking for up to ten minutes at a time in only knock-knock jokes, puns, and funny faces.

Russ was only eight years old and stupid enough to think that everything was going along just fine, when one night, dinner dishes long done and the family watching TV, his mom jumped up during a commercial break to bring them all hot drinks. Coffee for the adults and Ovaltine for the beloved son. Having to walk past Russ to get to the kitchen, she gave him one of her most beautiful smiles. Maybe her last one. Russ felt so in love with his mom in that moment, he wanted to reach out and connect with her. In their own special language. He did the first funny thing he could think of. He stuck out his leg as far as it would go.

Over the next fifty years, the scene would play back in painfully slow motion whenever he'd let himself remember. Jutting his leg outward, giddy with how shocking this perfect joke was going to be, proud of himself for how quickly the idea had occurred to him, he was dizzy with the lightheadedness of a person about to become the center of all attention.

But she didn't right herself before she fell—or turn on Russ to tickle him until he begged her to stop. She just fell. And kept falling. Down the three wooden stairs of their step-up living room. The smack of her hitting the ceramic tiles of the hallway floor wasn't the most horrible part. Even the crack of breaking bone wasn't the sound that would keep him from ever loving another human being again. It was what his mom blurted out as she crumpled into her never-right-again self.

"Russ!"

She had named her attacker. The person who would put her into the hospital for the second time in her life. The first had been to bring him into the world, which he'd had no control over. But this time the choice had been decidedly his. Would he allow his mom to return to the living room for a cup of hot coffee and her favorite show, or make her spend the next couple of days in searing pain, and then months in a cast up to her thigh? What kind of person chose the latter?

As she lay on her back in the hall, holding her leg and rolling from side to side, she sucked in deep, gulping breaths. She let them out again in pinched, nearly silent squeals. Even at eight years old, he understood she was trying not to alarm him by crying out loud. He wanted to tell her to make as much noise as she needed to—to scream if it would help—but he didn't. He couldn't even do that.

At the hospital his dad disappeared with his mom behind the big double doors off the emergency room, not to return for hours, leaving Russ and his grandmother to sit in blue plastic chairs, speaking only when their bodies required it.

Why are you squirming—do you have to go to the bathroom?

I'm thirsty.

Here, have a mint, your breath stinks.

When the nurse delivered the news that his mother's X-rays looked bad, and she would need surgery, Russ closed his eyes. He relived the scene for the ninety-ninth and one hundredth times. His leg jutted out. His mom fell. Leg out. Mom down. He had almost convinced himself that it was only a crazy accident, one of those weird things that just happened sometimes. But he opened his eyes to see his grandmother wishing him harm with her whole puckered face.

Her voice was hospital-quiet but made of gravel. "Surgery. Your own mother. What is *wrong* with you?"

Russ tried to pretend he hadn't heard the question. But the words fused themselves to the inside of his skull and ate away the bone until only the phrase *What is* wrong *with you?* was left to hold his head together.

His mother, on the other hand, would later do everything she could to help him believe in his crazy accident theory. After calling his name in the passion of the moment, she never again blamed Russ for what he had done. But the indictment, though unspoken, refused to go away. It sat with the family at the dinner table from then on and squeezed in between every hug.

As awful as these days seemed, however, they were about to become awfuller still.

Three weeks later, Russ came bounding down the stairs, trying to identify what they were having for dinner by the smell. It was a game he played with himself all the time. But the only scent he could detect came from the roses in the foyer. He walked into the kitchen to find his mother sitting at the table, crutches in a V on the floor, her leg with the cast sticking out to the side at an odd angle. She was staring worriedly at a raw pork chop in her hand. When he asked what was wrong, she told him she'd been trying to make dinner, but had forgotten how. She knew baked pork chops with dressing was her favorite dinner. And she knew she had planned to prepare that tonight; but right at the moment, she had no idea how to make it happen.

It was the beginning of the frontal strokes that would plague her for the rest of her life. It was the end of everything else.

Russ became an expert at tucking his problems into tiny little pouches along the walls of his brain. The guilt of having broken his mother's leg, he kept over here; finding the set of metal measuring spoons hanging on the hook with the house keys, fit nicely over there; his dread of someday having to change his mother's diaper, he hid way back in a faraway corner. And he spent as much time as he could thinking in the *middle*, where he kept his four-square games at recess, his trips to the library with his dad, and playing alone down by the river. But on his thirteenth birthday, two of Russ' nightmares slipped from their pockets and crashed together with enough force to alter the course of all the other days after that.

He was lying on his bed, bouncing a tennis ball against the ceiling, generally feeling sorry for himself, because though last year his father had apologized for not having the time to give him a birthday party, this year he'd said nothing about it at all. Caring for Russ' mom had become his dad's second full-time job.

Russ reached into the tiny brain pocket where he kept his first memory of his mother's illness. The Night of the Pork Chop. He saw her abandoned crutches, her leg with the cast, and the way she stared at the raw meat as if it were a brick wall blocking all further thought.

And something made him tingly. The cast, the pork chop. The cast. The pork chop. Russ had broken her leg, and a few weeks later she had become sick. The broken leg had made her sick. He'd broken her leg. He'd made her sick. *It was him! He had made her sick!*

The doctors had claimed that her strokes were caused by a bad heart. But thirteen-year-old Russ knew better. It had been the bad fall that had started the strokes.

He'd ruined his mom's life. And he would kill her, too. Years later, Russ would discover medical records his dad had forgotten to hide. A prognosis. His mother would continue to get worse and worse and probably die from these strokes one day. So basically, Russ had killed his own mother.

Some kids could draw better than others, some could hit a faster ball, others could tell funnier stories. But most of them did an okay job of loving their mothers. It was supposed to come naturally for a kid. But not to Russ. Probably the most important thing in the world, he had gotten totally wrong. And his grandmother had seen him for the oddity he was. *What is* wrong *with you?*

He would rewind the question, playing it back at every stupid move he ever made after that—until he learned to stop moving. Stop trying. Stop loving. On the day he turned thirteen, crying deep into his pillow, Russ Pioske vowed never, ever to get close enough to hurt—or be hurt—again. And he kept that promise.

If he had awakened one day, suddenly an adult who could see the error in his thirteen-year-old thinking, maybe things would have been different. But Russ grew up gradually, one long day at a time and then the next, certain there was something wrong with him, never bouncing the theory off of anyone else who might have poked a hole in it. He was a bad person who needed to stay away from people.

His oath had restricted him to a life without friends. He would never have the chance to argue over picking up a check, or be the one to decide what to read at book club this month, or share popcorn at a movie, or switch jackets accidentally at a party, or jump into the back seat of a car to allow someone else to ride up front, or ask if he should bring red wine or white, or suddenly realize he'd been up talking with someone all night.

It was odd, he understood, the life he led. In his job as a postal worker he had personal contact with plenty of people, and every one of them probably thought (if they thought about him at all) that he had a friend or two someplace. Someplace else. But he was completely without human companionship—at first, because he'd decided it was the safest choice, and later, because turning someone who knew him into someone who liked him would require tools he did not possess.

There was a skill to making friends, he figured. A science that people probably mastered early on, and got better at as they aged, so by the time they reached adulthood, they could do it without thinking. But Russ' social progress had been halted at age thirteen. And now, at fifty-eight, making friends had been added to his list of abandoned dreams. He had, years ago, given up on the idea of working with dolphins, rapelling down the face of a cliff, and picking up the phone just to chat.

Best as Russ could tell, building a close relationship would have to begin by making himself vulnerable to rejection. By definition, moving from acquaintance to friend meant doing things together socially. And a social event required a first invitation, which, once spoken, would hang pitifully out in the open, waiting to be spat on.

Want to go get some coffee?

(Pause) *Right. Like I would go someplace with you if I didn't have to.*

It was a mystery to Russ why people would put themselves through it. So he had decided long ago to live with the loneliness, sparing himself the pain. Curiously though, the loneliness had now *become* the pain. Unbearable on some days. And that was when his thoughts would turn to the last person he'd ever allowed to comfort him. His mother.

Her frontal strokes would continue for another fifty years past The Night of the Pork Chop. She would live the last twenty of them as an angry, disoriented woman who Russ could barely recognize as his mother. And in one of nature's ironic twists, she had stopped recognizing him as her son as well.

The grown-up Russ mostly understood the implausibility of a connection between her broken leg and what had been happening in her brain because of her heart. But how did her heart become weak in the first place? Who could say it hadn't been caused by the trauma she'd endured—the trauma he had inflicted upon her, by being so stupid in the way he had shown his love? His love had wrecked everything.

And now here he sat, staring down into a bag of salami and Wonder Bread, crying for his mommy.

Kitty repositioned herself, stretching her neck between the seats to lay her head onto his lap. After several minutes of regretting acts he could never undo, he opened the package of greasy meat and gave his dog a single slice. He shoved the rest back into the bag, feeling as un-hungry as he could ever remember feeling.

"Let's see." He softly rubbed his puppy's eyes with his palm, the way she liked. "So far today you've eaten a cup of kibble, a Girl Scout Cookie, half a caramel roll, and some cold cuts. Don't tell Dr. Dunlop."

The rest of the afternoon passed without incident. Russ put his mom back into her proper pockets and got on with his route. He kept his hand on whatever part of Kitty he could reach as he drove, and when he left the car, he invited her to walk beside him. He always stopped to wait when she wanted to push her face through the fluffy snow or check some other dog's pee-mail.

At his more rural stops, unless he had to give a person a ride to the neighbor's place or deliver an item he'd picked up for somebody at the Farm & Home, neither he nor the pup would disembark much that day. It was too dang cold. Instead, he'd pull up to a house, stick his arm out the window, and shove whatever the federal government paid him to shove, wherever they told him to shove it.

Such was the case at a house out in the country that he'd reached by 1:44 that afternoon. He pulled a U-ey at the dead end of the gravel road, bringing the driver's side up to the mailbox. He opened the mouth of the gigantic wooden trout (one person's tacky was another person's cute, he supposed), put the bills and a box of designer checks to pay them with inside, and snapped the mouth shut. He was about to drive away, but didn't, glancing over at his grey travel mug. In a gesture that Kitty would soon come to expect at this house, he stuck the mug out the window, and raised it toward the upstairs floor, second window from the right.

29

"Whoa, that was a nasty one! I'm going back to cooking the lean hamburger meat in real oil. That spray stuff doesn't work very good," said Cleo, shaking a few drips from the frying pan before handing it over. "What do you wanna do tonight, Pookie?"

To dry the pan, Jeffrey was using a thin dishtowel patterned in strawberries with little faces. Girl strawberries with long lashes and red lips, boys in blue ball caps.

"I don't know. I'm open. There's nothing good on TV tonight. You want to go for a walk?"

"Oh, honey, I didn't tell you. We went twice around the whole park today. I'm kinda walked out, if that's okay. Boy, Patton, he sure loves it outside. There's nothing he won't smell. No matter how embarrassing. And then John Henry has to run over and check out what it is and describe it to me. You wouldn't believe how many disgusting things are in that park." Nodding her head, she picked a few waterlogged French-style green beans from the basket in the drain. "I'm gonna cleanser the sink. I bought a new liquid kind. It squeezes out pink."

She opened the bottom cupboard and poked around, breathing in smells of silver polish and baby wipes, while leaving herself head down and rump up—or as her mom used to say, *turnin' the other cheek for Jesus*.

"By the way, my little Faline," said Jeffrey. "I'm really sorry."

"For what?"

"For this!" Twisted strawberries spanked the part of her J.C. Penny jeans she had been saving for Jesus.

The first half of her squeal echoed in the space under the sink; the second half shot around the kitchen as she chased her attacker.

"Shhhh!" Jeffrey was laugh-whispering. "You'll wake up John Henry."

She belly-slammed him, jumping repeatedly for the towel he waved three feet above her head. She made one final leap, like an antelope on one of her nature shows, snatching a handful of terry cloth strawberries. But there she hung. Jeffrey was holding her around the waist, dangling her feet several inches above the linoleum.

"Put me down!" She squealed, halfheartedly wiggling to free herself.

"No way am I putting you down. Not 'til you kiss me."

"Kiss you? I kissed you yesterday." Cleo tried hard to sound as if this game came naturally to them.

Cleo, in her very favorite place, invited to do her very favorite thing, stopped struggling. She let the towel drop, wanting both hands for touching. She put one against Jeffrey's soft hair and slid the other down the center of his back, feeling the heat of his skin through his t-shirt. She forced herself to un-smile, wanting her lips relaxed enough to spread all the way across his. Consciously, she slowed everything down, coaxing him to enter this new mood with her. Tonight he came along willingly, eyes closed, seeming to want her body against his. They kissed once, twice, and then tilted their heads the other way to feel the newness of it—a second lover.

Cleo dared to let her tongue rest against the center of his lips, asking permission. His mouth opened to her. She inhaled the earthy sweetness of his breath as she slipped inside, timid, careful. His tongue, his gums, his cheeks—all cooler than hers—were growing warmer, the two of them heading toward a single shared temperature. She pressed her hand a little harder against the back of his head, wanting him closer, to feel like one person instead of two, fighting the urge to wrap her legs around his waist.

Need was stinging her, screaming up through her tummy to her chest, along her arms—everywhere she touched him. And between her legs. She could feel him there, bulging against her, thick and stiff, making her crazy. She kissed him more deeply, trying not to moan, not to move any other part of her body, trying not to scare him away, worried he could feel her throbbing. A tear left the corner of her eye. *Please, God.*

She slowly circled her legs around his thighs, pulling his hardness more tightly against her, arching her back to get closer still.

Jeffrey opened his eyes and drew his head back, ending the kiss. Ending the chance for more than a kiss. He smiled nervously, his grip on her loosening. He gave her a single peck on the top lip of her open mouth before dropping her softly to the floor.

Cleo hid her panting. She took in a deep, long breath, letting it out slowly through her cheerful smile. “I love you, Jeffrey.”

“I love you too, Faline.”

He spoke the words with love in his voice—she could hear it—but his eyes hinted at other things too.

“Hey!” she said, trying for perky. “You know what? I was looking at some of those old box games of my parents’ down in the basement. Maybe we could play one tonight. Would you like that?”

“That could be fun.” He picked up the dishtowel, letting it drape casually in front of his crotch.

“Great. I’ll go down and pick out some good ones.” She walked toward the basement door, aware of her wetness.

“Sounds like a plan. I’ll go in and check on the man-child. Meet you back at the kitchen table.”

She could feel the stack of games teetering, threatening to fall over as she made her way to the kitchen. She used her chin to steady the pile, which meant she saw only the ceiling as she stepped haltingly, feeling her way with her toes. The doorway. The toybox. The stove. And finally, a leg of kitchen chair.

“No, no, don’t worry about me. I’ve got it,” she said, sing-songy. She smiled, turning her body to see Jeffrey seated at the table.

She cautiously set down the games, her arms glad to be free of them. And that’s when she took a long look at Jeffrey’s face. He was pale.

“Are you okay, sweetie?”

“Yeah, I’m fine.”

She didn’t quite believe him.

“You sure? You look sort of funny.”

“No, I’m good. You’ve got a lot of stuff there. Are we going to play all of those tonight? I’d better make some coffee.”

“I wanted to give you a selection to pick from.”

“Scrabble, Probe, Mille Bornes. I know all of those. But what’s this for?” He pointed to the large leather-bound book on top of the pile.

“It’s a dictionary.”

“I can see that. But why?”

“My family used to play the dictionary game. We’d pass the book around, and somebody would pick out a weird word, the goofier the better, and then make up a fake definition for it, or maybe read the real one. And people had to guess if it was true or not.”

She hefted the dictionary and held it to her chest.

“I know you know a lot of words, but I still bet I can stump you. Really, there are some bizarre words in here.”

“We have smaller dictionaries, you know. I can’t believe you lugged that huge thing all the way up here.”

“I know, but I saw this big ol’ one of yours, way up there on that top shelf, and thought it might be kind of neat. Lots of crazy words in here, I’m guessing. I almost killed myself getting it down. I had to drag that red stool over. You want to play?”

“No. One of those others, I think.”

“Really? I know it sounds stupid, but it’s a fun game.”

She opened the front cover of the dictionary. Jeffrey’s hand slapped it closed, clutching both the book and the hand that held it.

“I don’t feel very well,” he said, looking even worse than he had thirty seconds ago.

“I knew it!” She placed the book on the table. “You look awful. Is it the ulcer?”

“No—maybe. I’m not sure.”

“Here, let me get you to bed.” She ran around behind him to help him stand.

“No. I want to sit here for a bit.”

“Okay. Can I get you some water? A Pepcid?”

“Please, Cleo. Just let me be for a little while.”

“Oh. Okay. Tell you what.” She lifted the dictionary to the top of the pile of games. “I’ll take these out to the living room and look at them out there. You can just rest.”

She managed to get the pile several inches off the table before he stood up to help her. He put one hand over the stack, one under, holding her in place. “Why don’t you let me take this stuff out there? It weighs about as much as you do.”

“No, honey, that’s okay. Really, you sit down, I’m worried about you.”

She turned away with her load, but he kept his grip; the pile collapsed and fell to the floor. Everything except the dictionary.

Jeffrey clung to as many pages of the book as his hand could hold, which was only about half. The book had flapped open, spilling its contents onto the jumbled mess below. Cleo watched the papers flutter free. She stared down at where they lay, strewn across a square yard of game boards, dice, and plastic hotels.

“Oh my gosh, I’m so sorry, Jeffrey. Honey, go lie down before you fall down. You look terrible. I’ll take care of this.”

She squatted beside the mound of childhood memories. Barely aware of the smells of aging cardboard and plastic Twister sheet, she picked through the debris to collect what the dictionary had given up. Pieces of folded paper—some small, some larger, some white, some not—and a number of used envelopes.

"What is this stuff?" She was intrigued by Jeffrey's stash. "Can I look at these?" She giggled.

And then she stopped giggling. She noticed the handwriting, the same on each of the notes. Someone with beautiful penmanship had written all of them. To Jeffrey. And he had been keeping them hidden from her. Away. In secret.

Cleo's hands moved over the pile, but her movements made no sense. She remembered how to open an envelope and did, pulling the brown, heavy stationery page out into the light of her kitchen. It had a border of blue swirls, probably hand-drawn by the same person who'd written the letter, in the same blue pen. She saw the words, *My Dearest Jeffrey*, then skipped to the signature where she read, *With more love than another person has ever given another person. -R.*

Cleo's eyes darted wildly around the page, stubbing themselves on words and phrases, *Your hands... life without you... tingle... see you laugh... on my skin... past poets... kissing, kissing—*

The squeak that escaped her came on the inhale she'd been forgetting to take. She stared up at him, wanting him to undo this. To make it not be happening. But he refused to help her. He dropped instead to his knees beside her, his arms wrapped around himself. Silent.

"No. No, Jeffrey. You have to talk to me. I don't understand this. You have to talk to me."

Jeffrey rocked forward and back on his knees, his head down.

The panic that had been chasing her for so many years had caught up and was tapping her on the shoulder. Familiar, but horrible. This was the moment. All those years ago, she had chosen Jeffrey, pretending not to notice he was broken. Thinking love would cure him. But tonight the train came. The one she'd been lying on the tracks waiting for.

Oddly, realizing her life was over, she relaxed a little. The wishing was done. She stood, letting the letter fall from her hands. She made Jeffrey stand too, leading him quietly toward the sofa. She sat him down, pulled up the footstool, and sat down to face him. And she waited.

"I wanted to tell you," he said, his throat sounding dry.

For the first time since junior high her voice was clear. Strong. "No, you didn't."

"No, I didn't."

"Who is she, Jeffrey? Who have you brought into this house? Into our marriage. You need to tell me that right now. I love you. I will always love you. But you have to tell me who it is."

"I can't. God, Cleo I can't!" And he cried, bawling full out, a lost child.

"Yes, you can." She took his hands to calm him. "Just say it, and then you will have said it, and that part will be over."

She waited for him to quiet down before she asked again. "Who is she, Jeffrey?" She cupped her hand along his jaw to lift his face. "Is it someone I know? It is, isn't it?"

He nodded. Her husband was in more pain than she'd ever seen him, but any comfort she might have offered him she was saving for herself.

"Who, Jeffrey?" She was almost whispering.

"I'm sorry. I'm so sorry. Please. Please, I'm sorry."

"Who, Jeffrey?"

"It's—it's Ryan."

She couldn't imagine who he was talking about. The only person she knew named Ryan was a guy. The cute guy Jeffrey had hired at the frame shop, about a year ago.

"Ryan who?"

"Ryan Lansing. From the store."

Cleo grabbed both of Jeffrey's knees and stared into his beautiful blue eyes. Then she pushed his legs apart, put her head between them, and threw up onto the floor.

30

"He's up. He scores!"

No other sound like it, the satisfying clack of frisbee-on-teeth signaled a good solid catch.

As Fritos began his quick descent to Earth, Jake snapped the photo and immediately studied his work in the display screen.

"Yes!" His fist shot into the air.

At long last, he had captured the complete airborne animal. Until then, he'd only gathered a cameraful of smeary, isolated body parts.

The photo was better than he'd hoped. Fritos' floppy ears stood straight up as exclamation points. His eyes caught at their widest O, the dog stared directly into the lens. And the vertical blur of the plummeting pup turned the frisbee into an exaggerated pair of bright red lips, letting the naked eye, at long last, see the goofy smile he normally wore on the inside.

"We got it, boy! We got it! Good boy!" Jake looked up from his camera, planning to lavish a massive belly rub on the six-and-a-half-month-old palomino puppy, only to find that his wayward charge had gone missing. "Fritos?"

Scanning the dog park, he caught sight of Fritos on a mad dash toward a young German shepherd who was, himself, on a headlong sprint to close the gap. Jake assumed the dogs to be intent on play, not violence, but just in case, took off after them at a full run. The small camera dangling from his neck banged against his chest on every stride.

"Fritos! C'mere, Fritos!"

From a distance came a tiny echo. "Fritos!"

Jake spotted a fourth runner en route to the same square yard of wet grass. John Henry. Which meant the German shepherd in question posed no threat to young Fritos, allowing Jake to slow his pace to a mad dash.

Long before Jake made it to the designated meeting place, Patton had crashed into his littermate and was now nipping at his brother's legs and poking him with his snout, trying to get him to run.

Agreeably, Fritos sped off, circumnavigated the nearby statue of some lumber baron whose name Jake could never remember, and returned back again to home base. Just as Patton caught up, Fritos spun to retrace the loop in the opposite direction. It occurred to Jake that this was the same activity Patton and John Henry had invented months ago as an inside game. *Ring Around the Rosie.*

"Hiya, JH!" said Jake, bending over to pick up the forgotten frisbee. "How's it goin'?" He stretched out his hand for a grown-up shake, and John Henry good-naturedly obliged.

"Okay." John Henry's voice was high and cute; Jake wondered if his own absurdly deep voice had ever sounded like that.

"So. You and Patton just headin' out for a pack of smokes or somethin'?"

"Huh?" John Henry seemed more interested in the two-dog frenzy than human conversation.

"I'm just messin' with ya, little man. Anybody taller than you along on your trip to the park today?"

The boy didn't answer, but Jake noticed a green bench about fifty feet away where Cleo sat watching. She offered one of those waves a person completes without fully uncrossing her arms.

"Hey, Cleo!"

Jake tucked the frisbee between his knees to free his hands and brought the camera up into position. The leaves of the giant catalpa tree had draped a polka-dot shadow blanket over Cleo and the wooden bench. The light looked touchable. But he lowered the Nikon as quickly as he'd lifted it.

"Don't!" She dropped her head, covering her face with her hands.

Jake jogged to the bench to plunk down beside her.

"Hi, you! What's up?"

He could see now what he'd been unable to see before. Cleo didn't look so good. Unhealthy, maybe. Granted, it was the first time he'd ever seen her without make-up, but that wasn't it. She seemed puffy. Like his friend Kenny after the kidney transplant. He studied her face, feeling the slow dawn of reality. She'd been crying. And for a long time.

"Oh, wow, hey, Cleo. I'm sorry."

"Sorry for what?" Her voice was even more hoarse than usual.

"Um, I'm not sure. Being happy, I think."

"Everybody's always sorry. What good is sorry?" She folded her arms again and gazed out at John Henry.

Jake changed the kind of day he was having, to join Cleo in hers. Of all the puppy people, she would be the last one he'd expect to find outside on a bench between cries. He spent a minute or so watching other people in the park, slowing his tempo.

"Y'know, it's actually good to find ya here. 'Cuz there's something I've been meaning to say to ya, but it's never been quite the right time at the radio station."

"Oh, really?" She sounded wary.

"Yeah. It's no big deal. Just an observation. Would you be interested in hearing something that I've been thinking about you?"

She tilted her head back, giving him a good long, sideways look.

"I don't know if I do or if I don't. I guess if it's not too negative, I'd like to hear it. But if it's negative, I think we'd both do better if you just kept it to yourself."

"I hear ya." He weighed his next words, deciding that they met her condition. "It's just this: I think you're the most *convivial* person I've ever met."

"Convivial?" She narrowed her eyes at him. "I'm going to go ahead and assume that's complimentary."

"I like words, and this one's a favorite. Especially now that I know someone who shows me what it looks like. A convivial person is someone who's extra pleasant. Like you."

"You think so?"

"No question. I always notice how far outta your way you go to make people feel good. Even when they're being kind of annoying. Or right out rude."

"Huh. Thank you for saying that."

"And the problem is I'd like to return the favor and say something right now to make *you* feel good. But I don't know what that might be, since I don't know why you're feeling bad in the first place."

"That's okay. You don't have to say anything."

"Y'see? There ya go again. Tryin' to make me feel good. You shouldn't have to do that. So… since you shouldn't have to say anything nice to me, and I'm not sure what to say to you, maybe we could both just sit for awhile, with you knowing I wish I did."

"Okay."

And that's how it went. Jake played with Fritos off and on when the pup would tear himself away from his brother long enough to check in. And John Henry came over for some animal crackers when he got hungry. But for the better part of fifteen minutes, the two of them sat side by side conversing in sad grins and slow nods.

In addition to his concern for Cleo, Jake's thoughts included: wondering if he should change the weight of the oil in his bike, realizing he hadn't showered yesterday, and imagining what a funny-looking couple they must make to the casual passerby.

Cleo seemed kind of uneasy with Jake there, but he sensed she would feel worse if he left. So he didn't. As they sat, their polka-dot shadow blanket slipped to the grass, leaving them open to the mid-May midday sun. And he'd dressed in too many layers.

From deep inside the frayed Tour de France sweatshirt that Jake was tugging over his head came a muffled call. "Look out! Circus clown warning!"

As his head was birthed through the neck hole, his frizzy, red ponytail sprang free of its elastic hair binder. He could feel a sphere of unruly locks bouncing in long corkscrews at varying degrees from his head.

"Oh!" she said, covering her mouth with her petite hand, letting what was likely her first chuckle of the day slip through her fingers.

"What? What's so funny?" He pretended to search the park, whipping his head this way and that, making his wild, curly tendrils bob and collide.

"Stop!" She was laughing hard, holding her stomach in another ladylike gesture.

He ramped himself down to a more somber place. "I'm sorry."

"*Now* what are you sorry for?"

"For making you happy, I think."

She cocked her head. "Isn't that a good thing?"

"I'm not so sure. You strike me as someone who stays cheerful pretty much always. And in my opinion, a person needs to wallow around in the sad stuff once in awhile. It's good for what ails ya."

One side of her mouth turned up a little. "Don't worry. I think I've got enough sad to last me for the next year or two."

"Oh, okay. Good." He smiled at her while trying to squeeze his hair back into the tight elastic band.

So now he knew for sure. He hadn't just imagined Cleo's distress. If he were a better friend, he'd ask her directly if she wanted to talk about it. But they'd only known each other for a few months, and most of their conversations had taken place in a large group of people with the entire county listening in. Could you call that a friendship?

Cleo was studying him, not unkindly, but as if she were trying to figure him out. Whether he was trustworthy, he guessed, since she obviously had a secret to tell. Or maybe she was wondering if it would make her feel any better to spill out the contents of her heart to someone she barely knew.

"Jake?"

"Cleo?"

"I'm in kind of a bad way."

"Yeah. I see that." He nodded slowly, wishing he had a handkerchief for the tears beginning their soundless trails down her face. He thought about offering his sweatshirt but decided that was probably gross. "Can I help?"

"I don't know. I don't know if you can. But I really don't know who else to talk to. My girlfriends wouldn't—well, there's just no one. And you always seem so—open."

She looked up for the hundredth time to make sure John Henry was okay. At the moment, the little man was kneeling in the grass, feeding broken lions and bears to a pair of suddenly well-behaved dogs.

"Well, I know I'm not as good as you at sayin' all the right things." He was making a point to look at the tree overhead instead of her sorrow. "But I feel awfully bad for you right now. And if it could help, I'd like to be the one you talk to."

"I'm just not sure. I don't know where to begin. I feel so—I don't know. Scooped out. I'm not sure if I have the energy to tell you everything that's going on."

"Ah, okay, well… you could just say part of it. And then take a rest. I'm not going anywhere."

She looked at him, her puffy lips moving toward a smile.

"I found out something really bad last night. My husband. Jeffrey. He's—" She drew in a deep breath then spent it all on the next two words. "A homosexual."

Jake didn't know what he'd expected to hear, but it wasn't that. Stealing a few seconds, he scratched lightly at the red heart on the Claddagh ring tattooed around his middle finger.

"Oh, no." Not much of a helpful response, but he'd always had a nasty habit of letting his gut start talking before his brain found its gear. There was so much pain ahead for these three people.

"Yes." She was nodding and kept nodding. "I didn't know that about him when I married him. And not for all these years, either. I didn't know how he was."

"Oh, man, Cleo. That's really hard. For all of you."

"No, not for Jeffrey. He's got everything. A wife *and* a—boyfriend!"

It was too much for her, he saw, having to say words like that. *Homosexual. Boyfriend.* She bent over, buried her face in her lap and gripped her knees, crying hard enough to make her head jerk with each mournful sound.

Jake stood up from the bench, bringing the frisbee with him. His back to Cleo, he positioned himself to block her from John Henry's line of sight. He began to toss the frisbee straight up into the air, a few feet at first, then higher and higher until he heard her cries quiet a little then stop altogether.

He turned around to find her digging through the same orange nylon bag from which she'd produced the animal crackers. This time she withdrew a brand new pack of travel-size tissues. One of her hands was committed to opening the slippery package, while the other took swipes at the tears and mucous on her face. Her inability to control even this single humiliating moment in her life seemed like a painting of her whole story.

He gently lifted the clear cellophane pack from her fingers. As he tore along the dotted line, she stared up at him, a drop of water stuck in her thick lashes. He handed her two tissues, which she took gratefully and pressed to her face. She turned from him slightly to perform the indelicate act of blowing her nose in public. He sat back down beside her.

"I. Am. So. Sorry!" she said, still not facing him, sniffing and dabbing at her nose.

"Everybody's always sorry." he said, lightly.

She turned to watch John Henry standing in hog heaven, his arm around a panting Fritos, with Patton stretched out, napping at his feet.

"I can't seem to stop feeling horrible. For John Henry, mostly. That's the worst part, for sure."

"Yeah, I can see why you'd feel that way."

"I mean, we're a family. We *were* a family. But now my baby's going to have to grow up without a daddy, and that's not the promise we made to him."

Her voice was getting higher. Hoarser still.

"But—Jeffrey adores John Henry," said Jake. "Anybody can see that. I'm sure he's gonna continue to be a huge part of the little man's life."

"No, he isn't! That's one promise I can keep." She opened her eyes wide and spoke more strongly than he'd ever heard her speak on any topic. "I'm going to protect my son from that. No matter what, he's going to be safe from that."

"So… you're saying you don't want Jeffrey to see him?"

"I'm saying I told Jeffrey last night that he had to leave the house, which is what he's doing right now. Packing. And that's it for him and

John Henry. That's it. We're better off without a dad than with that kind of dad." She stared into Jake's eyes. "Don't you think?"

He chose not to answer—not that there would have been enough time.

"And what about me? All I've ever been is a wife and mom. I'm not anything else, and Jeffrey knows that. And now he's gone out and gotten a whole 'nother life, and I'm still just the mom. The single mom."

She stopped talking while she folded the tissue into a perfect square, flattening it with her fingertips.

"I told him that making me love him was the meanest thing he could have ever done. Because my love is forever, and now I'm in love with—a gay person. How can that work?"

Jake turned to face her, stretching his arm along the back of the bench. He really couldn't decide whom he felt more sorry for, Cleo or Jeffrey, but he was here with Cleo, now.

"You know," she said, raising her voice, or trying to, but her throat was spent. "I lived all those years with him being who he was and I couldn't tell. What does that say about me? I mean, I knew he was sad—like—he had a story from his past he couldn't tell me about. But I never thought there was something wrong with him."

Jake waited a bit to see if she wanted to take back that last remark, but it didn't seem so.

Cleo touched the outside corner of each eye, checking for tears. "I guess I do feel kind of sorry for him. I hope he comes out of it. But I can't help with that. All I can do is protect John Henry until Jeffrey figures things out. At least I can do that much."

Jake stood up slowly from the seat beside her. Draping his sweatshirt over one shoulder he lowered himself to the ground, onto the cushion of new grass. He leaned back against the bench seat, noticing smells of plant life and dirt.

"You know, Cleo... I'm not saying this isn't a horrible thing to happen to you guys. Obviously, it's bad. Real bad. But I wouldn't say there's something *wrong* with Jeffrey, exactly. I mean—he's still the same great guy he's always been."

He saw Cleo working to tamp her sadness down into something harder. Like anger. At him. Or if it was actually at Jeffrey, Jake was getting in the way.

"I know that lots of people feel like you do, Jake."

Her words had an unfamiliar brittleness.

"And I'm sorry, but you're wrong about this. I know it like I know anything. Gay men put their—they let other guys—" She exhaled exasperation. "Oh, you know what they do. How can you sit here and tell me that that's normal?"

Jake could see he needed to stop talking. Nothing he could say would ever change the ideas built so solidly into Cleo. Everybody came to this Earth with a few beliefs factory-installed, no options allowed. For him, they were:

Outdoors is better than indoors.

Never buy it for twenty bucks if you can make it yourself for a quarter. And,

People should be free to be who they are.

So, that last one of his certainties was getting all tangled up with one of hers. And using words in a situation like this was just throwing rocks against a brick wall. He could see, though, that Cleo was suffering and right now needed more kindness than opinion. They both watched John Henry for awhile.

"I don't even know if Jeffrey has ever had man sex. I asked him last night, and he said he's only kissed. But I don't know if I can believe that. Or anything he says, really. I think that's the hardest part of all this. I knew Jeffrey had some dark feelings he kept private. And that was always okay with me because I thought they were just too painful for him to talk about. But it turns out that he *can* talk about them—just not with me." She had started to cry hard again and was trying to talk at the same time.

"Oh, man, Cleo. Here I am gettin' ya all upset, when what I really wanna do is help you."

She took a couple of deep breaths. "I know that's what you want." She reached into the orange bag for her sunglasses. "But like my mama says, 'God won't give us everything we want, 'cuz if he did, he'd never hear from us at all.'"

Jake spun around in the grass to face her. "Is that what you're worried about? That God won't like who Jeffrey is?"

Looking down at him she blinked hard enough to dislodge one of those eyelash teardrops. "God?" She gave this some thought. "No. I don't know if God cares about stuff like this. I mean, he's the one who made Jeffery this way."

"Oh." Jake pulled up a blade of grass and gripped the root end with his front teeth as he spoke. "What do you think God cares about, then?"

"I think… God's main thing is—he just wants you to love everybody, no matter what."

Jake nodded. "Yeah. That sounds about right."

Cleo let go of a sigh that sounded like it had been up all night looking for a way out.

"Not that you should take any advice from me," said Jake. "But advice from God—that seems like a good way to go." He shut one eye for a moment. "So… maybe this is how you might get your head to the right place when you talk to Jeffrey. When you see him, you could just try to remind yourself: Love everybody, no matter what."

Her shoulders shuddered as her body emptied itself of another sigh—which became the first downward movement of a slow, painfully, torturously slow nod.

"I dunno. Maybe."

She held a Kleenex with her fingertips, executing the most ladylike nose blow he'd ever seen, then hid the tissue neatly away in the orange bag.

Another part of a nod. "Maybe, I guess. Love everybody, no matter what. Huh." Her hoarse voice was hoarser still. "Y'know, come to think of it… I bet God's pretty pleased with Jeffrey right about now—since that man seems to love all *sorts* of people."

Jake shot a look up at her face and saw it was okay to laugh. Which he did. Not too much, but just until her swollen lips formed a small smile. He leaned back onto straight arms, grass between his fingers, and tilted his head up into the sun, or toward God, or whatever it was that made him lucky enough to feel pretty darn good on most days.

31

THE VERY FIRST BUNGEE JUMP
– by Anna Dunlop

A dare? A rubber research trial?
A suicide dry run?
What man lived life in such denial
a cliff jump looked like fun?
Who lashed his ankle to a rope
expecting it to work,
then plunged while clinging to the hope:
to feel—not BE—the jerk?

Curled up in a 1960s webbed lawn chair in her back yard, Anna sat by the blackish-blue river, a thick spiral notebook on her knees, pen in hand. She read and reread verse that hadn't changed for over half an hour.

Letting her brain stop trying so hard, she stared deep into the lined paper. She forced her wrist to move, to get ink flowing to the page. A circle appeared, becoming a wagon wheel, each spoke aligned precisely with a counterpart on the other side of the hub, perfectly spaced from one another. She drew a box, then inserted ten smaller and smaller concentric boxes. And below that, the word *Tony*. She stopped.

Even in her poor handwriting, there was beauty in the collection of letters. She felt their kindness. Their understanding. Their need to make her happy. And then she knew. He was here. With her. She could smell the sun on his skin. Feel his warm hand on the back of her neck. Hear his whisper, his constant reassurance that he'd felt adored by her always, in a way that words could never have expressed. And his wish for her was that she could let go of her worry.

She didn't want to move, or even speak, his presence there so gossamer.

With only the tips of her fingers she pushed the pen to inscribe the words. *I'm so sorry. I LOVE YOU, TONY, LOVE YOU, HAVE ALWAYS, WILL ALWAYS LOVE YOU.*

She closed her eyes, trying to hold onto the sense of him, but as usual, felt him slipping away in less than a minute.

He would stay only long enough to pick up as much of her sadness as he could lift and carry off.

32

"This might be some kind of record." Eddy grunted. "Earliest we've ever gotten it out, isn't it? Uhf!"

He dropped the four twenty-pound sandbags onto the riverbank, almost falling down on top of them. Straight-legged, he bent from the waist, touching his fingers to the scrub grass, stretching his back.

"What is it? May twenty-seventh?" asked Anna. "Yeah, maybe the earliest. But it's stinkin' hot out already. And when I get hot, I get cranky."

"Gosh, really?"

"You know, you don't have to carry those things four at a time. I'm well aware of how big and strong you are. You can stop trying to impress me with your burly man-self."

"Now ya tell me." He shook both arms from the shoulders down. "Does this mean I can stop watching Monday Night Football, too? 'Cuz I hate football."

She walked past him, carrying her own cumbersome load. In her hands she gripped a dark green plastic patio table, and around her waist she'd tied a mesh bag full of bottled beer. Without breaking stride she headed out into the water.

"Whee! Refreshing."

As Eddy watched the Milk River rush past her strong, freckled legs, he tried to remember if the Water Table had been his idea or hers. They'd been in sixth grade, he was sure of that, because it was Mr. Radke who'd said that launching the invention seemed like way too much effort for not enough fun. But Eddy and Anna had always been willing to trade effort for fun. Back in those days and still in these.

Anna worked the legs of the table down through the rocks, the water coming within about three inches of the tabletop. The water level would drop lower at times during the summer but rarely rose higher at this part of the river behind Anna's house.

Eddy tightened his sandal straps and waded in with two of the sandbags, placing his feet carefully, but still slipping constantly on the slick rocks that Anna seemed to glide over without a care. Half woman, half water nymph.

But they both paled in comparison to Storm, whose agility in the water seemed impossible. Even Anna couldn't run over the rocks without twisting an ankle. The dog, on the other hand, never walked. She ran or swam, depending on the depth. The white German shepherd darted in between Anna and Eddy with the ever-present stick in her mouth, begging for someone to please-oh-please give it a toss. The problem was, Eddy was busy at the moment trying to stay upright, and the dog had no concept of *once*. She knew only *throw* and *throw again.* It never stopped surprising Eddy that running for a stick could be so entertaining. And apparently, swimming for a stick against the full force of the river could be even more entertaining. If you asked him, it seemed like a whole lot of effort for not enough fun.

Eddy set both sandbags on the tabletop and steadied himself in position. He used his foot to search for the PVC pipes they'd installed as crossbars between the legs, several inches from the bottom of the table. Bending over with his chin close to the water's surface, he draped the first bag over a bar, pushing it down until he was sure it couldn't go anywhere. The river was shallow here, but it ran fast. Then, with one hand on the tabletop, he stumbled and sloshed his way around to the opposite side, where he secured that part of the table with the second sandbag.

On his way back to shore for more weights, he passed Anna, traveling the opposite direction at twice his speed, flaunting two yellow plastic chairs similarly outfitted with PVC crossbars. Marveling at her surefootedness, Eddy got distracted and lost his own. He went down backside first. Most of the way down, anyway. But with catlike reflexes, he reached out to catch himself on a boulder, springing up again with a dexterity that surprised him. But not before soaking everything up to his armpits. Sheepishly, cautiously, he rotated himself to see if she'd noticed, but Anna was hard at work, shoving chairs down into the rocky riverbed.

Oddly, his next trip out with more sandbags came and went with no comment from her, even though his tan T-shirt and charcoal shorts had become brown and black respectively. Granted, the activity of the day was to sit in the river with the intention of becoming completely drenched, but only on chairs, and only on purpose. It was unlike his friend to exhibit such verbal restraint.

It wasn't until they'd tied the lunch cooler to the table and the beer bag to a chair that the subject finally came up.

"Okay. I think we've got everything," she said, rubbing her hands together. "You ready to sit down? Again?"

Eddy grinned.

"You know, for a guy born on an island, you're kind of a klutz in the water."

"My people are salt water people, yeah? We require more buoyancy than you *haoles*."

"I see. But next time try to go all the way under. That hat could use a rinse."

Eddy took off his favorite ball cap, the one she'd given him, and studied it as he liked to do. The embroidered insignia had frayed over the years, but he could still make out the veterinary symbol; the rod and its entwining snake, behind the letter V. The hat itself had been white once upon a time but now bore smudges of memories too dear to erase: grease from the underside of his rebuilt Plymouth Duster, mud from sliding into third the only time they'd ever beaten the Burger Boy Beefeaters, and though he had no idea how it had gotten there, yellow mustard from the backyard party at Anna's house where she'd finally revealed unto him the secret behind The Dunlop family barbeque sauce.

He'd started begging her mom for the recipe way back when he and Anna were still in high school, but absolutely no mercy had been shown him. And when Anna became old enough to cook, she herself had carried on the proud Dunlop tradition of denying him the information. But one magical night, about a year ago, she'd taken pity on him and given in. He couldn't remember what precise combination of words he had used to convince her, which was too bad, because it would serve him well to know how to talk Anna out of something she'd set her mind to. Anyway, there was, indeed, a secret ingredient to the barbeque sauce. Instant coffee. Who woulda thunk?

He resituated his cap on his head, and they both seated themselves at the Water Table. He, warily. They sat in line with the river's flow, with Eddy's back facing upstream so Anna could see the water coming straight at her. It was their custom to switch sides every hour or so, meaning Eddy would have his turn next.

The depth of the water hid their bodies up to their chests. But the river would splash higher with any sudden movement or on an impish impulse from either party to purposely douse the other. Buoyed by the river and the company, they felt light on their chairs and spent the regulation amount of time oo-ing and ahh-ing over how great it felt to sit out in the river's middle again, where most people only swam and then left.

It was time to play.

"Well? Should we begin the beguine?" he asked, not entirely sure what a beguine was, but he liked the old big band tune of that name.

"Yeah. Do you have the cards?"

Eddy felt his face fall from elated, down through pensive, on its way to troubled.

"Eddyyy…? What did you do with the cards I gave you?"

He slouched in his chair, straightening his legs to fish around in his shorts pocket. He brought the pack of cards up slowly from under the water, watching with worried fascination as a quarter cup of the Milk River spilled from the disintegrating box.

Anna folded her arms across her chest. "Oh, perfect."

"Wait a minute." He cocked his head at her. "You're just pretending to look upset. Like one of us is going to have to go all the way back to the house and get another pack of cards."

"One of us? I can solve that little mystery for you right now if you'd like."

"But I know you, Anna. You've got another pack somewhere, just in case. You never do anything without a backup plan."

"I do not have another deck of cards on me! And what do you mean, I always have a backup plan?"

"Well, let's see." He counted the list on his fingers. "One. When you're asked to bring dessert to a party, you always bring at least three of them. In case somebody is allergic to nuts. Or gets migraines from chocolate. Or can't do dairy. Two. In the dog yard at the clinic, you actually installed a second fence around the perimeter of your first fence in case someone left a gate open accidentally. Which isn't very likely, by the way, since you drive Katie, Noah, and Brian insane, asking them if they've closed it every time they come inside."

"Well, I worry an animal might run away and get hurt."

"Uh-huh. Back up plan. I'm waiting for you to start digging a moat around the place."

"Ooooh, how much would that cost?"

"And three. I know for a fact that this has been true, ever since you were a kid. The first thing you do when you get into a car is memorize how the seatbelt releases. Where's the button? Do you push it from the top? Is it the kind where you have to squeeze both sides? You're getting ready, just in case you have an accident and have to unhook yourself in a panic. Even in your own truck, to this day, I still see you fondling the buckle. Practicing."

"One button. From the side."

"I rest my case."

"A very elaborate argument, Counselor, all to deflect the fact that you've totally ruined our cards."

"No. What I've done is prove that you have another deck on your person somewhere. Now please bring it out so I can whoop your wet patooty at the game of your choosing."

She exhaled in exasperation, pushed herself up from her chair and used a dramatic swoop of her arms to indicate her wardrobe: a tank top and cotton running shorts. No pockets.

"And just where would I hide them?"

But—he'd been so sure.

She took the soggy pack from his hand and squeezed, sending water shooting from the box. She had that, *Oh, you darn kid*, look on her face. The reality was beginning to sink in. Anna Dunlop had actually neglected to plan for all possible outcomes. He was going to have to haul his waterlogged body out of this river to go get some other cards. And just maybe this was too much effort for not enough fun, after all.

By the time he'd brought his attention back to real time, it was to see Anna enthusiastically shuffling a deck of cards, forward then backward. Smiling, she gave the edge of the deck two sharp raps on the dark green tabletop before slapping it down in front of him to cut. He stared at her, open-mouthed.

"Two words." And she enunciated them both with far more lip movement than necessary. "Plastic. Coated."

Though they loved cards of all kinds, they generally gravitated toward a game they'd evolved in their early twenties. A two-person version of Five Hundred, but not as Hoyle had defined it. Instead, they'd devised a way to play the game with two dummy hands that became fake partners. They had named the game simply *Cards*, with a capital C.

A couple of St. Pauli Girls were opened, four hands were dealt onto the Water Table, and very little conversation ensued for half an hour or so, save the occasional bid and the intermittent expletive or sassy remark. When the dialogue began again, neither of them was aware it had ever stopped.

"I'll tell you who's worse in the water than you are," she said, trumping Eddy's ace.

"Oh, jeez! You've still got trump? I musta counted wrong. And I'm not bad in the water."

"Brian Ardeen."

"Really?"

"He's scared to death of it."

"That's kinda sad. But I gotta say, I think it's neat that he's opening up to you about personal things like that. Sounds like progress."

"Only in spurts. That fear of water thing just happened to come up while he was telling us a story about beating the crap out of some sophomore when he was in eighth grade. Apparently, the older kid had tortured Ardeen by giving him a swirlie, and this was his payback."

"What's a swirlie, again? I know I've heard of it."

"Clearly, you've never gotten one. Somebody pushes your head underwater in the toilet and then flushes it."

"Whoa. Scary *and* gross."

"Yeah, I guess Ardeen thought he was going to drown and really freaked out. He's been afraid of water ever since and hasn't been swimming since fifth grade. Isn't that weird to think about, though, never going swimming? When there's a river in your town?

"Yeah. But fifth grade? I thought you said he was in eighth when he beat the kid up."

"Oh, I left out the best part. After the swirlie in fifth grade, he started to work out—with the specific intent of bulking up so he could take revenge on that older kid, which he did, three years later."

"Wow. Sounds like Brian can really hold a grudge. I'm not sure how to react to that story, so I'm gonna change the subject. Sort of. How has he been doing? I haven't heard much about him for a couple weeks." Eddy was tallying the score of the hand she'd just won.

"I don't know. He still bugs the crap out of me, but I guess it's going a little better than I'd thought it would. He's not complaining as much anymore. And I hate to say it, but he's not entirely stupid."

"High praise."

"And I've actually caught him going out of his way a few times to make an animal comfortable. Without being told to, I mean." Anna fanned out the cards she'd just been dealt.

"Hey, that's great. Do you think you're getting through?"

Eddy noticed that even after three full months of working with Brian, every time she talked about him, her whole tone of voice would change. Each word—like a check to the IRS or a dash over hot sand at the beach—was endured but unpleasant.

"Do I think I'm getting through? I don't know. I doubt it. Maybe. I don't know. We had a cat in last week who needed observation for a couple of days, and she was really miserable in her kennel. She'd cower in the back the whole time, shaking. And I know for a fact that at least twice Ardeen went in to play with her on his own free time."

"Yeah?"

"He even built a toy for her out of a roll of gauze and a fecal container."

"That does sound fun."

"But then he turns around and does what he did on Friday morning. He was watching me examine this sweet female husky. Thirteen years old, with bad arthritis. The woman who brought the old girl in was devastated. Trying not to cry, she asked me how long it would be until she'd need to put her dog down. And from behind me I hear, 'Christ, it can barely walk. How 'bout now?'"

"Oh, boy."

"What am I supposed to do with that? What I want to do is kick him out of the exam room. All exam rooms, forever. But if he doesn't observe the work, then he's not getting the exposure that's going to miraculously turn him into this bleeding-heart animal lover I'm waiting for."

"So what did you do?"

"I decided to make it a teaching moment and forced him to try a little of your *menemene*, y' know? I kept my voice calm, and said, 'Brian, if you had arthritis and could still get around, but only slowly, would you want someone to euthanize you?' To which he said, 'But it's a dog. And I ain't a dog.' And that's when I told him something I've had to tell him about once every week or so. I said, 'Yes, he's a dog. But dogs are a lot like people. Except they're not as mean.'"

"And he said?"

"He didn't really answer. I like to pretend he spends those gloomy silences absorbing my great wisdom."

Eddy laughed but then groaned as she took his highest trump with her joker.

"Honestly, I want to believe he's getting it. At least a little bit. But really, how do you measure such a thing? I don't trust him as far as I can throw him, I know that. And his two loser friends were in again yesterday. By the way, their names are Bo and Toot. Bo and Toot! Are those names or body sounds?"

"Five hearts. Whoa!" said Eddy, jumping as a fish shot between his feet.

"I've trained the trout to keep you off your game," she said, taking a second to look at the cards she'd been dealt. "You're going down again. Seven spades."

"Oh, man." He slid her the blind.

"And I'm telling you, that Bo guy is a nut job. Toot is a total doofus, but Bo—he's seriously criminal. Which is another reason I can't let my guard down with Ardeen. You can tell a lot about a person by his friends."

"I don't get it. Why do they come to the clinic? What do they do there?"

"They just hang around in the waiting room until he's free to talk to them on his break. And then they leave. I have no idea what they're up to."

"Up to? Maybe they just think it's a cool place. Or they're just giving him moral support."

"Eddy, I wish you could meet them. Even you, the man who loves everybody, would have a tough time with these guys." She held her next card high in the air, communicating that it didn't matter what he played; she was about to take it.

"I'm not loving everybody at this exact moment." He saw he was about to get skunked again.

Eddy got a kick out of how, every ten minutes or so, Storm would circle them, swimming, still holding her stick in her mouth in case someone might want to throw it.

"You can really see that peachy color on her back when she's wet," he said, watching the shepherd pull herself out of the water, give her coat a good shake, and lie on the grass. "She doesn't look so much like a white dog out here."

"Yeah, I'm not sure why. It's so subtle when she's dry. I think they call it cream, by the way. Not peach."

"Cream, peach. That reminds me. I'm hungry. What kind of sandwiches did you make?" He tipped his head in the direction of the cooler. "Please tell me there's something in there besides tofu and wheat sprouts."

Anna brought one leg up, resting her bare heel on the edge of the weathered Adirondack chair. She glanced in Storm's direction when the dog sighed heavily, her head and front paws overhanging the top porch step in one of her favorite napping positions.

The rural Wisconsin quiet (that Anna never tired of) had yet to give way to the evening's frog song. So with nothing to hear and a wall of blackness beyond the porch, her mind had room to paint freely. She tilted her head back against the chair and closed her eyes. The day had been filled with all of her favorite things. The river. The sun. The Water Table. Not just *some* cards, but Cards. A cuddly dog. And Eddy.

Jeez. Eddy. She'd been leaning heavily into his friendship lately. She'd ring him up at odd hours wanting comfort, counsel, or conversation. And without fail he would sound happy to hear from her. She had to wonder what amazingly selfless act she'd committed in a past life to have earned such a loving companion in this one. Eddy was her keeper of old private jokes and her co-creator of new ones. He was her mentor, her sidekick, her confidant.

She played all of those roles for him, too, of course, but lacking the altruism that came so naturally to Eddy, she worried that she shorted him a bit.

And then her mind flitted to another question. Being in Eddy's company had felt effortless since they were kids—but had it always been as restorative as it seemed to her now?

Today, during her morning ritual of dark roast coffee and murky thought, she'd begun feeling a bit sorry for herself. Her veterinary practice had burgeoned as a result of an ever-growing number of people tuning in to the radio program. And the increased income was a relief. But it also meant working nights and weekends just to keep up. So as she'd sat at the kitchen table this morning, waiting for the sun to show her the river, she'd brooded about having to schlep into town to order more cat laxative and doggie de-wormer, when the rest of the world nestled deeply in predawn bedrooms, hearing the Sunday paper softly thump against the front door.

But then she had remembered. Her day. The reason she'd had to rise so absurdly early in the first place. She'd made late morning plans with Eddy, and he'd be there in a few hours.

This cheeriest of thoughts had brought her straight to her feet. She mixed two cups of kibble with a tablespoon of yogurt, chirruped *Enjoy your brekkies!* to Storm, snatched her steaming mug, and hummed her way off to shower up. The simple notion of playtime with Eddy had done for her what an hour of slumping over a bucket of Italian Roast had failed to.

Lately she'd found herself wishing for his company more and more often. In his Eddy-like thoughtfulness, seeming to sense her emotional void, he had moved in to fill it. She made a mental note to be careful not to impose on him and his many kindnesses.

Where would her life be right now if Eddy hadn't been in it? Could she have survived these past five-and-a-half years? She thought back on that first year after watching Tony die. If she hadn't had her friendship with Eddy—something solid to tether herself to—she would have wiggled out from under this mortal coil and drifted up and away.

She knew precisely when it would have happened. Not immediately following Tony's death, when she'd had the numbing shock to protect her from the realness. And not during the next few months, when people had buzzed around her, wanting to help, wanting to keep her talking. Her demise, were it to have taken place, would have happened between the fourth and seventh month following her husband's death.

During the roughly ninety-day period, she had, for some reason, been granted mental access to her biological ON-OFF button. She could have given her body permission to go, and it would have gone. She had been able to *feel* how to do it. Similar to the decision she made every night to let herself drop off to sleep, she could have decided to drop off forever. No overt action required. No pills, no razorblades. A simple system shutdown, which somehow she'd been aware would not have happened instantly with a theatrical collapse to the floor. Rather, it would have taken shape as a steep and steady physical depletion over the course of the next few months.

Looking back on it now, the oddest thing about this life force power button had been how entirely inborn the knowledge had felt. As if she'd had the ability to shut herself down all along but hadn't looked behind the right door in her mind to find the switch.

She'd wondered at the time what the doctors would have diagnosed as cause of death. Only the most spiritually aware physician would have called it for what it was. A suicide. How would her death certificate have read? Inexplicable organ failure? A rare blood condition with an unknown cause?

And to this day she had no idea why she had made the choice to live. If she'd succumbed to the unrelenting heaviness pulling on her, she would have been allowed to join Tony and not been trapped here without him. To *stop continuing* at that point would have been the easier path. Staying here had been the chore.

Once Tony had died, there'd been no single thing that had kept her among the living. She hadn't stayed for Eddy. Not for her mom. Certainly not for her job. It had been the sum of all the parts of her remaining existence that had outweighed the alternative. The grand total of good things had added up to a number high enough to keep the Life/Death Balance Sheet tilting in the direction it always had. And so she had stayed.

But what if she hadn't had her long history with Eddy to bolster her? How many life units was such a friendship worth? If the critical Eddy factor had been removed from her life/death tracking form, would the delicate balance have shifted, favoring the opposite column, shunting her toward the other fate?

On a regular basis during those months, when she'd wobble over the pencil-thin line between here and there, she would consciously ask herself the question. *Should I just go?* Each time she had decided to stay because she assumed she could pull the plug at some time down the road if things got worse. And after awhile, she found herself asking the stay-or-go question more infrequently, still considering her choice carefully before deciding to hang on a little longer. Then one spring day—and she could remember exactly where she was standing—she posed herself the now familiar question, and she was alarmed to realize that the window had been closed. And locked.

The knowledge of how to slip down the celestial drain had been snatched away after about three months of disuse. Perhaps because she'd crawled far enough out of her depression to fire up the brain function necessary to restore her self-preservation mode. She wasn't sure. But she was sure of this: if she wanted to die now it would require active endeavor, not mere surrender. She remembered feeling cheated back then. If she'd known the opportunity clock had been ticking down, she would have felt more urgency to decide one way or the other and might well have chosen to relax herself into the ebbing organic tide.

Certainly this was why older couples died within months of each other. Less ambivalent than Anna, with a balance sheet so bereft of positives it nearly toppled to one side, the surviving partner made a concrete choice. To act before the chance to act was lost.

Anna took a sip of Bailey's and then wrapped both hands around the Flintstones jelly glass to warm it. The creamy liqueur was Eddy's favorite, and he preferred it cold, so she made a point to keep the bottle in the refrigerator. Anna's inclination, on the other hand, would be to pour it over ice cream, which Eddy would consider disrespectful. He was so funny, Eddy. A simple person in the best sense of the word. It was on her top ten list of traits she loved most about him.

Extending Eddy the smallest consideration (like a surprise after-dinner Bailey's) felt like a gift for *her*, because realizing his good fortune, Eddy would respond in a particular voice he had—a warm, verbal hug of a voice. Originating from deep in his most earnest place, the words came to her in his lower register, softly, and held just a hint of the Hawaiian accent he'd been taunted into giving up as a grade schooler. Like running in flip-flops, and tiny wax bottles of colored sugar water, Eddy's musical accent filled her with the joy and loss inherent in all sweet childhood memories.

And just how many of those memories had taken place right here on this old front porch? Where friends and family had splayed themselves out to cool down on hot afternoons and huddled close together when days were stormy. Made of ancient, unpainted wood with its velvet patina, the porch was open to the elements on three of its four sides, but enchanted by an odd geological phenomenon. When rain-like-wild-ponies pounded the earth, and wind blew—in however many directions wind could take—no one within the cocoon of this wraparound shelter had ever gotten wet. Not in Anna's full forty years, nor presumably, in the years before that. Except, of course, on purpose, when she and other daring kids over the past eleven decades had darted out to feel tiny hooves pelting their bodies for a few brave seconds.

The screen door opened, and out came Eddy carrying his faded gym bag. He looked perfect to her. The sun today had deepened the rich brown of his skin, and there was a vulnerability to his face when he got sleepy that always made her smile.

"Thanks for letting me dry my other clothes. You're almost out of dryer sheets."

"'Kay. Thanks."

"I should get goin', yeah?"

"Eddy, wait. Turn off the porch lights for a second."

Without questioning, Eddy leaned back through the doorway to flick off both switches. No stranger to the blackest black of Wisconsin nights, he weaved his way without incident through wooden side tables, flower pots, and wind chimes to stand beside her chair.

"Look toward the woods." She spoke in the hushed tone nighttime asked for.

The first frogs were ramping up, but no one else spoke for about half a minute, until Eddy's revelation.

"Lightning bugs!"

"Isn't that great? I thought I'd seen one last night but wasn't sure. Tonight there are tons of them. Hey, sit down for a minute, can you?"

Without bothering to turn on the lights, he moved around her, slipping into the other Adirondack as smoothly as if he could see it. She inhaled his smells of soap and river water, two of her favorites.

"What's up, Buttercup?"

Clearly, his mind was in a less pensive place than her own.

"Oh, here." She fumbled for his Bailey's. "Give me your hand."

Eddy touched her arm. She put the juice glass into his broad palm, pushing his fingers around it. This amount of intimacy had been common in their relationship forever, but tonight the touch of his hand felt different on her skin. Her body had come to alert.

"What's this?"

She heard him sniff. She waited.

"Oh, Anna."

It was the Hawaiian voice hug she'd been hoping for.

"You're too good to me."

They watched the fireflies turn off and on. Some white. Some greenish. She had finished her drink and was considering running her tongue around the inside of the glass when he spoke again.

"Did you know that there's a kind of firefly, where the female sits in the grass flashing her light to attract a mate, but she's imitating the flash of some other species? It's a trick, yeah? And when the male flies down to mate with her, she eats him."

Anna's first thought was a continuation of her last several minutes of thinking—that she was lucky to have this extraordinary person in her life. "No, I didn't know that. I used to think lightning bugs were just cool. Now I'm a little scared. I mean, what else could they be planning?"

"I'm trying to remember the species. Oh—it's the Femme Fatale."

Like a quick kick to the shins for enjoying herself too much, Eddy's words brought thoughts of Tony front and center. Femme Fatale had been the title of one of her poems that he had so lovingly put to music. The song was about the difference between women and men: how only women tortured themselves by plucking their hair, waxing their skin, and cramming their feet into pointed, high-heel shoes.

We do it. We're Femme Fatale. Just Mary. Not Peter. Or Paul.
We do it. We're Femme Fatale. Not Desi. But Lucille Ball.

It had been a gentle kick, though. A warning blow. As was the norm, the farther down the calendar she moved from the anniversary of Tony's death, the lesser the pain of each recollection. She did, however, experience her familiar twinge of guilt for never having confessed to Eddy her hobby of writing those idiotic poems. Tony had been the one person she'd ever shared her secret with.

As the gentle blinking of green and white lights filled the space around them, Anna found herself wondering if she should write a poem about that trickster firefly. She could call it "Lightning Bug Love."

"I should really get going," said Eddy, standing up. "And you should go to bed. We've got a show to do tomorrow, you know."

She rose too, and in the dark they completed the intricate maneuver of passing the small, empty glass from his hand to hers.

Stretching, he said, "Ho, brah! What a day! I think we squeezed about everything there was to squeeze out of it, yeah?"

"Indeed."

Anna was distracted. Not sure why she wanted him to stay so badly, she resisted the urge to request it.

Eddy used his arms—not his voice—to hug her goodbye, picked up his bag, and stepped off the porch. She listened to his fading steps crunching gravel until they came to a stop by his car. Opening the door brought the dome light on, a small white glow in the distance. If she only had a flashlight. She would click it on and off at him, knowing he'd get the firefly joke, that she was trying to trick him into coming back.

It would be mostly a joke, anyway.

33

"*Plastic. Coated.* She said it just like that." Eddy laughed as he spoke. A contagious, bubbling laugh. "Funny, yeah?"

He looked through the studio window out at Anna in the hallway, who was smiling but shaking her head. He knew he'd pay dearly for his decision to tell that particular story on the air, since she preferred not to have her personal life broadcast over the radio. But since so many parts of her life overlapped with parts of his, especially lately, if he couldn't talk about Anna, he might not be able to talk at all.

"So, what I learned from my humbling experience out on the water was that plastic coated cards can take a fair amount of liquid abuse and still work just fine. At least they worked pretty well for Anna. I, on the other hand, lost every single game.

"Okay, I only have one final entry on *The Things I Learned This Weekend,* and then we'll get right to what I'd say most of you are wishing I'd, please, just get to. Your chance to catch up on the lives of our five hopelessly happy canines and the people who love them. And by that, I mean the next installment of our serial drama: *Days of Our Dogs.* I mean, in some ways it's evolved into a bit of a soap opera, hasn't it? With characters we've come to know and root for. And cliffhangers, too: *Will the twins, Rain and Snow, ever recover from their mysterious amnesia and remember that garbage is called garbage because it's not food? Is there truth to the rumor that Fritos has mastered the pole vault?*

"One tiny plot problem, though, keeps our show from reaching true soap opera status. Everybody in the cast of characters is way too wholesome. There's no villain committing dastardly deeds. But hey, it's early today yet. Let's see what happens.

"I'm talking, of course, about our segment coming up at eight o'clock, called *All of Us Animals*, with that veterinarian card shark Dr. Anna Dunlop. Most weeks it's a call-in show to answer your questions about the animals in your lives. But on the first Monday of every month, we check in with the adopters of those abused puppies who are now, unbelievably, seven months old. Not very puppy-like anymore, they've hit that gangly adolescent stage.

"But in these last few minutes before eight, I'd like to tell you something important about my Saturday. And for those of you who dislike it when I talk about the part of my life I guess you'd have to call spiritual, I'm sorry. But I'll try to keep it short.

"I've read a lot of books written by people who, in my opinion, demonstrate pretty remarkable psychic abilities. You know who they are 'cuz you see them on TV, and either you believe they could be legit, or you're positive they're scamming you. And trust me, I know that lots of dishonest actors work the phone lines pretending to be psychic, stealing your hard-earned take-home pay at two bucks a minute.

"But as most of you know about me, I believe there are trustworthy people out there, too. People who use more of the human psychological potential than most of us allow ourselves. I firmly believe we're all capable of communication on a bunch of levels we could tap into, but we don't, 'cuz we've been told our whole lives that it isn't possible.

"I can say this with some conviction, because I've personally had enough extrasensory moments in my unperfected life to know that even a schlump like me can be communicated to through media even more magical than Twitter. Across town, across country, and even across the boundary between the here-and-now and the hereafter, if the wind blows just the right way. Or if I can sit still long enough to listen.

"I know it's tough for a lot of people to accept the notion of hearing from those who have passed on to the Great Next. So I'm going to go ahead and gloss right over that particular idea today. But as an aside, if you ever want to hear the things my tutu has told me since she died, give me a call. She's only poked her head into my clay foot world a few times so far, and only when I've really, really needed her to. But I'm hear to tell ya, it has definitely happened. And I was wide awake. And not under the influence of any mind-altering substance, unless you think SnoCaps count. I know I'm about the only weirdo who actually eats those tiny chocolate buttons with the white sprinkle topping, but I seem to keep the company in business. Anyway, back to what I learned this weekend, yeah?

"There seems to be a consensus among experts of the psychic persuasion that it's entirely possible for any of us to sense when certain people are thinking about us, if we just open our minds to it. And like playing the banjo, or making a flaky pie crust, or parallel parking, if we practice this skill, we can get pretty good at it.

"So here's the exercise. If you're going about your daily whatevers, and the thought of someone you know randomly pops into your head—stop for a moment. Quick! Try to trace the thought back. Where did it come from? What made you think about old Uncle Irving all of a sudden? Was it because you happened to be looking at your brand new box of SnoCaps, which reminded you of how your third grade teacher, Mrs. Benassi, loved SnoCaps? And then thinking about Mrs. Benassi you remembered how embarrassing it was that Uncle Irving was so sweet on her, that whenever he saw you, he'd ask you to describe what she was wearing that day? Or did Uncle Irving just jump into your consciousness totally uninvited, with no reason you can trace back to? If that's the case, you're supposed to pick up the phone and give old Uncle Irv a call to ask him why he was just thinking about you. He'll think you're some kind of psychic, which of course you are.

"I've been practicing this little exercise from time to time. And having what I might consider modest success. So, I decided to give it a whirl again on Saturday night, because I knew I was in the right mood to be receptive to such things. Y' see, I've found that when I'm in a particularly creative mood, feeling like I want to drag out the watercolors or head down to the metal shop, I seem to be more capable of other mental stuff, too.

"So there I was on my walk home from the station Saturday night and feeling kind of inspired. And instead of pursuing one of my few artistic outlets, which I'm not very good at anyway, I thought I should take the time to exercise my otherworldliness."

Eddy glanced out at Anna again, maybe for the encouragement to share something so personal, which she gave him with her whole, sunshine face. For a fraction of a second, her presence derailed him. Had he ever felt so cherished from a whole room away? Her friendship was—oxygen.

"I stopped walking and sat down on that bench in front of the diner. Mom's Kitchen, yeah? I got myself all comfy and closed my eyes. I tried to think of nothing, which by the way, is kinda hard for me, 'cuz I spend most of my time trying to think of everything. But after awhile, thoughts of certain people started trickling in. I ended up sitting there for about forty-five minutes, I guess, and a whole slew of people made appearances. Almost everybody, though, I could trace back, using the well-known SnoCaps method. Except for three people. One was Anna. Dr. Dunlop, yeah? Another was Ben Steener. Big Benny, my brah who works over there at the Napa store in Cumberland. And the third person I couldn't trace back was a guy whose name I didn't even know. The likable young man who rides on the outside of the garbage truck from Murphy's Sanitation when they come to get my trash. Tall guy. Blonde, movie star hair. Anybody on my route knows exactly who I mean.

"So. Sitting there on that bench, I took the pen from my pocket and wrote down those three untraceable names. Anna, Benny, and Blonde Guy. Wrote them right on the back of a gas station receipt I had in my pocket. Hey, I just realized I've got that same hoodie here today. Hang on a sec, I'll get it."

Eddy removed his headset and left his post. He opened the small metal cabinet close to the studio door. Reaching into the front pocket of his black hooded sweatshirt he pulled out a white rectangle of paper covered in scribbles. He waved it at the many creatures out in the hall who were waiting to pack into his studio. Bunny and Jake waved back, Russ eyed him suspiciously. Anna didn't look up at all, since she was holding Storm's leash, watching John Henry hang from the dog's white, furry neck.

Eddy, in no particular rush, made his way back to once again fill the airwaves under his care.

"Yup. Says it right here. Anna, Benny, Blonde Guy. Proof! Anyway, so I walked the rest of the way home, stopping at the store, 'cuz I needed milk. I've decided to eat a little healthier, yeah? Thought it might be good to switch to skim milk on my Lucky Charms in the morning." He chuckled.

"When I finally got to my house, I did all the usual stuff. Put away the milk, looked through the mail, popped some leftover grilled chicken into the microwave. And eventually, I got around to listening to my phone messages. I had two. One from Anna and one from Big Ben. Both of those people had called me some time between when I left work and when I got home. I'm tellin' ya, I was so shocked, I had to sit down.

"I know what you're thinking. *So what? They're friends of yours!* And Anna, okay, yes. But Big Benny? Last I heard from him was when he wrote in to the station here, six or seven months ago, wondering if working double shifts to buy himself a motorcycle was a good idea. Remember that? No contact since. And then all of a sudden, the night I write his name down, he happens to call? It's at least intriguing, isn't it?

"But okay. That might not be amazing enough for you hardboiled skeptics out there. And being skeptical about this stuff is a good idea, by the way. But this morning was garbage day at my house and Murphy's comes early. I heard the truck and ran outside. And here's where I need to apologize to my neighbors. With what I wasn't quite fully wearing yet,

I'm afraid I made a bit of a spectacle out there. Hey, I just used *skeptical* and *spectacle* in the same story. Skeptical-spectacle. Skeptical-spectacle. Ha!

"I did create a spectacle, though. Here it is, six a.m., and out of the darkened house bolts this big Hawaiian guy, barefoot, zipping up his pants, open shirt flapping in the wind, bellowing at the garbage truck to, 'Wait! Wait!' And when I get up to the truck, totally out of breath, the first thing I blurt out to the handsome young man is, 'Were you thinking about me Saturday night?'"

Eddy paused, not for dramatic effect, but to luxuriate in the memory of the moment.

"I wish I had the right words to paint you the picture of his face when I asked him that question. His name is Josh, by the way. We had a very nice talk, Josh and I, after I buttoned up my shirt and stopped foaming at the mouth. It was toothpaste, technically. I explained my odd little question, and though he seemed more inclined to toss it off as simple coincidence, Josh said he was pretty sure it was indeed Saturday night when he'd been thinking about me for several minutes. He'd been considering asking me about the scrap metal sculpture in my front yard. If you don't know, I have a big metal rooster out there. Seems Josh is interested in making something like that for his dad, since he's got access to a lot of junk metal, and he's pretty good with his hands. So on the very same night I was writing the name *Blonde Guy* on this receipt, he was thinking about asking me how to make a rooster. Do with that information what you will.

"Anyhoo. That's what I learned Saturday night."

Eddy and Anna exchanged meaningful looks through the glass. He knew that a lot of his listeners were right now poo-pooing his mystic leanings, but Anna was a believer. She hadn't been at all surprised when he'd called her that night to tell her about his psychic phenomenon.

"And thanks for indulging me. It just felt like an encounter I should put out there in the world, because it seems bigger than the standard body-bound way of looking at things. Because maybe we have all sorts of ways to remain intimate with people, if we leave ourselves open to it. And I don't mind telling you, I'm starting to wonder what other sorts of talents lie dormant inside of us, waiting to be nudged awake.

"Moving on. I know it's a little cliché to say so, but—*now for the part of our program you've all been waiting for.* Hey, come on, it's the truth, isn't it? By far, the biggest percentage of you who are tuned-in to our show right now are going to tune out again as soon as *All of Us Animals* is over, yeah? It's the only thing you really come to WLCM for. And that's fine, by the way. No offense taken. I'm just glad you're here. In fact, by my highly scientific system analysis—meaning I asked around a little—it seems that during the four-plus months since these puppies were adopted out, our listenership has increased on Monday morning by seven times its normal self. That means we have *septupled* our listening population. And if our past is any indication of our future, by next month we might actually octuple or even nontuple our numbers, yeah? And by the way, a couple of 'uples have stuck around for the whole week, too, so our overall WLCM audience has officially at least doubled, thanks to the people who have adopted these puppies. And by that, I mean all of you listening here, because in a way, the whole county seems to have opened their arms to the little cuties.

"Even though these pups didn't start life this way, they are now the most cared for dogs in America. We get phone calls. We get emails. We get people stopping by the studio, and Dr. Dunlop gets well-wishers dropping by her clinic. Townspeople are approaching our adopters every time they go out in public, trying to give them a few bucks for a new collar or a special squeaky toy. Everybody, even from places outside of our radio signal range, is asking after these five littermates and their mom, who are, by the way, right now bouncing off each other out in our hallway, spreading mirth—and some other stuff we'll probably never get out of the carpet.

"It's true though. Your kind words, suggestions, questions, and thoughtful gifts have been thoroughly appreciated by every one of us. So thank you.

"And personally, I just love the idea of all of you out there waiting for it to be eight o'clock so you can catch up on the continuing saga of Storm and her brood. I'm picturing those old photographs from back in the forties, before TV, when the whole family would huddle around the radio for their night's entertainment. Be sure to send in your boxtops, kids, for your secret puppy decoder ring.

"But if you'd like to do more active huddling today, you can call in to our show. In the spirit of giving you another way to participate in the lives of these adopters and adoptees, we'll take a few of your questions, live on the air. I've hesitated to do this before, because we always fill the whole hour just with stories our human guests tell about their canine dependents. But I've decided to extend the show by another half hour from today on, so we should be good.

"Let's get to it. I'm gonna put on a little music, allowing all of our guests to enter the studio and get settled. So how 'bout an old favorite of mine? While I let the dogs in, have a listen to "Who Let the Dogs Out?" by the Baha Men."

"Oh, we're all having a gay old time, the two girls and I," said Bunny. "We've worked out a nice little arrangement for ourselves. Rain and Snow have hired me as their cook and housekeeper, and in return, they let me function as their chauffeur."

"You know, it's probably just as well you haul them around," said Anna. "Dogs make lousy drivers."

"Yeah," Jake said. "It's dangerous to drive with your head stuck out the window!"

As usual, the show today was filled with laughs and good news. The puppies Anna had worried about, so long ago now, were utterly adored and adoring.

"But, Bunny," said Anna. "I've been wanting to ask. Have you had any particular problems raising two dogs instead of one?"

"Well!" Bunny said, as its own little sentence. "I have finally figured out it is a little less confusing and more effective if I use a specific name before giving a command. Like, 'Snow, come.' 'Rain, sit.' 'Rain, don't chew on the wall.' 'Rain, stop rolling in the dead thing.' 'Rain, put down that wine glass.'"

She took Rain's head in both hands. "Do not let this face of sweet innocence deceive you. She is constantly on the prowl for ill-conceived schemes to drag her sister into. But luckily, I only have to remain vigilant over the ringleader to keep them both in line. Having two dogs hasn't been that difficult, truth be told. Of course, it should have been twice as expensive, with two times the vet bills for vaccinations, check-ups and such. But thanks to you, Anna, I have been relieved of that concern. You know, this might be a good time to remind our listeners about the contract we've all signed. I'm of the mind that we do not give that part of this arrangement enough regard."

"It's not a big deal," said Anna.

"It is a very big deal. We're all getting a tremendous financial deal here. Free medical care for our dogs. For life."

Jake started the round of applause, but everyone readily followed suit. Even Bitter Russ showed his appreciation.

"Oh, please," said Anna, embarrassed. "You get the much tougher job. The day-to-day care and feeding. But thanks, Bunny. Everyone."

Eddy interjected. "Dr. Dunlop?"

"Yes, Disc Jockey Rivard?"

"My three sad little phone lines are busting at the seams. Lots of people trying to get through. You think we can take a call or two?"

"Oh, that might be fun. Sure."

Anna was accustomed to fielding phone calls on the air, but Eddy's other guests were in more of a flurry at the prospect. A great shuffling of feet and clearing of throats could be heard throughout the studio (and from radios around the county, no doubt).

"Hi," said Eddy to the first caller in his characteristically interested tone. "You're on *All of Us Animals*, with Dr. Anna Dunlop. And a whole bunch of others. Talk to us."

"Hello? Eddy, my name's Marion Allwin," said a soothing, middle-aged voice Anna knew well.

Hers was the kind of thick Midwest accent relatively few people actually possessed, but movie makers and stand-up comics assumed to be ubiquitous. The back of Marion's tongue stayed high in her mouth, squeezing single syllables into two or three separate parts, slowing her words from rushing out into the world too abruptly. Her sentences mewed out sweetly in slow motion. A symphony of vowels, her sing-song voice was the stretch of warm taffy.

"Y' knowww, Anna and I go back a-ways, but it's sure nice to talk to you in person, Eddy. You've been talking to me for a long time now, dontcha know."

"I have? That's so nice. I'm glad you're calling in."

Anna nodded in recognition. "Hi, Marion." And then to Eddy and his listeners she offered a few words of introduction. "Marion owns a dog grooming business on the south end of town. The Woof-Woof."

"Yea-ahh, dogs ask for it by name," said Marion. Leisurely.

"She does a lot of other things for animals in our area too," said Anna. "She runs a rescue organization for cats and writes the newsletter for a shelter over in Balsam Lake. How's it all going, Marion?"

"Oh, good, good. Yea-ahh, everything's real good, Anna." Her words poured like brownie batter into a pan. "I'll tell you why I'm calling, though. You knowww, I've been thinking and thinking about how I could help out a little with these puppies, and your Storm, too, of course."

"Marion, you've already sent us tons of coupons for half-off at the Woof-Woof."

"I knowww, honey," she exuded. "But maybe something else, too. I don't have a lot of money, but I do have some dollars in the Woof-Woof advertising budget I haven't spent yet. And I've been thinking about spreading some promotional posters around. So what I'm wondering is if everybody there would be interested in doing a professional photo shoot with all five pups and their mom, against a real pretty background. We'll get them all dolled-up. Beautifully groomed, you knowww. And maybe with a few simple accessories. The girls in little hair bows and boys in bowties of different colors. Things like that. And the caption could read something like, *The Woof-Woof. Fun for the whole family.* I mean, everyone around here knows their story, so it's good for the Woof-Woof. But this way I can also give each doggie one hundred dollars cash as a fee. And we'll take lots of cute photos that day, and everybody can have copies. They'd make sweet Christmas cards, that's for sure."

Everyone in the clan was nodding and smiling.

"Marion, that's so nice of you," said Anna. "And just so you know, the idea seems to be meeting with mass approval over on our end."

Most everybody spoke up at once. Some thanking Marion. Some joking about their puppy in a bowtie.

"Hey, Marion, this is Jake. How ya doin'?"

"Real good, Jake, hi."

"You want me to bring the top hat I got Fritos for his six-month birthday party? It's silver with shiny sequins. Photographs great, the way light bounces off it."

"That sounds like a good idea," said Marion. "Everybody, bring whatever outfits you have. It'll be fun!"

"Outfits?" said Russ, lifting his lip in a sneer. The rest of his face, however, had difficulty hiding his keenness on the photo shoot idea.

"And one other thing I was thinking, too," said Marion, butterscotch puddingly. "I'm going to want to put some of these posters up more permanently in dog-friendly places around the county, so I've also got some extra money in the budget for framing ten of them. And Jeffrey, I know you own a frame shop over there in Turtle Lake, so of course, I want to be sure to bring my business over to you. I just need to know, what's the name of your store?"

Twelve human eyes, two of which were John Henry's, turned toward Cleo. Jeffrey had become the first puppy adopter ever to miss a radio session. Cleo had explained to everyone before the show that there'd been a family emergency, so Jeffrey wouldn't be able to make it today. When Anna had first gotten the word, while waiting out in Eddy's hallway, doggie siblings were arriving at the family reunion one by one, welcomed by the greeting committee with its customary sniffs and pounces, so she'd been distracted and had taken Cleo's news at face value. On further reflection, however, she'd become a bit concerned for Cleo, whose demeanor was oddly somber.

When Marion requested the name of Jeffrey's business, Anna would have expected Cleo to speak up immediately. To nod her head in that affirmative way she had, give Marion precise directions on how to get to the frame shop from Milk River, and provide an alternate route in case of construction. Instead, Cleo was still staring up at the speaker mounted high on Eddy's wall from which Marion's inquiry had issued. Anna was tempted to fill the dead air with an answer, to tell the caller that Jeffrey hadn't been able to come that day. But she could see Cleo wanted to respond. She made the conscious decision to stay out of Cleo's way.

Anna noticed something else during the year-and-a-half it took Cleo to answer. The petite woman with eyes like Bambi's wife turned away from the wall speaker to level a bottomless look on Jake, giving and taking little pieces of something. The crusty-biker-tattoo-guy placed his hand over his heart, tilted his head slightly, and rolled his shoulders a bit inward, cupping himself toward her.

When Cleo was at last ready to respond, she pulled John Henry onto her lap. She straightened her back and looked once again up at the speaker on the wall. As usual, her voice was hoarse, but today it was also absolute.

"Marion. This is Cleo, Jeffrey's wife. Jeffrey's not here today, and as I told all the folks here, he couldn't come because he had a family emergency. Which is true. But what I didn't say is that the family with the emergency is ours. The three of us. Which is now just the two of us."

People held very still in their seats.

"So I'm sorry he isn't here to answer your question. I know if he were, he'd sure tell you how grateful he was for your offer. I'm—" She started to lose control and stopped talking. Cleo bent her head to rest her eyes for a brief moment in John Henry's thick, brown hair. She inhaled deeply as she again looked up at Marion's speaker. "Sorry. And I want you to know, I'm grateful for your offer, too. Our shop is—his shop is called Frameworks, and it's right in downtown Turtle Lake."

Nothing. No one spoke. Most everyone stared at anything other than Cleo's humiliation. Except Eddy. Anna saw her friend's big, open face studying the young mother, probably trying to feel her misery along with her.

"Tell you what, Marion," said Eddy, with more than his usual abundance of serenity. "Why don't you send me an email to eddy@wlcmfm.com. Then I can shoot you out everybody's contact information, including specifics like the address of the McCoy's store. Then all these photo arrangements can be made off the air, yeah?"

"Oh, right, sure Eddy," said Marion, quickly for her, sounding distressed. "That's just what I'll do. And thank you—all of you—for what you've done. The world is so very proud of you, you know. Real, real proud, Cleo. And—I'm sorry. So sorry. G'bye, now."

"Wait, Marion?" said Eddy, so tenderly.

"Yes?"

"What you called for, it was a generous act. And Cleo is a remarkably strong person. And she and Jeffrey have us here—and a lot of you out there—pulling for them. So you take good care."

"Oh, okay. Okay, good, Eddy," said Marion, her voice a serving of mushroom soup hotdish on funeral day. "Talk to you all later, then. Bye-bye now."

A click. A dial tone. A giant balloon waiting to pop.

Cleo gazed at a fixed point in space, her arms limp in her son's lap. From that position she was unable to see John Henry's eyes squeezed shut, emptying themselves of tears. The boy's grief shot through Anna as a memory from her own childhood; John Henry was trying to close his eyes tightly enough to keep the bad stuff on the outside from getting in. Mercifully, his silent agony would be passing unnoticed by Eddy's listeners, though it rocked every person in the studio.

While Anna scrambled for what to say, Storm stood and walked delicately over to the child. She pushed her slender muzzle under the crux of his knee and held it there, looking up into his face.

As no surprise to Anna, it was Eddy who could speak first, his manner direct and soft. He brought the microphone closer to his lips.

"I think it was just after our last gathering, or maybe the month before, when Anna told me she'd come to an important realization about the individuals gathered in my tiny alcove here. That the men, women, and children, biped and quadruped, have formed themselves into an official clan. And that's just what we have here, isn't it? Six blood relatives and the families extending out from them. I've thought about that concept a lot since then, and the more I think, the more I like it. It's just right. Let me see if I can explain what it feels like to be part of this grouping.

"Okay—here. Take a minute to picture your spouse or significant other. Now picture that person's sister. And now that sister's husband. Got it? Yeah, that guy. Let's call him Charlie. I'm gonna guess that even though Charlie's a nice enough fellow, you wouldn't necessarily have chosen him as your good friend if he weren't related. Am I right? I mean, he's different from you in a number of ways. But he's part of your clan and that means something. You don't share actual blood, but there's a rope looped once around your waist, once around his. Not a physical one, but a *meta*physical one. And if he loses his foothold on the mountain, you're gonna keep him from falling all the way down, aren't you? 'Cuz that's what clan does.

"And ol' Charlie, he's got another thing goin' for him, too. Both of you have seen a fair amount of each other over the past several years. You've shared so many holidays, weddings, and near-death slips down mountains with him, that it's done something to you. You've come to realize that some of those highly unusual traits of his are actually kind of interesting. Refreshing, even. Maybe *different* isn't so unpleasant after all. In fact, it's the thing you now like most about him.

"Let's face it. This particular group of highly unusual human beings in the studio today never would have started hanging around together if it weren't for the blood that bound them. But now that they're all here, and have been here, and are going to be here, every single clan member watches out for the others. Bad stuff is going to happen as we make our way up the mountain. But when it does, the whole family takes it on."

Anna noticed Eddy pull his eyes from Cleo to smile over at Jake.

"I think I want to get myself a glass of ice water. In fact, glasses and bowls of ice water all around. So that'll take a few minutes. And in the meantime, how 'bout you listen to a song that's been on my mind this morning? Seems like it might make a good theme song for our little clan here.

And out into a forty-mile circle of Western Wisconsin, Eddy sent the opening guitar licks of Bob Dylan's "If Not for You."

34

"Holy, man! Did somethin' die in here or is that your new perfume?"

Brian tugged the red strings tight, pulling the plastic garbage bag closed as fast as he could, tying the knot. Situation normal, Katie made the face she always did when he tried to joke with her, half-squinting her eyes and blinking a few times, like he was speaking in Bolivian or something.

"We changed Toby's bandages again. That's what's in there. His leg is still infected."

"The big poodle dog?"

Katie nodded and turned back to digging through her desk drawer. "Anna thinks the leg might have to come off."

"Damn! Awesome."

This time she gave him the other kind of look he'd gotten used to. People got all pissy when he showed any excitement about surgeries. Like he was glad the animal was sick or whatever. No matter how many times he'd explained that it wasn't even about the animal for him, but about the operation, no one got it. Or if they did, they didn't like it. So with all the other stuff he was learning around here, he was also learning to stay quiet. But sometimes he forgot.

What sucked, though, was that it was totally okay for other people to get jazzed up about cool surgeries. Like the time a dog had come in with a sore on its ear, and they'd had to sew an actual button onto it to keep the wound from closing up. A button, like from a shirt. Everybody talked about it for a couple of days. And that's when Brian learned that when *they* got interested in a surgery it was because it was good science or some damn thing. But when he got interested, he was the bastard who liked to see animals get cut into. He wanted to get mad about that, but mostly, it made him feel bad. These people still didn't know him. Or even seem to want to.

He yanked the plastic bag from the can and headed out of the room. He stopped himself in the hall just before ramming into Noah.

"Hiya, Brian. Whassup?"

"Nothing. Garbage."

"You're doing great, by the way, dude. Hey, you think you could hose out the waste basket in there, too? Probably all of them could use a good cleaning, actually. You know where the disinfectant is, right?"

Let's see. He'd only scrubbed all eight of these goddamn trash cans about five times each since he'd started working here, so yeah, probably he could figure out some way to get the job done. But he would choose his words carefully.

"I'm on it."

Noah was the closest thing he had to a friend around here. At least the guy wasn't always waiting for him to mess up.

Garbage can in one hand, plastic bag of stink over his shoulder, Brian opened the back door with his hip and started down the cement steps. A sound off to the left stopped him halfway down the stairs. Lying in the sun was the white shepherd. His ex-dog. Dr. Giant's dog. It raised its head with its ears back in that pitiful way, like it was ready to get beat or something.

That made two nasty looks he'd gotten in just under two minutes on the job. Seemed about par for this place.

As he stared over at the dog, he got one of those weird déjà vu feelings. He set his load down and sat on the step to think. Which was when it came back to him. Walking down the stairs, hearing something, stopping, seeing the dog. It was exactly the same as on that morning at his house when the puppies first showed up. When this same dog got him into the trouble he'd been trying to get out of ever since.

It was seven months ago and seemed like a dream to him now. He never spent much time thinking about that morning. Everything else that came after he'd buried the puppies, yeah, he'd thought about that a lot. The cops coming to get him at work, his night in jail, all the court shit. But not the deed itself, really. It just hadn't seemed that big of a deal to him, one way or the other. It was the rest of the world that had taken it so damn seriously.

But sitting there, pushing his mind back to that morning, he could remember random parts of it. Coming down his back steps, hearing a squealing sound, seeing all those wiggling puppies, and feeling angry at the dog for screwing him over. Jeez, he'd been pissed about that. The weird thing was, right now, he couldn't figure out why he'd been so mad at the dog. He could see being ticked-off about having to deal with all those puppies and being forced to make a decision about what to do, but that was different.

As he continued to think, he remembered feeling scared about being late for work again too, afraid he might lose his job. But his strongest memory was of being totally furious with the dog itself. Bellowing at her. Thinking about kicking her (which he had never, ever done), but kicking the doghouse instead. Totally pissed off at her for how she'd screwed up his life.

But now, today, he couldn't quite get that. It seemed stupid to be mad at the dog. She'd been knocked up and going to have those puppies no matter what. If anything, it was probably his own damn fault for letting it happen.

He took a minute to picture the same thing happening to him today—coming down the stairs to see those puppies. What would he do? He didn't know. But he really couldn't picture being mad at the dumb animal. That whole long ago morning just seemed totally bizarre.

Brian had been staring in the direction of the dog over there on the grass this whole time, trying to sort things out. But he hadn't actually been seeing her. Now that he let his eyes focus, he realized she was freaking out about him staring at her for so long. She was flattened to the ground, pushing her belly into the dirt, dragging her chin through the grass, moving her head from side to side like a snake. A snake trying to hide, but too scared to take her eyes off him. She seemed kind of—pathetic.

"Come here, you." He spoke quietly, patting his lap. "Just come here."

The white shepherd stood partway up and slunk over to where Brian sat. She brushed up against his legs before falling to the ground, rolling onto her back in a show of pink skin.

"Oh, that's what you want. One of these."

He rubbed her belly for a good long time, wondering if she'd always been this soft.

"I pulled him out of my oak tree," said Mrs. Korhonen. "That old thing is completely hollowed out, and I've been meaning to have someone come and take it down before it falls on the house. But before I got around to it, I noticed that a feral cat had birthed a litter of kittens in there. Six of them. I looked in on them once but mostly figured I should let them be. And then this morning I heard such a racket, I went to see what it was all about. There this one was, inside the tree, all by his lonesome. Bawling like crazy. A good way to get eaten by something, if you ask me, squealing like that. Maybe that's what happened to his brothers and sisters, I don't know."

"Maybe, or maybe their mother moved them."

"I wondered that too, so I waited and watched from the house for a couple of hours. But she never came back. And the whole time this one kept bawling."

Anna held the tiny grey kitten up by her face to look into his eyes. They seemed clear.

Until today, Anna had known Bess Korhonen only through her annoying son. Now forty years old, Pete Korhonen had headed up what one would call the popular group in high school. His good looks and superior attitude had probably gotten him into the clique, and his bullying nature had kept him there. Pete and his sister, Sarah, who was even more good looking and arrogant than her older brother, had eventually grown out of their self-absorbed childhoods, into their self-absorbed adulthoods.

Anna had recently learned that neither Pete nor Sarah were making any attempt to care for their failing mother. Mrs. Korhonen, on the other hand, had done everything she could to care for them, including working seven days a week at the crappiest jobs in town, trying to save for their college education. She bussed dishes at the motel. She cleaned toilets at the factory. She helped her kids build good, comfortable lives for themselves, which they promptly relocated to faraway states, where the phones must not work very well.

Bitter Russ did whatever he could to help out Mrs. Korhonen, taking on minor repairs and picking up groceries once in awhile. Anna had learned this from the neighbors, of course, not from Russ.

So today, when Mrs. Korhonen called to say she'd found a stray cat and wanted to schedule an appointment to do whatever a person was supposed to do with a new pet, Anna was relieved. With a cat, at least the woman would have someone around the house she could talk to. And Russ would be checking in with her off and on, noticing whether or not the animal was being properly cared for.

"He's probably about three or four weeks old," said Anna. "Not really weaned yet. You think you're up to the task of feeding him a couple of times a night, then every few hours during the day?"

"Time is what I've got the most of. I have nothing to do all day, I don't really leave the house much, and none of my friends are alive anymore. I think it might be nice to be needed."

Anna glanced at Katie then back at her client. The woman's comment about being friendless had not been, in any way, a play for sympathy. Mrs. Korhonen had been simply stating a fact, as she might have mentioned the time of day, described her interest in the garden show, or reported that her sleeve was caught in the wood chipper, and she could use a little assistance please. She was what Anna thought of as a *flat-liner*. Unshakeable. Not a person concealing her emotion, but someone who absorbed the hard realities of life—and kept on moving.

"Okay, then. Let's check him out. His weight is good. He must have had a mother tending to him until fairly recently."

"He was hungry when I brought him inside, though. I gave him some warm cream from the corner of a wash rag."

"Smart. We can help you out with feeding. Brian, would you run and grab me some feline milk replacer, please?"

When she heard herself ask Ardeen for the milk replacer, she flashed back to the *canine* milk replacer she had needed for the puppies he'd tried to kill. She couldn't help it. Something would trigger the memory, and she'd find herself right back in October, trying to breathe air into Kitty's tiny, unresponsive lungs. The emotion she felt these days was nowhere near as raw as it had been on the morning she'd brushed death and dirt from the barely living. And the waves of distress were coming further apart. But when they arrived, they still rocked her.

On some days, this Ardeen undertaking seemed futile. No one—not Mother Nature, not his parents, not even his wife—had gotten him to evolve much of a social conscience. But Anna had blithely grabbed the baton and now wondered every morning if she'd have the stomach to finish what she'd started. She had, however, seen a few glimmers of hope along the way—such as the rare supportive word for an emotional client.

His over-the-top obsession with invasive surgery still troubled her, though. She wanted to believe it was just his new-found passion for veterinary science. Or maybe she didn't want to believe, and that was the problem. But his fervor for watching an animal get cut open unsettled her. She couldn't let go of his history and couldn't rely on his present. So far, there had been no dramatic confrontation, though she lived most every day on the verge.

Anna focused her attention back on the fuzzy kitten. It didn't take long to palpate his body. She began edging her fingers along his short frame and within moments discovered a problem.

"Oh. There's a bump on the side of his neck."

From the breast pocket of her white coat Anna pulled the reading glasses she was using more and more lately. She held the kitten in the palm of one hand, parted his fur, and put her face close to his neck. She was distracted only briefly by the shrinking of the exam room when Ardeen returned. “Oh, yup. I had a sneaking suspicion.” She looked back over her shoulder at Katie. “Cuterebriasis.”

“Really?” Katie stepped forward.

Anna pulled her head out of the way for Katie to get a good look. The vet tech examined the area, lightly feeling all around the bump.

“Yeah. There he is,” said Katie, before heading out to get the instruments Anna would need.

“Mrs. Korhonen,” said Anna. “He’s got a cuterebra larva in the subcutaneous tissue of his neck.”

“Okay.” The older woman waited calmly to hear what that meant.

“A big fly, it looks kind of like a bee, likes to lay its eggs right at the openings of animal dens—like on the hole in your oak tree. The kittens rub up against the eggs, which then attach themselves to their fur. And eventually, the body heat from the cats hatches the eggs. The larva gets itself inside of the body, either by being licked, or by crawling in through an opening, like the nose. Or sometimes it just burrows down through the skin.”

Anna heard a gasp of air from the corner of the room. She turned to see Ardeen clenching and unclenching his fists at his sides. His eyes were wide open.

“So there’s a worm under that bump,” said Mrs. Korhonen, matter-of-factly.

“A fly larva, yes. More like a big maggot. It makes a fistula in the lump. A little hole. And that’s what it breathes through. If you look closely, you can see it come up and take a breath.”

“No shit!” said Brian, unable to contain himself. He mumbled a quick “Sorry.”

“You want to see it, Brian?”

“Yeah!” He lunged for the exam table.

Anna held her breath against his cloying cologne.

“Oh, jeez, it just rolled over, then came up and breathed right through that freakin’ hole. That’s the most disgusting thing I’ve ever seen.”

“Will it eat its way out?” asked Mrs. Korhonen, seemingly unbothered by the prospect.

“Actually, it’s not really eating anything in there. It’s just waiting. And growing. Left to its own devices it eventually breaks through the skin and falls out. But it’s better to remove it.”

“You want to shave him?” asked Katie.

Anna studied the opening. “Um, I don’t think we’ll have to.”

Katie handed Anna the scalpel, then moved in close to hold the silent kitten flat against the metal tabletop. Anna scrubbed the area, made a small incision to enlarge the opening, which the cat didn't seem to notice, and then went after the grub with a forceps.

Mrs. Korhonen, her hands in the pockets of her baggy cardigan, peered over the top of her glasses watching Anna work.

After a bit of probing around in the hole, Anna pulled out the wriggling larva and held it up for a close look. It was dark brown and covered in spines.

"Jeez!" Ardeen's mouth hung open.

"Yeah, it's probably, what, almost half an inch long? That's about as big as they get."

35

“No way!” said Toot. “You seen ’em do it?”

“A bunch of times. Dogs and cats both. I’m not kidding. Ya just squeeze the bag and the nuts pop right out.”

Toot’s dorky guffaw made Brian laugh too. Even Bo smiled so hard that his left eye slammed shut. He never smiled on the right side, probably to keep his three broken teeth under cover. But the half-action smile fit with every other minimal motion about Bo Beaudry. Slow and planned. The Savage Sloth was what Brian liked to call him, when it looked like Bo was in a mood to be messed with.

“What,” said Toot, still laughing. “They just pop ’em out onto the floor?”

“Christ, you dipshit.” Bo shoved the heel of his hand against Toot’s shoulder. “As much as you play with yourself, you don’t know your nads are attached? Obviously, they gotta cut ’em off.”

Bo looked at the surgical instruments laid out in a perfect line on the blue towel. He picked up a scalpel and turned it slowly in his fingers.

“That’s it!” said Brian. “That’s what they use to cut ’em off with. They stop the blood first, though, with one of these.” He pointed to a clamp without touching it. Brian was doing his best to keep from looking cocky, but he had hardly ever gotten to show Bo anything.

The Savage Sloth never took his eyes from the sharp blade on its long stainless handle. His tongue played with the toothpick in his mouth.

“Okay, you guys, my break’s almost over,” said Brian. “See you at the plant later?” He leaned his body toward the door, lifting his arm in that direction, but nobody budged.

“Hey, look,” said Toot with a laugh, grabbing a forceps from the line-up, knocking another one to the floor with the ping of metal on trouble.

"It's like a little pliers or somethin'. For when the nuts don't pop out so easy, and ya gotta *yank* 'em out!"

Brian picked up the forceps from the floor and put it into the sink. He snatched the other one from Toot's hand. "It's for suturing, dickweed." He turned to the silent Bo. "You guys are gonna have to go, okay? I gotta get back to work."

"You know, Ardeen," said Bo, still studying the scalpel. "I think you've inspired me. A blade like this... makes me wanna try a little surgery."

In a fraction of a second Bo had closed the distance between Toot and himself, leaving zero inches between their two chests. Toot was immobilized, hunched over, Bo's talons digging into his shoulder, the scalpel's tip against Toot's scrotum.

"You and those damn baggy jeans." Bo's toothpick scraped against Toot's chin as he dragged one half of his mouth into the smiling position. "Who woulda guessed they'd save your balls some day?"

Toot breathed a light, high-pitched laugh. "Yeah."

"Seriously, Bo," said Brian, taking half a step in their direction. "I've gotta get goin' here. C'mon."

"What the *hell*?" Anna's appearance snapped two heads toward the door.

Bo drifted slowly away from his target, his gaze shifting casually to Ardeen. Anna did not exist.

"What's going on here? Brian, what are you thinking?" Anna took several steps into the room. "They can't be back here."

"Why? What's wrong?" He was keeping his voice strong.

"What's wrong? You know what's wrong. These guys are wrong. They're not allowed back here, and you know it. Everybody out!"

The sheepish Toot slid past Anna and disappeared. Bo began a ridiculously slow departure, piercing Brian with his stare. Clenching his toothpick in one half of his mouth he formed the word *pussy* with the other.

"Brian, you are way out of line here!" Anna's voice was still raised. "This is a big problem!"

"Yeah, Brian," said Bo. "This is a big problem." He turned to look at Anna threateningly, continuing his advance straight toward her.

"Oh, please," said Anna. "What's that, the evil eye? Does that actually work for you? And what do you have in your hand?"

She saw the scalpel and only later would wonder if a person with a stronger survival instinct might have reacted more cautiously. But seeing that slippery creature holding *her* knife—and noticing the disturbed instruments on the counter—her anger ratcheted a notch higher.

"Oh, my god. Give that to me, you delinquent! This isn't your little play room."

Bo feigned handing her the scalpel but pulled it back, slipping it theatrically into the breast pocket of his skin-tight, shiny shirt. As he moved past Anna, closer than necessary, he placed his palm over the pocket and made a loud kissing sound by her face. Anna rolled her eyes skyward.

"See you at work, Ardeen, if your mommy will give you a ride."

"Yeah, go screw yourself, *DeWayne*," said Brian to Bo's back.

Without turning around, DeWayne Beaudry pushed his arm high above his head in a furious flip of the bird.

"I don't know what to say to you," said Anna, and she really didn't.

Emotions were competing for use of her tongue, triggered by conflicting thoughts of how he was letting her down, and she, him. Also, at the moment, the look on his face was pissing her off. Where she should have been seeing regret and humility, she saw hostility. Defiance. The muscles in his compact body flexed and released. Off and on. His jaw, his arms, his fists, his legs. Contract. Release. Contract.

She started to take a step toward him, to shepherd him out of her space, but was stopped by a quick tug on her heart. Clearly, he was furious, and as usual, his reaction to a perceived threat was expressly physical. But to be truthful, she wasn't without blame here. She had embarrassed him in front of his creepy little friends instead of looking for a more professional way to handle the intrusion.

Bulges appeared and disappeared along Ardeen's body as he tensed and relaxed. A lion waiting to pounce, the animal's muscles rehearsing how they would work once the wildebeest was in grasp.

She could at least make a conscious effort to lower her volume. "What did you think you were doing? Honestly, I can't even imagine how you thought it was okay to bring those—people back here."

His face flushed, Ardeen began to breathe harder. And though Anna rarely felt kindness toward him, she did feel something like pity at these moments when he seemed to hesitate, afraid to violate some social norm he had never actually learned. "All right, look. I want to make this simple and keep the emotion out of it. You don't get to bring your friends back into my surgery. Period. Same as the last three times I've told you. This place is off limits to them. I mean, seriously, I can barely stand *you* back here."

Brian's eyes flashed, and his chest puffed to half again its normal size.

"Okay, wait. I'm sorry. That was really unfair. I'm sorry."

"Jesus!" he said, more as a ball of air than an actual word.

"I know. You're right. That was a bad thing to say." He seemed to be shivering; she knew it wasn't from cold. "What I want to say is this. Please, do not ever bring your friends back here again. This is a place of business. You get that, right?"

"Would you shut the hell up?" As he yelled, he pounded the metal table with his fist. "Stop talking to me like I'm ten years old. Yeah, I know this is a goddamn place of business, okay?"

Noah appeared in the doorway.

"Wow, hey. Is everything all right in here, you guys?"

Anna, without turning around, said, "Yes, we're fine. We'll be out in a second."

She heard Noah linger a moment before heading back down the hall.

"Okay, you're right." said Anna. "That was condescending. Sometimes with you, I don't think, I just react. I've got to work on that, I know. I do. And I will. You have to understand, though, this is a big deal for me. It's hard enough to see those guys hanging out in the waiting room for hours at a time, for some unknown reason. But then I come back here and see them in my surgery—I've gotta tell you, Brian, my first thought was, 'That's it! He's done. He's out of here.'"

Ardeen snorted. "Yeah, that fits with every other decision you've ever made in your life."

"What? What do you know about my life?"

"Oh, come on. You think people don't talk about you? And, shit, you force me to follow you around watching you all day, so I see how you roll. It's totally obvious that if you can't be perfect at *whatever*, you just stop playing. Like right now. You can't turn me into your good little robot, so you wanna dump my ass."

Anna opened her mouth, wishing something would come out.

"And from what I hear, that's just you being you. You got sick of your job last year, so you just quit and went home. Before that, it was the whole marriage thing. It wasn't some happily-ever-after-blah-blah-perfect story. So you swore off men for the rest of your life. I mean, god, get over yourself!"

"I can't believe you just said that to me." Anna felt frozen in place.

"What? The marriage thing? You think people don't talk about that? I know exactly how he died, and that you were there, and how you, the fixer of the world, couldn't save him. You screwed up, just like the rest of us poor slobs who do that sometimes." The look on his face was disgust. "Us mortals, though, we have to suck it up and move on. But not you. You'll never have another man, ever. Very dramatic. And too goddamn bad, too. Because you'd be a lot easier to get along with if you'd get laid once in awhile."

Anna squinted her eyes. "No, really. I can't believe what you just said to me."

"Christ! That's the problem. Nobody has the balls to say nothing to you. Maybe they think you're too pitiful or something. So let me say it. You're a spoiled bitch."

The twist of the key, the clicking of tumblers, the crack in the door. Sunlight.

Truth bounced between the walls of her hollow chest until it found a spot to settle. And that's where his pronouncement would live forever now. *She had done it* wrong *with Tony and wasn't willing to do it wrong again.*

So simple, but that was it. She had resigned herself to a life without a relationship, not because everything with Tony had been so perfect, as she had always told herself, but because she had screwed it up so royally. And if she couldn't be good at the whole romance thing, then she would just stop trying.

Ardeen was completely right. It was her fatal flaw. The fear of being bad—at anything. And he was right about something else, too. The night of Tony's death had sealed her fate, stuffing her down the rabbit hole where no other love could ever get at her.

But the greatest piece of wisdom to come from this wholly unlikely oracle was the idea that she could—should—stop fighting the guilt. *Suck it up.* She was guilty. She. Was. Guilty. But the revelation dawning was that she wasn't going to die from being guilty. She had spent the past five years flattened under the burden of her failure, letting it push her further and further into the ground. And the whole time, the answer had been so simple: *Get out from under it, pick it up, accept it as mine, and keep on walking.* There was life after guilt. She had honestly never considered the option.

Ardeen was completely mistaken, though, about one fundamental point in his rant. Her shame about Tony had had nothing to do with how she had let him die—but with how she had made him live.

36

Tony knew the curving gravel road well enough to drive it with one hand, even in the dark. He glanced down at Anna, who lay with her head in his lap, while he used the tips of his fingers to trace a path from her eyebrow to her hairline on the side where the migraine had taken hold. Keeping his pressure light, he stroked only in one direction, helping her picture the pain being swept up and out the top of her head. When drugs failed her, and sleep wouldn't come, this was some small relief.

Tony kept his voice soft, knowing sounds could make things worse. "Sweetheart? We're almost home. Will you want to lie on the couch or head on up to bed?"

"What time is it?" She parted her lips only far enough to let the question out.

"About nine-thirty."

"Couch."

No surprise there. Anna maintained that only old people went to bed before eleven o'clock on a Saturday night. Of course, sick people did too, but having a migraine didn't make her a sick person; she was only a person with a migraine. He smiled then, making a mental note to add that particular axiom to the Anna Dunlop Handbook he kept threatening to write.

The canoe trip had been great, but he was relieved to be heading home. He let his body relax further into the seat.

He was worried about the number of freshly fallen trees along the road, though; a serious windstorm must have blown through while they were gone. As he maneuvered the truck to avoid ruts in the gravel, he took mental inventory of the buildings on their property. The barn and workshed were only a couple of decades old and built sturdy. They'd be fine. But through how many centuries could the farmhouse be expected to survive nature's worst? He'd thought about replacing the roof this past summer, but in the end had decided to let it go one more season. A quick twist of his gut made him push a little harder on the gas pedal.

Tony looked over at the exhausted Jackpot curled up on the floor of the truck. The massive Rottweiller hadn't even put up a stink when Anna had commandeered the entire seat to lie down on. The dog had just wrapped all 130 pounds into a tight little ball and gone to sleep. Tony couldn't wait to do the same.

He thought back over their past five days on the water. Crazy enough to canoe in Wisconsin's late October, they hadn't seen a soul from the time they'd put into the Wolf River until they'd taken out, ninety miles down. The run was just as he'd remembered it. As the river wended, the clear, fast water would gain speed, launching them into some of the most challenging rapids in the Midwest. Which probably wasn't saying much. Their dream was to do the Colorado some day, and by next summer they'd have the money saved up to make it happen.

He was pretty sure he would still be unpacking the tin camping dishes from this adventure when his thoughts would turn to the next one. He loved absolutely everything about canoe trips with Anna. Pushing themselves to the limit physically, paddling fast and hard for long stretches, then drifting through others, sometimes with Anna lying back on the warm metal of the canoe, her face to the sun, arms dangling, fingertips cracking the glass of the river's surface.

Then at night they would sit by the fire with his arms around her; he would gladly make the trip for those moments alone. Like she was hypnotized, Anna would stare into the flames and feel comfortable letting him in on personal thoughts too fragile for daylight.

A few nights back, she had told him about an experience she'd had when she was ten years old. She'd come downstairs in the morning to find her dad asleep on the couch, naked and sprawling, his clothes in a pile on the floor. She'd heard him come home drunk the night before and had made a point to get up early to see if she needed to fix anything before Greggy woke up. She'd gotten a blanket and tried her best to cover him up, keeping her head turned the other way.

Bit by bit over the years, Anna was showing Tony what she considered the most horrible parts of herself, probably to see if they would make him un-love her. He rested the palm of his hand against her soft cheek, feeling the weight of her head on his thigh, and thinking what he had thought so many times before: that he wanted to spend the rest of his life mining the odd little wonders of her.

About a quarter mile from their house, a vehicle at an intersection caught Tony's eye. He clenched his jaw, studying the rusty pickup on the shoulder of the deserted road so far out of town. And so late at night.

Passing the truck he had his suspicions confirmed. The door to the cab was open, the driver just climbing back in—from doing what, Tony had no idea. But the dome light revealed two other young men inside, one of whom chose that particular moment to toss a beer bottle into the ditch. Another camouflaged form sat in the bed of the truck with three anxious coonhounds pacing around him, the butt of a rifle between his legs, barrel straight in the air. All four teenagers were laughing as Tony drove by. A quiet grunt escaped him when he realized what was going on. These guys were out coon shining.

He slowed down, watching his rearview mirror. The truck with its four rowdy hunters and one headlight was on the move. He watched to see where it was heading, hoping he was wrong. But he wasn't. The truck veered down an old cattle path and disappeared onto the outer reaches of Tony and Anna's property. What he wanted to do was follow them and order them the hell off his land. But he needed to get Anna home first.

They had chased plenty of hunters off their land over the years, and she'd always insisted they do it together. In her opinion, if they were going to be stupid enough to yell at drunk people with guns, they should be smart enough to use the buddy system. Though Tony always hated to involve her, Anna was Anna and couldn't be kept home. Besides, he had to admit that watching her assault on trespassing hunters was a thing of beauty, especially if the perpetrators had coon shining in mind.

He and Anna made a good team. He would use his physical size, aggressive gestures, and threats of police action to scare them off, while Anna relied on her deep arsenal of blistering adjectives, literary allusions, and vile pejoratives. She could verbally field dress a full-grown hunter in under two minutes. But not tonight.

He wasn't sure what to do. No way would he go home to bed and let a pack of boozing rednecks carry out their macho bullshit on his property. He looked down into Anna's flushed face, her lips pursed in pain.

He got her settled on the couch with a big glass of water, no ice. He took the stairs two at a time, running up to snatch the magic sheep from her bedside table. Stuffed with rice and lavender, the small cotton animal was some kind of headache comfort he'd never quite understood. "I've got the sheep."

When he put it into her hand, she gingerly positioned it across her eyes and forehead. She made minor adjustments to the sheep's position before laying her arm back across her stomach as if both body parts were made of handblown glass.

Her *thank you* was barely a mumble.

Tony squatted beside her, gently placing his hand over hers. "Anna May? Honey? I've got to run out for a bit, okay?"

"'Kay."

He was glad she hadn't asked any questions; he was a terrible liar. "I saw something outside I want to check out. I won't be long."

No answer.

Her lack of interest clued him in to her pain level. He touched his lips to her cheek, which felt cold. Stepping into the den to pull the throw from the desk chair, he noticed a piece of paper rolled in the ancient typewriter. He switched on the desk lamp; it was one of her poems.

Of course, she'd freak out if she knew he was reading it, but he'd never seen any of her work in progress before and couldn't help himself. The poem seemed to be a riff on spelling and grammar, titled "Proper English Ain't Easy."

'ENOUGH' and 'PLOUGH' and 'COUGH' and 'THROUGH'
They all should rhyme, and yet none do.
And that word too, it's 'DO' you know,
But spelled like 'THROUGH,' we say it 'DOUGH'

He laughed out loud and forced himself to stop reading.

Tony draped the blanket across his wife and bent over, putting one hand on the back of the couch, one on the arm. He spoke in the voice people use near sleeping babies.

"Okay, Anna. I'm going."

"Cooler?" She spoke the word through gritted teeth.

It took Tony a second to figure out that she was worried about the camping food spoiling in the cooler.

"Yup. I'll take care of it when I get home. I won't be gone long. I love you, Corazón." He stood as she smiled so imperceptibly that only someone who knew her would notice.

Tony took the flashlight from his duffle in the truck. He thought about getting his dad's rifle from the closet upstairs but knew Anna would throw a holy fit if she guessed what he was doing. Instead, he put the tailgate up and headed down to the river at a slow jog. It was the quickest way to the ravine where he would no doubt find those guys shining coons. Thinking about the poor raccoon in this type of hunt, he felt the muscles in his body gearing up to deal with these assholes. He ran without getting winded.

The dogs would find the scent of a raccoon and charge off, terrifying the animal on a chase through the woods. If the coon couldn't go to ground, it would take to a tree. Scared for its life, the prey would eventually look down at its pursuers. And that's when the hunter would shine a big light into its eyes; the animal couldn't help but freeze.

The shot was an easy one, adding to Tony's contempt for this particular brand of hunter. Once in a rare while, the raccoon's pelt was what they were after. But more often, these guys were just out for the sport of it—if you could call armed people with dogs and lights that paralyzed a confused creature *sporting*. Usually with these jokers, the dead or wounded raccoon was thrown to the dogs.

Worse, the chase usually hurtled forward on a stream of alcohol—meaning other poor choices could be made out here tonight too. Even if Tony were to ignore the torture of animals on his land, which he would not, these guys were getting liquored up and could be firing rifles within range of where Anna lay in the living room.

As he ran along the narrowing path, water on one side, a high ridge on the other, a sound began working its way into Tony's consciousness. It was the river, but louder than it should have been. He turned the flashlight toward the water and came to a quick stop. Directly ahead of him lay a massive jumble of fallen white pines, their tops jutting into the river. The water churned into a mound of interwoven waterfalls as it rushed over and around the branches. He used his flashlight to examine the obstacle blocking his path.

One of the 150-foot giants had been rotted and half dead, making it vulnerable to the straight-line winds that must have torn through here. But best as he could tell, the other two trees seemed perfectly healthy. They had apparently stood in the path of the toppling behemoth and been dragged down as collateral damage. He winced slightly at the loss of what might have been a combined total of six hundred years of old growth.

The three trees had crashed together, forming a snarled nest of twisted and broken branches keeping him from what he needed to do. The pines had been growing high on the ridge and had slid only partway down after snapping off. So the barrier was almost twenty feet high on the ridge side, decreasing as it neared the river to seven or eight feet in both height and girth. Even at his athletic, six-foot-four build, Tony was daunted by the hurdle.

He raced mentally through possible plans of action, coming up with only three. He could climb over the obstruction, or wade thirty feet out into bone-chilling water to circumvent it, or head all the way back to the house to access the ravine from the road. Before he could decide, the chase intensified.

Tony had always been particularly keyed in to sounds of any kind, which served him well as a musician but could be a curse in other ways. When the hounds began to bay, he felt his stomach flip, realizing he might be too late to prevent the first casualty. He ran his hands through his shoulder length hair as he studied the layout of the massive branches. Hearing the hunt happening just beyond his reach, he couldn't stop the scene from playing out in graphic detail between his ears.

The bellowing dogs were obviously hot on the trail of a raccoon. The terrified animal would be ripping through the woodland, its familiarity with the terrain not much advantage over the dogs with their faster speed and inbred lust for the hunt. Every fraction of a second lessened the distance between the pursued and its pursuers.

Then again, Tony thought he might be as hell-bent on stopping the kill as the dogs were to complete it.

Directly above his head, a thick bough, dagger-sharp at its broken tip, protruded as a likely handle. Below him, any number of limbs could work as serviceable footholds. He tucked his flashlight into his jacket pocket, glancing up at the moon, grateful it was nearly full and the sky around it cloudless. He gripped the branch and heaved himself up onto the spongy pile of pine boughs, hoping to land on all fours, but failing to gain a firm purchase. His left arm shot down through the web of interlocking branches up to the elbow, almost toppling him back to the ground. He righted himself and squinted through the dark to study the eight-foot plane of jagged mesh ahead, strategizing which part of his body to place where before risking another maneuver.

The fervor of the coonhounds swelled, their cries rising to a crazed pitch of anticipation, and Tony's gut tightened. Instead of carefully plotting his next move he simply made it, somehow finding support for both hand and foot as he scuttled across the snapping, elastic structure of the dead trees. Without much thought, he half-shinnied-down, half-jumped-off the bulging wall, landing better than he'd imagined he might. Hands sticky with sap and tingling from tiny scratches, he took off running before the flashlight was clear of his pocket. The sound he'd been dreading had begun.

The long, howling calls of the dogs had shifted dramatically to a series of choppier, more urgent barks, meaning the actual chase had come to an end, but the animal was still in play. The panicked raccoon had likely climbed a tree in desperation. All three dogs barked impatiently, probably lunging up at him from below, his scent thick in their nostrils, his flesh infuriatingly out of reach. The hounds voiced their frustration, signaling the hunters to hurry and come finish the job.

Tony leapt over logs and fought his way through dense thickets, working himself upriver toward the animal he imagined clinging to a branch, searching for options. Closing in on the action now, maybe fifty yards of tough terrain from where the dogs demanded their blood, he let himself hope he might arrive on time to change the outcome.

The beam from his flashlight, bouncing wildly as he ran, fell across something large and on the move just a few feet away. Tony brought himself to a quick stop, training the light in its direction. A raccoon, almost a yard-long, hurtled down the trunk of an old ironwood tree, bolting toward the river faster than Tony would have guessed possible. The animal slipped silently into the rushing water, crossing swiftly toward the other bank. A strong swimmer, the raccoon did well against the current. Tony shut off his flashlight, wanting to keep their little secret. By the hounds' continued barking, he could tell they still believed they had the animal trapped. But the coon had likely jumped to an adjoining branch, then traveled tree to tree before coming to ground. And now it had taken to the water, further confusing the scent trail.

Tony, puffing hard, smiled.

"Perfect." He exhaled the word, picturing the hunters sweeping their high-power flashlights over an empty tree.

This wooded land, forty of the few thousand acres of old growth left in Wisconsin, was home to a rich variety of wildlife. It attracted all sorts people looking to bag themselves an easy kill. But he and Anna took their role seriously as landlords to the white-tailed deer, grey foxes, pileated woodpeckers, river otters, and scores of other creatures making up the population, down to the last snowshoe hare and white-footed mouse. So now, with tonight's first potential victim safe and away, it was time to do what he had come out here for—run these drunken dirtballs off his property.

Some of these face-offs had gone more smoothly than others. But no matter how unruly the group, Tony never feared guys like these. If anything, he felt overconfident. This was his turf, and though he wasn't particularly proud of the urge, he was driven to protect it from people who had no damn right to be here.

He flicked his flashlight back on, waving it in the direction of the barking dogs. As he drew close to the hunters, he would yell a few words of greeting, making it perfectly clear that this approaching animal was no ten-point buck looking for a wall to hang its head on.

The rifle shot woke Anna with a jerk, dropping the magic sheep to the floor. She'd been able to push herself down into a deep sleep, the likeliest way to lessen the migraine's grip. A forced nap after four ibuprofen usually tucked a thick layer of cotton between the pain and her ability to feel it.

Jackpot had also sprung up at the sound and now paced between the couch and the window facing the river.

Anna was accustomed to hearing gunshots in the area, especially around this time of year, and lowered herself back into the prone position. She placed her palm against the side of her head and lay there in the darkened room, still aware of the migraine, a throbbing pressure having replaced the pain.

The gunshot had seemed particularly close.

It came from upriver. How far, she couldn't tell. Was it on their property? She tensed. And where was Tony? She didn't bother to call out. She was pretty sure he wasn't home; it was a weird sixth sense she'd always had with him. There was herself and Jackpot here now. No one else.

She pushed the blanket aside, standing up quickly enough to bring spots to her vision.

"What? Wait." She squeezed her eyes shut.

Tony had said he was going out. Out where? She looked through the picture window toward the river, but everything was black. *What had he said?* He'd seen something outside and wanted to check it out. Why hadn't she asked him to explain that? What time was it, anyway?

She glided slowly on stocking feet toward the kitchen to check the clock on the oven. Jackpot followed behind, nails clicking on the wood floor. 11:30. She'd been down for a couple of hours.

"Tony?" She thought she'd try, just in case. Her voice echoed in the Tonyless farmhouse.

"Where is he, Jack?" The one-eyed Rottweiller acted as if he'd like to know, himself.

Slightly disoriented, Anna forced the anxious dog to wait inside while she went out to poke around in the garage. She glanced at the truck, still packed tightly with camping supplies. She dropped the tailgate and lifted the lid on the cooler, seeing what she knew she would. Their leftover food. Her anxiety rose. Tony hadn't been home since he left her more than two hours ago.

A second shot, loud as the first but more alarming. Jackpot barked and continued to bark from behind the door. She knew for certain now, there were hunters by the ravine, just as she knew Tony was out there with them. Without her. And though she would torment herself about it for years to come, she wasted precious seconds closing the cooler, the tailgate on the truck, and the garage door. She ran to get her shoes.

Barely in need of her small Maglite, Anna sprinted along the water's edge, her childhood playground. Her body knew when to duck, jump and turn sideways. She did all of it at a dead run, her panic the taste of old pennies.

She noticed both things at once. The huge mass of fallen trees, and Tony standing in among them, watching her approach. He stood a few feet off the ground, branches up to his waist, one arm outstretched, casually, as if along the back of a couch. Moonlit and smiling, his presence was her instant cure.

"Tony!' She came to a halt, bending over to put her hands on her knees as she tried to catch her breath. "Oh, my god, I'm so glad you're okay. I heard those guns and kind of freaked. Wow, these trees. We must have missed one hell of a storm." She breathed in deeply, held the air in her lungs, and released it.

When he didn't reply, she straightened.

"Tone? Are you okay? What are you doing up there? You're not trying to move these things are you?"

She found his face with the tiny flashlight beam, and though nighttime tried to trick her, she could see he was the wrong color. His lips had faded to match the rest of his face, all of it too pale. In affirmation, his chin dropped to his chest, the strain of keeping his head upright for her apparently too great.

Before the next beat of her heart Anna was scrambling up the woodpile to get to Tony. Kneeling in front of him, a thigh on either side of his waist, she could see his legs heading straight down into the network of crisscrossed branches. She warmed his freezing cheeks with her flat hands, then covered his forehead and chin.

"Tone? Tony? Please?" She spoke softly, trying to keep herself calm. "Can you wake up, Tony?"

She put two fingers over his carotid artery and felt nothing. Then just a suggestion of a pulse. Where was he hit? She needed a light. Where was the damn light? She all but threw herself the eight feet to the ground, grabbed the flashlight where she'd dropped it, and scurried back up. Though he didn't open his eyes, she noticed him wince as she disturbed the branches.

"Sorry, Tone. Sorry, sorry. But you're awake, that's good."

She fumbled in her jeans pocket for the cell phone she had bought after 9/11. Teased incessantly by Tony and all of her friends for carrying it everywhere over the years, but never turning it on, she had not been swayed. *Just in case of an avalanche,* she used to say. She dialed 911, described where they were, and refused to continue to talk with the operator. Without turning off the phone she let it drop to the ground.

"You're shot, Tony, right? Where did they shoot you?"

No response. She started beneath his thick, curly hair, using the flashlight to look for entrance wounds. By the color of his skin and thready pulse she knew his blood loss to be substantial, but where was he bleeding from? She slipped a hand behind his neck, exploring the skin's surface by touch. Some powerful force of nature kept her sane as her hands flew over him, *searching her husband's body for bullet holes.*

She tucked the flashlight under her chin and moved inside his sweatshirt, slipping both palms up and over his shoulders to grope along his back. Nothing. From the front she yanked up his sweatshirt and layers of clothing beneath, placing one hand against the skin of his belly, wielding the light in the other, trying to spot the gut shot she feared. Quickly checking the front of his torso, she used both hands to encircle his waist, probing his lower back.

His voice was thin and dry. "Mmm, nice. But—is this really the time?"

Anna sat back on her haunches, gripping both of his shoulders, poring over his ghostly face.

She could tell he was trying to open his eyes for her but couldn't, and she thought about using her own fingers to help, so desperate she was to see them.

"Tony! God, Tony. I called an ambulance. Can you tell me? Where are you hit? Where's the bullet hole? I can't find it."

Without waiting for an answer, she leaned in to resume the hunt, investigating his smooth, frigid back.

"Anna," he whispered, raising his head, forcing his eyelids to half mast. "Sweetheart, stop."

She did, against her better judgment.

"My leg. Left leg." He slurred the words before falling again into unconsciousness.

She backed up a few inches, running the light beam down along his hip, then moving inward. That's when she saw. A branch, maybe as big around as her ring finger, disappeared into a hole in his jeans, half-way down his inner thigh. She used the flashlight to make a quick sweep of the nested trees, noticing how many branches had splintered off in the fall, shaving themselves into pointed weapons. Tony must have been trying to climb over this mountain of trees and slipped. Landing in the worst possible way. Impaling himself.

With the flashlight beam she traced his legs down through the tangled branches, startled by how very straight they were, his feet seeming to rest comfortably on a perfect ledge. He looked to be just—standing there, though his butt actually rested against a structure of limbs holding him in the upright position.

He was one of the strongest people she knew. He could easily have lifted himself free, she was sure of it. And he must have been tempted to heave himself out. But Tony knew a lot of things, including, certainly, the danger of removing an object piercing him this deeply. It must have been torture, feeling himself grow weaker and weaker, wondering if she would ever come. Maybe yelling for her to come. *God, please, let him be okay. Please.*

She grabbed at his belt, unzipping his fly. She didn't dare pull down his pants for fear of jarring the stick, exacerbating the damage. And she had nothing sharp with her to cut the jeans free. Gently, so gently, she slid her hand down across his groin, letting her fingertips explore the area, where everything seemed as it should be. It wasn't until she reached the very top of his thigh that she felt the long, hard branch barely palpable so far beneath his skin, angling its way deep into his body. How long was it? Eight inches? Ten?

Silently warning herself not to let the crying begin, she continued feeling down his leg, a fraction of an inch at a time, the stick taking on more and more dimension as she neared the entrance wound. She could feel lumps and imperfections in the branch through Tony's skin. At last, about four inches from his groin, she came upon the limb where it protruded from his leg. She ran her fingertip around the rim, feeling almost no moisture. Kneeling as tall as she could, as closely as she could, she directed the flashlight's beam down inside of his pants, seeing the surreal image of the branch invading his body. There was hardly any blood—which meant he was bleeding out internally.

Where was the goddamn ambulance? She closed her eyes, trying to recall her human anatomy. Based on the angle of the stick, depending on its length, it may have punctured his femoral artery, or if it were a little longer, maybe his iliac. Either way, since he was still alive, after being hoisted here for a couple of hours maybe, it must be a nick to the artery instead of a complete sever. All of his blood had been slowly draining—while she slept *(don't think about that)*—into the planes of tissues in his pelvis. And now that she was here, what the hell good was she?

Was there a siren in the distance? She whipped off her mackinaw and tucked it gingerly around him, wishing she'd chosen a warmer jacket. Anna sat down and moved in, encircling his waist with her legs, his chest in her arms. His face lay against her neck. She turned to smell his hair.

Campfire. And his clove-and-fresh-bread Tony smell. She breathed him in, again and again. She wanted desperately to rock him—soothe him—which would be the very worst thing to do. She put her lips against his icy cheek and whispered to his soul.

"Oh, Tony, please, please, please, please, please. Not yet. Not yet. Not yet. I can feel you going, you're going, I can feel you going. Can you stay? Is there any way you can stay? Can you stay with me? Please? Can you stay?"

She nuzzled her face up under his chin, opened her mouth as far as she could, and huffed warm air against his throat. Another.

A gun shot blasted from the other side of the ravine. People were hunting, but beyond their property line. Tony had dealt with the hunters, had been coming home to her. *Trying to come home to her—*

He was dying, and she knew it. Nobody in that ambulance would have any idea of how to help him, even if there were time, which there wasn't. He'd lost too much blood. He was too white. Too empty. Too gone. He was dying. *Like this? Tonight? Standing up in the cold? He was dying?* She knew he was, and no bargaining with the entities who controlled such things would stop it.

She peeled her upper body away from his, hungry, frantic. Desperate to see every moment of his face he had left to give her. As she pulled away, his head flopped to his chest, and she cried out. Her shaking hands tenderly cupped his cheeks as she memorized him, drank him, willed his seeping energy into her body to cover her heart. He was the human all humans should try to be. An improver, a rescuer, a pain absorber. But he was leaving, and no one could help him, and the world was becoming poorer.

Unfamiliar on her tongue, rarely heard as a child and never mastered as an adult, the words streamed from her now, overflowing.

"Tony. I love you. I love you. I wanted to say it—I meant to say it. Please know how much I have always, always loved you."

Tony's head jerked up, his dark eyes moistened, and he peered into her with a profoundness only someone half in heaven could summon. She saw—knew—he was having trouble believing what he had heard. He looked shocked, grateful, and as always, selflessly hers. She would wish later that his eyes had accused her.

She couldn't bear that his final act, his final thought, his final connection to her, to this *life*, was to remember how she had always cheated him out of those words. It would temper every thought she formed about herself from that night on. Love's Misfit had been granted the devotion of a good, good man and would send him off to ashes and dust with a deep regret to cling to. Never worthy of him in life, she had failed him in death as well.

But Anna had been wholly, disastrously wrong about Tony's last thoughts. Her loving words had shot through him on a bolt of electricity, giving him the charge he needed to open his eyes for one more look at the most beautiful part of his whole beautiful world. Anna.

Oh, Corazón. I accept your gift with both hands. But I hope you know I was never left wanting. Everything about you was love. Your voice, your touch, and that running-through-the-candy-store laugh. I knew the very first day I met you that I wanted to be with you for the rest of my life. And I was.

Tony gave her a tired smile and drifted off to sleep without speaking. He slipped quietly, forever away a few minutes later, as two men with a gurney trotted toward them downriver.

37

It had started out as a pretty good show, at least to Eddy's tastes. Jake talked about going swimming with Fritos one hot Saturday, having forgotten to bring his tennis balls (the most beloved *slobber-ons* and *bringy-backs* since the icicles had melted). That was the day Jake had discovered his dog would actually chase after rocks, diving down to fetch them off the river bottom. A couple of fisherkids got such a kick out of watching the dog's antics that they eventually put down their poles and got into the act, throwing stones for Fritos until Jake had to call his friend out of the water to rest. He was worried the dog would go on forever until he was too tired to swim to the surface with a big ol' rock in his mouth. And, of course, the idea of dropping the bringy-back would never occur to the pup.

In other news, Jake, to everyone's surprise, had gotten both of his missing teeth replaced. With as much smiling as he did, people noticed right away, of course. But no one mentioned it, except for Bitter Russ, who couldn't wait to.

"Could you tell me that story again, Rock Hudson? I was a little distracted by all them pearly whites."

This caused Jake to burst out in a full, thirty-two-toothed laugh.

Bunny was in rare form too, swearing up and down that Rain had become some kind of music aficionado, cocking her head to listen intently when certain songs were sung to her. Rain's favorite tunes seemed to have rhyming words that came close together. Like in *When the Red, Red Robin Comes Bob, Bob, Bobbin' Along*. What with a dog's limited attention span, thought Bunny, a rhyming word would have to quickly follow the word it was rhyming *with,* before the first word was forgotten altogether.

But it was Russ and Kitty who made Eddy laugh the hardest. Situation normal, Russ had come prepared to let Kitty fill most of his airtime with her latest trick, allowing him to get away with more showing and less telling. But the big bonus for Russ was that a well-designed dog trick, properly executed, could both amuse *and* affront. Had Russ found himself a protégé who could assist him in the art of offense? Was he grooming a Bitter Kitty?

Russ had squatted down in front of his dog, mostly blocking her from the rest of the room. He appeared to be rubbing her neck, maybe whispering into her ear. It was hard to tell. Eventually, he got up off the floor to sit back down in his chair, as if he'd lost interest. Kitty sat directly in front of him, her eyes riveted on his. Russ looked leisurely around the room, a man waiting for an oil change, perhaps. He squeezed his hands into his pants pockets and yawned.

Just as Eddy saw Anna about to intervene, Russ snapped his focus to the adoring Kitty. They locked eyes, and with a jerk of his chin Russ directed the young dog's attention toward Eddy. Kitty looked over at Eddy, who straightened himself in his chair, starting a smile he couldn't stop. Kitty looked back at her Russ for confirmation, which he gave with a repeat move of his head. Kitty stood and walked directly toward Eddy, her unknown intentions tickling the kooky uncle until his smile hurt his cheeks.

Kitty walked with a presence he might have called *regal*—slowly, but not shyly, head held high. Eddy pivoted on his chair to face her full-on as she came. She walked up to his knees, bent her head, revealing the arc of a particularly long and graceful neck, opened her mouth… and deposited a slobbery pile of plastic puke right onto his lap. Chunky, with just the right mix of brown, pink, and goo, the fake vomit had apparently been wadded up inside of Kitty's mouth and now sprang free, with laws of physics and strings of spittle pleasing the crowd in equal measure. The clan erupted into big whooping laughs—Eddy's the most boisterous of all.

The racket had distorted his audio, he was pretty sure of that. And it took him a long while to explain to his listeners what they had been missing out on. He started by saying that he'd just received the ultimate *gag* gift, causing everyone in the studio to crack up again. It was a minute or so before Eddy could thread enough words together to make a full sentence.

Eddy would look back on this day and realize that it was at this very moment when the show had taken a turn. Cleo's turn, to be exact.

There was a pronounced sadness wafting off of her that morning. If trauma had a face, thought Eddy, then this was it. While she spoke, her eyes darted from Anna to him, to the others, not landing long enough to take anything in. And every few seconds she'd reach down to touch John Henry as he played with Patton on the floor. She'd straighten his hair, brush off lint no one else could see, or tidy-up the collar of his shirt.

Eddy imagined Cleo as a woman who had never officially gotten mad at anyone in her life. And maybe to this day, still, had not gotten mad at Jeffrey but was throwing a whole bunch of mad around *about* him. Her hoarse voice cracked time and again as she talked about trying to get a job—and trying to find daycare for John Henry so she could go out looking. She'd brought him to a summer camp for a week, but when the older kids teased him about his dad getting kicked out of the house, that had been the end of camp.

"What am I supposed to do? Make kids stop saying true things? And I'm afraid that—" Cleo lowered her voice as if John Henry couldn't hear, "—that one of those kids is going to find out everything about everything, and tell my baby boy the whole story."

Last month Cleo had told the clan—off the air—about Jeffrey being gay. But she hadn't yet announced that fact to the rest of the world, and Eddy would see to it that she didn't today, either. In better times, the gracious Cleo would be the last person Eddy would worry about on the air. But it was hard to tell what a person in such upheaval might do. So, as Cleo went on and on about personal topics wholly unrelated to her dog's life, Eddy kept his mind on her stories and his finger on the mute button. He ended up silencing large parts of Cleo's stories, leaving holes in the broadcast audio, but Jeffrey's private life mostly in tact.

Sitting here listening, it occurred to Eddy that Cleo—and others in the clan—were coming to use this show as a sort of therapy session, or at least a massive coffee klatch, with the whole county as confessor, advisor, and mother hen.

As a concept, a two-way radio show with hundreds of neighbors helping to solve your personal problems and celebrating your good times right along with you appealed to Eddy. But in Cleo's case, the talk was too intimate. Too raw. Eddy figured this information was better kept as nobody's business, not everybody's business. Cleo, becoming madder and less guarded with every passing minute, might need someone to save her from herself.

Both Eddy and Anna spoke at once, vying for Cleo's attention. Eddy let Anna take the lead.

"I'm sorry, Cleo, that everything's so hard for you guys right now. Let's get together after the show to talk about it. In the interest of time today, though, how about if you go ahead and tell us what Patton has been up to this month?"

Cleo was barely listening. "Oh, and that's another thing. Patton, here." She moved her hand from the top of John Henry's head to the head of the large dog. "I feel so stupid. But it wasn't until just this week that it finally hit me why Jeffrey wanted to get this exact puppy—the one who looked like a German shepherd. And why he tried to get Patton into that killer dog training class, or whatever it was. He wanted John Henry and me to have a big, scary guard dog to protect us—"

Eddy hit the mute button.

"—because he wasn't going to be around to do it himself anymore, y' know what I'm saying? Jeffrey knew he was leaving and thought this would make everything okay."

Cleo's voice crinkled in anger, but didn't break.

"Hang on a second now," said Anna, a tiny grass shack in the path of Hurricane Cleo. "I don't think we should talk about Jeffrey when he's not here to offer his own thoughts about—"

"I mean, don't worry," Cleo said, nodding her head in a circle as she spoke. "I love Patton and everything, and I'm going to keep him forever, but shame on Jeffrey for that. Shame on him."

Eddy had muted Cleo's rant on Jeffrey—while he was *watching* Jeffrey. No one in the group could see what he saw through the studio window, but the missing clan member had been pacing the length of the hallway for the past ten minutes or so, hearing the show on the speakers out there, but choosing not to come in. Once in awhile he'd stop pacing, wrap his arms around the front of himself, untie them and wrap them the other way around the back, then drop them to his sides and start pacing again. Eddy thought about tapping on the glass to invite him in. But things would always take as long as they took, and Jeffrey would join them if he got himself to a place where he could. In the meantime, Anna needed help with Cleo.

The somewhat rare sound of Eddy's voice interrupting the interview portion of the show made Cleo pull back on the reins for a moment. He released the mute button.

"Hey, Cleo? Anna? I'm sorry, but I wonder if you would let me butt in here. My measly three phone lines have been jammed since before the show began, so I'm thinking it would be good to take a few calls, yeah?"

Most of the people in the room brightened at the idea; Anna shot Eddy the *bless you* look and a signal to patch the first person through.

"One thing, though. Today I'm only one person in this two-person station." He pointed to a photo on the wall, where a young him—and a younger Jenny—stood holding shovels, about to break ground on the WLCM building. "My producer, Jenny, is off today, since her mother's not feeling too well—*Malama pono*, Mrs. McKeel!—so I'm just saying there's nobody here to help man the phones, or screen and prioritize calls, stuff like that, so a little patience might be in order as you're waiting for me to answer your call, yeah? Okay, here we go.

"Hi, you're on the air with the adopters and adoptees from *All of Us Animals*. How're ya doin' today?"

"Hello? Am I on?" The caller was probably a teenager by the sounds of him.

"Yeah, we're here," said Eddy. "Sorry for the wait."

"Uh, that's okay. Hey, I'm calling to say that—"

An eruption of background noise seemed to confuse the caller. He stopped himself, covered the receiver with his hand, and yelled at the other young men laughing and harassing him.

"Will you guys shut up? I'm finally on, here!" Then to Eddy he said, "Sorry 'bout that."

"No worries. What's your name?"

"Oh, sorry. Steve. I'm Steve."

"Do you have something you want to say to our little family, Steve?"

"Yeah. Well, kind of. It's a question. About the mailman guy. I want to know how come every night on my way home from work—I work nights and weekends at the SpeedyGas, so I get home late—I walk through the alley behind the post office, and there he is every night. Sleeping in his car. So, that's what I'm calling about. What's up with that? Why's he always out there in his car?"

Nobody meant to make a dramatic gesture of any kind, but in the confusion of the call, with so much laughing in the background, and such unthinkable news in the foreground, all heads turned in Russ' direction. Eddy saw the trapped animal look on the man's face and knew at once that the rumors he had been hearing were true.

It was three months ago that Eddy had been unable to stop Andrea Shart from telling him what he had had no business knowing. In a narrow aisle at the library, she'd cornered him to report that her husband had been hired to serve legal papers on Russ. Some kind of financial trouble, it had been, but Eddy had tried hard not to listen. The information had greatly saddened Eddy but had come as no surprise. He had already been hearing lots of unwanted gossip about Russ.

As Russ' mother had spiraled downward through her illness, her medical costs had spiraled up. And apparently, Russ had refused to put his mom into a state-run institution to relieve himself of the mounting debt. (Kimmy Branding from the privately owned Turtle Island Senior Care Facility had forced that particular bit of knowledge on Eddy.)

When he'd learned about Russ being served papers of some kind, Eddy had connected the two pieces of information. He thought briefly of asking Russ if he could help in any way. But he knew what the man would say, and that he'd be making Russ feel even worse by asking. So Eddy had done nothing.

And now this. Russ was living out of his car. Had he mortgaged his home to pay for his mother's treatment? Taken out a second mortgage, even? Hospital patients versus banker patience: the first would always outlast the second.

Eddy could see by the alarm on faces around the studio that he was the only person here aware of Russ' plight.

"What are you talking about?" asked Anna. "*Our* Russ?"

It was a meaningless question, Eddy could see. A time-filler as Anna's brain worked to put some order to the young man's words.

"Yeah, I know it's him for sure." Steve didn't sound accusing but prideful in his discovery. "'Cuz the dog's always in there with him, too."

Steve's friends began to snore, cartoon-style. "God! Shut up, you guys!"

As the malicious laughter burst out on Steve's end, Eddy remembered all too well what it had felt like to be tortured by high school boys and saw the familiar drop of Russ' head and the shake in his hands. Eddy hung up on Steve, the abrupt silence making things worse, punctuating the call and all of its implications.

As if the moment weren't complex enough, Jeffrey picked that precise point in time to crack open the studio door and slip inside. It seemed Russ didn't much notice, but all of the other reactions communicated to Jeffrey some combination of "Oh, my," and "Poor you."

Jeffrey walked all the way to the empty chair between Russ and Cleo as if only his feet wanted to go; the rest of his body floated obediently behind. He seated himself on a deep breath. He looked first to his wife, his head tilting toward her, asking permission. Trembling, he took her hand. Cleo's eyes filled with tears and impossible devotion. She shook her head and looked to her lap. But she let her hand stay held.

Jeffrey turned his attention to the wild-eyed Russ, and with his remaining hand, touched the mailman warmly on the back.

Russ exploded at Jeffrey, at the clan, at everyone listening to their radio that morning, with the message he'd been conveying in any number of ways his entire life.

"Mind your own son-of-a bitches!"

38

The river, running the color of liquid chrome, rejected the late June sun at sharp angles. Situation normal, the water's mood matched Anna's own again this morning. Bubbling energy. Over stimulated. Tense.

She'd been down at the river since before sun-up, awake half the night before that, wondering where Russ and Kitty were sleeping. Russ had been unwilling to accept—or even discuss—offers from clan members wanting to take him in. The best they could do for him was to change the subject.

For the past couple of hours she'd been trying to put herself in Russ' position, imagining the series of humiliations he must have endured leading up to being kicked out of his own home. She looked over her shoulder, back at the old white farmhouse, trying to picture the cops coming in to haul her out. Her home was her bedrock. Her nourishment. Her nightly reset button. If someone were to take that away from her, who would she be?

God, how had Russ been functioning? Still going to work. Solving daily emergencies for people like the aging Mrs. Korhonen, with their jammed garbage disposals and shutters-come-loose. All the while, he'd been suffering what must have been a tremendous amount of personal stress as he tried to live with—and conceal—his secret. And what about Kitty? Would she be safe out there? Anna would watch for signs of danger to the dog, but she strongly believed Russ would protect his best friend at all costs.

She walked briskly up the hill to her garage, whistling through her teeth for Storm at a volume her mother would have called unladylike. The fluffy white shepherd tore through the woods, passed Anna by, and was dancing at the door of the pickup before she got there.

"Good morning." Anna was glad to hear her voice sound more amiable than she felt.

"Hey." Brian Ardeen slipped into the truck beside Storm.

The dog was still wary of him; her tail wagged close to her body, and she kept her head low between her shoulders. But she offered Ardeen a much warmer greeting than Anna could have mustered. Storm licked his face a couple of times and wiggled up against him before turning to keep watch out the windshield. Every morning Anna was reminded of how much more forgiving this species was than her own.

"So…" Ardeen hesitated. "I heard what happened on the radio yesterday."

Anna was surprised to hear him mention the radio show at all; he'd always avoided the topic. And if forced to address it, he would refer to the program as *All of Us Assholes*.

"You did, huh? Which part are you talking about? The phone call for Russ?"

"That's the mailman?"

"Yes."

"Then, yeah. So what, he's freakin' homeless or somethin'?"

Anna adjusted her rearview mirror unnecessarily and cleared her throat.

"I guess so. I don't have a lot of information about it. He's never been too keen on talking about his personal life, and he shut down entirely after that call. But I spoke to Eddy later, and he seemed to know a little more. I think things must be pretty bad."

Ardeen puffed air through his lips in a sarcastic laugh; it was a habit that Anna detested, and this morning she let it get to her.

"What?" The word was a demand.

"Never mind. I'm not in the mood to fight with you today."

She softened her voice. "No, come on. Let's talk about this. I'm glad you listened to the show. So tell me. What's so funny?"

"Well, I think it's kinda—interesting," he had paused to choose the word, then seemed to review it after he'd said it, "that you took all that time to find the perfect homes for those puppies, and as of today, two of 'em are staying with some old lady who's gonna die before they do, another one lives in a broken home with some pretty serious shit goin' on, and now a fourth one lives out on the street."

Anna's temperature spiked. "Well, the operative word in that sentence is *lives*. Better to be out on the street than to be nowhere at all, which was your big plan for those puppies."

"You know what? Screw it. Forget I said anything."

"No, let's not screw it. Let's have it out. We dance all around this topic—*the* topic—day after sickening day. So let's just do it. Come on, I really want to hear what you're thinking."

He opened his mouth to speak.

"But I'll go first." She took a nanosecond to look inward, wondering if she should be heading down this path when she was already so worked up about Russ. Then again that's probably *why* she wanted to mix it up with Ardeen. She compromised with herself—she would take him on but would make an effort to keep her cool.

"All right. Here's how I see it. You made this dog live her whole life outside on a three-foot chain. And when she got pregnant, which only happened because—hey, did I mention she'd spent her whole life outside on a chain?—you stole her puppies and made her watch as you put them to a slow, painful death, or tried to, instead of just swinging by the humane society on your way to work, which would have been, you know, a little too much trouble."

"Go to hell."

"Clever comeback. But I really want to know, Brian. Enlighten me. How is it that a person comes to a decision like that?

"Jesus. How did we get here? I got in the truck and said, 'Hi, heard about the mailman,' and suddenly you're all over me. I don't get it."

"No. Please don't wiggle out of this conversation with one of your typical, refusing-to-answer answers."

Anna pulled the truck over to the gravel shoulder and turned to face him. "Wait. I don't mean to be so sarcastic." She took a deep breath, letting it out as a trickle while she forced her shoulders to relax. "However we got here, we're here, so why don't we finally have that talk that's been hovering over every conversation we've ever had?"

She turned the key and pulled it out of the ignition.

What the hell is this? Was he ever gonna be able to talk to her without stepping in it? He'd been feeling pretty okay lately too. Everyone except Dr. Giant had pretty much loosened up on him over at the clinic, and he'd been fitting in good enough. What did she want from him, anyway? How could she always make him feel like shit so fast?

"So now you're just going to sit there and stare at me," she said. "I was hoping we could talk about this like two adults."

Up yours, up YOURS! He pushed his feet hard against the floor mat, shoving himself deeper into the seat. He wanted to look away but knew it would piss her off even worse.

"Come on, Brian."

He wasn't buying that all-sweetness voice of hers.

"Why did you do it? Believe me, I'm not trying to trick you here. I really want to know. I honestly don't get why you would bury those puppies. And if I could understand what you were thinking, maybe that would be a good starting place for you and me."

Brian put his hand to the far side of his hot neck and pinched the skin hard where she couldn't see. That's what she wanted to know? What he was *thinking* back then? Jesus, really? He had no idea. He barely remembered what had gone down on that day.

"You can tell me." She folded her arms across her chest and leaned back against the door of the truck, smiling a little. "Think back to that morning. You come out of your house. You see the puppies. And at some point you decide you need to bury them. I just want to understand how you come to that decision."

The thing was, it didn't seem like there was any real reason. It was just something he'd done. "I don't know," he said, not mad and not sorry, but squirming under the feeling of her questions all over him. He could see by her face it was the wrong answer.

"You don't know? How could you not know? It was something you specifically did. It took a lot of effort. A lot of time. There must have been some kind of thought process going on there."

Thought process? Screw you and how you talk.

Whenever people had asked him why he'd done it, he never gave the question any thought at all. 'Cuz it was nobody's goddamn business, that's why. But was that really why? He wasn't sure about that, either.

"Oh, come on, just tell me."

Okay, okay, shut the hell up for a second—let me think.

And for the first time since that day eight months ago, Brian made himself think about why, exactly, he had buried the puppies.

He remembered standing there, looking down at them all in a row by Storm's belly, making those little grunting sounds. And the dog trying to cover them up with her head, and with her tail too. That was weird, come to think of it. Like she was hiding them. Like she thought he might do something to them. *God, that had pissed him off.* Her trying to protect those puppies from him.

And as he pictured himself there on that day, with those puppies, he went right back to the feeling he had worn forever but hadn't been noticing as much lately. His understanding of himself as someone who was worse than other people. Not as real. Something less. And even the dog had known it.

When he felt his mind trying to avoid thinking this through, trying to stop thinking altogether, he forced it back on track.

No way was he going to be able to keep those puppies. He didn't have that kind of money. Brian's hand started rubbing his mouth. He wanted to swallow but couldn't.

Not in words, but in the familiar weight of a dirty bathrobe, he slipped back into being the guy who never took care of shit that needed taking care of—like bills, and the house, and the goddamn dog. Other people would fix the loose doorknob or wipe the dust off the windowsill or go to the dentist. But for some reason he honest-to-god could not understand, he would always put that shit off until it was too late, and then bad things would happen. And every bad thing led to another bad thing.

So why hadn't he just taken the puppies to the shelter in Amery that morning? That's what she wanted to know. He tried to think. It just—hadn't felt possible. All those people behind the counter at that place, acting all holier than thou about him and what he'd done. No way. Not an option.

Aware of her still watching him, he rubbed his eyes, giving himself time to keep thinking. Why had he cared so much about what those assholes at the shelter would think, anyway?

He looked over at Dr. Giant still waiting for her answer. He opened his mouth to talk—when another memory from that day bitch-slapped him. He could remember thinking that burying the puppies wasn't going to be that hard. That all he had to do was put them into a bag and put the bag in a hole.

What? Jesus! Really? It seemed like he was remembering some dream where he was doing stuff he couldn't do in real life, like fly over trees or turn invisible.

He opened his eyes and looked down at his fingers digging into his knees. Right then, for some reason, he pictured the litter of kittens they'd had at the clinic last week. Abandoned by their mom, they'd been way too skinny, so he'd had to feed them by hand. And after a couple of days they'd gotten to looking pretty good.

Anna didn't know if she had ever seen Ardeen like this. It wasn't his angry look. Or his sullen look. Or even his *I want to hurt you* look which she might have expected, seeing as she was cornering him on their very hottest topic.

"Brian?"

His troubled eyes shifted back to hers from some point out in space.

"Did you want to say something?"

She knew she was seeing part of Ardeen he hadn't shown her before. Unprotected. Thoughtful. She had felt sorry for him in the past, but this was the first time she had ever almost liked him.

Brian heard her question come from far away.

Did he want to say something? Actually, maybe. But was he really going to tell her about that day? Was that a good idea? She didn't seem like she was trying to dick with him. And maybe if he talked to her, gave her what she wanted, she would relax her crack around him a little.

He pressed his lips hard together while he decided how to start the story. The best he could manage was to squeeze the words out one at a time, in tight little sausage casings, pinched-off deep in his throat.

"Yeah. Okay. You're right. I was an asshole." It wasn't as hard to admit as he'd thought it would be, so he could probably go on. He just needed a second to figure out what to say next.

But the look she gave him was all wrong. Her mouth fell open, and her eyes went down to little slits. And when she spoke, she mocked his tone, making it seem totally different than it had sounded in his own head.

"'You're right. I was an asshole.' Seriously? More sarcasm? God, that's so typical!" She sat up straight, shaking her head and shoving the key back into the ignition. "You know, for a second there, I actually thought you might say something real. Like a grown-up. But that just isn't in you, is it?"

Brian coughed out a single laugh, which got her even crazier, but he couldn't help it. He held his breath and clenched his jaw shut.

They rode without speaking for a long time. Then just before they reached the clinic, she said something in a soft, sad voice.

"Sorry."

She sounded like she was gonna cry, which made him feel kinda shitty. He turned to look at her; she was staring straight ahead with the most pathetic look on her face. He wondered what to say. And that was when he realized she was looking at something out in the road. He followed her eyes to the dead squirrel.

Brian Ardeen leaned his head out the open window, hating what it was doing to his hair, but needing the wind to hide the sound coming from his throat.

39

Anna fumed. She'd been sitting at her desk for ten minutes or so, doing absolutely nothing but jiggling the foot at the end of the leg crossed high on her thigh. Like the wing of a housefly, her canvas shoe fluttered madly, while her mind darted from thing to infuriating thing about Ardeen. She would relive each appalling act, get herself a little more worked up, and then try to figure out what else about him pissed her off.

His attitude. His long silences and angry outbursts. His inability (or at least unwillingness) to treat her clients with respect. Okay, yes, he'd been getting better at those things. But too slowly. Way too slowly.

Oh! And then there were his god-awful friends. They'd been waiting for him yesterday when she and Ardeen had walked outside on their way to his factory job. There they were, leaning their backs up against her truck as if they owned it. Toot, the big, dopey one, had jumped up when he saw them coming. But not the little feisty one. Beaudry. Bo, as his disciples called him. He'd held his ground, trying to stare her down, heel hooked on her front bumper, the cigarette as much a part of his face as his pointed snout. With great intent, he opened one half of his mouth and did not blow, but rather *oozed* smoke from his lungs into a screen he could peer through with those rat-like eyes. Anna knew he was trying to intimidate her; it was his typical M.O. And although she found his badass expressions laughable, she couldn't help but consider him dangerous. Or maybe *destructive* was a better word.

She worried when he hung around, not so much for her physical safety, but for her property. Her things. She never had gotten get her scalpel back. And now here was this jerk leaning against her truck, laying some kind of claim to it. *Her* truck. Her old-but-barely-scratched truck. Her used-to-be-Tony's truck. The truck she got proposed to in.

The truck they went camping with. The truck that had to stay pristine forever, because anything happening to it would snap another thread. This joker had his grimy jeans up against the hood, daring her to do something about it. She sensed that one wrong word might send the heel of the scumbag's boot straight through her front grill.

Beaudry, the leader of this pack, ruled by instilling fear; that much was obvious. Anna had noticed Ardeen miss a step when he first spotted the two of them waiting by the truck. She had watched Brian change shape, walking with shoulders slumped slightly forward. The tough guy who'd tried to terrorize her in her own parking lot just over five months ago was now looking anywhere but into Beaudry's eyes. If Ardeen were a dog, he might have rolled onto his back and peed on himself. And though Anna felt a bit sorry for her employee, or whatever he was, she knew enough not to let her guard down. Around this Beaudry character, Ardeen was especially likely to tick her off, doing whatever he could to stay on the headman's good side.

Two other times since she'd first chased Beaudry out of her surgery, she'd found the three of them in places Ardeen had known to be off-limits to his chums. She'd found them out by the backyard kennels where three dogs had later mysteriously turned up missing. It was only by luck she'd been able to secure all three animals from their reckless spree through the neighborhood.

She'd also had to shoo Ardeen's friends out of the basement storage area, where she'd later discovered pilfered boxes of office supplies and obscenities carved into cartons of paper towels.

And now the vandals had returned. Sprawled across her truck, touching her things. Cockroaches. On the swarm and spreading disease.

As it turned out, Ardeen was the only one to speak, his voice a step higher than usual.

"Hey, Bo. What's up?"

Beaudry said nothing. He pushed his shiny boot against the bumper, peeling himself from the truck, which Anna immediately scanned for damage. Beaudry swaggered off, his minions trailing in his wake. He led them to a point just around the corner of the building, still in Anna's sight but out of earshot. The three of them huddled together conspiratorially, with Beaudry no doubt masterminding the next ill-doing the unholy trinity would undertake.

Thinking back on how testy Ardeen had been after he'd said goodbye to his friends and returned to the truck, Anna brought her fluttering foot to a sudden halt. She had questioned him on why Beaudry and Toot had been waiting in ambush, and he'd responded with his signature heated eruption.

"Oh, I get it. If they were your friends, they woulda been waiting for you to get off work. But my friends, they wait in ambush."

He'd had a point, of course. These were his friends, such as they were. And she couldn't exactly prove they'd been here specifically to make trouble. But no matter how he chose to spend his time *off*, she'd made it abundantly clear after each destructive appearance that these guys were not welcome on her property. Period. And yet again, yesterday, they'd shown up. And Ardeen hadn't made them leave; he'd entertained them while she'd waited to chauffeur him to his next job.

She could see now that nothing she'd ever say to Ardeen would keep those losers from coming around, intruding on her business. On her life. With him she got them. This was not the arrangement she had struck with the judge. Didn't she have a right to safeguard her livelihood? And a responsibility to protect her clients?

What she really wanted was to let Ardeen go. She wanted to fire him, or lay him off, or whatever one did to a court-ordered employee. The experiment wasn't working for her. After all this time, she still couldn't trust him, and she was bone tired of having to live life on the defensive.

But then again, he *had* seemed to be inching away, slowly, from his animal-equals-garbage position. And wasn't that the point of having him here in the first place? She knew she should grit her teeth and resolve to carry on for one more month. She, Katie, and Noah had each caught him in acts of kindness toward their patients, usually performed on the sly. Oddly, he seemed so uncomfortable when spotted, the staff had adopted a *don't ask/don't thank* policy. And if she were completely honest with herself, she'd have to admit that Ardeen had proven a fast learner, and he shared her sense of wonder for the science of veterinary medicine.

But his marginal enlightenment had come at too great a cost for her. It didn't seem worth it, having to feel this bad five mornings a week until she could dump him off at the factory and breathe freely again. Or was she being oversensitive? The rest of the staff seemed to accept him. Was the problem actually hers?

She was torn from her internal squabble by the unmistakable sound of a large, panting dog tearing down the hall toward her office. The yellow cannon ball shot past her door, then having seen her, skittered to a sloppy halt in a great flurry of nails and hardwood. Fritos barreled into her office and joyfully threw the upper half of his body (including drooling maw, fresh from the water dish up front) onto her plaid bermudas.

"Thank you!" Anna said, cheerily. She mopped her shirt with one hand while scratching his head with the other, in the same back and forth motion.

"Anna?" Katie's voice came through the intercom on her phone.

"Let me guess. My 11:00 is here."

"You got it." Katie clicked off mid-chuckle.

Anna stood as Jake appeared at her office door.

"Hiya, Anna." That rumbling bass of his still made her smile.

"Jake, hi. Hey, no beard!"

They hugged warmly, as all clan members—except Russ—had been doing for a couple of months now.

"Yeah. Turns out there's skin under here." He ran his rough hand over clean-shaven cheeks. "It's been pretty much rumor-only for about ten years, y' know?"

Anna was once again struck by how radically Jake had changed his looks in the five-plus months she'd known him. His recent tooth replacement had given him a gorgeous smile. But he'd also been keeping his hedge of unruly, red locks mostly tied back, and had dramatically lowered the ratio of shreds to viable cloth in his everyday wardrobe. And now this.

"Wow. You look so young. What ever possessed you to shave it off?"

"I looked so old."

"Ah, right. Well, have a seat." She took one herself. "You want coffee or a coke or something?"

"No, thanks. I don't really do the caffeine thing."

"Y' know, I always forget that. It's hard for me to remember such nonsense words." She took a sip from her WLCM-FM coffee mug. "But you do drink water, if I recall."

"Eight glasses a day, but I'm good, thanks."

Anna spent the first half of the brief pause that followed wondering why Jake had made an official appointment to talk with her today when he might just as easily have shown up at the clinic unannounced, as he and Fritos had done every week or so for some time now, just to say *Hey*.

But the tiny window of silence also made her more aware of her clenched muscles, nervous stomach, and general unease—leftovers from thinking about Ardeen. She had to make a decision about that guy. What the hell was she going to do? She hated the idea of feeling like this for another whole month.

Anna found herself wishing she possessed even a fraction of Eddy's ability to live solely in the moment. She forced her attention back to the always-surprising Jake.

Her ginger-haired friend had something so big on his mind he could barely stay put in his chair. He wiggled, twisted, and shifted himself up, over, and nearly out a few times. And because Jake's fertile mind was the playground where far-fetched ideas went to get crazy, Anna knew that whatever he was hatching would at least amuse, and more likely amaze, her.

"So, Anna."

"Jake?"

"Here's somethin'!"

Jake Ellertson often began his presentations in just that way. Like last month: *Here's somethin'! I'm thinking of installing a feeding system for Fritos, where he has to jump into the air and whack a lever to dump kibble into his dish. Good fun and a good workout, dontcha think?*

Or, *Here's somethin'! What if a guy like me was to build a doggie car? You know, that Fritos could sit in and drive all by himself? It'd be electric, y' know? And all he has to do is put his front paws on the steering wheel to get it to go. And he steers it by leaning in one direction or the other, right? Can a dog drive? Whaddaya think?*

But, of course, it rarely mattered what people thought, because Jake acted on most of his ideas that ever made it to the *Here's somethin'!* stage.

"Okay," said Anna, already feeling an *Oh my god!* welling up inside of her. "What now?"

He paused in thought before heading in, rubbing the backs of his fingers along his newly exposed, square jaw line. Anna had always suspected the presence of a handsome man under the scraggy façade; it was a treat to meet him.

"Okay. Okay. Here's somethin'!" He was working himself up into the big pitch. "I'm thinking we should do a run for the homeless. Y'know? For Russ. Well—for homeless people everywhere, really. Whaddaya think?"

"Are you saying that we'd host a run and give the proceeds to Russ?"

"Right! And I was thinkin' we could get the rest of the clan to help out with it, y' know? Hey! And all the puppies could run, too. In fact, everybody who runs can bring their dog, dontcha think? Oh! We could call it *Home Is Where the Bark Is*. No, that's lame. Wait—maybe just *The Dog Run*. Whatever. Anyways, whaddaya say? Wouldn't it be great? Maybe we can even get enough money to buy Russ' house back for him. That'd be so cool, wouldn't it? And Eddy could use the radio station to promote it on the air!"

In five months of playing audience to Jake's harebrained propositions, this was the first time she was having trouble getting there with him. She had to concentrate on keeping her mouth shut, because every other part of her body was screaming for him to stop. When Jake finally drew breath, she reluctantly put the pin to his bubble.

"Jake?"

Her dubious tone tugged down on the corners of his smile.

"This is a charity run we're talking about?"

"Yeah, I guess so."

"For Russ. Charity for Russ. That we'd be promoting to the whole world. The fact that Russ needs charity."

"Oh." His face drooped from the Comic thespian mask to the Tragic one. "Oh, cripes. That's not gonna work, is it?"

"No." She was nodding slowly. "Probably not."

"Huh." He pushed himself back in his chair, slapping his palms to his lap. "That can't work at all."

But even as he kissed his big idea goodbye, she could see him fish around for another.

"I've got to say, though, I love that you're working on creative solutions for Russ. I'm still slogging around in the desperation part."

And that was exactly why she'd always looked up to people like Jake. Eddy too. It wasn't that they didn't feel awful when horrible things happened. But they corralled those feelings, allowing them only a tiny corner of the brain to gnaw on, while the rest of the system went to work on solving the problem.

"Okay, how 'bout this!" Jake's newly-hatched plan brought him again to the front of his seat. "We've got that photo shoot with your friend coming up, right?"

"You mean Marion? The poster for her dog grooming place?"

"Yeah. We're getting a hundred bucks per pup, y' know? And Storm, she's getting a hundred too, right?"

"Yes…"

"Well, maybe we could all give our money to Russ. It's not a ton of dough, I know. Six hundred total. But it'd be a start. Then again—I dunno." He seemed to lose faith in this idea too. "He'd prob'ly never accept it, would he?"

"But wait!" Anna was back in her familiar role as Jake's sorcerer's apprentice. "I think we should get Marion in on this. I'm sure she'd be willing to tell him a little white lie. What if she told Russ that she's decided to pay *everybody* six hundred dollars."

"Not sure if I get ya."

"Well then she gives Russ the entire amount of money she was going to pay out to all of us."

"Sweet! Kind of devious thinking for the straight-laced Anna Dunlop, isn't it?"

"Desperate times and all that."

"It's an awesome plan."

"Only if the others are willing to give up their shares." She was thinking Cleo could probably use the money for herself.

"I bet anything they will. The photo shoot was always more about the fun than the money."

A soft knock on the door carried Katie in on a whisper.

"Anna? Can I talk to you for a minute?"

"You know what? Hey," said Jake, gently lifting Fritos' head off his lap to stand up. "We're pretty much done here anyways, right? I'll get outta your way."

"Really?" said Anna. "Because I can come right back."

"Naw, I'm good. I'm gonna go call Cleo and Bunny, see what they think. I'll get back to ya."

"Okay, if you're sure."

She rose to give him a quick hug, and then Jake grabbed Fritos by the collar to lead him out of her office.

"You know, Jake, they make these long, ropey things now called leashes. You can just buy one right at the store and snap it onto that collar-dealie thing."

His infectious laugh, always crouched in the ready position, tumbled out into the room.

He nodded at Anna and spun to leave. As he slipped by Katie in the doorway, an arc of electrons sizzled between them. He took her hand and gave it a quick squeeze as if he had done so every day of his life. Katie gave him a smile that glowed with a light Anna had never noticed in her before.

So that explained Jake's recent attention to his looks! His new teeth, his new face. His new love! Excellent. They were perfect for each other.

"Um… Anna?" Katie looked grim. "I think I need to tell you something."

"I'll say you do!" Anna plunked herself down into the chair behind her desk, motioning for Katie to take the one on the other side.

Katie remained standing.

"How long have you and Jake been an item? And why exactly haven't we been giggling about what a great kisser he is? And scribbling *Mrs. Katie Ellertson* all over your notebooks and stuff? You're cheating me out of my best girlfriend due, and I tell you, I won't have it!"

"Yeah." She exuded her usual amount of cynicism. "That whole giggling and scribbling thing. That would be me. Jake and I—we—I don't know. We're something, but I don't know what just yet. We've been seeing each other for a couple of months or so. I guess it might be kind of serious or something."

"Katie, that couldn't be better news. I'm so happy for you. I want details. Gimme."

"Okay, sure. Later, though. We've got to talk."

"All right." Anna sobered up. "This sounds serious."

"It is. I kept hoping it wasn't true, but it really looks like—someone has—well, a vial of ketamine is—missing."

The pen Anna had been playing with came to a halt. Then slammed to her desk.

"What?" She stood up. "Missing? What are you saying?"

"I'm saying one's disappeared. Recorded in the book as *definitely should be here,* but not here. Missing."

"How can that be?" asked Anna, already gone from the room.

40

Brian closed the exam room door to get to the puddle of pee. Kneeling down with a roll of paper towels, he finally figured out what a basset hound kept in that long, mutant body. The world's biggest bladder.

He finished the job and stood up just in time to keep from being knocked unconscious. When the wooden door slammed open, he jumped farther than he would have had to and got instantly mad at himself for being such a pussy. It was only Dr. Giant, but she was a lot more worked up than he'd ever seen her.

"That's it!" She was using some freaky-ass yell that was also a whisper. "You're out of here! Oh—and P.S.— you're going back to jail!"

He was pissed, but wasn't sure why yet. It was always a wild ride with this chick. Some days she'd treat him like he was an actual employee, teaching him things, even laughing with him. And other times she'd get all righteous, using words he'd have to look up in the dictionary if he gave a good goddamn. But this angry dragon thing was new.

"What's your problem?" He held as steady as he could, trying to smirk a little, but he couldn't lift his eyes from the yellowed paper towel in his hand.

She closed the door, trapping him in a rat hole with a crazy person. He set the piss-soaked towel on the metal table to give himself two free hands.

"Oh, gee," she said, bowels-of-hell sarcastic. "You want to know what my problem is. Okay. Let's see. My *problem* is, I've told you about a million times not to bring those criminals around here, but around they come anyway, a couple of times a week. That's a problem. And I've made it quite clear that you're never—ever—to touch our controlled drugs, but I come to find out you were rummaging around in that cabinet just last Friday. That's a problem."

"Hey! Katie was busy and gave me the key to go get her some—"

"Then surprise, surprise, your creep show friends make their next and *final* appearance here yesterday out in the parking lot, and suddenly we realize we're missing a bottle of ketamine. *Special K*, as you call it."

"As *I* call it?"

"Oh, give me one large break! Don't you dare deny this, Ardeen."

As pissed off as he was getting, he was Yoda compared to her.

"Fifteen years I've been in practice, and never once have I had anything stolen. You're here four months, and the strongest hallucinogen I've got turns up missing. I know the street value of that stuff. And then yesterday, with me standing right there, you go huddle up with your loser pals behind the building—my building—so you can hand the stuff off to them. Just how stupid do you think I am?"

"You're not stupid, *Dr. Giant*." They both heard the name out loud for the first time. "You're goddamn nuts!"

She stopped railing on him, cocking her head, giving him time to think. This was bad for him. Really bad. Could Toot and Bo (those assholes) have gotten in here and taken that stuff somehow? Toot could never have dreamed up a job like that, but Bo was always planning things, and Toot would do what he was told.

"You know what?" She took her voice down a couple of decibels. "You know what?" she said again, bobbing her head up and down, and she was sort of smiling. "You're exactly right. That's what I've been. Goddamn nuts."

She took a step closer to him. As casually as he could, Brian moved around the end of the metal table, putting it between himself and whatever the hell was happening here.

"As bent of a person as you are, you still made me believe—off and on, anyway—that maybe this could work, even though you push people. You offend them, because maybe you never learned any better. But, come on—even you know it's not okay to steal."

She braced herself with both arms, hands flat on the metal tabletop, leaning as close to him as she could. He could smell the cherry cough drop he'd seen her open awhile ago.

"The real you just can't stay hidden for very long, can it? God, whatever made me think you'd be able to function like a normal human being?"

And that's when he started to shrink. It was weird how fast his real self could take over again. Smaller. Less solid. He'd been hoping to outgrow the snakeskin, but mostly he knew that he'd never be more than what his dad called *a smear of shit on their pretty white shoes*.

He felt his lip start to quiver, so he pinched the skin on his upper thigh, twisting it as hard as he could. The pain made him grunt, but Dr. Batshit was too on-a-roll to notice.

"So here's what we're going to do." She was talking slowly, with too much space between words. "I'm going to take you to the door, and you're going to walk through it—forever—and never touch my things again. Okay?"

His eyes were stinging. She was kicking him out. He dug for his anger, knowing it would do him more good than feeling sorry for himself. "What, you think you can just fire me?" Hearing his voice sound stronger than he thought it would made him stand a little straighter.

"Um, let's see..." she said, tapping her mouth with her finger and looking up at the ceiling. She came back to stare him right in the face, smiling. "Yeah, I'm pretty sure I can."

Her nasty attitude was helping him stay mad. "And the fact that just maybe I didn't take your bullshit drugs doesn't even count, right?"

"I should have figured you wouldn't admit it. Wow, Ardeen, you are nothing if not consistent."

"You know, you can't even do this. You've got a court order. You gotta let me work here until my fine's paid off, and that's not for another four weeks."

"Wrong again." She had this sickening smile he wanted to slap off her face. "You don't think I've looked over that paperwork about a million times since you've been here?"

"Looking for a loophole to kick my ass through?"

"Wanting to know my options. And the agreement clearly states that I can choose to terminate your community service at any time if I let the court know, which I'll do, first thing tomorrow. And meanwhile, you can get yourself out of my life."

Brian opened his mouth but nothing came.

She opened the exam room door and stood there waiting for him to lead, *her face so puckered, it matched her asshole,* he heard his dad say.

He took his time and scooped the wet paper towel off the table, jamming it into the trashcan on his way out the door. He felt her breath on his neck as he walked by.

This whole thing was a total pig screw. After all the crap he'd pulled around here when he first started—he finally stopped being a prick, and *that* was when he got shit-canned? It would be funny, if this weren't the worst he'd ever felt.

He heard her walking behind him, squeaking the boards of the warped floors, and he missed this old building already. It had been cool to work in a firehouse where so much life and death shit must have gone on. As he passed his desk he saw the wrestling magazine he'd been reading on break and the guinea pig's water bottle holder he was trying to fix.

This was it. He was done. He was a factory worker. And for no good reason. That was the pisser of it. He hadn't taken a damn thing, and if Bo had, then Bo was the asshole, right?

He could see into the waiting room at the end of the hall and realized the sun had faded the schnauzer rug. It needed to be moved away from the glass front door. But, hey. Not his problem anymore. Which made his throat squeeze shut and his eyes start to water. He shoved his hands into his pants pockets but had trouble grabbing his skin through the slippery cloth.

Noah came to the door of the surgery and stood there watching his walk of shame. Brian looked down at the floor. Just this morning they'd been talking about going out to do some drinking, maybe next week. And now that wouldn't happen either, which really sucked, because he and Noah were getting kind of tight. Yesterday, in the middle of working on a stray cat messed up in a fight, Noah had given him this serious look and told him he was glad to have him there. Just like that.

Right after the cat had shown up, Noah went to collect the drugs Dr. Giant was gonna need to whip up a batch of *kitty magic*. Brian loved that term, *kitty magic*. The concoction turned a cat into a mellow sack of jelly while they did all the stuff to it that would hurt like hell otherwise. Like having to clean out and sew up the cat's ear yesterday. It'd been ripped almost all the way off.

And when Brian had held the cat for Dr. Giant, Noah had said how expert he was at holding animals down without stressing them out too much.

"Dude, you're the Cat Whisperer," Noah said, which everybody got a good laugh out of, even Dr. Giant.

God, he was gonna miss this place so bad. If things had been different, maybe he could have been a vet himself. He was good—really good—at memorizing stuff, like all the ingredients of kitty magic. He mouthed the names of the drugs, trying to ignore the sound of her footsteps behind him. Metoclopramide for nausea, enrofloxacin as an antibiotic, and the sedatives, medetomidine, torbugesic—

And ketamine.

Brian stopped walking, and Dr. Giant almost rammed right into him. He turned slowly around to stare up into her face, which looked surprised that he had halted her little death march.

"Wait a second." He said it to himself, not her.

"What?"

"Wait one goddamn second!" That one was for her.

He pushed by Dr. Giant and took off at a trot back up the long hallway. He'd already made it to the surgery before he heard her heading after him. By the time she got to the surgery doorway, he'd already gotten around Noah and was pawing through the high wooden cabinet where the non-controlled drugs were stored.

"What do you think you're doing?" asked Dr. Giant. "Get out of there!"

"Keep your panties smooth."

She moved in and grabbed his arm with both hands. Though he could have flicked her across the room if he'd wanted, he let her pull his arm out of the cabinet. His hand was in a fist, which made her look at his face to see if he meant to hit her with it. The truth was, this was the first time in the last ten minutes he *hadn't* wanted to punch her.

He turned to face Dr. Giant, and making a big deal out of it, lifted the fingers of his fist, one at a time, to reveal the bottle of ketamine in his open palm.

"I don't get it," she said, taking the vial and holding it up to see that it was just about full.

He could tell she was pushing around the same puzzle pieces he'd just snapped together himself.

"Whoa, dude!" said Noah, coming toward them. "The ketamine." He took Brian's right hand in both of his, pumping it and smiling.

"Yup."

When Noah finally let go of Brian's hand, he slapped him on the back.

"Seriously, Bri. How'd ya know it was here?"

Dr. Giant didn't say shit but obviously wanted to know the same thing.

"That cat yesterday," said Brian. The one that got all tore up from fighting?"

"Yeah. The stray one the Paulsons brought in?"

"All hell was breaking loose at the same time, remember? We had to hurry up and finish with him 'cuz that Weimeraner was puking in the next room?"

"Yeah…?"

"So I got to thinking, what if in a big hurry you picked up the ketamine with all the other non-controlled drugs and put it back in the wrong cabinet?"

"Wow, dude. But what's weird is that I already checked in here this morning when we saw it was missing."

"I don't know what to tell ya, except that it'd fallen over onto its side, so I couldn't see it. I had to feel for it."

"Good job, Sherlock!" Noah laughed, grabbing Brian in a huge bear hug.

"Okay, okay. Get a girlfriend." Brian tried to sound mad but didn't pull away.

Noah let him go.

"I'm just so glad you didn't have anything to do with what happened, y' know? Except of course, for being the big brainiac who figured it all out. So, hey, get back to work."

"Yeah, I've only got four weeks left. See if you can keep your hands off me 'til then, all right?" Brian couldn't stop smiling.

Dr. Giant finished locking the ketamine in its cabinet and marked something down in the controlled drugs record book. She put her hands in the pockets of her white coat.

"Brian," she said, worried-looking. "I don't know what to say. I'm—sorry. I feel so bad. I just—assumed—"

"Assumed I was pulling shit. I get it." He lowered one shoulder and stretched his neck by turning his head in the other direction. "It's okay. I guess. But maybe next time you could take a few breaths before ripping me a new one."

"Brian. The thing is—this doesn't really change anything."

"What? What are you talking about?"

"I still need you to go. I'm ending your community service with us. I'm sorry. I'm sure the court will let you work off your fine somewhere else. In fact, I'll talk to them about that. But I need this to be over."

His chest felt too heavy to get the volume he needed.

"You are *shitting* me!"

"Come on, get your stuff. I'll take you to the plant."

Noah looked at Dr. Giant, then back at Brian. "Dude. I'm sorry. Really." He put a hand on Brian's upper arm for a moment, then gave it a tap, shaking his head. "If you guys can't work this out—well, call me. I'll buy you that beer we've been talking about."

Noah gave his boss a sad smile as he left, closing the surgery door behind him.

Ardeen hadn't said a word since they'd gotten into the truck, which was preferable to how he'd bellowed, back at the clinic. But Anna wished he would talk to her now. She wanted to know if he understood why she was letting him go. Making him go. She had tried to explain how sorry she was. For everything.

His only response had been, "My shift doesn't start for an hour yet—I don't need any bullshit questions from the douchebags down there. Just take me home."

She had no idea how he would get himself to the factory, if that was even his plan. But it was none of her business anymore, so she didn't ask.

She looked over at him now, on this, their final truck ride together. His body was turned, crescent shape, toward the door, his left arm gripping the top of his right arm, his forehead tipped against the window. It was the closest he could come to not being there at all. Why he didn't roll down the window to catch the breeze in this eight-five-degree weather was beyond her.

Storm lay between them, her face against his backside. As was her way, the perceptive canine seemed to be reacting to the amount of misery in the truck. And if her body language was any indication, she was siding with the underdog.

Though Storm was wary of Ardeen, especially when he moved his hands too quickly, she loved it when he petted her, and she tried to do what she could to please him. His foul mouth, his sleazy clothes, what he had done to her in his past—none of it stopped this dog from wanting to be close to him.

As she watched Storm stretch her neck out a little farther, pressing her head more deeply into Ardeen's back, Anna realized that showing this guy the smallest kindness would cost her nothing. It was probably what he had been missing his entire life, and she knew it. "Brian?"

She thought his body stiffened, but she couldn't be sure. "Brian, I'm sorry. I know I've already told you that, but I don't think I was sorry enough when I said it. I can't imagine how it must have felt to be accused of such a terrible thing. I was way out of line. And I know I'm too paranoid around you."

After a little more driving, she spoke again. "I also want you to know something else. During these past few months I've seen a lot of change in you. You've learned a ton about veterinary medicine. I was constantly surprised by how many questions you asked, trying to absorb as much as you could. I saw a passion for the work I wish I'd had myself when I was your age. Or even now, for that matter."

He didn't move a muscle.

"You came a long way in how you talked with clients too. She smiled. "I'll never forget that day early on when Mr. Hammersheid showed up with his new pet bunny. He said it was pooping all over his house, and he was wondering how he could fix that. To which you said, 'Teriyaki marinade, four minutes each side.' I mean, that was wholly inappropriate; but Brian, you're really clever."

Ardeen lifted his head, tilting his chin over in her direction. He searched her eyes before returning to his I'm-not-here position.

As she pulled up to the last stop sign in town, she looked in her rearview mirror. No one coming.

"I'm just trying to say that—I know you won't believe this—but now that it's over, I'm glad you came to work with us. I'm not the easiest person to be around. And I was especially hard on you. I'm not going to make any more excuses for that. I think I probably—no, I'm sure—I didn't give you all the breaks you deserved. And I realize that my decision to force you to leave is way more emotional than rational. But it's such a strong feeling in me, I can't ignore it. And, hey, believe me, I'm the expert at ignoring my feelings, so this must be huge."

Jeez, Dunlop, can't you get through one significant moment in your life without cracking wise?

"Anyway, I want you to know that I think you're on the way to becoming a good person, but I just can't live through every second of that evolution with you. Oh, god, that sounds pretentious. I'm sorry. I'm screwing this up." She shook her head and started driving again.

As Anna wondered what to say next, the sweet scent of fresh-cut alfalfa drew her attention out through her open window. She took a moment to study the houses they were passing. All of them small, tidy, built in the '60s. That was back in the day when new houses were less likely to feature beige vinyl siding. The exteriors here were light pink, grey, dark green, and lavender. As kids, she and Eddy had named this neighborhood Easter Egg Park, and she could think of it as nothing else.

She glanced over at her passenger, unprepared for what she saw. His eyes, drilling into hers. Apparently, she wasn't the only person in the truck filled with loathing at how she had treated him. She'd had it coming, but the look of pure hatred startled her, pushing her attention back to the bumpy road.

His two-word sentence seemed to stretch on forever, starting softly and rising quickly, the roar of a lion.

"You BITCH!"

"I know," was all she said. Without looking, she reached down to lose her fingers in Storm's soft fur.

"You are so full of shit. Why the hell did you even drag my ass through this? To be some kind of hero, right? But when it comes down to having to actually do what you said, you just blow me off. This is so—goddamned—typical!"

He slammed his fist onto the dashboard, making her jump. By the grief in his voice, she wasn't sure if he'd meant that this was typical of her behavior, or this was typical of his life. He was biting down hard on his bottom lip.

"And now everything's gone." His voice cracked. "All of it. I'm totally screwed. Because of you."

"Okay, all right." She was trying to see all sides of this. "Yes, your life is screwed up. And I helped to screw it up. And I'm sorry. But let's not forget how this whole little party started. You screwed your life up first by doing what you did to those puppies. You want to talk screwed up? That was seriously screwed up."

"Jesus, I can't believe you!"

The fury of his yell forced Storm up into the sitting position.

"You and those goddamned puppies! Yeah, I shouldn't've done it, okay? I don't know why I did, okay? But you crazy bitch, they're goddamn dogs, all right? Animals! Not people, you get it? Christ! Yes, it's wrong to kill 'em, but it's wrong to live your whole *life* for 'em, too. What's it gonna take for you to get that?" He puffed air through his lips in a sarcastic laugh. "What am I saying? You're never gonna get it. I mean, shit, it still makes total sense to you that your own husband got himself killed over a goddamn *rodent!*"

The engine of Anna's truck went silent. The alfalfa lost its smell. She couldn't feel the steering wheel in her hands. She turned to study the vile creature on the other side of the large German shepherd. And didn't see the whitetail doe in the road until it was too late.

Anna slammed on the brakes and yanked the wheel hard to the left, sending the truck through the rusty railing of the Potts Road bridge, nose first into the deepest, most sunless part of the Milk River.

The deer leapt unharmed into the hedge.

41

He tried to remember where he was. In the truck. Right.

Off the bridge. He was sitting in water now, cold on his stomach. And rising. Coming in from below. And in from her window. Was he gonna die here? He couldn't find the door handle, but then he did find the handle, and the door wouldn't open. He pushed and pushed, but it wouldn't open. The water was up to his chest now, cold.

Dr. Giant looked dead. Was she dead? Her window was open. Why hadn't their airbags gone off?

Where was the button to roll down his window? He had to get out. *Shit! Think!* He put his face up by the ceiling where there was still some space left. He took a big breath. And another one. One last breath.

Just go. Go! Crawl over her. Out her open window. Do it. He had to get out. The river was trying to keep him in, but he had to get out.

He got past the floating dog. Onto Dr. Giant's lap. He had his feet on her shorts. *Just do it. She won't feel it.* He pushed himself out through her window, feeling her legs give way under him. There's light up there. *Go. Get up there.*

This was it. What he'd been swimming toward his whole life. In a hundred nightmares he'd been right here in this exact spot, not knowing how to move his arms and legs, clawing at cold water, silence everywhere except for the screaming in his head, sunlight straight up, but getting dragged downriver, not able to get to the surface.

A memory flickered—drowning was supposed to be a good way to die. Once you gave yourself up and sucked the water into your lungs, you became peaceful and even got pissed off if somebody tried to save you. That might be true, but everything before that moment was goddamn torture.

Being right below the surface was the worst, when he thought he'd have to give in and let the river have him, just a foot away from oxygen.

But then he was up. His head broke through into daylight. He pushed the old air out of his lungs, which seemed to take forever, before he could heave the new stuff in. And in and in. Making high, squeaky gasps.

He twirled his arms around in jerky circle movements, kicking his legs in a kind of spasm pattern. It seemed to be working. He was still above water. The current was taking him toward shore. He hit against a huge tree branch and stopped about twenty feet downriver from the truck. He could stand here, the water only to his waist, but the bank was too steep to pull himself out.

He began half walking, half pulling himself upstream by grabbing first one handful then another of the prickly weeds growing along the river. He could see the truck now, its roof about five feet below the surface. He kept going, passing under the bridge because just on the other side of it, the bank was flatter and he'd be able to pull himself out. There was a fallen tree jutting into the water there, too. When he reached it, he'd be able to hoist himself up and out of this nightmare.

But she was still down there. Trapped in the seatbelt, her arms drifting out at her shoulders. That gash in her head.

Was he going to do it? He couldn't believe he was going to do it. He took two deep practice breaths. Then a third one and held it. Down he went. He let the rushing river bang him into the back gate of the truck, then began pulling himself along with his hands, moving like a sliding magnet along the vehicle. He turned the corner, letting the river help move him toward her door. He tried the handle and was surprised when it came right open.

It was hard to sort out what he saw inside. A tangle of floating crap. She was leaning a little sideways toward the other door, her butt still strapped to the seat. The dog hung above her, its back against the ceiling, white legs dangling over Dr. Giant's body. A huge travel coffee mug bobbed in front of the dog's face, in the drinking position. There was hair everywhere, her dark stuff floating up and out in a big nest, mixing-in with the white, silky fur of the dog. A pencil, a granola bar, and a pair of sunglasses were caught in all that hair. And the whole wad of stuff was moving back and forth altogether, like some creepy helium balloon. When he saw his own plastic comb trapped between her head and the back window, he stared for longer than he should have. He was running out of air.

He groped along her seatbelt until he found the buckle. A button, on the side. He popped it open. Her body arched and drifted upwards, stomach first. Long, half-naked legs trailing. He grabbed her by the arm, but the touch of her warm, bare skin in his hands made him freak. He let go and shot to the surface, hooking his feet on the window frame to hold himself in place, leaning forward for balance in neck-high water, gulping for air.

"Holy Christ!" He tried to beat down his panic. He looked up at the bridge, wanting to see a person up there. A swimmer. But there was nobody.

"Oh, come on!" He smoothed back his hair with both palms. He took the biggest amount of air he could into his lungs, but fear had made his breaths shallow.

He bent from the waist, forcing his head back into the water. With the river hammering his side, he took hold of the roof, unhooked his feet and pulled himself farther underwater, his arm muscles starting to hint that there would come a limit. He put the left side of his body against the door frame, keeping himself from being shoved downriver. He could see into the truck again where things had gotten worse.

He came nose to nose with the floating dog. Dr. Giant had spun so her head was now banging up against the passenger side window. The worst part, though, was that she was flat up against the dog's belly, all four of the animal's white legs drooping down around her, holding her in some kind of face-to-butt death hug. Her head disappeared into the long, swirling fur of the dog's tail.

He could use only one hand since he needed the other to grip the truck, to keep himself from being pushed downriver, or worse, back into the cab himself. That idea made the panic rise again, so he stopped thinking and started to move.

He grabbed her by the leg, but when he pulled, the dog came toward him too and pushed up against his face. He froze. The dog was probably gonna die if it wasn't dead already. But he couldn't think about that.

He grabbed the dog by its collar and spun it sideways, dragging its front legs over her thighs, so now the dog straddled her across the middle, with its head pushed up against the back window. The two of them were still hooked together, and with only one hand, he was having trouble getting them apart. He considered, for one second, pulling the more easily moved body—the dog—out of the truck and out of the way. But that meant *into* the river, which would carry it off forever and wash it up dead on some bank somewhere, which weirded him out. He couldn't save it, but he wouldn't kill it, either.

He put his palm against the dog's side and pushed hard, bending halfway into the deathtrap. The dog glided over her and thumped softly against the passenger side window. His window. God. But its legs came free, and the dog released its hold on her.

He needed air. Desperately needed air. He shot up and grabbed a breath, but stared below him the whole time, afraid she might slip out the door and disappear downriver. He had to keep going.

Partway back into the truck again he wrapped his arm around the bend in her knees and pulled. Her legs with all that white skin knocked against his hip as he hiked his arm up farther, catching her around the waist. Could he hold his breath long enough to do this? He had to. He used his other hand to push against the truck, heaving her the rest of the way out. The easiest thing seemed to be to sling her over his shoulder, and he shot to the surface gasping for his next breath. The river pulled them both downstream, and he grabbed for the tree branch he knew to be there.

Was she dead? Was he carrying a dead person? How long had she been down there? One minute? Two? Time was all screwed up. And for all he knew, it was the crash through the rail that had killed her, not the water. He'd seen that gross slit in her forehead. Under the water it didn't look like it was bleeding. It was just this deep, two-inch opening in her skin, gaping like another mouth in her head.

But what the hell was he supposed to do next? With his shock wearing off, his fear was trying to take over. Get out of the goddamn water, that much he knew. As he'd done before, he used the thick growth of plants along the bank, this time to pull them both upriver toward flatter ground. He felt her head hitting against his back with each step and wondered if her gash was bleeding all over him.

Hauling her around wasn't easy. She kept slipping off his shoulder, so he had to stop a few times to push her back into place. It wasn't very far to the other side of the bridge, but the walk over the slippery rocks was doing a number on him, making his back and arms ache. And he couldn't catch his breath. What he wanted more than anything was to get out of the rushing water, but instead he lowered himself farther into it as he trudged along, forcing the river to hold more of Dr. Giant's weight.

"Whoa, shit!" He shot back upward, realizing he'd been dragging her head underwater.

He made it past the point where the truck and its bobbing contents lay below the surface just a few yards out, but he purposely avoided looking in its direction. Under the bridge was tougher going. With no plants to pull against, he was completely on his own power, fighting the current and about 150 pounds of dead weight as he tried desperately not to get sucked away to wherever it was the river wanted to take them. The water was higher here, almost up to his chest. He repositioned his load, checking over his shoulder to keep her face from going under again. She wasn't breathing, he knew that. But a person's face should be up where the air was.

He held her bare legs to his chest with one arm, using the other to steady himself against the concrete wall. Under the shell of the bridge, the echo of his heaving lungs made it impossible to ignore how tired he was getting. Shaking now, he couldn't stop his teeth from chattering, even when he hit sunlight on the other side of the bridge.

In a few more seconds he was grabbing onto the broken tree trunk where he could heave himself out, climb the slope, and be done with this river forever. If he were alone. But he couldn't get out while carrying her extra weight. He studied the situation, racing through his small list of pathetic options. He could try to shove her up the bank and climb up behind her, but as tired as he was, no way could he toss a floppy giant up onto a hill. Option B was to leave her down here in the water, crawl out himself, then pull her up after him. And far as he could tell, there was no Option C, so that would have to be the plan. His next problem was to figure out how to keep her from drifting downstream while he got himself up onto the bank.

The tree trunk angled down into the river from its break point ten feet in the air. If he could put her across the log high enough up, she'd be hooked in place without having her head in the water. He needed to grab her from behind to make that happen. He hiked her down the front of his body, feeling her get lighter and lighter as the river took her in. He held a hand against her wet hair to keep her head from falling to the side. Her face pressed against his chest, she was finally buoyant enough for him to turn her around. Barely. She was all elbows and knees.

Holding her in the spoons position, he squatted down until her head tipped back over his shoulder. With his feet he searched for flat sand between the slippery rocks. He spread his legs wide like he was about to clean and jerk the barbell, gripped her waist with both hands, and jumped as high as he could out of the water, pushing her up into the air. Just as she left his control, when he could do nothing about it, he realized how hard she was going to hit that tree. The full force of her body weight would come slamming down onto it with nothing there to soften the blow. Which was just what happened.

She landed on the tree right below her ribcage, forcing the water that was inside of her to come out in a coughing jag that spilled only a few teaspoons of the Milk River back into its interrupted flow downstream. He was surprised it was so little.

But she was alive. Alive and awake. He was the luckiest son-of-a-bitch on the planet. Except for her.

She hung there bent in half, arms dangling toward the water, wheezing and gulping for air, which Brian could see she would never get if he didn't take her down. He wrapped his arms around her wet, white legs and pulled. She didn't budge. And there wasn't any use in ducking under the tree to push from the other side. She was too high, and he was too short to make the angle work. He had to get higher than she was.

He grabbed a fistful of riverbank weeds and pulled as he jumped, taking hold of the tree above where she was draped, pushing against it for extra leverage. Without her weighing him down, it was no problem to get up onto dry land. He felt heavier than he'd remembered, though, as he dropped to his belly and reached for her body. He pulled her by one arm and the back of her shirt. Once he'd freed her from the tree, it was easier to pull her up the bank than he'd thought it would be, probably because she was able to help him a little. He dragged her up onto level ground, flipping her onto her back so she could inhale, which she did in deep, noisy breaths.

"Jesus, are you okay?" He pulled himself up to sit cross-legged beside her, afraid to touch her, even though he'd groped pretty much every part of her body in the last couple of minutes.

She didn't answer. She turned her head to look over at him, eyes wide and crazed, but didn't speak. The head wound wasn't bleeding. It was a deep, open slit in her skin, but clean.

At last she lifted her arm and dropped it limply into his lap. She wrapped her fingers around one of his ankles as she choked out the word.

"Storm."

He didn't know what he expected her to say after coming back from the dead, but he should have guessed. She wanted to know about her dog. The one bumping around inside the cab of that truck.

"It's—she's gone." He shook his head.

Dr. Giant looked deep into his eyes now like she was trying to figure out what he was saying, or maybe to decide if he was lying. He had to make it more clear.

"She's dead. Drowned."

"Where is she?" She lifted her head to look around.

"In the truck. She's still in the truck."

Dr. Giant sat bolt upright and tried to push herself into a stand. Weak, dizzy, or half unconscious, she fell back onto her ass.

"You have to go get her!" She wheezed out the words.

"What?"

He couldn't believe what he was hearing. Even from her, this was insane.

"You have to go. Go get her. Hurry up—my god!" She started a hacking fit that shook her whole body.

"Are you nuts? Go back down there? For a dog? A dead dog? Huh-uh. No way."

"I don't think I can do it." She was coughing between sentences. "But someone has to do it. You've got to go do it!"

"Give it up, yo! She's gone, okay? Dead and gone."

"Wait, Brian, wait." She gasped. "We don't know for sure she's dead, right? I'm not dead. Maybe she's not dead, you know?"

She was trying to breathe, and cough, and talk all at the same time but gave up and devoted herself to coughing only. She went on as soon as she could.

"It's possible, right? Can you do it? Somebody has to go do it. Can you go?"

"No! I'm not goin' nowhere!"

He jumped up and walked away from her into the trees, trying to figure out what the hell was going on here. He had just saved her life, but he was the bad guy again. How did that happen? How did that always happen? But, whatever, they had to get out of here. She needed a doctor. Maybe she had a concussion or something, and that was why she was talking crazy.

He jogged back to find her stumbling toward the water. Swaying back and forth like a bowling pin trying to decide, she fell before he could reach her. She got herself to all fours and began creeping toward the water. He ran around front to block her way. She tried to crawl around him, and he took one step to the left, keeping her from moving forward. She tried to move around him the other way.

"Stop!" He bent down to put his hands on her shoulders. "Will you stop?" He got down on his knees in front of her. He wanted her to see him speak. "Look, we gotta get outta here. The dog is gone. Storm is gone."

And then Dr. Giant did something he'd never seen her do. She burst into tears. Loud, sobbing cries. She pulled at his arms and rocked back and forth, wailing in a deranged, hoarse voice.

"Please—please, Brian. You have to go do this. Please!"

She looked up at him then, with those green eyes. He was still kneeling there in the dirt, trying to figure out who this person was. Dr. Giant. Crying.

She grabbed a handful of his shirt, took a gulp of air, and cried, and talked, and coughed.

"Brian?" She gasped, her eyebrows in a triangle shape. "I'm in trouble here, and I need your help. I—don't think I can get down there and come back with her—but you can."

"But I won't."

"Okay. I hear what you're saying. And that's your choice." She coughed so long she had to stop and spit. "But before you decide on that for sure—before you choose not to help where maybe you can—I just want you to know something.

"That dog down there—we're together. She gives me everything she has." Her words were croaks. "And counts on me for everything else."

He was having trouble making out what she was saying.

"They need us, Brian—dogs." She heaved in another lungful of air. Her face was red and wet.

He thought about using the tails of his shirt to wipe her cheeks.

"Please. Please! I—I put her in that truck today. I did that to her. And—" She drew in two long breaths before she could talk. "And now here I am—up here where she isn't—and *it feels like part of me down there!*"

She was back at it, bawling, now with both knees up and her face buried between them, rocking side to side.

He stood up, turned his back on all that crying, took a deep breath, and slid down the slope into the water.

42

"Lift on three. One. Two. Three!"

Anna pulled from above with Brian pushing from below to get the ninety-pound, sopping wet dog up onto the river bank. The exertion made Anna dizzy, and another wave of nausea swept over her.

"Okay, quick, Brian. Jump up here. I need your help."

Brian was beside her with surprising swiftness, considering how he'd already exerted himself that day. Anna opened the dog's mouth and looked inside.

"No obstruction." She'd stood too quickly and thought she might vomit, but the urge passed. "Help me get her up. Upside down."

Anna had Brian lift Storm by her back legs, pulling them over his head, while she wrapped her arms around the dog's middle. Water poured from Storm's long, white coat, and though it was difficult to tell, Anna hoped some of the liquid hitting the ground had come from her windpipe.

She and Brian lowered the dog and held her in a standing-on-all-fours position. Anna straddled her back, placed her fists below Storm's ribs, and jerked upwards a few times, trying to expel water from the dog's lungs. But nothing happened.

"All right. Downhill." She gasped for air enough to talk. "Let's face her downhill."

They positioned Storm on her right side, angling down the slope of the bank. Anna knew what she would feel when she placed her fingers on the dog's chest cavity above her heart. Nothing.

"I'm sorry, Brian, but I'm going to need you to get back into the river."

Without hesitation he skidded down the small hill into the chest-high water.

"Cup your hands around her muzzle to keep air from coming out."

He did.

"Right. Like that. Now put your mouth over her nostrils and blow."

The pained look he shot her wasn't trying to tell her that she was crazy. It was asking if she thought he could do it.

"You'll be good at this," she said, and meant it. "Take a breath."

He wrapped his lips around the dog's nose, blinking hard at the sensation, and began to empty his lungs into hers.

"Okay, stop. That's about the right amount of air, got it?"

He nodded.

"Give her a few more."

Brian breathed for the dog who was unable to breathe for herself.

"Good. Now wait."

Brian pulled his mouth away from Storm's nose, loosening his grip on her muzzle. Anna put one hand on top of the other between Storm's third and sixth ribs. She gave her ten quick compressions and felt for a pulse. She looked at Brian.

"Two more breaths."

Anna watched the dog's chest rise and fall both times. And not another. She gave Storm's heart ten more compressions before nodding at Brian to do his part. She checked for a pulse. Back and forth they went until the miraculous moment when Storm's head jerked in a watery cough. And then another. Anna felt for a heartbeat and beamed down at her helper.

Brian Ardeen gave a whoop that echoed out over the river.

"All right! All goddamn right!"

43

"I wish you'd take a few more days off, Anna. Tomorrow seems too soon to go back."

Anna chose not to respond to her mother's wish as they stepped out onto the wraparound porch and seated themselves in a couple of Adirondacks. It was precisely where the Dunlops had relaxed after summer lunch for the past century or so.

The Adirondacks had been replaced over the years, the current three painted periwinkle, red, and yellow, but apart from that, Anna had stayed true to tradition and would often pause in one of them with a final glass of iced tea before getting on to whatever chores needed tending.

"It does smell lovely out here, dear, but I've never much cared for the look of those weeds you call a lawn."

"They're not weeds, and you know it, Mom. They're prairie plantings. And I don't call it a lawn; you do."

"Ah-ha. But I remember the days when you and the boys would run around on our beautiful, soft, green grass, playing freeze tag and lawn darts. It just seems sad that no one could play anything out there now with all of those four- and five-foot *plantings*.

"That's okay, Mom. It's hard to get my friends interested in freeze tag these days."

Smiling, Anna put the glass to her mouth, hearing one of her favorite sounds, the tinkling of ice on its way to her lips. She closed her eyes to smell and then taste the fusion of black tea and fresh lemon. Especially keen senses distracted her today. The Adirondack cupping her body so comfortably, the river tumbling noisily behind the house, her mother's mint-scented shampoo, bumblebees and their shadows bobbing over the globe thistle. Surrounded, included, connected, nourished. Pono.

"Speaking of your friends, dear..." Her mother's voice had that tone she would use when her words would say one thing and mean two or three things. "It certainly seemed as if Eddy spent every one of the official visiting hours with you at the hospital. And a few of the unofficial ones, if I'm not mistaken. That was nice to see."

Anna meant to use her own tone to stop the interrogation before it began, but her mind was elsewhere. Truth was, Anna had been touched by Eddy's attentiveness. More than touched. Stirred. Astonishingly, guilt-riddenly, soul-ticklingly stirred. And the feeling wasn't letting up.

Now that she was home with her dog-like awareness and rightness with her surroundings, she was experiencing more clarity than she'd known for years. Tony, Ardeen, her career, Eddy—all of it was making more sense to her now.

"He's a good friend, Mom."

"I'm glad, honey. Eddy has such a sweet soul. You know... I do wonder why he never married."

"More iced tea, Mom?"

"Don't worry. I let go of my dream for a love connection between the two of you more than twenty-five years ago after one of your grand, *We're Just Friends* lectures. You remember the one where you told me to quit bringing it up because the very idea of kissing Eddy Rivard made your guts want to squeeze out through any available orifice in your body? I let it drop there and then, ending my string of ill-fated *Please Date Eddy* campaigns."

Anna couldn't remember the specific conversation in question, but knew many of her adolescent rants had been aimed at disabusing her mother of romantic ideas about Eddy.

They sat watching the hummingbirds bang into each other in a frenzy for the two feeders. It always startled Anna to hear their papery wings mesh together at those speeds. She could never relax until they parted safely after the skirmish.

"Why do you think he did it?" asked Anna. "A guy with a fear of water and nothing but hatred for me. Why would he make the decision, all on his own, to come back down to get me?"

"He has more than hatred for you, Anna. He looks up to you."

"What?"

"He's imprinted on you, like a chick to its mother. I think what he feels for you is masked in hatred, yes. But actually, it's a desperate need to please you, which manifests itself as anger when he can't do so." Her mom took a drink of iced tea. "Frankly, if you ask me, most of his hatred he saves for himself."

"Huh. So you've been practicing your *menemene* on Brian Ardeen then."

"I beg your pardon?"

"Nothing, sorry. You've found the key to his soul?"

"In the hospital, two days ago, watching my nearly drowned daughter sleep. And trying to sort out every little detail, to make sure it would never happen again. I replayed everything I knew about your Brian Ardeen and came to some astonishing conclusions."

"So you're telling me that he risked his own life and faced his horrible phobia because he thinks of me as his mentor?"

"No, I'm not saying that at all. That's why he went down for your dog, yes. Because his mentor was begging him to, and he couldn't disappoint her. But I believe there was a very different reason he ignored his own safety to save you."

"Well, come on, oh, Great Seer. Why did he do it?"

"Because he had to."

"Okay..."

"Your friend, Joseph Campbell, had the answer. Remember him talking about the man who tried to commit suicide by jumping off a cliff in Hawaii?"

"Oh, yeah. How did that go, again?"

"A police car pulls up, and the officer on the passenger side flies out of the car and grabs the man right as he jumps. The man's weight pulls the cop over the edge with him, and the only reason neither of them dies is because the other officer gets there in time to pull them both back to safety. But the question is, why was that first cop ready to die for a man he had never met?"

"Didn't he tell reporters that he *couldn't* let go—that if he had, he couldn't have gone on living, or something like that?"

"Exactly. And Joseph Campbell ties it back to what Schopenhauer, or some famous philosopher, said about traumatic experiences."

"Traumatic experiences like being trapped together underwater?"

"Right. He said that in a life-threatening situation, the most primal part of yourself takes over. And on some core level, we humans know we're all part of the same one life. And so you do whatever you can to save that life. Self-preservation. Ardeen had to do it."

"He had to come back down and get me because he *was* me?" Anna almost laughed, and then remembered begging Brian to save Storm because the dog felt like *part* of her.

"Well, that's the theory. I can't seem to come up with a better one."

"Ah-ha," said Anna, poking at an ice cube. "I think I'll just ask him why he did it."

"Yes, you do that. I'd love to hear his reflections on Schopenhauer."

"Mom, be nice."

"You're right. I owe him—whatever he wants, really."

The two of them drank a little more. Then Anna tipped her head back and closed her eyes.

"So... have you seen Mr. Ardeen since that day?"

"I haven't actually seen him, but I've called him a bunch of times. The last time he didn't answer, but I'm guessing he was home. He doesn't do well with people thanking him for things."

"Oh, really? I have a daughter like that."

"I need to get in touch with him again soon, though."

"Honey, if he doesn't want to be thanked, stop thanking him."

"I suppose. But I have an important message to deliver. I've been meaning to tell him something."

"And what would that be?"

"That raccoons are procyonids."

"Pardon me?"

"What sent us over that bridge in the first place was him proclaiming that Tony had died to 'save a goddamn rodent.' And raccoons aren't rodents. They're procyonids."

"Ah-ha." Her mother looked up to the few clouds for strength. "So what's going to happen with the two of you now? Are you going to have him finish out his time at the clinic? Would that be too odd?"

"Yeah, it'll be odd. What I've told him is that I'd like to pay off his fine to the courts myself and then hire him on as an official employee. Full time. If he wants the job, that is. I could use the help, the way the business has been growing. He hasn't said yes yet, but I think it's because he doesn't know how to."

"That's kind of you, Anna."

"Not really. He's a hard worker—challenging, but hard. And obviously I owe him a lot. I've got no idea how he's going to act around me now, if he even wants to be around me at all. It's weird, but I feel like being dunked in the river cleared up a lot of things. Like what a whining jerk I was to him. And how much he's actually done for me—besides that pesky saving-my-life thing. You won't want to believe this… but he helped me find a way to cope with my guilt about Tony."

Her mother turned around to look into Anna's eyes.

"You have guilt about Tony? I knew you were grieving, but—and Brian Ardeen helped you? Anna, tell me about this."

"Yeah. I think I can, now. I should. But not today, okay?"

"All right, dear."

Anna looked down to fidget with the peeling periwinkle paint on the armrest. Joey laid her smooth arm along Anna's own, skin to skin. Anna twitched only the slightest bit at the contact, and then both of them stared out into the rustling prairie grasses with the peppering of purple, orange, and yellow flowers.

"Oh!" said Joey, patting Anna's hand. "Bunny came over to my unit on her way out for a walk with those two dogs of hers, yesterday. Like everyone else, she wants to know how you're doing and sends her love. She looks fabulous, by the way. What a cackle that woman has."

"Yeah, she's great. I've been thinking about her and the other puppy people today."

"Have you?"

It's Russ I really worry about. Where's he going to be a year from now? He won't let anyone help him, and—"

"Anna?" The male voice came from out of nowhere.

Both women jumped. They turned to see Eddy coming from around the side of the house. Sweaty and panting, he'd apparently run over from the radio station.

"Eddy?" Anna tried to hide her smile from her mother. She stood to give him a hug, but he stopped before coming up the steps of the porch. Normally his same height, she towered over him now. "You okay?"

"Yeah, sure. I'm great. Hi, Mrs. D."

"Hello, Eddy." Her mom pushed herself up and out of the wooden chair, then straightened her skirt with one hand while handing her glass to Anna with the other. "I think I might leave if that's okay with you, dear. I've got errands to run. And now that Eddy's here, you won't be alone."

"I don't mind being alone," said Anna, wanting to mean it.

"Just the same. I'll call you later," she said on her way down the porch to her car. "Goodbye, Eddy."

"See ya, Mrs. D."

"So—hi!" said Anna to Eddy who still stood down on ground level.

"Hi yourself." Panting a little from the run, his words were breathy and a bit Hawaiian-accented, fashioned into that verbal hug she couldn't get enough of.

"Wanna come up and sit down?"

He trotted up the stairs and found a seat.

"Why are you here? I mean—*how* are you here? Isn't Jenny still at her mom's? Who's on the radio?" Seating herself, she reached to turn on the small, green transistor she kept on the windowsill.

Dead air.

"Eddy!"

He shrugged and smiled. She watched his lovely brown hands pat the wide arms of the yellow Adirondack to a rhythm she couldn't hear.

"Actually, Jenny's coming back this afternoon. She'll hop on so I can stay here through the evening."

"Oh. That'll be good. Hey, I need a refill on my iced tea. You want some?"

Eddy popped to a full stand faster than she'd thought a person could peel himself out of one of these chairs.

"Sure. But let me get it."

"Wow. Okay. There's sugar for yours in the pantry."

He took her glass, and her mom's, and went inside.

She called in after him. "I'm totally fine, you know." And then in a thick Russian accent she added, "Strong like bull!"

44

"Quit staring at me."

"No. No, I don't think I will."

Anna was petting Storm's big sleeping head. The dog lay curled up on her favorite woolly bed, tucked between the fireplace and the television. Red-orange sunset dribbled in through the old window screen, tinting a swath across the white canvas of Storm's body.

"Seriously, Eddy. I can feel you back there. You're messing up my hair with your eyes."

He chuckled, getting up from the couch and coming over to join her on the floor.

"How's she doing?" He placed his hand on the center of Anna's back, rubbing lightly, up and down.

"She's good. I've pumped her full of antibiotics. I'm a little worried about pneumonia. She took a lot of water into her lungs."

"Really? So what about you? Could you get pneumonia?"

"No. Brian said I didn't cough up much water. I think my trachea slammed shut right away to keep the water out. As a reflex. Actually, that happens a lot."

"Hopefully, not to you."

On his lifetime list of most surreal conversations with Anna, this one, talking about what her throat was doing while she was drowning at the bottom of the river, probably ranked up there in his top three.

Anna leaned forward to run all ten of her fingers through the long fur on Storm's side. Eddy kept his hand on his friend's back as she moved. He wasn't done reassuring himself yet, needing to feel her solidly there with him. Warm and strong. He was watching her run her hands down the length of Storm's two front legs, gently cradling the dog's feet when she got there. "I can't believe I almost lost her," she said.

"I can't believe you almost lost *you*. That *I* almost lost you." He softly touched the bandage on her forehead, feeling the wiry stitches below. He smoothed her wavy hair from the top down, leaving his hand on the back of her head. "I wish you would have stayed in the hospital longer. The doctors thought you should."

Anna tilted her head back into his palm, closing her eyes for a good long time. A single tear rolled down her cheek. Eddy stopped it with the fingers of his other hand. He put his mouth by her ear and whispered.

"Shhhh. Anna. *Ku'u ipo.* Tell me what you need. I'll take care of it, yeah?"

Without opening her eyes she said, "The truck. It's gone. Totaled."

"Totaled? I'm so sorry, honey. Oh, no."

"Oh, yes."

Anna turned to sit cross-legged, knee-to-knee with Eddy. She put one hand onto each of his muscled legs. "I think—he took it back." Another tear fell; this one onto her shorts.

"Who?"

"Tony. I don't think he wanted me to have his truck anymore."

"Really? Why would he do that? It's so important to you."

"Yeah, too important. I guess it's time to let go a little."

They sat together in silence. Anna squeezed his knees, staring into his eyes. She wanted something from him. He wanted to give it to her. He didn't know what it was.

"Eddy?"

"Yeah?"

"I love you."

"I know. I've never doubted that. Your love of me is pretty much my favorite thing."

"No, Eddy. I'm not talking about our friendship love. Or our kindred spirit love. I'm talking about the kind of love that's hard to admit to. The kind that's supposed to spark when you first meet a new person, and you both feel it, and it jumps—really quickly—into the I-need-you-forever kind of love."

"Oh. That kind." He paused. "So... *jumping quickly* for you means, like, in thirty-three years or thereabouts?"

"No! That's exactly my point. This can't possibly be the right way to do this. But I fell in love with you little awhile ago. And I've been waiting for it to pass, but it won't."

"Ah. *Our love is like a kidney stone.* It would make a nice Hallmark card."

"Eddy. Can you be serious? Who do you think you are? Me?"

He clamped his lips together, dropping his head to his chest. And while he was down there, he sent up a silent prayer of gratefulness to his tutu for what was happening here.

"I know this is totally weird." She let go of his legs and slipped her hands into her shorts pockets. "And believe me, I've tried to talk myself out of it. But when you leave I can't stand it, and when you're with me I'm worried you're going to leave. And the weird thing is, I think about kissing you all the time. And I don't mean our usual old-buddy-old-pal kisses. I mean, real, actual, long, sexy kisses. I think about your *tongue*, Eddy!"

He did everything he could to keep from smiling. He wanted to laugh so badly, and if he smiled he knew the laugh would come. And then his own tears would start—the fast, unstoppable kind that the soul releases when it's finished one of its critical missions and can relax a little.

As she spoke, Anna unfolded her long legs, repositioning herself into a kneel, then resting on her haunches. "I'm sure you're sitting there thinking that I'm only feeling this way because I could have died the other day. But I'm telling you, I've been feeling this way for months, and I'm only *saying* it because I could have died the other day. Yeah-yeah-yeah, life is short and all that. It's so cliché. But clichés are based on universal truth, you know, or they wouldn't get to be clichés. Trust me; almost drowning hasn't changed my opinion on anything. It's just made me brave enough to tell you about it. And my opinion is that I want to stop being your dearest friend and become your dearest—everything."

Eddy put a finger on her lips to help her stop talking. And he let himself smile.

"Anna. I have loved you as my Dearest Everything for as long as I can remember."

"You—have?"

"I have."

She slapped his legs. "Why didn't you tell me? I can't believe this."

"I didn't tell you because I knew I wasn't *your* Dearest Everything. And our relationship was—and is—the most perfect thing in my life already. I'm a happy man because of what I already get from you. I hope you know that you're the most meaningful part of me."

"I can't believe I'm hearing this." She shook her head, careful not to lose contact with his eyes.

"You need to believe it. Every place I go is more interesting because I know I get to come home and tell you about it. I'm a gentler person because of the kindness you've shown me. I'm a funnier person, because

I want to see you laugh. I care more about animals, not just because you've opened my eyes to that, but because you are one of them."

"So—when did this start? I mean—how long have you felt this way about me?"

"Let's see." He narrowed his eyes and raised his eyebrows as he pondered the question. "Y'know, what I feel for you has never really grown. It started as big as love gets, I think, and nothing seems to make it any smaller. Not you bossing me around at recess, not you alphabetizing my spice rack, and not you marrying another man—nothing changes it. It lives for you, waiting for you to take it. Or not. And until then—it's enough for me."

She reached over to cup his cheek in her soft, freckled hand.

Eddy leaned in to kiss her. Finally, finally to kiss her. But at the last moment she pulled away.

He cocked his head a little. "Um, I'm no expert on this kissing thing… but I think that if you want a long, sexy one, you're gonna have to get a little closer."

"I know. I do. I'm sorry, Eddy. It's just that it's all happening so fast. Of course we're going to kiss. But—what if you don't like it?"

He chuckled. "This is so wonderfully you. I'm pretty sure I'm gonna like it."

"No, really. It's possible you might not like the kind of kisser I am. And then what do we do?"

"Well—maybe in just this one thing, you could take the risk of not being exactly perfect the first time? And just look forward to all the laboratory testing where we improve the process? That's my plan, anyway."

Anna was quiet. Eddy could see her thinking. Of Tony. He sat back a little to make room for him.

Then Anna burst all the way forward, covering him with an impassioned kiss he had never imagined for himself. As it turned out, he quite liked the kind of kisser she was.

But before he was completely through enjoying it, she pushed against his legs with her hands, throwing her full self into the air, standing and walking without looking back. He watched her pass through the doorway into the den, open the bottom drawer of her desk, and pull out a stack of notebooks and bulging colored folders. She studied them for a moment before turning to bring them in. Bending from the waist, she placed the unwieldy pile on the floor in front of him, steadying it before standing up again.

"I write—poems." She pointed with her forehead toward the stack. "Stupid ones." She crisply folded her arms across her chest and gave him a stiff nod. "Okay?"

He looked up at her with eyes that prickled, his vision beginning to blur. "Okay."

"Okay."

"So…" He lifted the flap of the top folder. "Is there one in here anywhere on the topic of kissing? I mean, reading about it would be better than nothing."

She gave him her hand and let him pull her to the floor.

EPILOGUE

A mother with her two young children passed by them on the sidewalk, heading in the opposite direction. Russ took no special care to be sure they were out of earshot.

"I've never much cared for kids," he said to Kitty. "I don't mean to speak for both of us, though. You might actually like them. They're short, you know? So their hands are down at your mouth level, and they're always holding some soggy piece of food. And every kid loves to feed the doggie."

He had rigged up a new hands-free leash system which attached to his belt. He looked back at Kitty who'd found something in the grass that made her tail curl up at full attention.

"You kill it, you clean it."

He already had the old woman's mail ready. Nothing from her kids again. There never was, but he checked every day. He mounted the few front steps, making a mental note of the chipping cement. It would be a pretty easy fix. That was his first thought. His second was of his trowel, trapped back in the garage he didn't own anymore.

He pushed her small stack of junk mail into the black metal box mounted next to the front door. He sensed a ghostlike motion and looked up to see her standing behind the screen.

"Sheesh, lady! You scared the crap outta me. Warn a person next time."

Clutching the small, grey kitten to her chest, she opened the door between them. "I made coffee."

"In a clean cup? Oh, boy." He passed by her into the foyer, making sure Kitty got all the way in before the door closed.

He went to the kitchen and sat at his side of the table. There was tea in a cup on her side. A few Lorna Doones waited on a small, unbreakable plate. He took a sip of tepid instant, waiting for her to shuffle herself in.

"I heard about your house," she said, dropping into her wooden chair with a little grunt, moving the kitten to her lap.

"Yeah, you and the rest of the county."

They sipped awhile, the only sounds the clinking of cups on saucers and the hum of her dusty wall clock.

"I could use someone around here," she said. "To keep the place up."

"Keep the place up? Bess, it's almost time to tear the place down."

More sipping. More clinking.

He narrowed his eyes. "The dog gets to lie on the couch."

She thought for a moment about that before nodding.

Bitter Russ picked up a Lorna Doone, gave half of it to Kitty, and pushed the rest into his mouth.

***

ABOUT THE AUTHOR

Carrie Maloney is a freelance writer and video producer with a passion for animals—human and not. She began her career at the PBS station in St. Paul, Minnesota, producing for the national Emmy Award-winning science show, Newton's Apple. Around this same time, she also won a regional Emmy as a producer on a documentary. After that, she worked in corporate America as a creative director—but the business environment never quite felt like home. So, today Carrie is back to following her heart, working on projects in the non-profit, education, and health & wellness worlds. In her free time she volunteers for Can Do Canines, an organization that trains assistance dogs for people with disabilities. And she's recently become the Marketing Manager for the Grey Muzzle Organization, working to improve the lives of homeless and at-risk senior dogs.

Carrie lives in Star Prairie, Wisconsin, with her husband, Mark, and two senior shelter dogs, Gracie and Rose. The latter two live for a chance to play in the river.

Look for Carrie online:
breathtobreath.com
facebook.com/breath2breath
@maloneycarrie

READING GROUP DISCUSSION GUIDE

1. What makes Milk River, Wisconsin, feel like a small town (certain relationships or situations)? Would this story have unfolded the same way in an urban setting?

2. If you had to describe Anna's personality to someone, what would you say?

3. If you had been sitting at the community gathering where Anna explained the "deal" she was offering puppy adopters, would you have stayed or walked out? Would you ever consider sharing parts of your personal life on the radio?

4. How did you feel about the scenes involving veterinary medicine? Did they enhance or detract from the story? Would you have preferred a different balance?

5. Does the way Anna views the relationship between humans and other animals differ from your own?

    a. Did this book shade your opinions about animals in any way?

    b. Is the topic of the human/animal relationship handled fairly by the author as part of Anna's personality, or does it feel "preachy" in parts?

6. How did *menemene* (may-nay-MAY-nay) shape the behavior of various characters?

READING GROUP DISCUSSION GUIDE (cont'd)

7. How do Eddy's Hawaiian sensibilities help him navigate his Midwestern life?

8. How would you describe Anna's relationship with her mother?

    a. How might Anna's upbringing have influenced the way she interacts with people as an adult?

9. How do you feel about Brian Ardeen as a person?

10. What helped Anna turn the corner on her grief over Tony?

11. How is Anna's relationship with Eddy likely to be different from her life with Tony?

12. Just for fun… if you were going to make a movie from this book, which celebrities would you cast in major roles?

13. Which of these characters would you like to spend more time with in another Milk River book?

Made in the USA
Charleston, SC
15 November 2014